STAR TREK®

THE
LOST YEARS

STAR TREK®

T·H·E
LOST YEARS

J.M. Dillard

POCKET BOOKS

New York   London   Toronto   Sydney   Tokyo

Another *Original* publication of POCKET BOOKS

POCKET BOOKS, a division of Simon & Schuster Inc.
1230 Avenue of the Americas, New York, NY 10020

This book is published by Pocket Books,
a division of Simon & Schuster Inc.,
under exclusive license from Paramount Pictures Corporation.

ISBN: 0-671-68293-8

First Pocket Books hardcover printing October 1989

10 9 8 7 6 5 4 3 2 1

POCKET and colophon are trademarks of Simon & Schuster Inc.

Printed in the U.S.A.

Acknowledgments

———————————— ☆ ————————————

On December 13, 1987, a little bit of *Star Trek* history was made. Quite literally.

That was the day that *Trek* authors Brad Ferguson, Irene Kress, and I met with Pocket editor Dave Stern and DC Comics editor Bob Greenberger in Pocket's New York offices. You see, Bob had come up with this incredible idea: Why not "fill in the gaps" between the end of the *Enterprise's* five-year mission and the events chronicled in *Star Trek: The Motion Picture?* After all, *ST:TMP* may have answered some questions as to what our heroes were up to during that time, but it left many unanswered, such as: Just what was it that drove Spock to pursue the discipline of Kolinahr? . . . And why did James Kirk allow himself to become one of those "paper-pushers" he so despised? *The Lost Years* answers these, and more.

Neat idea, huh? Bob has a tendency to come up with those. So does Dave Stern, the guiding force who put it all together. He worked out a rough guideline of the events that needed to occur in each book, and helped Irene and Brad and me to figure out what happened when, and who was where doing what. . . .

And the nicest thing about the whole meeting was that we realized that we all got along really well, that we were all excited to be doing this project, and that, not only was it going to work, it was going to be *great.*

So if you enjoy *The Lost Years,* just wait . . . because the series continues in a few months with Brad Ferguson's *A Flag Full of Stars* and Irene Kress's *The War Virus.*

I'd like to thank those who critiqued the manuscript in its early stages. I am especially indebted to Kathleen O'Malley for loaning me her concept of "esper-blindness." Kathy read the first draft of this manuscript and gave helpful comments, and came up with some nifty last-minute exits from certain corners I'd written myself into.

Thanks are also due Martha Midgette, whose eminently logical brain (she is, after all, a Spock fan) and knowledge of all things military (and a Picard fan) greatly helped improve the book.

And then, of course, there's George, whose overdeveloped right brain always provides instant relief for all my plot headaches.

Now, if I might indulge in some personal business . . .

To the zillions of you who have written me at the post office box in McLean and haven't received a response: There are one or two reasons for this.

One, I've since moved to Florida. (Surprise.) They do forward my mail, but it takes a good long while. Those of you who'd like to write with comments, please do so . . . but the safest place to send letters is in care of Pocket Books (1230 Avenue of the Americas, New York, NY 10020—the address is on the copyright page of every book they publish). I'd like to give you my current P.O. box, but chances are my address will change again within the next year.

Two, you didn't enclose an SASE (self-addressed, stamped envelope). I know I didn't request one the first time . . . but then, I never expected to get hundreds of letters the first few months the book was out. I enjoy hearing from you—but after the first month, I began to realize that the only way to answer all this mail was to quit paying the rent and buy postage stamps instead. I'd like the chance to respond to each and every one of you personally—so if you want an answer, please remember the SASE.

And speaking of letters . . . A lot of people who have read my *Trek* novel *Bloodthirst* (or *Demons* or *Mindshadow,* for that matter) have inquired about the fates of the characters

Lisa Nguyen, Ingrit Tomson, Lamia the Andorian, and Jonathon Stanger.

In response, I say: Read on. . . .

—JEANNE M. DILLARD

Tampa, Florida
October 1988

STAR TREK®

THE

LOST YEARS

THE MOUNTAINS
OF GOL

———————— ☆ ————————

140005 V.O.D.
(Vulcan Old Date)

PROLOGUE

─────────────── ☆ ───────────────

Zakal spent the first half of the night coughing up green-black blood and listening to the wind hurl sand against the side of the mountain fortress. The cavernous chamber was windowless and dark, save for the feeble light emanating from the initiates' room, but Zakal had seen enough sandstorms to picture this one clearly in his mind's eye: a huge, vibrating column of red sand that blotted out the sky until nothing remained but moving desert. Any creatures foolish enough to venture unprotected into the storm would be found the next day, mummies leached of all moisture, their skin crackling like parchment at the slightest touch.

Around the middle of the night, the stains on his handcloth changed from dark green to bright, the color of a *d'mallu* vine after a rare spell of rain. Shortly thereafter, the healer left him, a sign that there was nothing more to be done, no more easing of pain possible; a sign that he would be dead before sunrise. The relief on her drawn face was all too evident. She was not of the Kolinahru, and had attended her charge with a mixture of loathing and terror. For this was Zakal the Terrible, the greatest of the Kolinahr masters, with a mind so powerful he had twice used it to melt the skin of his enemies into puddles at his feet.

He said nothing to stop the healer from going, merely closed his eyes and smiled wanly. It was fitting to lie here and listen to the roar of the storm on the last night of his life. Eight hundred

3

and eighty-seven seasons ago, he had been born in a storm like this one, and so his mother had named him Zakal: the Fury, the Desert Storm.

He was drowsing off when an image jolted him awake. Khoteth, lean and young and strong, furling himself in his black traveling cloak, his expression severe, brows weighed down by the heaviness of what he was about to do. Khoteth was crossing the desert, Khoteth was coming for him. Zakal knew this with unquestionable surety, in spite of the three initiates in the next room who stood guard, not over his aged, dying body, but over a far more dangerous weapon: his mind. Even their combined efforts to shield the truth from him could not completely sever his link to the man he had raised as his own son. Khoteth had sensed his master's impending death, and would be here well before dawn.

The new High Master was risking his life by crossing the desert in a sandstorm . . . and oh, how Zakal listened to the wind and willed for Khoteth to be swallowed up by it! He tried in vain to summon up the old powers, but fever and the continual mental oppression caused by the initiates made it impossible. Zakal contented himself with cheering on the storm as if he had conjured it himself. Even so, he knew that Khoteth would complete his journey successfully.

So it was that, a few hours later when Khoteth's soft words drew Zakal from a feverish reverie, they brought with them no surprise.

"Master? I have come."

Outside, the wind had eased, but still moaned softly. Zakal kept his face toward the black stone wall and did not trouble to raise his head. The sound of his former student's voice evoked within him a curious mixture of fondness and bitter hatred.

"Go away." He meant to thunder it with authority, but what emerged was weak and quavering, the ineffectual wheezing of an old man. He felt shame. Could this be the voice of the Ruler of ShanaiKahr, the most powerful and feared mind-lord of all Vulcan? He had known more of the secrets of power than the rest of the Kolinahru put together, but fool that he was, he had entrusted too many of them to the man who stood before him now. He turned his head—slowly, for any movement made him dizzy and liable to start coughing again—and opened fever-pained eyes to the sight of the one he had loved as a son, had chosen as his successor, and now despised as his mortal enemy. "Leave me,

Khoteth. I may be your prisoner, but you cannot tell me when to die. There is time yet.''

"My name is Sotek,'' his captor admonished mildly. Khoteth drew back the hood of his cloak, scattering rust-colored sand onto the stone floor. Such a young one—too young for a High Master, Zakal thought disapprovingly—but the responsibility had prematurely etched the first lines of age between his brows. Khoteth's severe expression had eased into one of calculated neutrality, but Zakal could see the emotion that smoldered in his eyes, the one sign of the highly passionate nature Khoteth had been born with. As a child, he had been a true prodigy at the secret arts, devouring everything Zakal dared teach him, always hungering for more. In spite of his own appetite for power, Zakal had early on glimpsed the unpleasant truth of the matter. This child would grow into a man who would surpass his teacher, the greatest of all teachers. If you cannot defeat your enemy, then bring him into your camp. Zakal designated the lad as his successor, for one day Khoteth's abilities would lead him to much more than rulership of a single city. One day, he would be master of all the western towns, perhaps someday even Master of the entire continent. And Zakal, the wise teacher and adviser, would have to be content to ally himself with such power if he could not be the source of it himself.

Even with his powerful imagination, Zakal had never thought his protégé's incredible talent could be thwarted, wasted, perverted by the simple-minded philosophy of a coward.

"Sotek," Zakal hissed, and raised his head just enough to spit on the floor in Khoteth's direction. The young master did not flinch at the ominously bright green spittle at his boots, but a flicker of dark emotion shone in his eyes. Zakal's thin lips curved upward with irony. So Khoteth was at last afraid of his teacher again . . . as he had been years ago, when he had first confined Zakal here. Only this time it was not mental sorcery that made Khoteth cringe. Lunglock fever made cowards of them all.

Zakal found his breath for an instant. "What kind of name is that for a Vulcan? And what are your followers called now? Sarak? Serak? Sirak? Sorak? And how many Suraks altogether, please? Tell me, how long do you think this can last until you run out of names for your children?" He emitted a wheezing cackle that deteriorated into a coughing spell.

He was far too weak to sit up and so lay, hands pressed tight against his aching ribs, and choked helplessly on the vile fluid seeping up from his lungs. Khoteth watched dispassionately, hands still hidden beneath the folds of his cloak, which would be burned, Zakal knew, as soon as Khoteth left the mountain stronghold.

"How can you bear to see your old teacher like this," Zakal managed to gasp at length, "knowing that they do not permit me to ease my pain?"

"I regret that your pain is a necessary consequence." Khoteth came no closer. "But to permit you access to any of the mind rules would be very foolish."

"Foolish!" Zakal croaked. "Where is your compassion?"

Khoteth's eyes were intense, though his tone remained cool. "I operate according to the principles of logic, not compassion." He struggled to keep a wry smile from curving his lips, and was not entirely successful. "And I know you, Master. You merit no compassion. I have seen you kill without mercy or guilt. Given the chance, you would murder me here and now without a second's hesitation."

The piteous expression on Zakal's face shifted into a harder one. "I would. And that is also why you are here, to kill."

Puzzled, Khoteth raised an eyebrow at him.

"Perhaps," said Zakal, "not to kill my body . . . but my spirit. You have come to deny me the second life."

"You misunderstand, Master." The folds of Khoteth's cloak parted, and with both hands he drew forth a shimmering globe. "I have come to keep the promise I made so long ago."

Zakal's dimming eyes widened at the sight of the *vrekatra,* the receptacle in which his eternal spirit would rest for all eternity. "But Nortakh—" he began, until the heaviness in his chest left him gasping again. Nortakh, one of Zakal's initiates with no particular talent for mental sorcery, had been Khoteth's sworn rival ever since the new High Master chose to follow Surak's teachings. Zakal had been taken prisoner and hidden in the desert so that Nortakh and his followers could have no more access to the secret knowledge. Indeed, Zakal had expected the new High Master to deny him the vrekatra—for to do so was the only way to ensure that the secrets would be forever lost, safe from Surak's enemies.

"Nortakh grows more powerful each day." Khoteth brought the glowing orb a step closer to the dying Vulcan. "I will confess that at first I considered setting your katra upon the winds . . .

but I am bound to keep my vow to you. And . . . I need all of your knowledge, Master, if I am to defeat him."

Zakal found the strength to taunt him. "I thought the followers of Surak took no action against their enemies. Aren't you supposed to deal peace with Nortakh?"

A slight grimace rippled over Khoteth's serious features. "I will do no physical harm to Nortakh or any of his Kolinahru, but that does not preclude my taking certain . . . precautions. Nortakh must be rendered harmless if Vulcan is ever to be at peace."

Zakal coughed into his handcloth again and idly watched the stain spread through the fabric. "Surak's utopia of peace is a childish fantasy, a refusal to face reality. All creatures must prey on others, and compete among themselves; this is the way of survival, the way of all life. Surak would have us deny what we are." A spasm of pain clutched his chest, making him wheeze. His distress was so desperate, so unfeigned, that Khoteth forgot his composure and, alarmed, moved toward his old teacher, but Zakal waved him back with the bloody cloth. After a moment, he managed to speak.

"Surak will not succeed. His followers will come to their senses, just as S'task did. And S'task was his closest disciple."

"S'task and his followers are leaving Vulcan," Khoteth said quietly, his eyes searching the old master's face for a reaction, "so that Surak may be successful. Even S'task acknowledges the folly of more strife, more wars."

"Leaving Vulcan!" Zakal cried, enraged at the cowardice of S'task and his followers, humiliated that such common knowledge could be kept from him by the three initiated idiots in the next room. The outburst caused another spasm of pain, a hot, heavy fire that shot up from his solar plexus to the back of his throat.

"Twelve thousand are preparing for the journey on the first ship. It is expected that more will follow."

For an instant Zakal forgot his anger in the face of supreme agony. The achingly heavy fluid in his lungs seemed turned to acid, burning him, eating at him. Without the mind rules, he managed for a short time to transcend the pain with sheer hatred. "So . . ." he gasped. "The planet is in the hands of sheep . . . while true Vulcans surrender their birthright. I swear to you—before the Elements—were I free, I would convince S'task to stay and fight. I would kill Surak myself—"

"I know that, Master. That is why I have taken care that your katra does not fall into the wrong hands." Khoteth held out the globe. "It is time."

"No!" Zakal tried to shriek. "I will not be used to help Surak!" But the words came out an indistinct gurgling noise.

Even so, Khoteth understood. "Master," he said sadly, "would you see all of your knowledge scattered on the winds? This"—he nodded at the shining vrekatra—"this is your destiny."

Bitterness filled Zakal's mouth and he began to choke furiously, spraying blood in all directions. In the midst of his desperate fight for air, a ridiculous thought struck him: *I am drowning. I am drowning in the middle of the desert, where there is no water.* . . . And in spite of his pain, the irony of it shook him with fevered, silent laughter.

A gentle force propelled him into a sitting position, so that he was able to suck in air. Khoteth was next to him, holding him up, and he was dimly aware that Khoteth was risking his own life to do so. The vrekatra sat at the foot of the bed.

"I can force you, Master," the young Vulcan said. "But I will not. If you wish to join the Elements, I will not prevent you. Your knowledge would be most useful to me, but I can find a way to render Nortakh harmless without it."

And so, Zakal realized, Khoteth had jeopardized his own life, not out of a desire to attain the secret knowledge to defeat his enemies, but out of a sense of duty, to fulfill his promise to his old master. And in the midst of Zakal's swirling, dying thoughts, one single, disgusted refrain stood out with perfect clarity: *How did I manage to raise such a fool?*

Eyes closed, Zakal lay against Khoteth's strong arm and used the last moment of his life to consider his options. Attempting a mental takeover of the young master would be foolhardy; the three initiates would prevent it, and even without their help, Khoteth was likely to emerge the victor from such a clash of wills. The choice was simple: utter annihilation . . . or eternal life on the mental plane. Despite his fury at the idea that his secrets would be used to further Surak's aims, Zakal was far too selfish to contemplate nonexistence. Perhaps Khoteth had known it, had counted on it, when making his "noble" offer. Perhaps the boy was not as stupid as he had thought. . . .

"The vrekatra," Zakal sighed. And as Khoteth pressed cool

fingers against the desert-hot skin of his master's temples, Zakal's final thought inside his body was:

I shall have my revenge on you, Surak, for stealing my pupil, my city, my world from me. I shall have my revenge, if I have to wait for ten thousand seasons. . . .

Outside, the wind became still.

SPACEDOCK,
EARTH

————— ☆ —————

Stardate 6987.31

ONE

Jim Kirk sat in the captain's chair on the bridge and watched as Spacedock gradually grew larger, rotating slowly on its axis like some gigantic burnished metal top. Beyond it, suspended in the void of space, hung a sphere of marbled blue-white: Earth.

The *Enterprise* was coming home.

Impossible not to feel a tug of nostalgia at the sight: it had been no fewer than five years since he last stood on Earth, five years since he last witnessed this very sight—only then, Earth and Spacedock had been receding as the *Enterprise* moved away toward the unknown reaches of space.

Good Lord, Jim remarked silently. *Knock it off before you get maudlin.*

The past few days, as the ship drew closer to its final destination, he'd been alternating between wistful regret and restlessness—he refused to admit that it was fear—yet there it was, full-blown, irrational, waking him in the night to stare up in the darkness. The feeling that what was most important to him— the captaincy, the *Enterprise*—was on the verge of slipping through his fingers.

Not that he would let it.

Kirk ran a finger under the too-tight collar of his dress uniform and promised himself that as soon as the ship was safely docked, he would head for his quarters and deal directly with the source of the anxiety: a certain Admiral Gregor Fortenberry, director of assignments at Starfleet Headquarters, more popularly known as the Detailer.

Spacedock loomed a bit larger on the main viewscreen. Jim stared at it, feeling the self-conscious, heightened awareness that came with the realization that this was the *last time* for something. He'd experienced the same emotion—the need to commit every shred of detail to memory, to focus on what was happening so intently, time slowed—his last day at home before leaving for the Academy, and again, his graduation day at the Academy . . .

He stopped the thought; the situation did not apply to this ship, this crew. *Not the last day. I'll be back in this chair in a year or so, that's all.* A year or so, and the *Enterprise* would be refitted, recommissioned, and, hell or high water, Kirk would be commanding her. He refused to recognize any other possibility.

"Lieutenant," Kirk said, his gaze still on the screen. "Advise approach control, please."

"Approach control," Uhura said, seated at the communications console behind the captain's chair. No doubt she had been poised, anticipating this particular order. "This is the USS *Enterprise*, ready for docking maneuver." Her voice was calm, steady as always, but Kirk perceived a trace of the anticipation that permeated the bridge. Even Spock had quit pretending to be busy at the science station and had swiveled in his seat to stare frankly at their destination.

The response signal was strong, clean of interstellar static at such close range. *"Enterprise,"* came the young masculine voice of the controller, "you are cleared to dock at Bay Thirteen." A pause. "Welcome home."

"Enterprise confirms," Uhura replied, "and thank you. It's good to be back."

Kirk glanced over his shoulder to see her smiling, and smiled himself. It *was* good to be back . . . still, it would have felt better if Jim knew that, while the *Enterprise* spent the next year or so in Spacedock being refitted, another ship awaited him. While he would never feel quite the same pride and loyalty he felt for this ship, his first command, at least there would be a ship; at least he would be out there, in space.

"Mr. Sulu. Slow to one-quarter impulse power." Kirk sighed. "Take us home."

"Aye, aye, sir. One-quarter impulse power." Sulu's expression was placid, but his dark eyes shone with keen excitement. Like his captain, he wore his formal dress tunic, satin-sheen gold for Command. Sulu appeared to have no regrets about returning home; within a matter of days, he would receive official notification that the promotion Kirk had sponsored him for had been granted, and that he was no longer Lieutenant Sulu, but Lieutenant Commander. It would not be many more years, Kirk reflected, before Sulu captained a ship of his own.

The *Enterprise* slowed as it approached Spacedock and assumed a spiral orbit until it reached the huge hangar doors that shielded Bay Thirteen from the radiation of space. As the ship neared, the hangar doors silently parted; the *Enterprise* glided easily into the massive bay.

Behind her, the great doors closed. Inside, the bay's interior was vast enough to accommodate dozens of starships, and did— some of them, as the *Enterprise* would soon be herself, undergoing refits; others, maintenance; still others, new ships, lay in various stages of construction.

As the *Enterprise* neared Docking Bay Thirteen, the controller spoke again. "*Enterprise,* please stand by for final docking procedure."

"Standing by," Uhura responded.

"Mr. Sulu," Kirk said, resisting the desire to jump up and pace until they were safely into port. He wanted no part of the upcoming festivities, wanted only for the docking to be over, for the chance to pressure Fortenberry into reassuring him that the *Victorious* would be his to command. "Activate moorings. Stand by with gravitational support systems."

"Moorings activated, Captain. All systems standing by."

Seated next to Sulu at the navigational console, Chekov did a double take at the screen, his round cherubic face reflecting awe. "Captain, look . . ." He emitted a low whistle.

Kirk followed the navigator's gaze to the viewscreen, which showed the blinking lights of Bay Thirteen and the row of small ports along the bay's upper level. As the ship moved closer, Kirk could just make out the crowds of people pressing against the port, all trying to catch a glimpse of the *Enterprise* as she arrived home at the end of a successful five-year mission.

"Some reception," Sulu remarked *sotto voce* with a pleased grin.

Kirk did his best to appear unmoved by the spectacle. "Activate gravitational support systems."

Sulu forced himself to look away from the screen and down at the helm control panel. "Activating now, sir."

"There must be a lot of reporters," Chekov mused to no one in particular.

"Gravitational support systems locked on, Captain."

"Disengage engines."

At the engineering station which sat directly opposite Spock, Ensign deRoos, a thin, angular human female, gave Kirk a grim look. "Engines disengaged, Captain."

It seemed to Kirk that the ship sighed as she eased into the bay and then stopped, though someone who knew her less well would not have been able to tell that she was no longer moving. "Well," Kirk said. It seemed somehow anticlimactic. "So here we are." He leaned down to press the toggle for the ship-wide intercom.

"Ladies and gentlemen, this is the captain. Let me be the first to congratulate you on a safe arrival home." He paused, confused by his own reaction to arriving home: he should have been exhilarated, or at the very least, relieved, instead of this oddly nagging disappointment. And perhaps he wasn't the only one to experience it; the times he had pictured this moment in his imagination, the crew always cheered. But there were no cheers on the bridge, only smiles, and almost—or was he projecting his own feelings onto those of his crew?—reluctance.

He continued awkwardly. "Let me also say that I am proud to have served with you, the best damn crew in the Fleet. My commendations to all of you." Another pause. "Tomorrow at 0900, Admiral Morrow will conduct a review. Until then—let the firewatch festivities commence."

He snapped off the intercom and was about to get to his feet when the entire bridge crew—Sulu and Chekov at the helm, Uhura at communications, deRoos at engineering—rose as one, turned to face their captain, and applauded solemnly. All, that is, with the exception of Spock, who rose, hands clasped behind his back, his expression grave but managing nevertheless to convey the fact that, although he did not follow the custom, he agreed with the sentiment.

"Not for me," Kirk said, rising. He raised a hand for silence, uncomfortable with the tribute. Modesty, false or otherwise, had nothing to do with it—but the ovation seemed to him misdirected. The applause thinned. "Not for me. For those who didn't make it back with us."

The second round of applause was restrained; this time, Kirk joined in.

* * *

Austerely elegant in his blue dress tunic, Spock stepped onto the turbolift with the captain. The others, as if picking up on the fact that the captain might have a few things to discuss with his first officer, remained on the bridge to shut down their stations.

Kirk spoke the instant the lift doors closed. "Spock, I want you to know that I've sponsored your promotion to captain. It should come through in a matter of days."

Spock opened his mouth and drew in a breath as if to reply, but Jim didn't give him a chance. He'd expected a protest—the Vulcan had often enough voiced his lack of desire to command. "Look, Spock, there's no need to repeat that business about not wanting a ship of your own. You *deserve* it—you've earned it— and a newly commissioned research vessel, the *Grissom,* is in need of a captain. I've recommended you for the job."

Spock stared ahead at the turbolift doors for a few seconds, apparently weighing his answer. At last he turned his head to regard Kirk with sober dark eyes. "I appreciate the gesture, Captain."

Jim waited for more; when it did not come, he frowned. "You appreciate the gesture . . . but *what,* Spock? Don't you have any opinion on the matter?"

Spock blinked and looked back at the lift doors. His long, angular face was composed in an entirely inscrutable, unemotional expression, but Kirk got a fleeting impression of mulish stubbornness. Spock was not in the mood to discuss it because he'd already made up his mind, and that was that. "I shall . . . consider it, along with another offer."

Kirk felt a surge of surprised irritation. Was *everything* at Scheduling being done behind his back? "What offer? No one at Starfleet mentioned the possibility of your receiving another assignment."

Spock's coal-black brows rose slightly as he half-turned his head to glance at the captain. "An assignment as an instructor at Starfleet Academy. The information is available from the Detailer's office." He hesitated. "Did you ask?"

"No, but—" Kirk broke off and tried to return to the topic the Vulcan had so successfully led him away from. "Look, Spock, the point is that it makes no sense to stagnate where you are. Command is a challenge—but you've learned a lot over the past five years. You'd make a damn fine captain, whether you'll admit it or not. It's the best thing for your career—"

"Captain." There was the faintest tinge of irritation in the first officer's voice as he turned to face Kirk, but it disappeared before Kirk could be certain he'd really detected it. "My desire to remain at my present rank has nothing whatsoever to do with a lack of confidence as to my fitness for command. And while I appreciate your concern for my career, I remain somewhat puzzled by your insistence on my promotion. I respectfully point out that *you* are in the same position as I at the moment—under pressure to accept a promotion you do not want. I am frankly at a loss to understand your reasoning, as you yourself have requested a lateral career move, to the captaincy of the *Victorious.*"

Kirk felt a flush of warmth in his neck and face. "I haven't told anyone except the Detailer about that. How did you find out?"

"I asked," Spock replied simply. "Such things are public record." The turbolift began to slow. "May I speak openly, Captain?"

Kirk reached out for the control and brought the lift to a halt. "I wouldn't have it otherwise. You know that, Spock."

"Then may I know why you have not requested me as first officer aboard the *Victorious?*" Spock's deep-set eyes narrowed slightly as he studied Kirk's reaction to the question.

I'll be damned, Kirk realized with amazement. *He's angry about it.* "I already told you, Spock—it wouldn't be fair for me to hold your career back. If I requested you as my first officer, it would be a purely selfish move on my part. And I was afraid your sense of loyalty wouldn't let you put what's best for you foremost."

A shallow crease appeared between Spock's upward-slanting brows. "You are making the assumption, Captain, that what is best for my career is also best for me. However, you do not make the same misguided assumption in your own case. Why did *you* refuse promotion?"

Kirk didn't have to consider the answer for even a second. "Because I'm doing what I love best. I want to be in the middle of the action, not stuck behind some desk as an administrator—"

"And *I,*" Spock countered, "am a scientist. As science officer aboard a starship, I am constantly exposed to new life forms, new scientific discoveries—it is an opportunity for field research which is unparalleled. I therefore submit that my request to continue to serve as your first officer and science officer is quite reasonable."

"I understand that. But the *Grissom* is a research vessel—" Jim began, but he knew his line of attack was doomed to failure.

"If I were science officer aboard her, the scientific opportunity would be an excellent one. However, a captain's duties do not permit the luxury of research."

"Mr. Spock, I can't withdraw my recommendation—"

"I quite understand, Captain. But I wanted you to understand why I shall most likely refuse it . . . if Starfleet decides to permit me, which I believe it shall, considering the other option it provided me with."

Kirk acknowledged defeat with a sigh. "Understood, Spock—and no hard feelings." He smiled grimly. "Actually, after arguing with Fortenberry and Admiral Morrow the past few weeks, it's refreshing to talk to someone who shares my point of view about a promotion to the admiralty." He paused. "That is, assuming you feel I'm justified in refusing one."

"You would be foolish," the Vulcan said deliberately, "to accept it. Your temperament ill suits you for an administrative assignment."

"You make it sound like a personal failure, but I'll take it as a backhanded compliment. And I'll remember that when I talk to Fortenberry. I was just on my way to talk to him. Since you've obviously been in touch with him, then you also know I still haven't received my orders."

Spock gave a nod.

"Opinion. What are they trying to pull by delaying my orders?"

"My best hypothesis is that they intend to pressure you into accepting the promotion—but as to what precise action they intend to take in order to do so, I am at a loss."

Kirk touched the control. So . . . he wasn't being paranoid after all. A very small relief compared to the greater worry of being right. The lift began to move again, very slowly, then eased to a halt. "My thoughts exactly. Not that pressure will do them any good—I can play that game as well as they can."

Spock tilted his head, puzzled. "I scarcely see what pressure you could bring to bear on Starfleet Command—with the sole exception of threatening them with your resignation."

"If necessary, that is exactly what I intend to do."

The lift doors opened. "Then by all means, Captain," Spock

replied slowly, "I suggest you prepare yourself for the possibility of having to carry out your threat." He stepped out into the corridor.

Startled, Kirk watched him go. "It won't come to that," Jim said, more to himself than to Spock. He stepped from the lift before the doors closed over him.

He caught up to the Vulcan. "It won't come to that," he repeated, more loudly this time.

Spock glanced sideways at him with hooded eyes. "Perhaps not," he said, but his tone was noncommittal. He did not speak again until he arrived at the door to his quarters, where he stopped and turned to face Kirk. "I have . . . deeply appreciated the opportunity to serve under you, Captain. It is my hope to do so again."

"I guarantee it," Kirk said emphatically, but as the Vulcan disappeared behind the door to his quarters, Jim found himself wondering whether he would be able to keep that promise.

In the privacy of his own quarters, Jim pulled the damnably tight collar open and sat at his desk to stare at the dark terminal screen.

Dammit, Spock was wrong. If Jim threatened to resign, Command would never risk calling his bluff. The Fleet couldn't afford to lose him. . . .

He thumped the intercom toggle with his fist. "Lieutenant Uhura—"

A bass voice answered. "This is Vigelshevsky, sir; I just relieved Lieutenant Uhura not two minutes ago."

"Vigelshevsky, raise Starfleet Headquarters. The Detailer's office. I want to speak to Admiral Fortenberry himself. And pu it on visual."

"Aye, Captain."

Kirk fastened his collar and grimaced irritably. The encounter with Fortenberry was bound to be uncomfortable in more ways than one.

The response came faster than he expected. He had forgotten that the distance between Command Headquarters and the *Enterprise* was now negligible. In fewer than thirty seconds, Vigelshevsky's voice filtered over the intercom again.

"Sir, Admiral Fortenberry's secretary informs me that he's in his office, but not to be disturbed."

Kirk hunched forward, his forearms resting on the desk,

both hands curled into fists. He had waited long enough, dammit, and he wasn't going to be put off by someone's secretary. "Put me through to his secretary, then."

The terminal on Kirk's desk brightened as the secretary, a gawky young ensign with protruding eyes and a prominent Adam's apple appeared on the screen. He stared wide-eyed at Kirk.

"C-Captain. I'm sorry, sir, but Admiral Fortenberry is eating lunch. He doesn't like to be disturbed—"

"Who's in there with him?" Kirk demanded, scowling. While he despised bullies as a rule, at the moment he was desperate to get through to Fortenberry, to do whatever was necessary to get another ship—even if it meant making this quivering ensign miserable.

"No one, sir, but he's eating lu—"

"Ensign," Kirk said slowly, drawing ominously close to the screen, "did the admiral give you a direct order that he wasn't to be disturbed?"

"W-well, sir"—the young man's hands fluttered nervously— "not specifically, but—"

"I'm a captain, and I'm giving you a direct order *now*," Kirk said, not at all nicely. "Put me through to him."

"Sir . . ." The Adam's apple bobbed alarmingly as the ensign swallowed, and his huge eyes grew even huger as he contemplated which fate was worse. "With all due respect, Captain, he's not going to appreciate—"

Kirk interrupted out of pity and managed a faint half-smile. "I'll tell him I pulled rank on you and threatened to drum you out of the Service."

"Oh, *thank* you, sir," the young man breathed, and fumbled for the control. His image vanished, replaced by that of a human male whose skin was the same color as the pumpernickel on the oversize egg-salad sandwich he was eating.

The admiral looked up, startled, but recovered himself immediately. Middle-aged, lean, dressed in a neatly fitted dark gray tunic, Fortenberry was noted for his meticulousness, a quality that made him well-suited for the job of Detailer. He chewed his bite of sandwich leisurely, thoroughly, then swallowed and dabbed at his neatly trimmed salt-and-pepper beard before saying:

"I'm not in the habit of doing business during lunch, Captain. Ensign Moroz knows that."

"It's my fault, sir. I pulled rank on your secretary," Kirk said, trying to maintain his anger and not be distracted by the two tiny pieces of egg white caught in Fortenberry's wiry beard. "Admiral Fortenberry, I filed my assignment request with your office a full ten weeks ago and have heard nothing. Nearly all my crew received their orders a month ago. The *Enterprise* just docked, and still the computer lists no assignment for me. Sir . . . just what exactly is going on?"

Mouth closed, Fortenberry ran his tongue over his teeth, probing for bits of egg salad, and eyed Kirk coldly for a full minute. Then he folded his hands on his desk, cleared his throat, and said, "Obviously, *nothing* is going on. But then, that's the problem, isn't it?"

"Is that supposed to be a joke, sir?" Kirk struggled to keep his tone polite and even. The Detailer was full of quirks—after two conversations with the man, Kirk couldn't decide if Fortenberry was simply strange or having fun with him. Though technically an admiral, the Detailer was considered "beyond" rank— an attitude dating back to the old Navy tradition of having a civilian serve in the post. But Fortenberry seemed to relish the power he wielded over those in the Fleet.

"No, indeed." The Detailer's amber eyes regarded Kirk soberly. "I suppose that at this late date there's no harm in telling you that your assignment request has been put on hold."

"On *hold?*"

"For review." Fortenberry stroked his beard with long, spatulate fingers; the nails were tastefully manicured. A crumb of egg white tumbled onto the white breast of his tunic.

"For *review?*" Kirk stood up and hunched over, shoving his face into the screen. Review was for those candidates whose career records were spotty, mediocre, whose chances for promotion or for the requested assignment were in grave doubt.

"Yes." Fortenberry's tone was one of icy disdain. "Are you going to repeat every one of my answers back to me, Captain?"

Kirk felt a flush of heat on his face, and opened his mouth to say, *As long as you keep baiting me, you arrogant ass,* but he closed it again. Fortenberry saw, and was pleased; he knew, Kirk realized with a pang of honest hatred for both himself and Fortenberry, that the captain would say nothing to jeopardize the Detailer's goodwill—and thus his assignment to the *Victorious.*

"Admiral Fortenberry," he said, with hostile civility, discovering that it was possible to say the man's name with one's teeth firmly clenched, "I really have only *one* question, to which I would sincerely appreciate an answer. Who ordered the hold—and review?"

The amber eyes narrowed. "Fleet Admiral Nogura."

Nogura, Kirk almost repeated, but caught himself in time. He'd expected to hear the name Morrow—the admiral who'd sponsored him for his captaincy and was now pressuring him to apply for a promotion to the admiralty. But he'd never expected Nogura . . . Nogura, recently come out of retirement to be the head of Starfleet Command. Nogura, the highest-ranking admiral in the Fleet, referred to by his underlings as the Old Man, and sometimes, not all that jokingly, God Himself. Kirk had prepared himself to do battle with Morrow over this, but taking on the head of Starfleet was not something he'd expected at all. Morrow he could deal with, but Nogura . . .

For a split second he remembered Spock's words—

I suggest you prepare yourself for the possibility of having to carry out your threat

—and just as quickly dismissed them.

It won't come to that. If Nogura's involved, it just shows how badly Starfleet wants me. There's got to be some kind of deal I could strike with them. . . .

Surprisingly, the Detailer's dark features aligned themselves in an expression of sympathy. He spread his large sable hands. "I'm sorry, Captain. There's simply nothing I can do until Admiral Nogura lifts the hold on your file."

"I understand," Kirk answered abruptly, scarcely seeing Fortenberry in front of him; in his mind's eye, he was already arguing with Nogura. "Thank you for the . . . information, Admiral."

Fortenberry said something which Kirk did not bother to understand; he touched the intercom toggle and signaled Vigelshevsky again.

"Lieutenant. Get me Fleet Admiral Nogura."

A surprised pause, and then Vigelshevsky replied, "Yes, *sir.*"

Kirk saw that he was clutching the viewscreen terminal with both hands, and forced his arms to drop to his sides. He wasn't afraid of Nogura by any means, but the fact that the admiral was involved meant that Jim would have to argue that much harder to obtain the *Victorious.*

Let him try, dammit. I'll find a way to convince him to see my side of it—

Vigelshevsky came on the intercom again. "Sir, I'm sorry, but Admiral Nogura is out of his office."

"See if you can track him down at HQ."

"He's left Command HQ, sir. His aide said she's unable to get in touch with him at the moment. Shall I leave a message, Captain?"

Kirk paused. "No. I'll get in touch with him later."

"Yes, sir."

Kirk closed the channel and stared at the empty screen. The encounter with Fortenberry had done nothing to reassure him, had only served to blacken his mood and increase his anxiety. Obtaining captaincy of the *Victorious* would be ten times more difficult than he had anticipated—

By God, I'll find a way. He rose and walked over to the wall mirror to refasten his collar.

The last damn thing he was in the mood for was a party, least of all a farewell party, least of all a farewell party for the *Enterprise*. He paused on his way out to sweep his gaze over the modest captain's quarters, over the packed suitcase unobtrusively set in a corner of the bedroom.

Goddammit, this isn't *good-bye. . . .*

McCoy's quarters were disturbingly bare: the inner bedroom was empty with the exception of two huge suitcases lying open on the bed, the outer office stripped save for two liquor bottles and two large whiskey glasses on the desk. The doctor, dressed in a pale blue civilian worksuit that accentuated his blue eyes and the first hints of silver in his dark hair, rose grinning from his chair behind the desk. One of the glasses was already one-third full of amber liquid.

"From the looks of things, you've started without me," Kirk said. He meant to say it lightly, as a joke, but in his darkened mood it came out sounding like an accusation.

McCoy's ebullient spirits remained undampened. "Hey, I did my best to wait for you, Jim." He picked up the glass and gestured at Kirk with it. "But when you made that formal proclamation—well, hell, I *had* to drink to the best damn crew in the Fleet." He picked up one of the bottles, an old dust-covered flask, and uncorked it. "Let me pour you one."

Kirk didn't protest. He deflated, sighing, into the chair

opposite McCoy's and swiveled his head to study the bleak surroundings.

"Kinda depressing, isn't it?" McCoy's cheerfulness ebbed slightly; he kept his gaze on Jim's glass as he poured. "You live someplace for years, and in twenty minutes you're all packed up and the place looks like a damned hotel room." He handed Jim his drink, then sat down to nurse his own. "Maybe we should have had the drink in your quarters."

"They look the same," Jim answered shortly. He'd hoped McCoy would cheer him up; instead, he seemed to be bringing the doctor down with him. He nodded at McCoy's clothes. "Dressed for shore leave already, I see." For the past several weeks the doctor had expressed his eagerness for an extended leave to anyone who would listen.

McCoy looked down at himself and spread his hands demurely. "What, this old thing? Just practicing. I wanted to see what it felt like to wear civvies again."

"Brings out the color of your eyes. Looks good with the silver in your hair too." Jim took a swallow rather than a sip of his drink. Cognac, and a very good one—it went down too easily. Kirk breathed in the aftertaste of fire and vanilla and apricot.

"Silver?" McCoy scoffed, defensively running his fingers through the hair near his temples, as if trying to smooth away the traces of gray. "What silver?"

"Don't tell me your eyes are going too."

"You're just jealous because you're stuck wearing that monkey suit for our last drink together, and *I* get to be comfortable."

"Do you have to make it sound so goddamn *final?* It's not like we'll never see each other again," Kirk snapped with a bitterness that surprised both of them.

McCoy's blue eyes widened slightly, then narrowed again. "Jim, are you really that mad about my wearing civvies, or is it something else?"

"Something else." Jim set his glass down, closed his eyes, and drew a hand across them. He felt suddenly exhausted, unwilling to face the remainder of the day's festivities.

"They gave someone else the *Victorious?*" McCoy's voice was grim with concern.

"Almost that bad." Jim looked up and stared at his drink for a minute before picking it up and taking another sip.

"For God's sake, Jim, don't keep me in suspense—"

"Nogura put my request on hold."

"The Old Man himself, huh?" McCoy took another sip of his bourbon and savored it. He seemed unimpressed by the fact, which frustrated Jim even further.

"They're going to pull out the stops to try to pressure me into this promotion, Bones—I can feel it."

"Now, don't give up so quick, Jim. You let the ol' doctor help you out on this one."

"Who the hell said anything about giving up? With you as my witness, Bones, I swear, whatever they're planning, I'll never give in."

"Just calm down and listen to me for a minute, will you?" The doctor set down his glass. "You're forgetting that in a case like this, the chief medical officer's recommendation has enormous impact. So much so, in fact"—McCoy leaned across the desk and lowered his voice like a conspirator—"that my opinion has already been sought. By the Old Man himself."

"Nogura contacted you?" Jim blurted angrily; he very nearly leapt to his feet. "And you didn't *tell* me about it?"

McCoy motioned for him to keep his seat. "For God's sake, don't get in a huff, just *listen*. I didn't *tell* you because I didn't want you getting all worked up like you are now. Nogura's office contacted me a couple days ago, all very confidentially. He'd seen my report on you which recommended *against* your promotion. After the way Morrow raved about you, he figured you were a shoo-in for admiral, and my report shocked him. I guess he figured you had some deep dark character flaw that I was too polite to mention directly."

Jim saw that he was gripping his glass so tightly that his knuckles had turned pale yellow. He consciously tried to relax his hand. "So what'd you tell him?"

McCoy wagged an admonishing finger at Jim and picked up his glass again. "Ah, ah. You know better than that, Captain. These things are strictly confidential. But since I've piqued your interest, let's just say it had something to do with the wasting of an exceptional talent for field command. I let him know in no uncertain terms that promoting you would be a criminal act. I also told him if I heard about any such promotion going through over my head, civilian or not, I'd personally hightail it over to Starfleet Headquarters and let him know what I thought about it. Threatened to resign myself." He grinned toothily, relishing the memory. "I was pretty vehement about it, and Nogura came away mightily impressed, if I say so myself."

While the doctor was speaking, Jim felt the tension in his face and neck ease. By the time McCoy finished, Jim's expression had lightened and he was almost—almost—smiling, for two reasons. First, because the chief medical officer's report was always weighted heavily in such instances; if McCoy had been *that* emphatic, Nogura would definitely think twice before he overrode the CMO's report. And second, because he could picture McCoy chewing out Nogura and not giving a good goddamn if he *was* the Head of Starfleet. Still, Nogura had had two days in which to think it over . . . why no decision yet?

"Well?" McCoy demanded. "Feeling any better?"

"Somewhat, thanks."

"*Some*what?" McCoy feigned outrage. "I threaten God Himself, and you're feeling only *somewhat* better?"

Jim smiled at the doctor's good-natured tirade. No point in explaining that Nogura's failure to make a decision within two days was in itself cause for concern; he changed the subject. "I hereby formally appreciate what you did for me, Bones. Thank you. Now, why don't we change the subject to something more pleasant? Like the fact that you're running off to have some fun."

"Damn straight," McCoy agreed with gusto. "Hey, did I bother to tell you Chris has decided to go back for her medical degree?"

"At least twice. But you still haven't told me where you're headed. Any idea?"

"Oh, yes . . . a very definite idea." McCoy's lips curved in a sheepish little smile.

"Well, don't keep me in suspense, Doctor, after all the noise you've been making lately about looking forward to six months' leave—"

The doctor's smile widened. "Oh, all right, if you insist. . . . You remember Natira, don't you, Jim?"

"How could I forget?" Natira, high priestess of the planet-ship Yonada, and descendant of the Fabrini race, had fallen in love with McCoy and temporarily taken him as her mate when the *Enterprise* landing party beamed down to prevent Yonada's collision with an asteroid. "Don't tell me—"

McCoy's cheeks took on an uncharacteristically red hue. "Well, you know that I've been meaning to do some research on all the medical documents contained in the Fabrini records, and I figured since I was headed out there, I might as well pay Natira a little visit—"

"Of course," Jim deadpanned, nodding.

"Anyway, to tell you the truth, I'm a little nervous about it. The Yonadans have settled on a new planet, but the conditions there are pretty . . . primitive. No subspace communications. They're pretty uninterested in our technology—plus, there's the Prime Directive . . ."

"She'll be happy to see you, Bones. You know that," Jim said, finally distracted enough by McCoy's worries to relax.

"Let's hope so." But McCoy sounded dubious.

"Doctor, I do believe you're blushing."

"Go to hell. Finish your drink." The doctor threw his head back and drained his glass, then set it down on the desk with a *clunk.*

Jim did likewise and stood up.

"Only one drink?" McCoy asked, surprised.

Jim nodded at the liquor bottles on the desk. "We can finish those off later. Right now, I've got some farewell parties to attend."

McCoy rose. "I'm going with you."

"I thought the chief medical officer had a party of his own to conduct."

"I do. But Chris and M'Benga are keeping an eye on things till I get there. I told 'em I might be a little late. This is my last day aboard the *Enterprise,* and by God, I'm going to enjoy it. My prescription is for you to do the same." McCoy rubbed his hands together gleefully. "Now, where do we start?"

TWO

——————— ☆ ———————

Security Second-in-Command Lieutenant Jonathon Stanger stood in front of the closed door and adjusted the collar of his dress reds, then gave his carefully trimmed black mustache an unconscious nervous stroke. He was on his way to a party, yet his mood was anything but festive. He reached for the buzzer, stopped himself, and took a second to close his eyes and try to think of something pleasant.

In his current dark mood, he couldn't think of a damn thing to smile about.

Hell, yes, you can. You've just been promoted. And you're going to be security chief aboard the Victorious. *Now,* that's *something to smile about.*

True, he was happy about that; but at this particular moment it was still hard to smile. As Stanger opened his eyes again, he forced a broad insincere grin, then let it fade slowly so that his expression wouldn't look artificially cheerful, nor quite so glum as it had appeared in the mirror back in his quarters.

He drew in a breath and pressed the buzzer. For several seconds nothing happened. Stanger was just getting ready to press the buzzer again when the door slid open abruptly. He stepped back, startled.

"Lamia," he said.

She stood in the doorway of her quarters, dressed in the same scarlet satin tunic and black breeches Stanger wore; the braid on her sleeve indicated the rank of lieutenant, junior grade. Lamia was almost his height (and Stanger was tall for a human), with a silver-white cap of straight, silky hair; her skin was the powder blue of Earth's sky. She wore a grimace as unnatural as the one that had graced Stanger's face an instant before, but she had better reason: on her home planet, Andor, smiling was unknown. Even so, Andorians were an extremely adaptable people who took pride in mastering other cultures' customs; when Lamia was honestly happy, Stanger knew, her smiles looked perfectly human.

Of course, she was not happy now.

"You look great," he said with false cheerfulness.

"So do you." Her voice was whisper-soft. She stepped out next to him and touched his hand; her skin was pale and cool against his own dark brown flesh. He formally offered her his arm. She took it, and together they walked down the corridor, each shyly avoiding the other's eyes, as if afraid even a look might destroy their tenuous resolve to be cheerful.

After an awkward silence, Lamia spoke. "I want you to know that I've made up my mind to not be sad." She glanced at him with light celery-colored eyes.

"That's good," Stanger said, still looking straight ahead. "I've made up my mind not to be sad, too." He paused. "But it isn't all that easy."

"I didn't mean that it was. But I think it's the best thing for both of us. For our careers, that is." She was referring to the fact that Stanger had accepted the position of security chief aboard the *Victorious;* but in order to secure a promotion, Lamia had accepted a deep-space assignment aboard a different vessel, the *Exeter.* A temporary separation was the only intelligent solution. Even so, he resented the fact that he could not have both her and the promotion to security chief.

"Yes," Stanger said with the faintest tinge of bitterness in his voice. "The best thing."

"It'll only be for a year, maybe even less if an opening comes up on the *Victorious.*" She was studying him intently. "Please don't be upset, Jon."

"Lamia." He sighed, stopped walking, and faced her. "I'm trying not to be upset, okay? I'm going to do my damnedest to have fun at this party, to do what I can to make saying good-bye easier on both of us. Just don't expect me to act deliriously happy when the subject comes up."

"I understand. I feel the same." She took his warm hand in her cool one.

He gave it a gentle squeeze. "If only you didn't have to ship out so soon—being alone on leave isn't going to be much of a leave at all." He'd accrued an entire month's worth, which began immediately, after which time he'd begin a five-month assignment Earthside, and then ship out on the *Victorious*. Lamia's assignment, however, required her to report for duty aboard the *Exeter* tomorrow and defer her accrued leave to some later date. As much as he'd looked forward to shore leave, now the thought struck him:

What the hell am I going to do by myself for an entire month?

He'd find something to do, of course. He'd always been an independent sort, and he wasn't going to let a year's separation get to him. He'd been through far, far worse things than this. . . . Day after tomorrow, when she was gone, he'd be all right. It was just that looking at her now, and knowing she was leaving, was difficult.

Lamia laid a delicate blue finger across his lips. "We've talked about this before. Repeating it isn't going to help."

"I know it's all for the best," he said quietly, his lips brushing against her slender finger. She drew her hand away. "And I'm not complaining. It's just that . . . I guess it didn't sink in until just now, when I realized you really are leaving tomorrow." He stared at her for a moment, so that later he'd be able to conjure up the image of what she looked like here, now. "Damn, I'm going to miss you."

"It's only for a year or so." Her tone was firm. "We can survive that long. Now, stop it, Jon, before you make me sad again." She let go of his hand and took his arm, a signal to start moving again; he did so reluctantly. They walked silently, arm-in-arm, the rest of the way to the Security Lounge.

At the entrance, Lamia let go of his arm and moved to a discreet distance from him; while their relationship was hardly a secret, public displays of affection between officers were considered unprofessional. Stanger smoothed his tunic one last time, then stepped inside.

The chairs in the Security Lounge had already been moved to one side; in the center of the room stood a buffet table covered with platters of hors d'oeuvres. A small crowd of Security personnel had already gathered, so that the room was a moving sea of red.

"Geezus," Stanger muttered. "Have you ever seen so many redshirts in one room?"

"Yes," Lamia whispered next to him. "At my graduation ceremony at the Academy." She waved at someone on the other side of the room.

"Stanger! Lamia! Over here!"

Stanger turned his head at the sound of his name; what he saw made him do a double take. He gave the Andorian a discreet nudge and said, out of the corner of his mouth, "Take a look at that, will you?"

In a far corner, Security Chief Ingrit Tomson—all six feet, six inches of her—stood behind a portable servitor bar waving a half-empty flute of champagne. Her thin straw-colored hair was twisted into its usual tight bun, but today a hospitable smile replaced her normally dour expression. As was the custom for the head of each department, Tomson was playing host and bartender—and it seemed she'd found enough time to have a drink herself.

Stanger grinned in earnest as he and Lamia headed toward her. When he'd first met Tomson, he'd despised her: a pale, oversize scarecrow, the woman had a cold, mistrustful disposition and a well-earned reputation as a martinet. But after working for her for a few years, Stanger had earned her trust and her goodwill. Tomson was still a stickler for regulations, and could be damned uptight, though she was also fair: screw up, and you'd pay dearly for it, but if she decided you'd earned something—as in Stanger's case, a promotion—then she'd move heaven and earth to get it for you.

Of course, there was nothing she hated more than getting caught doing something nice for someone. Ruined the tough, coldhearted image, Stanger supposed.

As they approached, Tomson punched a code into the servitor and leaned down seconds later to lift out another crystal flute goblet, which she handed gingerly to Stanger. The flute was frosted, ice cold, and his fingers left prints where he touched the glass.

"Here you are, Lieutenant. Part of the required uniform of the day." She turned to Lamia. "And you, Lieutenant . . . ?"

Stanger gave Lamia a warning look. Andorians were extremely susceptible to alcohol poisoning, a fact Stanger had discovered on an evening's shore leave with Lamia, an evening he—and no doubt she—would rather forget. She hadn't touched a drop of liquor since that night, but he was suddenly worried that she might forget caution and be reckless: after all, she was leaving tomorrow. But Lamia returned his glance with a cool "don't-you-trust-me" look of her own before answering Tomson. "I'll have some Thirellian water . . . in a champagne glass, please."

"Coming right up," Tomson said. She wasn't at all drunk, Stanger realized; not even tipsy. At most she'd had a sip or two from the champagne glass resting on the bar. What gave him that initial impression was the fact that she was smiling and exuberant—both cause for amazement—and the fact that her normally milk-white complexion was flushed. Her skin was so translucent that the vascular dilation caused by a mere half-glass of champagne had turned the end of her nose a vibrant rosy pink. Stanger realized he was staring at it, and when he looked away, he caught Lamia's wide-eyed gaze: she'd been staring at it too. He felt a sudden ridiculous urge to giggle, and turned his attention to the bubbles rising in his glass until the impulse passed. Blithely unaware, Tomson hunched down a bit to code in the request, then bent over to retrieve the glass when it appeared in the servitor opening. "Here you are."

"Thank you." Lamia took the proffered glass and began to take a sip.

"Ah." Tomson raised a warning finger. "Before you do that . . ." She raised her voice and called out, "Atten*tion!*"

The noise level in the room fell immediately, tapering off quickly to impressive silence as those speaking recognized the voice of their security chief.

Tomson's expression and tone became entirely serious. "Now that all of you are here, I'd like to say a few words. First, congratulations to Second-in-Command Stanger for his promotion to full lieutenant, and his coming assignment as security chief of the *Victorious.*"

Polite applause. Stanger did his best to smile graciously and not fidget.

"And to Acker Esswein and Martina Vorozh, on their promotions from ensign to lieutenant, junior grade."

More restrained applause. Tomson raised her glass solemnly. "A toast, to all of you: to echo Captain Kirk, the best damn

security crew in the Fleet. It has been my pleasure and privilege
to serve as your commanding officer."

The clapping grew thunderous. In a graceful, fluid motion,
Tomson tilted her head back, emptied her glass, and set it down.

Suddenly caught up in the spirit of things, Stanger took a
deep breath and drank his champagne in three fast swallows. He
saw Lamia's slightly shocked expression out of the corner of his
eye, but he didn't care. He wanted to get blissfully, painlessly
drunk, and he had every right in the world to: to mourn the fact
that his lover was leaving him tomorrow and this was his last day
aboard the *Enterprise,* and to celebrate the fact of his promotion.

He stepped up to the bar and set the glass down. Tomson
was already setting out more champagne for those who had
finished off theirs for the toast; Stanger took one, waited for a
few people to come up and get fresh glasses, then raised his drink
aloft and said:

"To Lieutenant Commander Ingrit Tomson: the best security
chief in the Fleet."

The door opened and closed behind him, but Stanger didn't
react; he polished off his champagne, again in three swallows.

"I'll drink to that," a voice behind him said.

"Captain," Tomson said, quickly setting down her empty
flute. She sounded the tiniest bit stricken, as if she'd just been
caught flagrantly violating a regulation; but she recovered
quickly. Stanger turned his head and caught a glimpse of light
blue and chartreuse amid all that red.

"Welcome, sir. And welcome, Dr. McCoy." Tomson took
two full glasses from the bar and walked over to hand them to the
captain and the doctor.

Stanger got himself another drink and followed. The champagne was just beginning to have effect; the room seemed suddenly warmer, the people friendlier, and the soles of his feet
tingled faintly, as they always did when he was pleasantly tipsy.

The captain smiled up at Tomson as he took the flute. He
gestured expansively with it at the others. "Let's not forget the
toast: To the best security chief in the Fleet." He took a small
sip.

"To the best security chief," Stanger cchoed, along with
others, and drained his glass yet a third time. Lamia, standing
next to his right elbow, spoke into his ear.

"Jon . . . you're going to get terribly drunk."

He ignored her and instead grinned at the captain. He felt a surge of warmth for the man and suddenly wanted to explain to him just how very highly he and everyone else aboard the *Enterprise* thought of him, just how much he appreciated the chance to serve under such a legend.

But Kirk was busy talking to Tomson. "And congratulations on your new assignment. Command was very lucky to get you."

"Thank you, sir. It'll be a little strange being Earthside, but the opportunity's worth it." Tomson turned her attention to McCoy. "I see the doctor couldn't wait to wear his civilian clothing."

McCoy took a sip of his champagne before replying in his Georgian drawl. At times it was scarcely noticeable, but when the mood struck him, the doctor could lay it on so thick Stanger could barely make out what he was saying. "I just couldn't stand the thought of having to put on my dress uniform again. If they didn't make the collars so damn stiff . . ."

He trailed off, his shrewd blue eyes focused curiously on Tomson's face. The nose, Stanger realized, and bit down hard on his upper lip to keep from grinning. McCoy noticed, and, apparently on the verge of smiling himself, looked over at the buffet, down at his feet, anywhere but at Tomson's face.

"So, Captain," Stanger said quickly, to distract himself. "We're all very interested to hear what you have planned, sir." He expected to hear Kirk's formal announcement that he was planning to take command of the *Victorious;* after all, the word had been out for a month that Kirk had personally relayed the request to the Detailer's office. It was one more reason Stanger looked forward to serving aboard that particular vessel.

"Nothing at all, Lieutenant." Kirk took his second sip of champagne. "Six months of R&R with absolutely nothing to do."

Later, when he was sober, Stanger would hate himself for being so stupid as to press. It was clear—or would have been clear if he hadn't been drunk—that the captain had avoided mentioning it because he didn't want to go into it. But no, he had to be stupid and ask. "And then, sir . . . ? The *Victorious?*" Very faintly, he was aware of Lamia giving him a surreptitious kick on the side of his boot, but his mind was too numbed to connect it with what he was saying.

Kirk smiled, but the smile did not extend to his eyes. Stanger thought he saw a flash of veiled anger, and something very like bitterness there . . . or perhaps he had only imagined it. Kirk looked down at his glass, and when he looked back up, the anger was gone, the smile still frozen in place. "We'll see," he said.

It was obviously all he was going to say about it. Both McCoy and Tomson looked away; the doctor shifted uncomfortably. There passed an awkward silence.

"Well," the captain said finally. "You'll have to excuse me, but I'm afraid I have many more parties to attend. My best to you all." He went over to the bar and set down his almost-full goblet; Tomson followed and picked up a fresh glass, which she raised in another toast.

"To Captain James T. Kirk."

He and McCoy left while everyone was still drinking.

As he finished his fourth round of champagne, Stanger had a revelation. Kirk's puzzling behavior became blindingly, exquisitely clear. Stanger stood staring at the doors that had just closed over the doctor and the captain. "That," he announced rather thickly to no one in particular, "was the face of a man about to be kicked upstairs against his will."

"Engineering," Kirk said tersely into the turbolift control, then glanced at the doctor standing alongside him. Neither had said a word since leaving the Security party. McCoy still held his crystal flute and was just polishing off his champagne; he swallowed, wiped his mouth with the back of his hand, and belched discreetly.

Kirk looked away, at a spot on the lift emergency manual-control panel. "Good Lord, Bones, am I going to get the same question everywhere I go tonight?"

" 'Fraid so, Jim." McCoy's tone was matter-of-fact and surprisingly free of sympathy. "The crew's curious—they want to know. You can't blame 'em. So you'd better start rehearsing your answer." He paused. "I'd opt for the truth myself. Better you tell them than have the rumor mill invent something worse."

"Damn," Jim said softly, more in response to the situation than to the doctor's statement. "What could be taking Nogura so long to make up his mind?"

"Dunno. Why don't you ask him?"

"I will—as soon as I can find him."

The atmosphere on the main Engineering deck seemed even more convivial than that in Security—in part, Kirk decided, because Engineering was one of the largest departments on the ship, and thus there were more people, who managed to fill the huge deck so completely that Kirk and McCoy had to elbow their way to the bar. But there was no doubt that at least part of the credit was due to the chief of engineering, who, like Tomson, was serving drinks from behind a bar servitor.

"Gentlemen," Commander Montgomery Scott cried, his normally ruddy complexion ruddier than ever, "come and hae a drink." Like the others in Engineering and Security, he wore his red dress tunic; unlike the others, he forwent the black breeches in favor of a tartan wool kilt. He had been in the midst of an animated conversation with a slender blond officer, who turned to follow Scott's gaze. Kirk recognized Will Decker, son of the late Captain Matt Decker, Kirk's friend who had died in the line of duty. After Matt's death, Kirk had followed the boy's progress; Will showed every sign of having his father's talent for command.

"Now, this," McCoy shouted into Jim's ear in order to be heard over the talk and laughter (the acoustics in Engineering were perfect), "*this* is a party. Scotty sure knows how to throw one. Do you think we could skip the Science party and just stay here? I hate to think how dull that one'll be with Spock in charge . . ."

"I'll let you stay here," Kirk said.

"What?" McCoy cupped a hand around his ear.

But Kirk had no chance to repeat himself. As he and McCoy approached the bar, Decker stepped forward, smiling. Though the young man held a near-empty glass in one hand and was slightly flushed, he was totally sober.

"Captain Kirk. It's good to see you again, sir."

"Commander Decker," Kirk said, forcing a cheerful expression. "Will."

Scott pulled a glass from the servitor and shoved it into the captain's hand.

"What's this?" Kirk lowered his face to smell the dark honey-colored liquid.

"Single-malt Scotch," the chief engineer proclaimed with Gaelic pride. His burr was becoming particularly noticeable. "The only proper drink for such an occasion."

McCoy set his glass down on the bar. "I'll have a champagne."

"Champagne?" Scott grimaced derisively and eyed the doctor's glass with distaste. "Come, Doctor. Champagne is for children and weaklings. What *you* need is a good stiff Scotch."

He reached into the servitor again and set a glass down in front of McCoy with intimidating firmness.

McCoy looked uncertainly at it, then back at Scott, then over at Kirk, who leaned with one arm on the bar, enjoying the doctor's predicament.

"Help me, Jim," McCoy begged.

Kirk smiled. "You're on your own." He lifted his glass at McCoy. Though the doctor would never dare admit it in front of Scott, Kirk knew he passionately despised Scotch.

In the meantime, Scott had procured himself a glass; he raised it as well. "Gentlemen," he intoned. "To the *Enterprise*."

Decker lifted his now-empty glass.

"To the *Enterprise*," McCoy sighed, yielding. He picked up the Scotch, took a tentative sip, and shuddered faintly.

"To the *Enterprise*," Kirk echoed. He envied Scott, the only one who didn't have to give up the *Enterprise*—the engineer had received word of his assignment: the supervision of her refit. Jim sipped the Scotch. Despite McCoy's reaction, it was of excellent quality, full-bodied, with a smoky aftertaste. He took another sip.

"Ah." Scott smacked his lips with unembarrassed pleasure. "Now, *that's* a drink, eh, Doctor?"

"Absolutely," McCoy deadpanned, but he caught Jim's gaze and rolled his eyes.

"Speaking of the *Enterprise,* Scotty," Kirk asked, "what's your estimate of the time needed for her refit?"

"Year and a half," Scott answered confidently. "Unless they come up with some new technological improvements during that time, in which case it'll be two. At the outside. I assume you'll be asking to take her out again once she's ready, Captain?"

"You can count on it, Mr. Scott."

"As a matter of fact, Commander Decker and I were just discussing the *Enterprise*'s refit," Scott said. "Will here is verra knowledgeable about all the latest advances."

Decker smiled and gave a nonchalant shrug. "You could call it a . . . hobby. I like to read the technical journals. It's my way of unwinding. Before I decided on the command track, my first love was engineering."

"Which makes him perfectly suited to help with the refit," Scott said approvingly.

Decker nodded. "It's a great opportunity," the young man said, somewhat unconvincingly.

Kirk knew the reason for Decker's dissatisfaction.

"You'll get a ship of your own soon, Will," the captain said. "You deserve it." Yet, as he spoke, he became aware of the ironic contrast between himself and Will—Decker, the rising young star, eager, hopeful of getting his first command . . .

And Kirk, the seasoned captain, on the verge of losing his. He extricated himself from the thought with a repressed shudder of disgust at his own self-pity, and saw Scott gazing quizzically at him.

"And what will ye be doing in the meantime, sir?"

McCoy surreptitiously set his drink down on the bar and did his best to ignore it. "Don't ask him that, Scotty, unless you want your head bitten off."

Scott tilted his head questioningly and looked at the two of them.

"It's all right, Mr. Scott." Kirk sighed and paused to take another swallow of Scotch. McCoy had been right earlier: no point in withholding the truth, however awkward it might make Jim feel. "You probably heard that I requested captaincy of the *Victorious*—"

"I did indeed, sir, though of course I never take rumors too seriously—"

"Of course. Well, that was one rumor that happened to be true." Jim set his glass down next to McCoy's. The Scotch, good as it was, did not sit well on top of the cognac and the small amount of champagne. He knew better than to allow himself to get drunk this afternoon: in his current state of mind, it would only serve to make him depressed. "I don't know what I'll be doing in the meantime. I haven't received my orders yet. My file's been put on—"

He broke off. As he was talking, Scott had begun to somewhat distracted by a commotion on the other side of the deck. Scott tried to keep listening, but whatever was happening across the way became too much for him. "What the . . . ?" Scott muttered, finally unable to pretend to pay attention to the captain any longer.

"Good Lord," Decker said.

The deck grew quiet, save for sudden intakes of breath and whispers; even McCoy was staring, wide-eyed. Kirk turned.

Fleet Admiral Heihachiro Nogura was walking toward the bar. The head of Starfleet Operations was unimpressive-looking— a slight silver-haired man with dark eyes; the top of his head came barely as high as Jim's chin. He looked ancient—until he moved or spoke, and then he seemed a man of much younger years. In civilian clothes, on the street, no one would have guessed him to be anyone of importance.

But on the Engineering deck, officers were snapping to attention and sidling out of his way with murmured greetings as he made his way to where Jim and McCoy were standing. Even McCoy nervously smoothed out his civilian suit and straightened his posture—a fact that some detached part of Jim's brain noted as amusing and filed in order to tease the doctor about someday. McCoy had always claimed he didn't give a tinker's damn about rank and wasn't afraid of Starfleet brass.

But as unthreatening as Nogura's physical appearance was, the man had some intangible quality about him that forced others to recognize him as a leader. Jim tried to name it. *Confidence,* he thought at first, then decided that even though Nogura clearly carried himself with confidence, it wasn't quite the right word. *Presence.* That was it. Heihachiro Nogura had presence.

"Admiral," Jim said, and nodded graciously as Nogura came to stop in front of him. "Welcome aboard. This is quite a surprise."

It was one hell of an understatement. The only official visitor expected from Starfleet Command was Admiral Morrow, who wouldn't arrive until tomorrow. For the head of Starfleet to show was irregular in the extreme.

Jim's tone was one of total politeness, of course, but there was absolutely no doubt in his mind as to why the admiral had come: to talk him into the promotion. Nogura wouldn't make a personal visit just to tell Jim that his request had been granted. The captain smiled and Nogura smiled back: two friendly enemies squaring off for the fight.

"Good to see you, Jim," Nogura said heartily, offering his hand; Jim gave it a firm shake. Nogura matched his grip. "I didn't mean to interrupt the party . . ." He turned to the silent crowd behind him—"At ease. Please continue"—then turned back. "But I did want to come to offer my congratulations on your safe return, Captain, and the end of a successful mission."

"Thank you, sir." He started to ask at first how Nogura had managed to get aboard without Vigelshevsky or someone else alerting him, but realized immediately that there was no point in asking; if the head of Starfleet asked to come aboard without the captain's knowledge, no officer in his right mind would dare stand in his way.

"Lot of reporters out there. A real circus. You're wise not to let any of them in. But I think they intend to wait until you come out."

"Sir," Scott breathed. He stood rather comically at attention, chin tucked under, chest thrust out. "Commander Montgomery Scott, sir. Admiral Nogura, may I offer you a drink, sir?"

"Admiral." Decker nodded gravely.

Nogura smiled benignly. "I see you're all having a little off-duty celebration, eh? What's that servitor stocked with, Commander Scott?"

"Scotch, Admiral." Scott paused, and then, as if confessing a great secret, added, "Very *good* Scotch, sir. Old Laphroaig. Single malt, the best there is."

"Hm." The admiral seemed unmoved. "You wouldn't happen to have some black tea, would you, Commander? I'm afraid that, unlike the rest of you, I have to report back to my office this afternoon."

"Tea?" Scott's expression sagged ever so slightly. "I'll bring you some from the officers' lounge, Admiral, right away."

"No, no, if the servitor isn't stocked, don't bother. It was just a thought." Nogura turned from him to face Jim and McCoy.

Kirk gestured at the doctor. "My chief medical officer, Dr. Leonard McCoy . . ."

McCoy bowed formally from the shoulders, as if he'd never seen the man before in his life, but Nogura said, "Ah, yes, the doctor and I have met."

Kirk smiled thinly. *Damn straight you have. So let's get down to why you've come.*

"I'll be honest, Jim." Nogura's deep-set eyes regarded him with complete sincerity and openness, which made Jim worry even more about what he was up to. "I didn't come just to join in the celebration. I wonder if I could bend your ear for a few moments." His gaze swept over McCoy, Scott, and Decker. "In private, of course."

"Of course," Kirk said easily, but inside he felt a ripple of familiar anxiety: they were really going to try to do it, they were going to pull out the stops and try to force him into the admiralty.

And he'd be damned if he'd let them. By God, if it meant threatening them with resignation, then he'd do it, regardless of what Spock had said.

He could see from the faint glimmer of angry distrust in the doctor's eyes that McCoy had picked up on what was going on, but there was nothing that could be done except meet the admiral head-on.

"Why don't we go take a stroll in the corridor?" Nogura suggested pleasantly.

On Earth, it was early afternoon on a weekday, but the *Enterprise* corridors, though brightly lit, were deserted. Everyone was off celebrating, a fact Nogura had no doubt noticed on his way to Engineering. Once outside, the admiral wasted no time.

Nogura folded his hands behind his back and began walking at a slow, steady pace. He regarded Jim with a calm, impenetrable gaze. "You know what I've come to talk about, of course." It was not a question.

"Of course," Jim said. He volunteered nothing further; he wanted first to hear what Nogura had to say, to know precisely what angle the admiral would be coming from. Trying to second-guess someone as shrewd as Nogura rarely paid off.

The older man looked away for a moment at the far end of the corridor. "This Rittenhouse thing has shaken Starfleet to the core. The media weren't kind, and the publicity hurt us badly, very badly. The words 'Starfleet Command' used to be held in esteem; now people shake their heads and whisper in the same breath of cabals, of unscrupulous admirals wielding too much power. They've lost any faith they ever had in the Fleet. Even Fleet officers and personnel have little trust in Command, and that can destroy us. Hell, even the Federation itself began to look at us with a jaundiced eye. If we lost Federation support, we'd be out of business."

"Admiral Rittenhouse and his power-hungry cohorts might have tried to take control of the Fleet—but you and I both know they could never have succeeded. Not in this day and age."

" 'It couldn't happen here,' eh? Don't be so sure, Jim," Nogura said. "He came damn close to pulling it off. Damn close."

"You didn't come here to talk about the Rittenhouse scandal," Jim said impatiently.

Nogura looked back at him. "To be perfectly honest, I didn't want to come out of retirement, Jim. I did so because I was needed. People knew me, trusted me. My name generated confidence and respect. For that reason, I came back. Your name, Jim, whether you know it or not, generates that same confidence and respect." He paused to let the words sink in. "I wouldn't have put your assignment request on hold if I didn't desperately need you."

A muscle in Kirk's jaw twitched. "You were right, Admiral. I knew what you were going to say; perhaps *you* know what *I'm* going to say now. Perhaps we could have avoided this entire conversation."

Nogura tilted his head, his gaze bright and birdlike.

"I appreciate what you're saying, Admiral. I, too, want to do what's best for the Fleet—which is to serve it the best way I can, as a starship captain. I have no talent for administration, sir. It bores me. I would be doing you and Starfleet a disservice by accepting such a promotion."

Nogura stopped abruptly and turned to face him. "Then tell me what it would take to get you to accept one."

"A ship," Jim answered.

The admiral began walking again, his fine, sparse brows knitting as he considered this. They continued in silence for a while; at length Nogura said, "What is it about commanding a ship that you find so rewarding?" There was no reproach in his tone, only curiosity.

Jim was taken aback by the question. It seemed so clear, so obvious to him, that he had never broken it down into specifics before. Haltingly he replied, "The chance to travel, to explore . . . to not be chained to a desk. To be where things are . . . happening. To be able to command."

"An admiral commands more than a captain. A captain commands one ship; an admiral can command a fleet," Nogura countered.

"It's not the same. Commanding long-distance isn't the same as being there, being able to see the immediate effects your orders have." Jim shook his head. "It's far more rewarding to be a captain. And frankly, sir, I have—had—a friend or two who made the transition from starship captain to admiral."

"Waverleigh," Nogura said.

Jim nodded. "He hated it, and warned me not to make the same mistake."

"I suppose if I spoke ill of the dead and said Waverleigh was always a bit of a misfit, that would do little to change your mind."

The admiral released a soundless sigh. "I take it you'll refuse the promotion, then?"

"I'm prepared to resign, if necessary."

The thin gray brows went up a few millimeters at that. "I see. That would be . . . unfortunate."

Jim didn't respond. Was Nogura threatening that it would come to that?

But the admiral switched the subject. "You've got how much leave coming up, Jim? Six months?"

He nodded.

"That's a lot of time," Nogura said, "to think things over. Maybe there's a way for both of us to get what we want. You think about that, Jim." He gave Jim's shoulder a friendly slap. "I'll be in touch."

And with that he disappeared down the corridor.

The doctor was in the middle of a dead sleep when the buzzer woke him. "What the devil . . . ?"

He struggled to a sitting position and waited, gasping, for the mental fog to lift enough for him to understand where he was and what had just happened. He and Jim had stayed up late the night before, drinking—an entirely morose experience, given the captain's mood; the more cognac Jim had, the more vehemently he swore never to give up the captaincy—and although McCoy had had the good sense to take a pill before retiring, to diminish the effects of the alcohol, he still felt hung-over, as if his tongue and brain were swaddled in cotton. It had been a rough night; he'd awakened several times from anxious dreams of Natira . . . and at least once, bolted upright in bed, pulse racing, fully alert a split second after waking, a single thought circling his brain:

Am I doing the right thing?

Of course he was. He'd always known he'd return to Natira someday, and that she'd be waiting for him. There had never been any doubt in his mind.

At least, none that he'd known about. He hadn't been able to go to sleep after that, not for hours; finally, when it was almost morning, he'd drifted off, exhausted.

Now the buzzer sounded a second time. McCoy rose grumbling, found his pants, and for decorum's sake pulled them over his underwear, then gave his black T-shirt a couple of mindless tucks so that it hung half-in, half-out of his pants. He staggered toward the door.

"Now, who in Hades would have the nerve to wake people up at this ungodly hour—" McCoy pressed the lock release without thinking to ask who was there. The doors slid open.

Spock stood in the doorway. McCoy scowled and rubbed his burning eyes with a fist.

"Good Lord, Spock." It came out a low growl; McCoy coughed in an effort to get his voice working again. "What are you doing up?"

"It is ten o'clock in the morning," Spock said evenly. There was something inexplicably odd in hearing him say *ten o'clock in the morning* and not *ten hundred hours*. McCoy blinked and realized that the Vulcan was dressed in civilian clothes, a sight which made the doctor's mind, if not his tired body, do a double take.

"Ten o'clock in the morning," McCoy repeated. For a moment, he was too confused to make sense of it.

Spock prompted patiently, "I have come to say good-bye."

It struck him then; like Jim, Spock was taking six months' leave before returning to duty. There was a very real chance that McCoy would never see the Vulcan again. He felt a painful and—because it was Spock—embarrassing tightening of his throat. "Oh. Well," he said. "Guess we won't be seeing each other for a long time, will we?"

Spock gazed at him steadily without answering. If the Vulcan felt any discomfort at the potential emotionality of the moment, he did not show it.

McCoy shifted his bare feet awkwardly and cleared his throat. "Look, Spock, I know I've teased you a lot over the years, and maybe we've had a few serious arguments, but I want you to know that in spite of it all . . . Well, hell." He thrust out his hand thoughtlessly, from sheer instinct. When he realized what he had done, he tried to pull it back.

If Spock's Vulcan sensibilities were offended by the doctor's bad manners, he did not show it. He took the proffered hand briefly, then let it go. His grip was strong, warm to the point of feeling feverish. "In spite of our philosophical disagreements, Doctor, I have a great deal of respect for you."

That did it. McCoy felt himself choking up, and was angry at himself for doing so. He cleared his throat a few more times and hoped Spock wouldn't notice the film of tears in his eyes. He did not speak until he was absolutely certain he had control.

"Good-bye, Spock," he said quietly, and then, unable to

contain his exasperation: "Dammit all to hell, I think that of everyone, I'm going to miss you most."

Spock smiled without smiling—something McCoy had seen him do once or twice before, and damned if he knew how the Vulcan did it; something with the eyes, maybe—and nodded ever so slightly in acknowledgment. "Live long and prosper, Doctor."

He turned and walked away down the corridor. McCoy watched him for a while and then withdrew to his quarters to wipe an errant tear and swear at himself for sniffling. He couldn't really help it; he had the strangest feeling he would never see the Vulcan again.

The atmosphere aboard the *Enterprise* was one of muted sadness in comparison to the previous day's gaiety. Most of the crew were gone now, so that the ship began to take on an empty, deserted feel. Those still aboard struggled with suitcases as they murmured good-byes, some of them in civilian clothing, headed at a leisurely pace for shore leave, others still in uniform, dashing to make the shuttle to their next assignment.

Jim Kirk stepped, suitcase in hand, from his quarters into the corridor and very nearly collided with his first officer.

"Spock." Jim stepped back. "I thought you had already gone." He had made his farewells the night before, and this morning had hoped to slip out unseen. Last night had drained him, and he had slept little after the confrontation with Nogura, a scene he replayed in his mind a thousand times, each time trying to figure out what he should have said, *could* have said to the admiral that would have changed the outcome, that would have guaranteed him the *Victorious* . . . and each time, failing.

"I was just leaving." The Vulcan wore a dark blue tunic of Vulcan style and cut; he paused, his expression guarded as he apparently considered the best phrasing for what he had come to say. "But I must admit, Captain, that I am curious."

Jim did not smile, but his tone lightened. "That does seem to be a characteristic of yours, Mr. Spock. Let me guess. You came to ask about Nogura."

"Yes. I understand he came aboard for a brief time yesterday afternoon."

The lightness vanished. "He did," Jim said. "They're putting pressure on me to accept the admiralty—nothing you and I didn't talk about yesterday, really. Nogura asked me why I didn't want a promotion to flag rank, and I told him. When he told me why he wanted to promote me, I threatened to quit; he asked me to reconsider. Told me to take time and think it over while I'm on leave." Jim saw that he was still clutching the suitcase, and set it down.

"Will you?" Spock asked.

He frowned, not following. "Will I what?"

"Think it over. Reconsider."

"No." Jim shook his head firmly, his lips thinning at the very thought. "I stand by what I said to you yesterday, Spock. If I have to resign my commission—"

Spock was gazing implacably at him; Jim averted his eyes. He'd almost said, *and join the border patrol, or become a commercial captain,* but both alternatives were impossible to voice, much less seriously consider. Jim couldn't really believe Nogura would push him that far. Was he being conceited, deluding himself to think that Starfleet would never risk losing him, that Starfleet needed him so badly—in whatever capacity—that they would let him call the shots? He forced himself to look Spock in the eye.

"—then, dammit, I will. And my answer will be the same six months from now."

"I see," Spock said.

"And what about you, Spock?" After last night, Jim was tired of fielding questions about his uncertain future, eager to let someone else do the talking. Besides, in the Vulcan's case, he was honestly curious. "Have you made up your mind yet?"

"No. However, six months is more than sufficient time in which to reach a decision."

"It is indeed," Kirk said. "And I hope you'll consider what I said about the *Grissom.*"

"I will. And if that is all, Captain, then I will again wish you farewell."

"Not exactly 'farewell,' Spock. 'Good-bye,' maybe, or 'till we meet again.' We'll be seeing each other in six months or so." He did not let himself say, *God willing.* Jim smiled, a grim little smile. "Give my regards to your parents."

"I shall. Good-bye, Jim."

"Take care, Spock."

They did not, as they had done last night, shake hands, nor speak formally of the privilege it had been for each to serve with the other. Spock nodded briefly and turned to go back toward his quarters.

Jim did not watch him go. He picked up his suitcase and headed briskly in the opposite direction. He did not, he told himself firmly, feel at all sad to be leaving his first officer, or the *Enterprise*.

After all, it wasn't really good-bye.

THE MOUNTAINS OF GOL

☆

155622 V.O.D.

THREE

───────── ☆ ─────────

Spock stood on the small balcony and watched the sunset paint the plain scarlet. In a far corner of the desert, a single steel-colored cloud spilled rain in huge drops that evaporated in the arid heat a meter before striking the ground. Such ghost rains were uncommon, though not as rare as the rains that soaked the ground. Nearby, to the east, Mount Seleya, the tallest peak in the Gol chain, blocked the view—not that there was anything to see in any direction except barren plain stretching to the horizon. The desert became eerily silent this time of day; not even a breeze whispered. The sky was untroubled by so much as a single blinking skimmer light. In Gol, technology dared not intrude. The desert had lain undisturbed except for the period several thousand seasons ago when the students of Kolinahr came and carved this retreat from the rock. The view from this particular cubicle had probably looked exactly like this to some other pilgrim two millennia before. The desert remained unchanged.

Such was not true for Spock. He had come here because his life had changed, because there was a choice to be made, a choice he had hoped never to make.

He had been on Vulcan not quite six months when he heard the news: Kirk had finally been persuaded to accept flag rank, despite his initial refusal to be "kicked upstairs." Spock had taken it for a rumor, nothing more, but a call to Starfleet Headquarters confirmed the impossible. There would be no chance to serve under Captain Kirk again. Perhaps it had been illogical of Spock to expect a human to be logical, to resist something he clearly felt strongly against.

Yet Spock had never considered the possibility that Kirk would not do as he had sworn. He had taken Kirk at his word: *I stand by what I said. Dammit, if I have to resign, I will. . . .*

For a human, Kirk had always acted most reliably. Yet Spock had felt—though he scorned premonitions and ignored them when he experienced them—that when he spoke to James Kirk outside his quarters that final morning aboard the *Enterprise,* it would be the last time they would speak together as captain and first officer.

He was considering the fact now. That, and the decision he had to make. Starfleet had offered him a promotion to captain, with the option of accepting a command of his own, or training Academy cadets for deep-space assignments. And when he had first returned to Vulcan, the Science Academy had offered him a teaching position, an offer he had neither rejected nor seriously considered. Now his six months of leave was nearly ended; the time for decision had come.

The sense of betrayal Spock felt upon hearing of Kirk's promotion surprised him. So, too, did his difficulty in choosing among his remaining options. In the tradition of his ancestors, he had come here, to Gol, to make a decision. And tradition had seemed curiously fitting: for the first time in his adult life, Spock was considering life on his native planet—to be a Vulcan among Vulcans . . . and, for the second time, was considering taking a Vulcan wife.

"Student," announced the low voice outside the door. Spock turned his head sharply. He had not heard footsteps outside in the corridor, in spite of the fact that he had left the heavy stone door to his cubicle ajar, anticipating that someone would come to take the supper dishes. The Kolinahr students waited on the retreat guests, availing every courtesy.

Spock withdrew from the balcony into the dimly lit room with its black stone walls. "Come."

The student slipped agilely through the crack without pushing the door open further, despite his bulk. He fit the stereotype of a Watcher guard perfectly: medium height, with a thick, muscular build. To allow Spock his privacy, he kept his eyes downcast and headed for the bowl sitting on the table ledge cut from the rock.

Spock scarcely glanced at the student, who had already

turned away with the bowl and was gliding silently toward the door—but something about the student's movement made Spock take a second look. He had seen the student before, when he was much younger, but still thick-necked and burly, and with anger etched on his broad, angular face. . . .

The background filled in, of an image thirty-five years old, of a twelve-year-old face barely capable of masking its fury, of that same burly build scattering Spock's six-year-old tormentors. . . .

"Sekar," he said wonderingly, and then berated himself silently for the surprise in his tone, something that a student of Kolinahr would be quick to hear and disapprove of.

Sekar turned slowly and regarded him. "And you are Spock." He said this without surprise, as if he had known from the beginning the identity of the guest in this particular cubicle. His expression was implacable.

Spock tried to suppress the surge of warmth that directed itself at the student. The child Sekar had come to his defense some thirty-five years ago, silencing the bullies who had challenged Spock as an outsider, as an Earther who had no business claiming his Vulcan heritage. Spock experienced an impulse to thank Sekar for his help after all these years, and reflected grimly that he had spent far too much time among humans.

Sekar wore the simple white robe of a student postulant; he had not yet undergone the Ritual, and was at the point where he was trying to break all emotional ties to others. "You have been gone a long time, Spock. Have you come back among us to stay?"

Spock hesitated. Until that moment he had not been sure of the answer to that question; now, when Sekar asked it aloud, his answer crystallized. He had feared returning home because he doubted whether he would be accepted; and yet, all that had happened since his return pointed to the fact that he was indeed accepted for what he was. His place in Starfleet had evaporated; his place was here now, on Vulcan. Why else had he been offered the job at the Science Academy? Why else had T'Sura offered herself to him? He had been made to feel welcome by her and by one of his former tormentors; what, then, was keeping him from making the decision to stay?

It had all been the misunderstanding of children, the cruelty, that had driven him to Starfleet. But he was an adult now, and so were the children who had once tormented him. Perhaps they had all grown in wisdom.

"Yes," he answered slowly. "I have decided to stay."

Sekar bowed his head in a gesture of respect. "Welcome."

Spock nodded back. "But what of you, Sekar? Do you undergo the Ritual soon?" Courtesy demanded that he ask the question. Before the Ritual, the student was given the chance to take his leave of all family and friends; it was a necessary breaking of ties, a severing of emotional bonds. By asking the question, Spock honored Sekar with the title of friend.

Sekar's hesitation was palpable—an unidentifiable flicker of emotion lit his eyes for an instant and then faded. But it was not friendship Spock perceived, but something closer to fear. Yet Sekar the child had been Spock's protector. Was this Sekar's reaction to the warmth he, too, felt?

"Yes," Sekar said finally. His tone was calm and even. How strange, Spock reflected, that of all of his childhood acquaintances, Sekar, the one who seemed least ashamed of his emotions, should be the one who now sought to rid himself of them.

Even more curiously, Spock got the odd impression that Sekar did not want him to ask the question; yet it was unavoidable now. "May I come to take my leave of you before the Ritual?"

Spock was offering him the chance to sever all ties to this one part of his past, to make the transition to adept easier for him. And yet he felt Sekar would prefer him to stay away, that there was some strange resentment at seeing him here, at this time. The question hung unanswered for a time.

Sekar spoke at last. "Of course. Come in nine days' time. On the tenth, I join with the High Master." He bowed. "Again, welcome home."

Spock returned the gesture. "I shall return in nine days to take my leave."

But first, he would take his leave of another.

SAN FRANCISCO 5:30 A.M.

It was still dark when Jim rose after a near-sleepless night of tossing, so dark that he could barely make out the blue-black outline of the bay against the eastern hills. He'd made only one change to Quince Waverleigh's old apartment, a change he knew the late owner would have approved: a picture window in the bedroom overlooking the bay. The window was almost as large as the one in the living room. Outside, only a few lights blinked against the shore, owing to the early—or late, depending on your point of view—hour. He felt lucky to get the apartment. When he'd contacted Quince's widow about the place, he'd done it on a hunch, even though reason told him she had to have sold it long ago. But Ke hadn't had the heart to live in it, hadn't even had the heart to list it with a realtor. Guilt, perhaps, over the fact that she had left Quince such a short time before his death. Or maybe over the fact that things might have worked out differently if she'd stayed. At any rate, she was glad, she said, to sell it to Jim. Quince would have liked for him to have the place.

Jim kept the lights off and dressed slowly in the dark. Turning them on would have obliterated the view, in which black was already fading to the deepest shade of blue. The chrono blinked softly at him in the darkness, and he swore mentally as he noticed the time: three and a half hours early. Could he stand another three and a half hours of waiting?

He felt as excited as a kid on his first day of school. He hadn't slept the night before he'd left for Starfleet Academy, either. And now he was going back to almost the very same place. Ridiculous, of course. He was thirty-six, too old for anything as juvenile as a case of first-day-on-the-job jitters.

But then, he'd felt the same way when he first got command of the *Enterprise.* . . .

Not nerves. Just a little excited, that's all. And why the hell shouldn't he be?

Your chance, Nogura had said. *Your chance to command more than just a starship, Jim. Think of all those frustrating times when you were a captain, when you wanted to get things done and couldn't because you had to wait for orders. Well, this is your chance to make up for all those times.*

Nogura had said it three months ago, when he'd finally had the nerve to come to the farm, where Jim had been staying with Mom and Peter. A social call, he'd said, and after all, he had known Winona for years . . . but he knew Jim had been waiting for him three full months. The shrewd old fox played it for all it was worth, too. . . . Jim watched and fumed silently while Nogura sat at the kitchen table and drank Earl Grey tea with Winona and chatted about old times and Jim's father, George. Jim wore a strained smile and sipped his tea without a word until they finished off the second pot. This time Jim let Winona get up to refill it.

"Enough of old home week, Admiral," he said finally. He

meant it to sound jocular, meant to keep the bitter edge out of his voice, and wound up failing altogether. "You didn't come here to talk to my mother. Get it over with. Make your pitch. I'll go ahead and refuse the promotion just as I promised, and if you want to, you can drum me out of the Fleet. But I won't be kicked upstairs."

"In some ways, you're a lot like your father," Nogura answered softly, unruffled by the anger in Kirk's voice.

Jim stood up quickly and slammed his cup down so hard that tea sloshed over the side onto Winona's blue gingham tablecloth. George Kirk had never been promoted beyond commander because, according to some, he feared the responsibility that went along with the captaincy. The rumor was that George had always found a way to annoy his superiors enough to delay that final promotion.

"Sit down." Nogura's voice rang with authority. Kirk stared at him angrily for a full minute before slowly, grudgingly taking his seat. The admiral held the Blue Willow teacup in both hands and peered through the wafting steam at Jim with black eyes that were at the same time ancient and very young. "I was referring to your defensiveness, and nothing more." His voice softened. "Just what is it about the admiralty that scares you, Jim?"

Jim weighed whether or not to lose his temper again, and decided against it. He had prepared himself for every possible tactic Nogura might try—except that one. He blinked at the admiral without answering.

Nogura's tone was fatherly. "I didn't come here to make you angry or insult you. And I'll take any excuse I can get to come see Winona again. But it's clear that the idea of a promotion frightens the hell out of you. Why? I want to know why."

"We've been through this before, Admiral. Except then, I believe your question was what it would take to get me to accept a promotion. And my response is still the same: A ship. You can insult me if you want, but we both know it has nothing to do with being afraid. I'm not. You've read my psych file. It would be . . . against my nature, that's all. I'll say it again: I want another ship."

"You're afraid to lose the *Enterprise*," Nogura said point-blank, without anger.

"You're twisting words, Admiral."

Nogura sipped his tea thoughtfully. "Regardless of what you think, I listened to what you said last time we talked. And I've been thinking, Jim. What if I couldn't give you a ship—but I could give you something even better?"

Jim began to shake his head skeptically.

"God knows," Nogura said easily, "I don't want you to resign if I can help it. But I can't stop you from leaving the Service."

There it was—the final card to be played, and the admiral was willing to take the risk.

Jim stared hard at the old man's eyes to see if he meant what he was saying, but the admiral's black eyes were hard, reflecting nothing. *Am I willing to do it? Am I really ready to leave the Fleet?* Command a crew of thirty on some rattletrap stationed near the Klingon border, or become a commercial pilot for the thrill of delivering cargo?

A hint of frustration crept into Nogura's tone. "Dammit, Jim, *listen* to me. Being a starship captain requires a person to become a hell of a diplomat and think on his or her feet. And you were one hell of a starship captain. What if I made you an admiral without chaining you to that desk? If I made you a special envoy, put you in Admiral Ciana's department as a troubleshooter? If it's excitement you want, we could have you warping all over the galaxy again. God knows, you've had more experience in dealing with alien cultures than anyone else. And if it's power you want, there's that too. Power to change things, make things happen, change the big picture—power that isn't limited to just a single ship. Think of the difference a man like you could make, Jim . . ."

"All right," Jim said slowly. "Talk. I'll listen."

And that was when Nogura launched into the *your chance* speech.

It began to make some sense. Jim agreed to think it over and to meet with Admiral Ciana to discuss the details of the proposed assignment.

He'd arrived at Vice Admiral Ciana's office feeling defensive and nursing the suspicion that Nogura's promise had been an idle one calculated to get him as far as Ciana's office. He'd dressed in civs that day—a mute threat—and had gone there, to the sixty-seventh floor of the main building of Starfleet Headquarters, believing that he would succeed in getting Lori Ciana to admit that there was, after all, a catch to Nogura's offer, believing that he was in fact prepared for the encounter with her. As he stood in the open doorway of her office, one glance convinced him that he was not.

He'd known *of* Ciana, of course—knew that she was one of the youngest vice admirals ever appointed (so far), knew that she was Nogura's right-hand adviser in current xenoaffairs, knew that she was reputed to be difficult to work with.

"Captain?" The voice was gracious, authoritative, distinctly feminine. "Please, come in." Behind the desk, Ciana rose. She was not a particularly tall woman, but she gave the illusion of height because she held herself so straight. Only five years Kirk's senior, she had already attained the rank of vice admiral, and with good reason; Jim had already studied her public file. Her records had indicated command material of uncommon brilliance.

Jim walked up to the desk and clasped her extended hand. Her grip was painfully firm, as if intended to illustrate her strength, and her dark blond hair, cut just above shoulder-length so that it swung without grazing her uniform when she looked up or turned her head, had started going prematurely gray several years back. Silver strands mingled with golden.

Beyond that, the vice admiral was, quite simply, stunning. It had both nothing and everything to do with her physical appearance. For she was not an especially beautiful woman, but she possessed an almost electric intensity that enhanced her native attractiveness and made Jim silently catch his breath at first sight of her.

Still, he told himself, he had enough self-control not to be affected by it. "Admiral," he said, nodding. He kept his expression carefully grim and did not return her professional smile.

"I've heard much about you. Please, sit." Ciana sat and gestured at the sleek chair on the other side of the desk. The office was uncluttered, stylish, black with gold appointments.

Kirk lowered himself into the chair and said nothing.

"Well, then"—Ciana folded her hands atop the polished onyx surface of her desk and leaned forward confidently—"shall we get right down to the business at hand, Captain? Unlike Nogura, I have no patience for small talk; I prefer to be direct."

"By all means, Admiral. I prefer directness myself." He managed to say it without a trace of good humor.

Her left eyebrow quirked up a bit at that, her one reaction to his scarcely contained hostility, but her confident graciousness never wavered. "Good. Here it is, then: I want you to work directly with me as a diplomatic troubleshooter. We'd go straight to the hot spots and attempt to negotiate a solution on behalf of Starfleet and the Federation. In terms of judgment, Nogura is willing to give us virtual *carte blanche*—though, of course, as senior officer, you would be answerable to me. But if you work with me, you'll find that I give a lot of leeway—and since we'll work together closely, you have the right to voice your opinion and advise me from the point of view of your starship experience." She paused and stared at him expectantly with intense dark eyes.

It was the same thing Nogura had talked about—and once again, it sounded too good to be true. There had to be a catch. Kirk looked at the darkening sky outside and took his time replying. "It sounds to me like you're giving the job description of a Federation diplomat. That's an entirely different branch of the Service."

"No." Ciana shook her head emphatically; Jim watched the gold-silver hair swing slowly back and forth. "I'm talking about crisis situations where Federation diplomacy has done no good, or where diplomatic relations have entirely broken off. We're expanding rapidly—too rapidly, if you ask me. There's been too much emphasis on soliciting new members and not enough attention paid to those members experiencing internal difficulty. Starfleet doesn't like to talk about Federation members who are disgruntled and want out—but that's what I'm talking about. A very special diplomatic task force . . . a diplomatic 'last resort.' "

"All right." Kirk started out calmly enough, but as he continued, he let some of the anger come out in his voice. "Then why me, Admiral? Why do you need a starship captain so desperately that Nogura is willing to let me walk if I refuse this promotion? Why haven't you simply gone ahead and done this on your own?"

It struck a nerve. Ever so slightly, Ciana stiffened in her chair, and Kirk detected a bright flare of honest-to-God anger that dimmed the same instant it appeared. Yet it seemed more directed at the situation than at Kirk. So . . . the rumors were true; the seemingly perfect vice admiral had an Achilles' heel in the form of a temper.

But Ciana had already forced herself to relax. Once again she gave the impression of coiled force beneath a surface of absolute control, absolute calm—though Kirk now knew it was possible to catch a glimpse of the anger, the white-hot drive that Ciana worked hard not to show. "A fair question," she said easily. "One that requires an answer. And I do believe in total honesty."

"I'm glad to hear it." Kirk's tone was noncommittal.

She paused to stare down at the glossy desktop and collect her thoughts. After several seconds she looked back up at Kirk. "The answer is rather personal, but since your future is involved, you deserve to know." Another pause. "I created this position with you in mind, Kirk. I asked for you specifically; I requested that Nogura put your assignment request on hold. I am, in effect, using you to get what I want."

The statement apparently had the effect she wanted; she smiled faintly at Kirk's shocked stare and went on. "You see, I need your 'hands-on' diplomatic experience. The bottom line is this: I've been working at Starfleet command for the past ten years . . . and I've loved it, but I want more. I want to be a Federation ambassador someday—and not just to some little backwater planet, either, but to Rigel or Vulcan. And here is my problem: I'm a xenopsychologist, so I've got the educational background necessary, and I've been adviser to Nogura as well as to Federation diplomats . . . but as far as in-the-field experience . . . well, many years back, I spent some time aboard a mixed-crew starship as a staff psychologist. I lasted nine months, not because I disliked deep-space travel—in fact, I loved it—and not because I found the job stressful. I left because I was bored out of my skull from the lack of challenge and because I hated the fact that there was nowhere to go, no way to advance beyond 'ship's shrink.' So I wound up here at Command."

"But there are several assignment possibilities you could apply for if it's experience you want," Kirk protested. He was beginning to feel a faint, illogical hope that perhaps he could talk Ciana out of her problem . . . and himself back into the command chair of a starship. "I still don't understand why you need to create a special task force." *Especially one that includes me.*

She glanced away from him toward the glass wall and spoke with a sad reluctance. "There *is* an assignment that I want, that I've been trying for for years—that of Starfleet's diplomatic liaison to the Federation. Nogura has made it abundantly clear that he doesn't want me to have it. He's been very evasive as to why—but he did say that I lacked 'subtlety,' which I suppose has to do with my . . . directness. Apparently he thinks I'm incapable of diplomacy. And then there's the lack of direct experience . . ."

She looked back at Jim with a determination that was fierce. "I've convinced him to let me do this, to *prove* to him that I *can* function effectively as a diplomat. Nogura trusts you, feels I can learn from you. If we're successful at this for a year or two—"

"Exactly," Jim said abruptly. "After a year or two, when you get the assignment you want, what becomes of me? Does my position dissolve? Do I get stuck at some desk in a dark corner?"

She gave a small knowing smile. "Hardly. After all, I wouldn't admit to using you so callously without returning the favor. What's the old expression: You scratch my back . . . ? If you'll teach me what you know, Kirk, I'll do whatever I can to help you. Once I'm gone, of course, you can be head of your own task force—or I'll give you a recommendation for whatever assignment you want." The mysterious smile widened slightly. "And my recommendation carries quite a lot of weight around here, a fact I'm sure you already know."

Kirk looked at her very, very intently, trying to see past her polished exterior. "And if, in that year or two, Admiral, I decide that I want a starship of my own . . . maybe even the refitted *Enterprise* . . . ?"

Ciana returned his gaze with unshakable confidence. "If you want the refitted *Enterprise,* I'll move heaven and earth to get her for you. I can't promise Nogura will let you have her—but I can promise an enthusiastic recommendation." She allowed him a moment to digest this, and drummed her fingers silently against the hard, shiny veneer of her desk.

After a time, she asked softly, "I've leveled with you, told you everything. So you tell me, now: do we have a deal?"

"How can I trust that you'll do as you say?" Kirk asked. He knew even before he said it that it was a naive question, one that could easily and truthfully be answered with:

Because you don't really have any choice.

Turn down Ciana's offer, and what would he have left? No commission, no ship, no future.

But instead, she replied, "Because I swear it on my honor as an officer." And for an instant her expression was so wide open, so honest, that he believed her.

"I see," Jim said. "Then the answer is yes."

Ciana's smile was sincere and almost beautiful. "I'm glad."

At the time, he decided, it was Ciana's aboveboard directness that finally swayed him (along with the fact that it was his best chance of getting the *Enterprise* back). . . .

In later years, when he remembered the instant of that momentous decision, he would admit that he could not recall exactly what was said . . . but what he recalled most clearly was the haunting image of her lovely face.

FOUR

☆

And so, Jim Kirk had left Ciana's office excited at the prospect of working with her. Like him, Ciana despised bureaucracy. Like him, she believed in getting things done. Nogura hadn't been leading him on after all. In the remaining few months of leave, he actually became impatient for the assignment to begin, actually began to look forward to working with Lori Ciana.

Even now, at 5:45 A.M. on this damp fall morning two weeks later, the enthusiasm she had ignited in him still hadn't worn off. And he was beginning to believe it never would.

Why *had* he been frightened of the admiralty, after all?

"Lights on," Jim said. The overhead light came on, reducing the view of the bay to a dark windowpane. Kirk squinted at the full-length mirror just long enough to be sure the dark-gray-and-white uniform with the extra braid on the sleeve was in place. Starfleet had recently issued newly designed uniforms that strongly reminded Jim of pajamas. At least the admiral's uniform was far more flattering than the pale, monochromatic captain's version. Rank still had its privileges.

He cut off the lights again to have another look at the bay. Since he'd come, he couldn't take his eyes off the water. This weekend he was going to buy a sailboat, dammit, and take her out on the bay.

He was glad to have the water.

He wandered out into the living room, turned on an old-fashioned nautical lamp, and got a cup of coffee from the servitor. He drank it looking out at the water. Old Yeller, the stuffed armadillo Quince had willed him, rested on the window ledge. "Back home again," Jim said absently, and rested a hand briefly on the creature. It squirmed and said, in Waverleigh's Texan drawl, "Hello, Jimmy."

Like listening to a ghost. Having Yeller was in a way like having Quince's spirit here.

Don't you ever let anyone talk you into a desk job, Jimmy. . . .

You were depressed when you said that, Quince, Jim answered silently, giving the armadillo another mindless stroke. *Ke and the children had just left you. And you were chained to your desk. You should have made a deal with Nogura like I did—*

A sudden inspiration seized him, and he picked Yeller up from the ledge. "How'd you like to come to work with me, old boy?" He tucked the creature under his arm and was headed for the transporter pad Starfleet had installed for Quince when the bells sounded.

Damn. Only six o'clock. Of course, as an admiral, he could report in anytime he pleased—but his first day, there would be little for him to do before Ciana and her staff arrived to brief him. *What the hell am I going to do with myself for the next few hours?*

With Yeller under his arm, Jim headed for the door. He'd get there on foot—take his time, check out the new neighborhood. And if he got there early, then so be it.

It was shortly after eight o'clock when he arrived at Starfleet Headquarters, the towering edifice that stretched up out of the fog bank. His uniform was clammy against his skin, wet from the heavy morning fog and perspiration. He hadn't realized just how steep some of the hills were in Oldtown. Or was he just that tired after five years out in deep space?

He walked in through silver double doors that opened as he neared. Invisible scanners recorded his entry, verified that he was allowed unimpeded passage. They were not quite sure what to make of the object he was carrying, but they could tell enough to know it was not a weapon.

He took the lift up to his new office on the sixty-sixth floor, one level below Ciana's, two below Nogura's, and wondered with some amusement about the correlation between office level and rank.

Off the lift, down the corridor to the left—it all looked unfamiliar after touring it only once, but he had forced himself to remember how to get there, at least. It took a full minute of indecision before he determined which of the offices Ciana had shown him the last time he was here.

The lights were on in the office, as if it had been waiting for him. Outside, the sun had risen and lit up the bay. The entire eastern wall of the office was glass; Kirk had insisted on a view of the water at all times, and Nogura had been more than willing to accommodate him. At first Jim had asked for Waverleigh's office, but it was a floor below this one, and the current occupant was disinclined to move.

He set Old Yeller gingerly on the desk, then started at the sound of steps behind him. Nogura or Ciana—

"Admiral." The voice was too young and surprised to belong to an admiral. Kirk turned.

"You're a little early, sir. I wasn't expecting you." The lanky young man who stood in the doorway to the aide's office seemed all sharp, awkward angles. From a distance, he looked like a teenager, but according to his file, Lieutenant Commander Kevin Thomas Riley was twenty-eight years old. Smiling broadly, Riley stepped into the room. "It's good to see you again, Admiral."

"Good to see you, Commander." Kirk made a point of using Riley's new rank; after all, he'd argued strenuously with Nogura in favor of promoting the young man. Since he'd transferred off the *Enterprise,* Riley's career as a navigation instructor at the Academy had been lackluster at best—yet when Riley served aboard the *Enterprise,* Kirk had spotted him as a man with great potential for command, a man with instincts as sharp as those of Kirk himself. The Riley Kirk knew now seemed to have little in common with the one who had served on the *Enterprise,* and Kirk intended to get to the bottom of it. Later, of course, after he had gotten reacquainted with the man and had the chance to ask such a personal question.

Kirk smiled and gave Riley's extended hand a firm shake. "Four years, hasn't it been?"

"Yes, sir," Riley answered, seeming pleased that the admiral remembered. "And we've all been looking forward here to your arrival."

"Thanks. Is that coffee I smell?" Kirk eyed the mug in Riley's right hand.

Riley peered woefully down into the spirals of steam rising from his mug. "I'm afraid all the servitors on this floor are malfunctioning this morning, Admiral. Some kind of central maintenance problem. I went down a level for this." Kirk watched indecision flicker on Riley's face as he wrestled with his guilt; altruism won out. He proffered the cup with an air of noble stoicism. "Here, sir. I haven't touched this one. If you like yours with cream and sugar, that is. I'll just go down and get myself another—"

Kirk frowned, not because of the fact that he took his coffee black, but because filtered sunlight was glinting off golden-brown bristles on Riley's cheek. "Good Lord, man. Did you run out of beard suppressor?"

The skin beneath the bristles turned bright pink. "Ah . . . no, sir. I just thought—with the promotion and all—well, I thought it might make me look more . . . distinguished. The curse of a baby face, sir."

"I had that once. Finally grew out of it."

"I'm beginning to think I never will, sir. But if it's any problem, I'll get rid of it."

The beard or the baby face? Kirk wondered, but he said, "As long as you keep it regulation, I have no problem with it. But I can't speak for Admiral Nogura."

"Thank you, sir." Riley's shoulders slumped with such visible relief that Kirk smiled again, although privately he felt a pang of concern. Riley had been a brash young lieutenant on the *Enterprise,* but Jim had figured that in four years the man would have . . . matured somehow. Not seemed so damn . . . green. *Just first-day-on-the-job nerves. Hell, you've got a touch of them yourself, remember?* "Ah, sir . . . ?" Riley delicately cleared his throat.

"What is it?"

He squared his thin shoulders. "Permission to ask a personal question, sir."

"Ask. I can't promise an answer."

"Why the promotion, sir? I understand you gave me a sterling recommendation."

"Because it'd look bad for me to have a chief of staff who was only a lieutenant."

Riley colored again. "With all respect, Admiral, I'd appreciate a serious answer. You and I both know I haven't done anything recently to merit it. Frankly, I'm confused. Of all the people you could have asked for—"

Kirk wavered for a moment between explaining his reasons and telling Riley he was out of line to question a superior's decision. He did neither. "You were a lieutenant for almost six years. Isn't that enough?"

"Six very undistinguished years," Riley countered. "I'm not trying to look a gift horse in the mouth, Admiral, it's just that ,. . well, it's a little irregular, this appointment. I greatly appreciate what you've done for me, sir, but I'd like to think that I've done something to earn it. And I know I haven't."

"Then why don't you start doing something *now* to earn it, Commander?"

Riley gave a small sheepish grin. "Yes, *sir,* Admiral. And thank you."

"And quit worrying about my reasons and make the best of it. If I asked you to be my chief of staff, then obviously I believe you're the best person for the job. The best thing you can do is to believe it too."

Riley digested this in silence before nodding. "Yes, sir." He turned to go back into his office, then stopped suddenly. "Oh, about the coffee, sir—"

"Keep it. I take mine black. But forget about the coffee. I'd just as soon get to work." Kirk moved behind the desk and sat down. "Do you always get here this early, Commander?"

"I'm usually here at eight-thirty, Admiral, but I thought I'd make an exception today. Just in case."

Kirk smiled briefly. "Good instincts. So, let's get started. What work do we have today?"

"I've set up some interviews with yeomen for the position of secretary; I've narrowed the applications down to four candidates. As far as other positions, I'm still looking at résumés, sir."

Kirk shifted in his chair. For some reason, it didn't conform to his body very well; he could tell it would become uncomfortable after sitting awhile. He would tell Riley to requisition a different one. "Did Admiral Ciana leave any instructions?"

"Not specifically, though she said she would brief you herself as soon as she arrived this morning."

Kirk scowled at the thought of yet another half hour of waiting. "Well, what about Nogura? Is he in yet?"

"I can certainly find out for you, sir." Riley went into the outer office. After a moment he appeared again in the doorway. "He's in, sir, and headed this way."

"Thanks." Kirk stood up nervously and frowned at his desk. It was perfectly clean except for Yeller. Was he crazy, putting something like this on his desk the very first day, before he had a chance to prove himself? *Ease up. Quince got away with it.*

Yeah, but Quince didn't work directly under Nogura. And you know what a stickler for protocol Nogura can be.

Well, the hell with Nogura if he couldn't take a joke.

Jim was absently stroking Yeller when Nogura wandered in, gingerly balancing a steaming mug of tea in both hands.

Today Nogura looked quite harmless, like a doting white-haired Japanese grandfather (which he in fact was, several times over—the mug bore the legend "Galaxy's Best Great-Grandpa"), but Jim had learned a long time ago that Heihachiro Nogura's artless casualness was a pose, contrived to make his enemies underestimate him. Nogura was a shrewd strategist who knew how to play people. He saw all and forgot nothing.

And right now he was staring at the top of Jim's desk.

"Good Lord, Jim," he said quite pleasantly, "what is *that?*"

Jim smiled. "An armadillo, sir."

"A what?" Nogura leaned over the desk to peer at the creature more closely, then shook his head. "I wouldn't want to know where in the cosmos you found it." He straightened and smiled up at Jim. "Welcome, Admiral."

"Thank you, sir."

"Nice view, huh?" Nogura gestured at the window with his cup. Before Kirk could answer, the admiral fired another question at him. "Coffee, Jim? Or are you a tea man?"

Jim opened his mouth to answer, but Nogura was already speaking into the intercom. "Riley. Bring Admiral Kirk a cup of tea."

Kirk heard the slight hesitation as Riley considered explaining about the broken servitors—but as it was Fleet Admiral Nogura talking, the hesitation lasted about three-tenths of a second. "Right away, sir."

He was midway through saying it when the sound of a hailing whistle came over the intercom. Ciana, no doubt, but then Riley's voice sounded surprised again.

"Sorry to interrupt, sirs, but there's a communication coming through for Admiral Kirk."

Kirk leaned over the intercom on the desk. "Admiral Ciana?"

"No, sir, it's from Vulcan. It's Mr.—"

"Spock!" Kirk finished, and then realized he was grinning.

Nogura gave him a pat on the shoulder. "Go ahead and take it, Jim. I'll wait." He wandered into Riley's office.

Jim hit the toggle with his fist as Nogura disappeared back into the outer office. Spock's face appeared on the viewer.

"Spock!" Jim grinned broadly at him. For the first time since the *Enterprise* crew disbanded, he realized that he had missed his Vulcan friend. "You old devil! What the hell are you still doing on Vulcan?"

"Admiral," Spock said by way of greeting. He made it sound quite natural, as if he had always addressed Kirk by that title.

"So when are you going to get yourself to San Francisco, Captain? Or am I going to have to order you here?"

The instant he said it, he knew it was the wrong thing to say. Riley hadn't mentioned Spock's rank—or any rank at all, for that matter—and the realization that Spock was out of uniform made Kirk suddenly suspicious. He searched the Vulcan's face, but it revealed nothing.

"That would be most ineffectual," Spock answered softly, after a beat's hesitation. "I have resigned my commission."

"Resigned? Why?" Jim asked, before he could stop himself. It, too, was the wrong thing to say, but he had to know. He had to find some way to change Spock's mind—

Spock actually looked away before answering, and Jim suddenly felt ashamed of himself. Who was he to demand an explanation from Spock? The Vulcan had the right to do whatever the hell he wanted, without having to explain himself, even more so now that he was no longer answerable to Kirk or anyone else in Starfleet.

"I have decided to accept a teaching position at the Vulcan Science Academy." Not exactly an explanation, but probably the closest thing to one the Vulcan would ever offer. Spock cleared his throat. "However, that was not my sole purpose in calling. I wished also to congratulate you on your promotion to admiral."

"My promotion," Jim said distractedly. "Yes. Thank you." He paused. "I'm sorry. I had no right to pry—"

"I did not consider it such," Spock answered, thus putting to rest any of Jim's notions that Vulcans were incapable of outright lying. "Perhaps in the future our paths will cross again."

"Yes," Kirk said, trying very hard to think of exactly what it was he wanted to say to Spock at this point, and failing. In the periphery of his vision he saw Nogura in the doorway, sipping his tea and pretending not to listen, then disappearing again into Riley's office. "Yes, of course." He paused. "Spock . . . I know there's no point in urging you to reconsider once you've made up your mind, but . . . well, at the risk of sounding hackneyed, you *were* the best first officer in the Fleet—the Service won't recover from your loss. I'll miss you, Spock. You've been a damn fine officer—and a good friend."

There was only the slightest hesitation in Spock's voice. "I appreciate the compliment, Admiral. The same can be said of your performance as captain of the *Enterprise*. I shall . . . miss serving under you."

Was there the faintest trace of recrimination in Spock's steady gaze? No, of course not. Just his own guilty imagination. Jim forced a smile. "Good luck in your new career, Spock."

Spock raised his right hand in the Vulcan salute. "Live long and prosper, Admiral."

The screen went dark. Jim let himself stare at it for only a second, mindful that Nogura would be back in. It had never occurred to him that Spock wouldn't accept the Starfleet Academy post. It had seemed . . . the logical thing for Spock to do. Kirk had never for a moment considered that the Vulcan might not come to San Francisco.

And why the hell hadn't he?

Nogura came back in.

"Everything all right, Jim? I hope it wasn't bad news."

Kirk forced a lighter expression. "Fine, sir."

"Too bad about Spock. A real loss for the Service."

"Agreed."

"I understand you two worked together quite well."

"Yes, sir." Jim changed the subject. He would think about Spock, deal with the disappointment later, back at Quince's apartment. "What time does Admiral Ciana normally arrive?"

"She should be here by now. I wonder what's holding her up," Nogura said, suddenly irritable. He went to Riley's office and barked something Kirk could not hear, then turned around to face Jim again. "She's on her way," he said triumphantly, and he had just enough time to say it and smile before Lori Ciana entered the room.

Jim stood up and walked around the desk without knowing he'd done it.

The vice admiral was unconsciously graceful, all eyes and legs, and so wary and alert to everything going on around her that sometimes Kirk expected her to bolt if startled, but she always managed to stand her ground and remain gracious at the same time. In many ways she reminded him of Nogura. There was a tough edge to both of them, and they were smart enough to keep that fact hidden from their enemies . . . and, sometimes, their friends. Ciana strode into the room on those long legs and extended a firm hand to Kirk. He shook it and let go of it far sooner than he wanted.

"Admiral." She smiled at Kirk.

Jim tried not to gape at her like a fool. She was a grade level above him in rank, and he was glad that the old axiom that one did not become romantically involved with someone in one's chain of command no longer applied by the time one made flag rank.

Out of the corner of his eye he saw Nogura smirk. "Admiral Ciana." Kirk smiled politely.

"It's great to finally have you here." She gave Nogura a nod. "Admiral." Nogura nodded back, his smirk now a polite smile. "So, Kirk," Ciana asked, "has Admiral Nogura been educating you?"

"Er . . . no, sir. There hasn't been time for that yet."

"There will be." Nogura glanced, satisfied, from one to the other. "Lori will do all the educating, Jim. I'm afraid I've got work to do myself. But let me know how your day went. Why don't you drop by my office around seventeen hundred?"

"Yes, sir," Kirk answered, thinking that if he took the stairs, Ciana's office was on the way to Nogura's, and wondering if she would still be there at seventeen hundred.

"Take care of him," Nogura said to Ciana, and left.

Ciana walked to the side of Jim's desk and flicked the intercom toggle, all in one smooth motion. "Riley. Did my aide give you those reports for Admiral Kirk?"

His voice filtered through the grid. "Yes, sir. I'll get them right away, sir." He appeared in seconds with a thick stack of flimsies in one hand and two mugs grasped by their handles in the other. "On the desk, sir?" he asked Ciana.

She nodded. Riley unloaded the flimsies and handed first

Ciana, then Kirk, a cup. "Your 'tea,' Admiral," Riley said to Kirk with a sly smile.

Jim bent his face over the mug and smelled coffee—black, the way he liked it. He smiled back at Riley.

"Is this what I think it is?" Ciana said approvingly into her coffee with cream. "Riley, bless you. All the servitors were out on the sixty-seventh floor, and when I went up a level for some, they were all out there too."

"No problem, sir." Riley hovered for a second to be sure he was no longer needed, then retreated into his office. Jim stared at the pile of papers on his desk.

Ciana looked back at him and did not smile. "I need you to wade through all of this as soon as possible. I realize the normal procedure would be for my aide to brief you, but I've got him tied up on another project right now. Oh, I know you probably can't wait to start troubleshooting, but you're of no use to us until you're educated about the specific trouble spots where we might use you." She paused before throwing down the challenge. "How soon can you get through these?"

"As soon as you need me to," Kirk answered instantly. He wasn't the slightest bit intimidated by the stack of reading, but he was mildly surprised by the fact that someone who had achieved the rank of admiral would have to prove himself. In any case, it wasn't important enough to worry about—let Ciana play games if she wanted. He could play along with the best of them. "Anything else you need me for today?" His tone was deliberately casual.

"Just this. After lunch I'll give you the traditional tour and introduce you to the staff; tomorrow I'd like you to accompany me when I meet some Federation Council delegates." She smiled. "Nogura thought you deserved a few days' rest before we started shuttling you around the galaxy. I know this isn't your cup of tea, but it has to be done." She gave him the serious look again. "How soon?"

Kirk eyed the stack warily. "I can try to read them all by this afternoon, if you'd like."

Ciana smiled again at that. "That's a bit optimistic, don't you think? I'd like you to *remember* some of what you read. I figure I can let you have two days to plow through it. No shortcuts, Admiral."

*   *   *

He had almost forgotten about the conversation with Spock when, two hours later, Will Decker called.

Kirk glanced up from the stack of flimsies at Decker's bright, confident face on the terminal screen. The younger man now wore the monochromatic blue-gray of a Starfleet captain's uniform.

"Admiral." Decker grinned broadly. "I just called to congratulate you on your promotion."

Kirk smiled back at him and absently stroked the crease between his brows, the result of squinting all morning at reports. "Same to you, Will."

Decker's smile grew even broader. "Which leads into the second reason I called. I know you recommended that I oversee the refit of the *Enterprise* as her new captain. Sir . . . there aren't adequate words to thank you."

"Those will have to do—along with the comfort of knowing she's in capable hands." Kirk allowed himself a small sigh. "Quite frankly, Will, I envy you. If I were still a captain, I'd do whatever was necessary to get command of my ship back."

Decker's smile faded slightly. "I understand, sir. I'll take good care of her—"

"I know you will. I didn't mean that quite the way it sounded. Congratulations, Will . . . and good luck. Matt would have been proud."

"Thank you, sir."

Kirk cut off the communication and did not allow himself to think of the *Enterprise,* or Will Decker, or Spock. . . .

At least, not until later that afternoon.

It was five o'clock by the time he got three-quarters of the way through the stack. He had intended to stay late and read them all just to get them out of the way—after all, the faster he got this behind him, the faster the real work could begin—when his intercom buzzed.

He pressed the toggle. "What is it, Riley?" It came out a yawn.

"Long day, eh, sir?" Riley asked knowingly, and then, hastily, as if afraid he had been inappropriately familiar, said, "Admiral Nogura wanted me to remind you it was seventeen hundred. Sir."

"So?" Kirk laced his fingers and stretched his arms above

his head. "Riley, could you requisition me a new chair? This one is killing my back."

"Yes, sir." Riley hesitated. "I think Admiral Nogura wants you to quit what you're doing and go up to his office, Admiral. Something about how your day went . . ."

"That's right." Kirk sighed. "Thank you, Commander."

"You're welcome, sir."

Kirk snapped the toggle. It was going to take a while to get used to the notion that the workday for most stopped at seventeen hundred. Or that it stopped at all. He stared listlessly at the dwindling pile of flimsies to be studied, and with great effort stood up and put them under his arm. He supposed he would have to break down and buy a briefcase like all the other—

He stopped himself from thinking the word *bureaucrat*. He wasn't a paper-pusher, dammit, and he didn't need a briefcase. This was the first and only time he'd be required to lug flimsies around with him. Only for a few days, Ciana had said. Only a few days.

Nogura's office was two levels up, and he took the stairs because his ass had gone numb from all the sitting. He took the stairs two at a time, and by the time he made it to the corridor near Nogura's office, he was breathing hard. The door to the aide's outer office was open, but the room was empty. The aide had either gone home early or was on some errand. From where he stood he could see that Nogura's office was open too, but from the angle he couldn't see into the room. He was debating whether to buzz or just poke his head in the door—after all, Nogura was expecting him, and maybe had left the door open for him—when he realized someone in the inner office was half-yelling. It took him a minute to register the presence of the voice; his subconscious had already identified it and its outraged tone as very familiar, and hadn't immediately alerted him to the fact that it was out of place here, in Nogura's office.

It was the impassioned voice of Leonard McCoy, ranting about God-knew-what.

Jim grinned and ran to the doorway, then stopped as his brain began to sort out some of the things McCoy was saying.

". . . he doesn't belong here. *I* told you, and every one of your damnable psychiatrists told you, and you've known about it all along. But you don't care, do you? You don't care about what's best for *him,* you only care about what's best for *you.*" McCoy had already begun to look more at home in civilian clothes than he ever had in a Starfleet uniform; other than that, he looked exactly the same as he had six months ago when Jim had last seen him . . . except that perhaps the circles beneath his eyes looked a little darker, as if he hadn't had much sleep lately. He was pacing back and forth in front of Nogura's desk and gesticulating wildly at the seated admiral. Nogura had narrowed his eyes so much they looked almost closed. His hands rested palms down, one on the other, on top of his desk.

"I care about what's best for the Fleet," Nogura corrected him patiently.

"*Hang* the Fleet!" McCoy blazed. "I'm talking about what's best for Jim!" He grabbed the edge of the desk and leaned forward to shove his face in the admiral's. Nogura did not flinch. "Do you know what a quarterdeck breed is, Admiral?"

"I probably know more of those old nautical terms than you do, Leonard. Of course I know."

"Well, Jim is a quarterdeck breed if ever there was one. He *belongs* in command of a starship. To stick him behind a desk is crim—"

"*Enough,*" Kirk said from the doorway. He was surprised it came out calmly, surprised that his voice did not shake with rage.

McCoy wheeled around, startled. Nogura's expression did not change, as if he had known that Kirk was there.

"I'm sorry, Jim," the doctor said, but the anger was still in his voice and eyes. "I'm sorry, but someone had to say something. Someone had to take your part."

The two of them glared at each other for a half-minute.

Nogura broke the tension. "Could I have one moment alone with Admiral Kirk, Doctor?" His tone was polite and composed, as if McCoy had just been telling an amusing anecdote instead of shouting.

McCoy shot him a dark look and stomped out of the room.

"I'm s—" Kirk began, but Nogura raised a hand to silence him.

"It's all right, Jim. He means well. He's upset because our staff psychologists disagreed with him on certain aspects of your psych profile." Nogura made a wry face. "He doesn't take being contradicted too well, does he?"

"He never did, sir."

Nogura sighed. "I'm amazed he stayed in the Service as long as he did." His tone brightened. "So, did you survive your first day?"

"So far."

"Ciana dump a load of briefs on you?"

Kirk smiled grimly. "That's a very accurate assessment, sir."

"She's funny that way. It's meant to rattle you, I suppose . . . or impress upon you just how much about the Federation you need to learn. I tried to discourage her from dumping it on you all at once, but she can be damned persistent sometimes." Nogura shook his head. "I don't want you to get the wrong impression, Jim. We're not going to turn you into a desk driver."

"Quite frankly, I wouldn't let that happen, Admiral."

Nogura sighed again, and for an instant he looked like the old man that he was. "Now, if you can just convince Leonard McCoy of that. We—Ciana and I—were going to take you out for a drink after your first day on the job, but she's gotten tied up. Tomorrow, maybe. Right now, maybe you'd better try to calm your friend down. I certainly couldn't."

"I'll do my best, sir."

A subdued McCoy was waiting out in the corridor. Jim headed for the lift without slowing down, and McCoy hurried to keep up with him. Jim looked at his surroundings, anywhere but at McCoy, and for the first time he realized that the interior of Headquarters was very like that of a starship. They stepped onto the empty lift, and for a moment Jim was tempted to pretend he was back in the *Enterprise*'s turbolift, arguing with his chief medical officer.

"Ground level," he said, and then McCoy finally spoke.

"Look, Jim, I know this is really bad timing—you're pissed at me—but I wanted to have the chance to talk to you. Can I take you out for dinner, or at least a drink?"

"That would be fine," Kirk said. It came out clipped.

McCoy's voice rose in exasperation. "Dammit, if I weren't concerned, I wouldn't have said anything."

Jim finally glared at him. "You didn't have to do it behind my back. Why didn't you come to me instead of Nogura? Why didn't you give me a chance to explain?"

He watched McCoy hesitate, then decide to say it anyway: "Jim, you can be damnably hardheaded once you've made your mind up. Obviously, Nogura found some sort of way to talk you into this—"

Kirk came very close to exploding. "No one talked me into anything. I *decided*, Doctor. How the hell can you s—"

"I can say it because I'm your friend. And I would say it about a total stranger if his psych file read like yours." He shook his head in disgust. "Nogura's whores, that's what they are."

"Who?"

"The psychiatrist or two he found to contradict me. Ciana and her ilk . . ." McCoy spread his hands beseechingly. "Dammit, Jim, you *swore* a dozen times that nothing could ever make you do it—"

"Ciana happens to be a damn competent officer." Kirk felt blood rush to his cheeks. "Did you ever stop to consider that maybe *you* were the one who was biased? Maybe you couldn't stand for it all to end. Maybe you just wanted everything to stay as it was, all of us still on the *Enterprise*. Well, grow up, Doctor. Things change."

McCoy's eyebrows rose swiftly in surprise. "That's a damn stupid thing to say, Jim. In fact, that's probably the one truly stupid thing I've ever heard. I'm going to try to forget I heard you say that."

"I'm sorry," Jim said, and meant it because of the honest hurt in the doctor's voice. "And I'll try to pretend I'm not angry that you didn't come to me first." *And that I never heard that remark about Nogura's whores.* "But you have to give me a chance to tell my side of it."

"Apology accepted," McCoy said, and something in his weary eyes made Jim think the hurt extended far beyond this particular argument, far beyond anything to do with Nogura or Jim. "How about I give you that chance to explain during dinner?"

The lift doors opened on the first-level reception area. Beyond lay the breath-catchingly steep hills of Oldtown San Francisco, the only remnant of the city to have survived the 2062 quake.

"I'm buying the drinks," Jim said.

FIVE

☆ ────────

The sun was setting over the Pacific, and its dying rays streamed through the glass wall of the restaurant into Kirk's eyes. He turned back to face McCoy.

"Take a look at that," he said, nodding to his right. "Beautiful, isn't it?"

McCoy squinted over his left shoulder, his face colored orange-red by the light. "Yeah. Beautiful," he said without enthusiasm, and settled back into the soft cushioned recesses of the booth. He was on his third drink, and he drained the last milliliter of George Dickel No. 12 White Label from his glass and motioned to the waiter for another.

Jim fingered his brandy snifter. The small talk throughout dinner had been strained. Bones and he agreed not to talk about Jim's promotion until the after-dinner drinks were poured. But the way Bones was downing the sour mash, Jim was surprised that he could still speak at all. And the more McCoy drank, the more morose he became. He had slumped so far down in the booth that his chin was a mere six inches or so from the table.

"We were going to talk about me," he began, but before he could add, *but I think we'd better talk about you first,* McCoy launched into it as if he had been electrically prodded into action.

"Here's the sum of it." He leaned forward. Kirk could hear the beginnings of a slur. "Nogura asked me for a psychological evaluation of you—standard procedure when they're considering a promotion like this—and then when I gave him my opinion, he proceeded to ignore the hell out of it. 'Smore than a little irregular to override the chief medical officer's recommendation, don't you think?''

Kirk didn't answer.

"So I resigned," McCoy said.

"You *what?*''

"You heard me. I resigned. I'm out of the Fleet. Didn't you wonder why I was out of uniform?''

"Yes, but—''

"Come on, Jim, we both knew it was coming. I won't play games with those damn bureaucrats. Hell, I'm glad I did it.'' The waiter set the drink down in front of McCoy, who paused to take a large swallow and then continued, glaring across the table at Jim, as if talking about it had made him angry all over again. "Nogura brought in his own people so he could contradict my report—one of his lackeys, Admiral Ci . . . Ci . . . ah, hell, I forget her name, but what the hell does it matter?''

"Ciana," Kirk told him. "She's no lackey, Doctor. I'll forgive you that because you're drunk. She's damn capable.''

"I see.'' McCoy narrowed his eyes. "And I'm not?'' He took another sip of the Dickel. "Well, it doesn't matter who did the damn report. The fact is, I'm mad because Nogura apparently doesn't give a damn about you. Or my opinion.''

"That I'm a quarterdeck breed.''

"Dammit, Jim,'' McCoy cried, exasperated. "What did they do? Bewitch you?''

A muscle in Jim's jaw started twitching. He took a long sip of his cognac before he answered. "Are you too drunk to listen to what I'm going to tell you? Because if you are, I—''

"Try me.'' McCoy's eyes glittered.

Jim shook his head. "I'm hurt that you don't know me better than that, Bones. Don't you know I'd never accept a desk assignment?''

"I think that Admiral Ci . . . what's-her-name's bewitched you.''

"Don't say that again,'' Kirk said very softly, and McCoy fell silent. "I'm going to say this only once. Nogura could never talk me into a desk job. They cut me a deal. I'm a troubleshooter, Bones. A traveling diplomat. I'll get to see some real action again . . . it's like being a captain, only better! I don't have to check with Command every five minutes about what to do next. I have some real authority to get things done! Nogura's too smart to waste me at a desk. Besides, after the Rittenhouse scandal, they need some fresh blood . . ."

"So you're going to sacrifice some of yours," McCoy said under his breath. Jim pretended not to hear it. "Like being a captain, huh?" McCoy asked, this time louder. "A captain without a ship, is that what he told you? Didn't look to me like you were traipsing around the galaxy in search of adventure today, Jim. Looked to me like you'd been sitting at a desk. How did it feel? Just tell me that. Deep down, what are you really feeling?"

"Irritation at a dear old friend. You're a hell of a one to talk, Doctor. There's nothing bothering me right now, but there sure as hell is something bothering *you*. And it's not just that Nogura overlooked your report."

McCoy recoiled into his booth until the shadows hid one side of his face. He stared down into his drink without answering.

Kirk's voice softened. "You've been awfully tight-lipped about what you've been doing for the past few months. Something with the Fabrini, you said. I suspect you didn't come all the way to Earth just to harass me."

McCoy sighed. "There was no point staying on Yonada any longer. I'd gathered all the information they had in terms of medical knowledge, verified what they had in their computer stores . . . Had an anthropologist helping me." He turned his face from Kirk and stared glassy-eyed at the bay. "I gave a lecture at Harvard and the Fleet Medical Academy, and now I'm headed for the Vulcan Science Academy . . . I'm catching the shuttle after dinner."

Kirk gazed at him steadily. "No point in staying . . . ? I thought you and Natira—"

McCoy shrugged, tried to smile, and gave it up. "I did too. Seems the lady had other plans."

"I'm sorry."

"So am *I*." McCoy took another large gulp of his drink, then adopted a more philosophical tone. "Well, hell, I deserved it, Jim. Why should she have waited around for me so long?"

"I can think of some good reasons," Jim said kindly. "For one, she was waiting for Leonard McCoy."

McCoy gave him a sheepishly grateful glance. "You can skip the others. I've already thought them all out. But she was right. And apparently there's some sort of statute of limitations on how long a high priestess can wait before producing a successor. She had a responsibility to her people . . .''

She had a responsibility to you, Jim almost said, but decided that McCoy probably already knew that too.

"Damn selfish of me," McCoy was still saying, watching the remaining disk of red sun slip below the water. "I just figured she'd always be there for me when everything . . ." He let the words hang unspoken in the air.

"Why don't you stay in San Francisco? Put up your shingle here?" Jim suggested.

The doctor shook his head. "No, thanks. This is a company town. Who wants to play physician to a lot of overweight, deskbound Fleet—" He broke off and half-grinned at Kirk. "Sorry. Must be the liquor talking."

"Actually, it sounds a lot more like your old self," Jim retorted, and smiled because McCoy was smiling for the first time that evening.

Still grinning, McCoy raised his glass at Jim and drank, but before he swallowed, his expression became one of surprise, then guilt. Kirk reached toward him, thinking he must be choking. "Bones?" And then he realized that the woman standing over them was not the waiter.

McCoy gulped hard, then coughed feebly as he glanced at the chrono on his wrist. "Dwen. Oh, damn. I'm sorry. I lost track of the time."

The woman with the free-flowing dark hair and decidedly casual civilian clothes folded her arms and glared at McCoy like a wrathful stone goddess. "You seem to do a lot of that lately," she said, and Kirk detected a faint British accent. "And you're drunk, to boot. Leonard, you *promised.*" Her dark blue eyes narrowed with disapproval.

Jim glanced quizzically from the woman to McCoy, who was carefully avoiding everyone's gaze. She was large-boned, with straight, simple features, a hawkish (some would call it aristocratic) nose, and looked like an outdoorswoman ready to go mountain-climbing on a moment's notice. But the doctor had seemed so truly heartbroken over Natira . . .

Reduced to a perfect nonplus, McCoy half-rose from his chair and gestured from Dwen to Kirk. "Uh . . . Dr. Keridwen Llewellyn, Admiral James T. Kirk." He paused as if about to offer more explanation, but seemed to decide better of it. He straightened and stepped around the table to stand next to her.

She almost matched him in height. McCoy's age, or thereabouts, Kirk guessed; she had a shock of silver at the left temple.

Dr. Llewellyn reached across the table, her long hair fanning from shoulder to elbow. "Admiral Kirk. Leonard speaks very highly of you." She smiled just long enough at Kirk to avoid being totally rude, then glowered at McCoy again.

"Uh, thank you," Kirk said, feeling somewhat awkward at being unable to return the compliment.

"Look, Jim, I gotta go. Keridwen's been waiting to leave for Vulcan—"

Jim checked his own chrono. "They leave every hour. I'm afraid you've missed this one. Why don't you wait it out here until the next one? Dr. Llewellyn can join us."

"Thanks, but . . . she's piloting. Has her own little shuttle." McCoy jerked his head in Llewellyn's direction. "Let me get this, Dwen. Won't take a minute." He motioned to the waiter.

"I've got this one. You can catch the next one." Jim got out of the booth and squeezed McCoy's arm. "Say hello to Spock if you see him." He nodded at the woman. "Nice meeting you, Dr. Llewellyn."

"Same to you, Admiral." Dwen was curtly polite, but obviously still smoldering at the doctor.

McCoy looked at Kirk sharply. "Spock—he's not taking the teaching position at Starfleet? I thought for sure—"

Jim shook his head.

"Well, I'll be . . ." McCoy said, but then he nodded. "Can't say I blame him. Not after the way I treated him. Maybe he'll be happier among his own people, after all."

He gave Jim's shoulder a quick thump and left with Llewellyn, leaving Kirk to stare in wonder after them.

T'Sura was a healer from a long line of healers who could trace their lineage back some hundred thousand seasons before the time of the Reformation. There was a serenity to her, an utter sense of security in who and what she was. She wore no mask to suppress her emotions; it came naturally to her, like breathing. She employed no artifice. She simply was who she was: a column of strength, of self-possessed calm. She made Spock feel like an impostor. And yet he was drawn to her, this idealized version of himself, of all he wanted to be.

But for some unaccountable reason, it was she who first was drawn to him. . . .

The Science Academy was hosting a reception to honor her appointment as a lecturer to the medical college. Sarek wished to attend, and for no reason Spock could surmise, bade his wife and son come with him. Spock went.

It was a typical Academy reception: the large stone hall that was the traditional place for such functions was brightly lit, uncluttered by furniture or the human propensity for food and drink. Even the sound was different from that of the social gatherings on the *Enterprise:* the cadence was different, no rise and fall of laughter and questions, simply the steady, low hum of calm Vulcan voices. The attendees queued up to wish T'Sura well. The entire affair would last perhaps an hour. Spock took his place in line and waited.

T'Sura was attended by her twin brother. Spock had known both when they were children, one year his senior. Spock knew little of T'Sura; he wished he had known Svonn less well than he did. Svonn had been part of a small but determined group that had once encouraged Spock to eat sand, on the basis that his stoic resolution to do so would in some scientific way decide which half of Spock's heritage was ascendant. Spock ate the sand—an unpleasant experience, though not nearly as much so as the humiliation of being forced to—but the group of budding scientists called the result inconclusive. The experiments continued irregularly until Sekar permanently discouraged the young researchers. On Svonn's behalf, it must be said that he was not the leader of the group, merely one of the curious followers.

Now, in the great reception hall nearly three decades later, Svonn's eye caught Spock's, and they nodded at each other briefly before Svonn turned to address some aged well-wisher. The derisive look Spock remembered in the boy's eyes was gone in the adult's.

Svonn was tall and bony, with the same severe handsomeness as his twin. Their parents had been killed many years before in a skimmer accident, two years after Svonn and T'Sura began their public education. Brother and sister were fiercely protective of each other. Even now, Svonn remained at her side through the entire reception.

When Spock reached the end of the line, he gave both the formal salute, which each returned. And then T'Sura took him completely aback.

"I wish to speak to you after the reception," she said. "May I call on you at your parents' home?"

Startled, he could think of no reason to refuse her.

Svonn had never tormented Spock openly as the other children had; like his sister, he was too reserved, too dignified even as a child to participate in physical violence or name-calling. Yet Svonn's cruelty had hurt most of all.

Six-year-old Spock had thought of Svonn as a friend simply because the full Vulcan had never joined the group of bullies that routinely waylaid Spock every day for the first few months of his first year of formal training. But Svonn was always in the background, aloof, watching, neither helping nor hindering Spock's challengers.

It was several months after the episodes had stopped. Spock no longer expected a daily reminder of his human heritage; he no longer needed one.

He had come home one day to find his pet *sehlat,* Ee-chaya, missing from his air-conditioned stall. The aged sehlat was used to more temperate northern climes than the equatorial desert of ShiKahr. If he escaped to the plains and became overheated, or the victim of a predatory *le matya* . . .

Spock's agitated search finally led him to Svonn—and Ee-chaya, cool and content in Svonn's family's sheltered garden. It was the year that Svonn's parents later died.

Svonn was unrattled by Spock's indignation.

"Why did you take him?" Spock cried, his training quite forgotten. He was close to tears of anger and relief, and far too outraged to care what Svonn might think of this display of temper.

"It was a simple experiment," Svonn answered coolly, sitting on his haunches in the sand next to Ee-chaya, one hand stroking the creature's woolly back, one hand offering the delighted animal a tidbit. "There was no danger to him at all."

"Experiment?"

"To compare your reaction with that of a full Vulcan's," Svonn said. "I was curious."

Spock became keenly aware of his clenched fists, his choked-back tears, and, humiliated, led Ee-chaya home. He was far too ashamed to ask Svonn the outcome of his experiment.

It was all so simple, so clear, so logical. She was alone, a widow without heirs, and she wished to bond with him. Most males Spock's age had long ago consummated their engagements and produced children. She understood Spock to be unencumbered; tactfully, she did not mention his divorce at the hands of T'Pring. He came from a noble family and she judged him to be a suitable candidate. If he were not, he must explain now. Otherwise, she awaited his answer.

He gave it. The next step was a six-month trial bond, a preliminary to marriage itself, which gave both parties the chance to test their compatibility before formally committing themselves. As they were adults, they alone had the right to choose . . . the families' opinions were noted but not necessarily crucial to the final decision.

Our family is honored, Svonn had said upon entering Sarek and Amanda's house. He waited inside now with Spock's parents, probably, Spock thought, making awkward conversation. His twin stood in the garden with Spock, the fierce midday sun at her back. The bright light gave her black hair a violet cast; it was tightly plaited and wound into a thick coil which covered the prominent bones at the nape of her neck. She wore everyday clothes, a simple beige tunic with black pants. Spock had never seen her, even as a very young woman, in bright colors.

"Shall we begin?" he suggested, feeling some awkwardness. There were no traditional words, no ritual for what they were about to do . . . and for a brief instant Spock felt something suspiciously akin to a pang of fear. Perhaps he had made the decision too abruptly; perhaps, in view of Jim's decision and the consequent radical change in Spock's life circumstances, he had not clearly considered all the implications of T'Sura's offer. . . . Indeed, what had possessed him to open his mind to this near-stranger?

She reached one hand up, gently, and rested her fingers against his temple. He squelched the wave of doubt and mirrored her action.

The first layer: calm, serenity. Reassurance. Peace. He rested there; there was no need to go deeper this first time.

Yet the images rose slowly in her consciousness, percolating up through the layers like bubbles of air rising through fluid, seeking the surface. At first the images were ill-formed, wavering . . . but then they took shape, complete, and shimmered before dissolving into vapor again. She was withholding nothing.

Fierce closeness to her twin . . . the trauma of growing older, growing apart from her brother, of finding her own identity as a

separate being. The sensation remained, permeated everything
. . . including the death of her parents.

New image. The damaged shuttle, its hull twisted, the soundless sensation of air being sucked from the cabin out into space.
He had not known that T'Sura had been on the flight, had
remained conscious long enough to place the oxygen filter over
her mouth. Her mother had been killed instantly, her father
critically injured . . . but she had not been able to crawl over the
wounded and the wreckage in time to get his filter in place. She
watched as he suffocated.

The image changed only slightly . . . to that of Starok, her
husband. A glimmer of pride. Starok was a healer, much honored
. . . in fact, her professor at the Academy and her elder by fifty-
five seasons. His first wife had died in an industrial accident.
Starok had become afflicted with a slow, wasting disease, an
inability of his blood to utilize even the simplest of nutrients. A
rare disorder, so rare that no cure had been found. Again, T'Sura
had watched helplessly as he died.

The images stopped. There were only order, calm . . . and
great loneliness. She was used to close attachments from birth,
but the bond with her husband had been unusually strong, one
that the comfort of a brother could not replace. She wanted the
family that had been taken from her—not just once, but twice.

She had revealed what was most important to her, at the cost
of great discomfort to herself, a bold gesture and an honorable
one. It merited a fully honest response. But what had come forth
so smoothly and promptly from her came forth from Spock
haltingly, and with difficulty.

There was the slowly dawning suspicion that he was somehow different . . . followed by the unhappy certainty brought
home when he entered formal training. He was sorely tempted to
edit some of the scenes that came to him, but restrained himself.
She learned of the childish fistfights, the name-calling, his disagreement with his father over his choice of career. The agony he
knew it had caused his mother . . . and how T'Pring's rejection
of him fueled his determination that he would never have a life on
Vulcan. And then he stopped the images.

All? He could sense her mind probing his. *Is this all?*

No. Not all. There was no sense in hiding the incident with
young Svonn from her. She was so close to her brother, no doubt
she knew of what had happened. He let her see the image of
Svonn, stroking the thick fur on Ee-chaya's back, blinking at

young, agitated Spock. The image of himself was most unclear
. . . he could not remember how he must have appeared; he could
only summon up the feelings of outrage, relief, and, ultimately,
his humiliation at Svonn's hands. He was not really a Vulcan.

The image faded.

A bubble of amusement rose up quickly through the layers
of T'Sura's mind and was gone.

*Svonn relayed the same incident to me. Like you, he feels
great shame because of it. Yet in his version of the tale, you
passed the test.*

They went inside to announce that the trial bonding had been
successful. The engagement would be announced and, in six
months, consummated.

SIX

─────────────── ☆ ───────────────

Spock found T'Sura out in her garden, exactly where he had known she would be. The link with her was immensely reassuring, somehow—perhaps because it in some way reaffirmed his own link to his Vulcan ancestors, in taking a Vulcan wife in the traditional manner—and oddly pleasurable.

Svonn had welcomed him at the door, and if he had ever experienced any guilt or discomfort over the past incident with Ee-chaya, it had clearly been resolved. He treated Spock comfortably, like . . . family, and led him back to the garden.

The family garden was more an animal sanctuary than a place for growing plants. T'Sura philosophically disagreed with the notion of keeping pets, yet she kept the garden filled with food for all types of creatures: insects, birds, mammals, even a poisonous *shatarr* lizard who lived under a great rock and was given wide berth by the other inhabitants. Svonn had said, with an air of saintly tolerance, that in times of severe heat or drought T'Sura left the door open so that the animals could take shelter in the cool house.

Now T'Sura was sitting on her heels in the sand, one arm outstretched and offering a tidbit to the fat *chkariya* less than a half-meter away. At the sight of Spock the animal stopped, sat on its sleek haunches, and raised a quivering brown nose to the air. T'Sura remained motionless, but her eyes darted in Spock's direction.

"He's all right," she explained to the weasellike creature. Her voice was low and melodic. "You're hungry. Come."

The chkariya slowly lowered its front paws and waddled up to T'Sura to retrieve the fruit.

"I give him his favorite every day," she explained to Spock while keeping her eyes on her dinner guest. "It keeps him from destroying the garden." She left the rest of the fruit on the ground, rose slowly, and dusted the sand from her legs.

Spock considered asking whether it would not be more logical to set a humane trap for the chkariya and release it elsewhere, but decided that perhaps, for T'Sura, such an action might not seem logical at all. He said nothing.

"It's fortunate you are able to accompany me to the Academy lecture this evening," she said, walking over to him. "I think you will find it interesting."

"I have always found Fabrini culture fascinating," Spock answered truthfully.

She studied him for a moment, then said, "I think you will find it interesting for more than one reason, then. The keynote speaker will be Dr. Leonard McCoy."

McCoy nodded at the polite applause (polite but restrained, since, after all, two-thirds of the audience were Vulcans) and loosened his grip on the podium. Beneath his trembling hands, the ink on his notes had smeared. He turned away from the audience and let his face sag.

"You were great." Dr. Keridwen Llewellyn, the other speaker for the evening, stood in front of her chair on the platform and applauded more enthusiastically than anyone else in the room. McCoy had met her on Yonada, where they were involved in very different types of research, she doing ethnographic interviews and poring over the ancient Fabrini records in her study of an artificially created religion. There were only rare instances of such in the galaxy, and Llewellyn lost no time in staking out her claim. She'd been on Yonada for over a year when McCoy arrived. When he'd first seen her from a distance, he'd mistaken her for one of the natives, dressed as she was in a long blue Yonadan toga.

He'd gone to see Natira the first day he arrived, of course.

Afterward, stumbling back to the room provided by the Yonadan government (which, ironically, consisted of Natira and her new husband), McCoy had wanted privacy, but the researchers' rooms were adjoining, and as soon as he'd thrown himself on the soft floor cushions that constituted his bed, a knock rattled the door.

"Who is it?" he groaned into the cushions.

The door opened. It was how he came to learn of the Yonadan disdain for locks. Llewellyn's face peered around the door's edge, and he at first mistook her for a Yonadan servant. Except that he had never seen a Yonadan with hair black as coal and eyes blue as cobalt.

"Dr. Keridwen Llewellyn, at your service," she said, with the vestiges of what McCoy decided was an English accent. "We've developed a bit of a custom here on Yonada. All fellow researchers must be welcomed with a drink . . ." She finally caught McCoy's tortured expression, and in a softer voice added, "And, by gods, you certainly look like you could use one."

"Go away," McCoy snarled, but Llewellyn had already pushed the door open. She held two glasses and a large chemist's flask of clear liquid.

"I'm leaving," she said as she entered, and while McCoy puzzled over the paradox, she set her burden down on a table. "But first I'm going to pour you that drink, and tell you that if you ever need to talk about it, I'm next door. Just one sip, and I'm gone."

Anything to get the woman to leave. McCoy sat up and took the glass offered him. He took the required sip and nearly choked. He was used to hard liquor, but this stuff burned like raw antimatter going down. "Good God, what *is* this stuff?" He wiped involuntary tears from his eyes.

She was good enough not to smile. "The local moonshine. The boys in the Federation ag lab make it. I prefer gin myself, but I'm afraid alcohol's quite against the local laws. Cheers." She splashed some into a glass and swallowed it without flinching. "And now I'll leave you to your private sorrow. You can keep the bottle."

And she disappeared through the door again.

Much later, he told her the whole awful business about Natira, whom she had interviewed. She had some interesting insights into the priestess's character. "Duty first, love second," Dwen had waxed philosophical one evening, "that's Natira's motto, and if she had to break a promise to an individual to fulfill her duty to her people, well, that isn't a very big sin for a high priestess, is it?"

McCoy was not so sure, but he became friends with Kerid-wen anyway. She kept him supplied with the local hooch and a sympathetic ear, played caretaker, making sure he didn't drink *too* much, pounding on his door when he overslept. And when she and McCoy started receiving invitations to lecture, it only made sense to coordinate their schedules and go together. After all, Keridwen was a certified pilot who owned a tiny shuttle. It only made sense for McCoy to go along for the ride.

They had lectured on Rigel, Earth, and now, the last and most prestigious invitation, the Vulcan Science Academy. Her attitude toward public speaking annoyed McCoy unspeakably: she seemed to think it was fun, and refused to indulge his attacks of stage fright.

"Absolutely great," Keridwen said now, still clapping, al-though the crowd's applause had stopped. For the first time that day, McCoy was relaxed enough to notice that she was dressed as formally as he had ever seen her, in a long black tunic and pants. The outfit was of Vulcan design (though the flowing hair definitely wasn't), which he decided made sense. Among the Fabrini, she had worn Fabrini clothing; on Earth, Terran; on Rigel, Rigellian. "Absolutely great."

"God," McCoy said through clenched teeth, when only she was close enough to hear him, "God, I hated that! Why do I keep doing this to myself?"

"Rubbish. You can't mean that," Dwen said reprovingly. "Were you nervous? I couldn't tell. You did just fine."

McCoy picked up his smudged notes and they walked to-gether to the stairs at the edge of the platform. "Quit trying to be so damn nice," he whispered, conscious of the room's perfect acoustics and all the Vulcan ears inside it, even though most of the crowd had already made their way to the exit. "Just get me out of here, okay? I need a drink."

Her self-consciously professional expression hardened around the edges. "Lately, you've been needing far too many of those." She squinted at the crowd. "Get ready. Here comes someone. Must be another question."

"Oh, no," the doctor groaned. "God spare me from any more Vulcans with well-reasoned questions."

"More rubbish. One more won't hurt," Dwen said cheer-fully. "Besides, you handled them all very well."

"I handle pain very well too, but I don't go out of my way—" McCoy broke off and dashed down the stairs into the crowd, his mouth stretched into a huge toothy grin. *"Spock!"* He shouted it so loudly he drew stares from the reserved group still filing out in orderly Vulcan fashion. McCoy stopped and waved his entire arm energetically, for the moment so glad to see his old friend that he almost forgot to be depressed about Natira.

Spock crossed to the front of the auditorium. He looked exactly the same as he had six months before, when McCoy had last seen him on the *Enterprise,* except that now he wore a dark blue tunic of the same cut as Keridwen's.

It was all McCoy could do to remind himself not to grab the Vulcan's hand and pump it furiously. Instead, he allowed himself a quick pat on Spock's arm. "Spock, you old son of a . . . I can't believe I'm saying this, but I missed you!"

"And I you," Spock answered, his expression reserved but kindly.

Surprised, then pleased at the response, McCoy beamed. "I just came from Earth. I'm supposed to tell you Jim says hello."

"The admiral," Spock said, as if reminding himself, and nodded. "I trust he is well."

"As well as can be expected. Nogura's fed him some cock-and-bull story about letting him be a troubleshooter. Giving him free rein and all that. Huh!" McCoy snorted. "I know they've supposedly cleaned house since that Admiral Rittenhouse scandal, but a bureaucracy is a bureaucracy—"

To his left, he heard Keridwen clear her throat. "Oh. Excuse me. Mr. Spock, my colleague, Dr. Keridwen—"

"Dr. Llewellyn," Spock remarked, nodding. "I found your lecture most interesting." He glanced back at McCoy. "As I did yours, Doctor."

There was an awkward pause, and then McCoy registered the presence of the Vulcan woman who was standing next to Spock. Quite an attractive woman, in a regal sort of way, though to the doctor's mind her looks were spoiled by her coolness, her lack of sparkle. "Forgive me, I'm being rude again. And may I ask who this is?"

"T'Sura, a healer, newly appointed to the Academy medical faculty." Spock hesitated briefly, then added something that sounded to McCoy very much like "my-aunt-say."

She looked awfully young to be Spock's aunt, but then, McCoy supposed it was possible. "Beg pardon?" He cocked an ear in Spock's direction.

"My fiancée," Spock repeated. He eyed McCoy intently,

watching for his reaction, as if—or was it just the doctor's imagination?—daring him to make a flippant remark.

Well, you can just knock me over with a feather, McCoy wanted to say, but he turned to T'Sura and bowed from the shoulders.

"It is an honor to meet you, ma'am."

The faintest flicker of warmth crossed her elegant face. "It is an honor to meet Spock's friend."

"Well," McCoy said awkwardly, "this calls for a celebration. I'm gonna take us all out for a drink."

Life is very strange, McCoy reflected as he sipped his Scotch with something less than appreciation. *Natira is married to someone else, which she swore she'd never do. Jim is in San Francisco, doing the one job he swore he'd never do, whether he knows it yet or not. And here am I in a bar on Vulcan, having a sociable chat with Spock and his intended.* The hotel he and Keridwen were staying in was on the outskirts of ShanaiKahr, the capital, but it was run by Vulcans and therefore a cut above anything else the tourist quarter offered. Unfortunately, McCoy hadn't realized the Vulcans leased the bar to another, less moralistic species. Alas, the bar stocked no sour mash or even bourbon—the closest thing was Scotch. McCoy grumpily ordered a Glenfiddich. It was very good Scotch—which meant it was just palatable enough for McCoy to get down without grimacing. Keridwen ordered a gin and tonic and wore a smug look on her face that said *At least this way you won't be likely to drink so much.* McCoy was tempted to kick her under the round table.

"Dr. Llewellyn," T'Sura said. She and Spock sat next to each other in unintentionally (McCoy assumed) identical position—leaning forward, folded hands resting on the table in front of unused cocktail napkins the grumbling Tellarite waiter had left even though the Vulcans ordered nothing. "I must confess that we came only to hear Dr. McCoy's lecture, but were early enough to listen to the end of yours. Religion is outside my field, but what you said was most intriguing. As a healer, folklore has always interested me, since, unlike doctors, we also utilize many ancient treatments once considered magical, until they were found to be based on scientific principles. Did I understand correctly that the Fabrini religion was based on magic?"

A gracious woman, McCoy decided. Reserved, yes, but not as cold as he had first thought. She was doing everything in her power to be hospitable to Spock's friends, even at the cost of sitting in a tourist-quarter bar with two humans and making sure the conversation stayed interesting. Very gracious. It made him think of Natira, and then he felt sorry for himself again.

"Not the state religion." Keridwen brightened like a firefly. "There is an ancient Fabrini cult, outside the official religion. And because unsanctioned religions require secrecy for survival, it is frowned upon, considered 'evil' by everyone but its practitioners. Every culture has its 'evil, magical' religion."

"Except Vulcan, I'm sure," McCoy interjected. Had only Spock been there, he would have tinged the remark with sarcasm, but for T'Sura's sake he said it with convincing sincerity. "I'm sure all their religions are logical."

"On the contrary, Doctor," Spock remarked. Up to this point, he had said very little. "Before the Reformation, many Vulcan provinces were ruled by so-called 'evil magicians.' "

"Quite true," T'Sura added helpfully. "Actually, these magicians—the Vulcan term for them translates roughly as 'mind-lords'—evolved into our modern-day students of Kolinahr."

"How fascinating!" Dwen exclaimed. "Now, *there's* my next project."

"The Kolinahru were not actually magicians," Spock corrected T'Sura. "They simply learned to expand their mental powers beyond those of the local populace."

"True," T'Sura admitted calmly, "but more than that, they felt they could control certain . . . natural forces, one might call them. I have never heard the term translated into Standard."

" 'Elements'?" suggested Keridwen.

T'Sura considered it. "Yes, I suppose it could be translated that way."

Dwen nodded knowingly. "I'm not surprised. The concept of elemental magic—and divination, too, for that matter—seems to be a true universal. I've written a number of papers on it."

McCoy snorted. "Dwen, this is all very interesting in an anthropological sort of way, but you're beginning to sound like you actually believe in this stuff."

Her cobalt eyes narrowed. "I do. There happen to be some very scientific theories on how divination works, Leonard."

"Jung's theory of the collective unconscious for one," Spock volunteered, "as well as the more reasonable explanation of Surak's—"

"I disagree with you Vulcans," Keridwen responded

quickly. "You say it's telepathy and nothing more. What if I could prove otherwise?"

Spock and T'Sura raised eyebrows in such perfect unison that McCoy looked down into his glass to keep from smiling. "We would be most interested," Spock said, "in seeing this proof."

"Then let me do a tarot reading." Dwen reached into her carpet bag and produced a small black bundle. At McCoy's shocked expression, she retorted, "For gods' sakes, Leonard, were you too nervous to pay *any* attention to my lecture?" She untied the scarf and displayed the contents. "Fabrini divination stones and Old Terran tarot cards. I was talking this evening— Leonard *should* have been able to explain this—about the similarities between the two systems. Both use archetypes." She set the stones and cards aside, picked up two corners of the silk, gave it a flick, and smoothed it out on the table. "Let me read for you, Mr. Spock. I know tarot best, so I'll use that."

"Tarot!" McCoy exclaimed scornfully. "Come on, Dwen, that's just an old parlor game. You can't be serious."

"Some doctor you are," she retorted. "You think nothing can work unless it's been scientifically proven. But people used aspirin for centuries without knowing how it worked."

Spock interrupted. A slight crease had appeared between his dark eyebrows. "Dr. Llewellyn, quite frankly, I don't understand. You say you can prove telepathy has nothing to do with divination. Exactly how do you propose to do so?"

Dwen's thin lips curved upward in a smile. "Very easily. Touch my mind, Mr. Spock."

He tensed visibly. "For such an unimportant issue, I would prefer not—"

"I'm esper-blind." Clearly bemused by his apparent distress, she leaned forward, elbows resting on the table, and closed her eyes. The pale skin on her lids was translucent, so that McCoy could see the tracery of fine blue veins beneath. "Give it a try. I dare you."

"Esper-blind?" McCoy wondered aloud.

Spock tentatively reached one hand toward Dwen's long face. His fingertips barely grazed her temple; then he, too, closed his eyes for a few seconds. He withdrew his hand and opened his eyes. "Fascinating."

Dwen looked at him, still smiling, as if in some odd way proud of her handicap. "You see? Nothing. Zilch. A total zero.

Of course, you could achieve a mind-meld and get inside my head if you were patient and you worked at it. But I couldn't be accused of annoying natural telepaths by broadcasting my thoughts."

"Incredible," T'Sura said. "I've heard of rare instances among certain Terrans, but I've never met anyone with the . . . condition."

"Will someone please explain what's going on?" McCoy persisted, starting to feel left out.

"Your *psi* rating, then," Spock said, ignoring the doctor, "would be zero."

"It is," she said, suddenly rueful. "The lowest test score I've ever gotten." She turned at last to McCoy. "You see, Leonard . . ."

"Her brain has no telepathic center," Spock said. "No specialized brain tissue to assist the development of telepathic function. A congenital defect, analogous to those extremely rare instances when humans born without a speech center are unable to acquire language. Naturally, telepathic ability is latent in most humans—quite undeveloped, since the evolutionary trend favored the development of oral speech—"

"Naturally. Thanks for the lecture." McCoy rolled his eyes at the Vulcan's interruption, but inwardly he was pleased at the opportunity to tease Spock again.

Dwen chuckled. "Actually, Mr. Spock's explanation is quite accurate. If you think of me as a radio, I can't send *or* receive signals. I haven't any transmitter or receiver." Her black hair swung gently as she gave her head a wistful shake. "So here am I, interested in magic . . . technically, I should make a pretty rotten magician—that is, if it's true that telepathy is all there is to it." She straightened in her chair. "Now, if you'll excuse me a moment . . ." She closed her eyes and took a slow, steady breath and released it. This she did three times while McCoy watched in amused anticipation.

"Frankly, I think," the doctor said good-naturedly when she opened her eyes, "this is all a bunch of hocus-pocus for show. Rubbish, as you would say."

Smiling, she ignored him and picked up the pack of creased, dog-eared cards and started shuffling them. "So can I read for you then, Mr. Spock? Past, present, and future? You can already judge my accuracy on present and past, but you'll have to wait and see whether my predictions come true."

Spock raised his eyebrows almost imperceptibly at T'Sura; McCoy didn't notice any change in her expression at all, but Spock apparently did, for he turned to Keridwen and said, "Very well. But first I would like to establish which facts you already know about me."

"All right." She nudged McCoy with a sharp elbow. "Tell him. What have you told me about him?"

"Hmm." McCoy grimaced in mid-sip and allowed himself time to swallow. "Well, I don't think I've told her much at all—just that we served together on the *Enterprise* until six months ago."

"And I know you have a fiancée. Upon my honor, that's it." Dwen's eyes were fixed on Spock as she shuffled and reshuffled the cards; her hands seemed to move independently.

"Then I am ready," Spock said.

Dwen assumed a businesslike air, quite unlike the one McCoy expected from a fortune-teller. "All right, then. First, some explanation. Tarot cards are divided into major and minor arcana. Major-arcana cards describe states of being; the minor arcana, situations—except for the royalty cards, which may signify actual persons. Now, the minor arcana consists of four suits: cups, wands, swords, and pentacles. The cups correspond to—forgive the expression, Mr. Spock—your emotional life; wands correspond to creativity or career; swords to your mental life; and pentacles to your material or physical situation." She put the cards down in a neat stack and shoved them across the table at Spock. "Would you shuffle these, please, then cut the deck with your left hand?"

Spock complied; to McCoy's surprise, he shuffled the cards with the practiced ease of an Arcturan casino dealer. "These are antiques," the Vulcan said admiringly.

She nodded proudly. "They're over two hundred sols old. Made on Earth, but I got them from a dealer on Rigel."

Spock cut the deck, then set one pile of cards atop the other and gave them back to Keridwen. "Why the *left* hand?" McCoy wanted to know, but Dwen good-naturedly shushed him and started to deal the cards from the top of the deck.

"One question," Spock said. "How can I be sure you're giving the correct interpretation of the card?"

She stared at him, wide-eyed, obviously amused by her position of power. "I guess you'll just have to trust me, Mr. Spock."

Dwen set the cards facedown on the black silk in three rows, four cards in each row. After the twelfth card, she set the rest of the pack down and looked up at Spock.

"This top row represents your recent past. From left to right"—she drew her finger along them—"the more remote past to the more recent, up to the present. This middle row is your present, and the bottom, your future. Generally, a reading only goes, at most, six months back in time and six months forward."

"I understand," Spock said.

She turned over the first four cards. Their faces were so worn and faded that McCoy had to squint at them to make them out. The images seemed to be of people in ancient Greek or Roman clothing. "Hunh," Dwen muttered distractedly to herself. "Very strange."

"In what way?" T'Sura asked, glancing down at the cards with such genuine concern that McCoy suddenly felt like giggling. Talk about life being strange! Not only was he in a bar with Spock and his fiancée, he was in a bar with Spock and his fiancée watching Spock get his fortune told. Both Spock and T'Sura seemed totally captivated by the cards. Leave it to Llewellyn to get a couple of Vulcans to take fortune-telling seriously. She was a very compelling speaker that way. Of course, if McCoy didn't know better, he'd almost think she was serious about all this— but after months of working and then traveling with her, he'd learned she took very little seriously, except her work.

"Remembering this is all within the past six months or so"— Keridwen pointed at the first card—"the six of wands is a great card to get. Wands, of course, refer to career. This is the card of victory. See, Jason bears the Golden Fleece on his shoulders."

McCoy squinted closely at the card. By gum, it *was* a faded picture of Jason and the Golden Fleece.

"So," Dwen continued, "the most faraway event that happened to you during this period of time was an auspicious one. Literally, the card represents the triumphant conclusion of a journey at the end of which you experienced public acclaim."

McCoy snickered. "Oh, c'mon, Dwen. You knew about the *Enterprise*'s mission being over. Everyone knows that."

She was unshaken. "I admit that freely, but *I* didn't pick the card. Spock did."

"Please go ahead, Dr. Llewellyn," Spock told her, his expression total seriousness. Something about the way he said it made McCoy have to bite his cheek to keep from grinning. "What did you find that was strange?"

"Well, the next cards don't reflect any sense of victory at all. Far from it. The five of cups—emotion—indicates you actually felt regret and betrayal after this successful journey." She glanced up at Spock as if seeking reassurance, but the Vulcan's expression betrayed nothing.

McCoy no longer felt like smiling. He'd been too upset to tell her anything about Jim's promotion to the admiralty—and even if he had, how in the worlds could she have guessed how it might affect Spock?

Dwen seemed slightly confused as she continued. "This event caused a mental dilemma, as evidenced by the eight of swords—meaning that you were forced to make a decision you did not want to make. The fourth and last card of the past is the Tower—it shows a past way of life crumbling, to make way for something entirely new." She looked up at the Vulcan again. "Well? Am I doing okay so far, or am I one hundred percent off-base?"

Spock was unruffled. "It seems that the cards allow for a very broad range of interpretation. Your comments have been quite general, and no doubt influenced by the fact that you know of the end of the *Enterprise*'s five-year mission; however, I am sufficiently intrigued to continue."

McCoy rolled his eyes.

"I'll take that as a compliment." Dwen smirked a little as she turned over the next four cards. "Now, into the present. . . . The six of cups means that you still feel nostalgic right now, wishing things could go back to the way they were—"

McCoy gave Spock a sidewise glance, but the Vulcan ignored it.

"Ah, the queen of swords. There is a woman in your life; swords indicate the mind, so the woman's primary mode is mental. No doubt she's quite the intellectual." Dwen gave Spock's fiancée a knowing smile.

"Indeed." Spock sounded entirely unconvinced. T'Sura shifted ever so slightly in her chair.

"Next," Dwen continued, "the two of cups. The card shows how Eros sees Psyche and is smitten by love. This indicates the beginning of an emotional attachment—please forgive the un-Vulcan expression—the 'falling-in-love' stage of a relationship." Her tone became extremely smug. "Of course, this could be *any* type of relationship: friend, lover, even business partner—but one you feel quite fond of. It augurs a good beginning.''

Spock's eyes grew narrower by the minute. This, McCoy decided, was getting ridiculous. "Come on, Dwen," he chided, only half-joking. "Admit it. You fixed the cards."

She looked up at Spock, her gaze open and steady. "On my honor as a scientist, Mr. Spock. I am not deceiving you in any way. No sleight-of-hand. No false interpretation." She seemed so sincere that McCoy began to think maybe she *was* serious.

"I believe you," Spock answered at last, though his tone was faintly grudging. "However, I still maintain—"

"I know, I know. The cards are so general they can be interpreted any way. . . . But think it over. That's all I ask." She dimpled suddenly. "This last one about your present is a tad interesting, if you ask me. The queen of cups. Interesting, that you should have a preponderance of cups . . ." Her voice lowered, became theatrical. "You will meet a mysterious woman with a great depth of feeling. . . .''

"Would this be," Spock asked slowly, "a tall, dark stranger?"

She chuckled. "Could be. Or maybe it's just a dark-haired Terran woman who will come along and read your tarot for you." Still smiling at her own joke, she glanced down at the spread again. "Let's try the future, shall we? Remember, only up to six months ahead." She flipped the last four cards over, and as she did, McCoy could feel her tense next to him. An odd light came into her eyes—*fear,* McCoy thought, though by the time she looked up at Spock again, it had vanished. If this *were* all just Dwen's idea of a joke, McCoy no longer found it very funny.

"Well," Dwen said finally, her expression very controlled, very sober, "bear in mind that the cards need not be interpreted literally. They only reflect trends, which can always be changed by appropriate action. The future we see reflected here may not come to pass."

"Then how shall I judge the accuracy of your prediction?" Spock asked, but Dwen didn't answer. She seemed mesmerized—in a strange, frightened way—by the cards.

"For God's sake, what do they *say?''* McCoy burst out, exasperated, unable to control his curiosity as well as the Vulcans did theirs.

Dwen shuddered as she returned back to reality, then began in a detached, matter-of-fact tone, and kept her eyes focused on the cards. "All right. First, the five of swords. This one is also called the Lord of Defeat. On the mental plane, you could—*could,* not *will,* you understand—experience a great sense of defeat, of loss. It ties in to the next card . . ."

She paused to catch her breath, which gave McCoy enough time to make out the picture on the next card: a black-robed and hooded figure carrying a scythe. He drew in his breath. If Keridwen were going to play a joke on Spock, this would not be consistent with her sense of humor.

"Death. Death is not usually interpreted literally. It generally signifies a drastic change, some sort of loss—"

"I am somewhat familiar with the tarot archetypes. It can also mean physical death, can it not?" Spock asked with a decidedly clinical air. Good Lord, was there anything the Vulcan *didn't* know?

Dwen glanced up at him, then quickly looked down at the cards again. "Conceivably. Oh, rubbish, I can't lie about it. It could indicate your death . . . or the death of someone close to you. Some great loss." She took a breath and went on hurriedly. "This next one is the Magician, ill-dignified—that is, upside down. It means . . ." She faltered, her voice suddenly husky. "Forgive me, Mr. Spock. I'm not quite sure what it means. It has something to do with the card before it."

"With Death," Spock prompted calmly.

"Yes. A power . . ." She did not finish the thought, but stared down at the cards as if too stricken to make sense of them. After a moment she managed to return to the businesslike tone.

"The last card is the four of swords; it indicates a need for reflection and solitude, the need to find a place where the mind can seek peace after the great loss. You definitely will need to spend some time alone." Dwen picked up her glass and took a very long drink. "That's it. That's all there is."

"Most interesting, Dr. Llewellyn," Spock said. "I shall wait to see whether your predictions come true."

She finally met his gaze. "Not *my* predictions . . ." she began, but did not finish.

McCoy shifted in his chair. The appearance of Death seemed to have cast an unpleasant pall over the conversation. Dwen sat back, looking distracted, and sipped her drink. It was unusual for her to fall silent. As soon as T'Sura and Spock were gone, the doctor promised himself, he would ask her about all this.

Uncomfortable with the silence, he tried to make light of the reading. "That prediction musta been for me, Spock, those last two. That's exactly what I need—solitude and reflection. Playing the hermit would suit me fine right about now. Say, does either of you know a nice quiet place around here where I could get away? This was the end of my lecture tour tonight, and I have some free time. If there's a quiet, restful place in the galaxy, I figure it would have to be on Vulcan . . ."

Spock and T'Sura exchanged glances; then Spock appeared to ponder something before finally speaking. "There is such a place. It is not one that many outworlders visit, but you have been there before, Doctor."

"Gol?" McCoy groaned and shook his head. "I thought only . . ." He searched for the right word, then gave up. ". . . only monks or whatever you call them were allowed there."

"There is a different area reserved for visitors. The Kolinahru—the monks, as you call them—attend to their needs. You would be free to relax, to meditate, to be alone."

"That does sound like exactly what I'm looking for," McCoy said, then flinched as Dwen got a piece of ice from her glass and started to crunch it. As much as the doctor liked her, she hadn't left him to himself for almost six months now. He was starting to feel smothered by her friendship, and he wanted the relief of not having to put up a good front, of being able to mourn the loss of Natira in private.

"I will be going there in a week's time," Spock said, "to visit a friend. I would be honored if you would accompany me as my guest. Naturally, you would have your own quarters and all the privacy you desire . . ."

Dwen was still subdued and playing with her swizzle stick, but at Spock's invitation, she brightened. "Spock . . . Would it be too rude of me to ask if I could go along? I would dearly love to interview some of the Kolinahru. I was quite serious when I said this could be my next project."

McCoy's heart sank.

"Of course you may come along," Spock replied, but the doctor thought he heard a trace of reluctance in the Vulcan's tone. "Still, I cannot promise that the Kolinahru will agree to discuss such things with you. In fact, I strongly doubt they will."

"It's worth the risk," Dwen insisted.

Later, after the Vulcans were gone, McCoy sat in the bar with Dwen, and toyed with his Scotch. She was still being unusually quiet, except for her aggravating habit of chewing ice.

"I've got this funny feeling," he said lightly, "that you really *did* believe in what you were telling Spock. If I didn't know you better, I'd say those damn silly cards upset you. And all this time, Dwen, I believed you were a scientist."

He expected a sharp, humorous retort, but Dwen turned to him and said very slowly: "Would you like to know something, Leonard? Right now, I wish to hell I didn't believe in what you call those 'damn silly cards.' " And went back to chewing her ice.

Something about the way she said it made McCoy order another drink.

SEVEN

---------------- ☆ ----------------

Riley was working a little late that evening. Nothing specific, really—just trying to learn a bit more about how an admiral's office should be organized. He started when the comm whistled, two sharp blasts to indicate an outside call. He was not surprised to see Anab's brown face appear on the screen. "Ah, my Nubian goddess, I was just about to finish up here. I'm sorry I forgot to call—"

"That's not what I was calling about." Anab was Somalian, and elegantly beautiful; her face reminded Riley of the elongated, stylized lines of an ebony wood carving. She kept her hair short, close to the scalp, which emphasized the sweeping curve of her neck. Riley stared at her in rapt aesthetic appreciation, as he always did . . . and noticed that something was wrong. Her full bottom lip trembled.

"Anab, what's wrong?"

"I was going to leave a message for you . . . but it would have been too cruel." She took a deep breath. "I'm shipping out tonight, K.T. I'll be gone by the time you get here."

"Leaving?" Sickened, Riley clutched the sides of his desk. "Anab, what the hell are you talking about? Is this your idea of a bad joke?" Yet, at the same time he was stunned by disbelief, part of his mind whispered: *You knew this was coming. She's been so preoccupied lately. You knew it, but you just didn't want to believe . . .*

"Kevin, please." The sound of his given name surprised him almost as much as her sudden announcement. In the year and a half that he had known her, six months into a one-year marriage contract, she had never called him that. Tears were starting to collect in her large brown eyes. "Please, don't act so shocked. Let's not go through everything again. We're not going to get anywhere. Just let me go."

"You're going on the *Starhawk*, aren't you?" he asked. Suddenly he felt hurt, bitter, and he wanted to hurt her back. She'd been planning this, and waited until *now*, when he had just started the new job. Ye gods, why would she choose *now*, when things were just starting to look up for him? "How long have you been planning this?"

"A long time. K.T.; you've known for the past eighteen months how much I've wanted a deep-space assignment. For your sake, I stayed here. But . . ." Her composure broke, and the words angrily tumbled out. "I've already turned down one promotion for you. I won't lose another. I won't ruin my career in Starfleet just because you don't give a damn about yours."

"What is *wrong* with you?" he cried. "I just accepted a promotion. I'm working for Kirk now! I did it just to make you happy, Anab. I didn't even *want* this damn job. And now you're going to leave me?"

"That's just it." She had control of herself again. "You did it because *I* wanted you to. You didn't want the responsibility, did you? You're afraid of it."

He felt his cheeks flaming, but he didn't deny it.

"I knew it." Anab shook her head sorrowfully. "K.T., you would have been content to stay a lieutenant and have a safe little job teaching cadets for the rest of your life."

"And what's *wrong* with that?" he demanded. She didn't understand how he felt, couldn't begin to understand, because he had never been able to tell her about Lana Shemry's death. *I don't* want *command, don't you understand?* he wanted to scream at her, to reach inside the screen and shake her. *They gave me command of a shore party, and a crewwoman died because I screwed up—a crewwoman who also happened to be my friend.* But he was too ashamed, too haunted by it, to tell her. *If she knew about Lana, she wouldn't blame me . . .* "Anab," he said, feeling like a martyr, "you just don't understand. And it's something I can't explain to you. But a career isn't everything. A career isn't as important as two people's lives together. At least, not to me. Of course, you disagree with me.''

She looked so hurt at that that he immediately felt awful for saying it, even if he *did* know it to be the truth. "Not more important. Not *more*. But you—you have no ambition. I can't understand you. What do you want out of life?''

"Security," he said, so quickly and vehemently that it quite surprised him.

"That's the one thing no one can ever have." She seemed to be receding from the screen. "K.T., please—can I just say goodbye?''

"We still have six months—''

"Maybe not forever. Just for a while. Who knows . . . maybe I'll be back in a year. Maybe one of us—or both—will change. But right now, I have to do this. I don't want to spend my life as an aide at Starfleet HQ. I want some starship experience. I want a promotion. Is that such a horrible thing to ask?'' She was trying very hard now not to cry.

"You always knew what you wanted," he said heavily, knowing that he had lost her. The thought of her on a starship, far away from him, exposed to unknown dangers, frightened him. How could he live if she didn't come back?

"You never did," she said. "A word of advice?''

He just looked at her, trying to memorize her face.

She told him anyway. "Get out of Starfleet. Find out what it is you really want to do with your life. Let someone who really wants it have your job. You're not doing Kirk any favors by working for him halfheartedly. And whatever you decide to do, do it for yourself, not because I or someone else thinks you should do it.''

She was leaving him. . . . *Don't go,* he wanted to beg. *One day my father and my mother left the house, and I never saw them again.* But Anab would not, could not understand his horrible, overwhelming fear that if she left, something bad might happen to her. He fought to maintain some semblance of composure, of self-respect . . . and to hold on to the small shred of hope that maybe, after that year or so on a starship, she might come back to him. "Just tell me one thing, Anab. Go ahead and leave, do whatever it is you have to do, but I must know . . . Do you still love me?''

She bowed her head. Tears spilled onto her cheeks. "I love you, K.T. I really do.''

"Then why are you leaving me?" he asked, but the screen had already gone dark.

He couldn't work after that, but he couldn't go home either. Normally he would have taken the tube straight to the apartment, but tonight he took the lift all the way down and stumbled out onto the sidewalk. Grief blinded him; his brain refused to make sense of what his eyes told him, so that finding his way down the dark, hilly street to O'Reilly's Publick House was extraordinarily difficult. He passed by it the first time without seeing it, and had to backtrack.

O'Reilly's was crowded in the evenings, full of Starfleet bureaucrats, Academy instructors, and occasional midshipmen, seniors who had, in their final year, earned the right to drink liquor. Riley looked at them without seeing any of them. He elbowed his way through the crowd and procured some standing room in front of the old-fashioned oak bar. Riley went there often and had become acquainted with the owner, Seamus O'Reilly. On the days Seamus was there, Riley's second Guinness was always on the house, because, as Seamus would say, even if Riley couldn't spell his own last name worth an Orangeman's damn, he was still family.

Hearing was as difficult as seeing. A bartender Riley had never seen before asked him what he was having, and it took the man three tries before Riley understood and requested a draft Guinness. He never drank more than two because three made him embarrassingly maudlin, but tonight he was not as concerned about his public demeanor, even though he thought he recognized a nearby cadet he'd once taught. He studiously ignored him, and drank four pints very quickly, and when he felt sufficiently numbed, he headed for home.

For a long time he stood shivering in front of the door to his apartment. He felt he could not face going inside and finding her things gone, finding himself alone in a half-empty room. He considered not going in at all, considered turning around and taking the tube back out to the street. But the fact was, he had no other place to go. He braced himself and stepped up to the sensor. When the door opened, he stepped inside.

Strangely, everything looked the same. The lithographs she had hung on the walls were still there. Some knickknacks she'd bought were still on the table. A sudden impulse made him dash to the bedroom and pull open the closet door. Most of her clothes were gone, but some remained, neatly pushed to one side to make more room for his things.

She wasn't completely gone; she might be talked into coming back. He sank weakly onto the neatly made bed. On her pillow was a handwritten note on rose-colored parchment. It was just like her not to use a terminal for such a personal message. One reason he had fallen in love with her was that under the military, no-nonsense exterior, she was very much a romantic. He picked up the paper and read:

> K.T.:
>   Be in touch with you after a few days. Please think about what you want.
>   I do love you.

He held the note to him very tightly.

He remembered the young cadet in the bar, just like all the other cadets he'd taught in navigation class, all flushed and full of excitement at the prospect of a deep-space assignment. Riley had felt that way himself, once, a long time ago. He had known what he wanted then . . . or thought he knew. Or maybe he was just following the path of least resistance, out to the stars. His parents had been killed when he was very young, and Riley spent his time between boarding schools and the restless company of his father's younger brother. But Uncle Joseph had been too busy with his career in the Fleet to be tied down with a child, and Riley had no other living relatives. He was a bright, capable lad whose teachers were always telling him to settle down, to apply himself, to focus his talents on one thing that he liked to do. . . .

Bright but unmotivated, that was Kevin Riley. He dreamed of adventure then, and any place other than boarding schools. It seemed sensible to enter Starfleet Academy, to follow his uncle into space, especially since he had no one, no family to tie him down. That was before he learned that adventure always involved responsibility and, sometimes, death. Now when he dreamed, it was not of deep space, but of Lana Shemry and the sickening feeling that came over him when he contacted her and all that came over the frequency was silent static. . . .

Anab was right: he didn't know what he wanted. For whatever childish reason he had entered Starfleet, it hadn't been the right one. After Shemry's death, he had wanted more than anything to get out of the Fleet . . . but he had been afraid. He had known nothing outside of the Fleet, had no civilian friends. It was safer to request a transfer Earthside and spend his time in a classroom, where no one got hurt, telling others how to make their way through the treacherous reaches of deep space.

And then he had met Anab Saed, and he realized that he no longer wanted to risk losing anyone else; he had done enough of that in his short life. What he saw in Anab was the chance to reclaim some of what he'd lost. He fell in love with her almost immediately, started talking about raising a family. A large, safe, happy family.

What is it you want, K.T.?

He put his head on his knees and wept. More than anything else, he wanted Anab, and he would give up everything he had to win her back.

0845 hours. It was going to be a great day, Jim Kirk decided as the lift deposited him on the sixty-sixth floor. He had made it through Ciana's damnable stack of reports and now knew everything about every dispute on every border planet in *or* out of the Federation. But even better, he was cheerful because there was something better to do today than sit and read at his desk. This morning, he and Ciana were welcoming delegations to a special Federation Council meeting, after which she had promised to brief him on his first real assignment. And at that thought, Jim started to whistle Gilbert and Sullivan, all the way down the corridor, to the left, into his aide's office. The door was open, which meant Riley was there.

At the sight of his aide, Jim stopped whistling. Riley was slumped in his chair, leaning over his terminal with one elbow on the keyboard, his head propped in one hand. He looked on the verge of total collapse. " 'Morning, sir." He turned a pale, puffy face toward Kirk.

Kirk stared. "Good God, Riley, are you ill?"

"I'm fine, sir." Riley stood unsteadily, one hand on the back of his chair for support. "Had a touch of insomnia last night. Can I get you a cup of coffee?"

"Black," Kirk said automatically, and then, after a second glance at Riley's swollen eyes, "but I'll get it myself." He walked over to the servitor in the opposite corner of the office, which, thank God, seemed to be working today, and produced a respectably hot cup of coffee on demand. Kirk sipped at it and paused to glance at Riley, who sat hunched over the terminal again, his back toward Kirk.

If Riley wasn't volunteering information, maybe it was none of Jim's damn business. But then, Riley appeared to have just been to hell and back. A simple case of insomnia couldn't account for his grim expression. The man looked as if his dearest friend had just died. "Ah . . . Riley . . ." Kirk began delicately.

Riley straightened in his chair and swiveled to face Kirk. "Yes, Admiral. Admiral Ciana is in and on her way down to meet you, sir." He started to his feet, but Kirk motioned for him to stay seated.

"Thanks, but . . . I wasn't asking about that. I wondered if there was anything wrong. You don't have to answer if it's too personal. But you seem upset."

"I do, sir?" Riley was visibly distressed at the news. "I apologize, Admiral. I had hoped that . . ." His voice faded and for a moment he stared back at his terminal.

"Is it anything I can help with?" Kirk asked gently.

Riley's shoulders expanded and deflated with a sigh. Still not facing Kirk, he said, "I'm sorry to be such a disappointment to you, sir—"

"Disap*point*ment!"

"—but I don't think I'm cut out for the Fleet. I'm not the officer you think I am. I'm sorry."

Oh, Christ, Kirk wanted to say with disgust, but he was too astounded for a minute to say anything. Riley was right. He *was* disappointed. And right now it took a superhuman effort not to show it. "Lieutenant Commander, does this have anything to do with that crewperson who died?"

Riley shuddered. "No, sir. It has to do with me."

"Are you telling me that you're resigning?"

"I haven't tendered it officially yet—"

"Then don't. Dammit, Riley, what have I done to make you want to leave?" Kirk permitted himself to show a small fraction of the exasperation he felt.

Startled, Riley finally looked at him. "Oh, sir, you misunderstand. You've done nothing. It's been a pleasure to work for you."

"Then what about the assignment do you dislike?"

"I like it very much, sir, it's just that . . ." Riley faltered.

"Lieutenant Commander, you have been on the job one whole day. If, after two weeks, you still feel you don't belong here, *then* you may submit your resignation. Until then, both of us will pretend this conversation never took place. Is that clear?''

He must have said it with greater vehemence than he'd intended, because Riley seemed to shrink in his chair. There was a long pause, and then Riley said in a low voice: "Understood, Admiral. Two weeks.''

"Good.'' Kirk felt the last vestiges of a good mood disappear. Today definitely wasn't going to be as pleasant as he'd originally thought. He was thoroughly frustrated by Riley's willingness to throw his promotion away—a promotion that Kirk had argued long and hard with Nogura about—yet at the same time, he was worried about the troubled look in Riley's eyes. Something had happened, something that he might get Riley to talk about in time. In two weeks the young man would be over it and able to think clearly again. "Now, were there any messages for me this morning?''

"Just Admiral Ciana saying that she was coming down—''

"Admiral Ciana is here.'' Smiling, Ciana walked through the open door. If she had heard anything of the foregoing conversation, she gave no sign of it. Her manner was briskly good-natured.

"Perfect timing, Admiral,'' Kirk said, making an effort to smile back. Riley rose to his feet and tried his best to look pleasant.

"Always.'' She looked pointedly at the mug in Kirk's hand. "If you want to finish your coffee, Admiral, you'll have to do it before we get down to the reception area.''

"I'm finished.'' Kirk took a huge swallow and set the mug down on Riley's desk. "Who are we greeting today?''

"Andorians first, then the Vulcans and the Iotians.'' She walked over to Riley's desk. "You go on ahead, Kirk. I'll catch up to you. There's something I need to go over with Riley first.''

"Of course,'' Kirk said, and stepped out into the corridor. Ciana had acted as if she hadn't noticed Riley's condition at all—but as a psychologist, she must have. He felt a surge of warmth toward the woman. Ciana was a class act. Obviously she had heard at least part of the conversation, but was too discreet to let on in front of both of them. And now, no doubt, she was going to offer Riley a sympathetic ear. He shook his head and smiled grimly. She was far more qualified to do it than he was right about now.

He flinched when the outer door to Riley's office slid shut.

* * *

Ciana marched up to Riley, tilted her chin up, and gazed steadily into his eyes. She was not all that well-acquainted with him personally, but she knew Riley the individual very well. She had pored over his records and his psych evals a dozen times back when Jim Kirk was arguing to have Riley as his new chief of staff.

"Off the record and forgetting rank," she snapped, letting Riley see some of the anger she felt, "I heard what you said to Kirk. What the hell do you think you're doing, resigning?"

To his credit, Riley didn't wince. Ciana approved. His psychs indicated deep insecurity, but also a tough resilience. The kid might be scared to death, but he would never show it. And he'd take action in a tight spot. It was this trait that had finally made Ciana back Kirk's decision. "With all respect," Riley answered, his face flushed—more from anger than surprise, Ciana guessed— "if we're forgetting rank, Admiral, then I'd just as soon not answer that question. My reasons are personal."

"Let's remember it, then. I want an answer."

Beneath the patchy beginnings of a beard, Riley's cheeks grew a brighter red. "I'm not the right person for the job. Admiral Kirk needs a real go-getter. My record proves I'm not—"

Infuriated, she jabbed a finger at him. "Admiral Kirk stuck his neck out for you! Don't you give a damn about lopping his head off? If you go through with this, you won't just be killing your own career. You'll be hurting his as well."

Riley's eyes widened. Obviously the thought had never occurred to him.

Ciana built up steam, punctuating her words with the accusatory finger. "Think about it, Riley. Think about all the trouble he went to in order to get you that promotion. Believe me, it wasn't easy convincing Nogura. Kirk argued long and hard to get you. How will *he* look if you resign the first week?"

Part of it was an embarrassingly simple ploy to make Riley feel guilty—a little guilt would do him good, Ciana decided. His psychs had also revealed a tendency to self-centeredness. But mostly she said it because she honestly wanted to defend Kirk. Nothing would happen to him, of course, except that Nogura would be mildly disgruntled over Riley's resignation. But she was learning to admire Kirk—for his brilliant strategist's mind, of course. Naturally, after meeting him, she found him attractive in other ways as well . . . but she did her best to keep their relationship on a strictly professional level. She didn't want

Nogura saying she had thought up the troubleshooter position just to get Jim Kirk near her.

"Admiral," Riley tried to say, "I—"

She interrupted him vehemently. "You *owe* it to Kirk to be a success, Riley. And, dammit, you owe it to yourself. I've seen your files. I see everyone's in my department. You want to know the truth about yourself? You've got *no* excuse for screwing up. Not one. You're damn fine command material. Kirk's smart—he sees it in you, and he's trying to give you another chance to show it. But for some reason, you keep refusing to believe it."

Riley's face quivered and then hardened. "If you read my file, then you know . . . a crewperson died because of me."

She shook her head. "A crewperson died under your command on a surveying expedition. It seemed to me there was no way you could have prevented it. It happens every day, Riley; it's something officers have to learn to deal with."

"I could have—" Riley began hotly, but she silenced him.

"If you look at it that way, then I, and Admiral Kirk too, are responsible for dozens of deaths apiece. Would you be so quick to accuse Kirk of negligence in the same situation?"

Riley did not meet her eyes. "Maybe not," he said finally.

"Good. A little honesty. Lieutenant Commander, I *know* what the record shows. You were not at fault. And I checked you out with a fine-tooth comb before you got here. You deserve this job and can be a great asset to Kirk, if you'll let yourself."

"Sir," Riley said earnestly, "Admiral Kirk gave me two weeks in which to make a decision. I'll consider everything that you said. But I need some time to think."

Ciana stared hard at him. "Just be sure that at the end of those two weeks you do the right thing by Kirk." She left before Riley had the chance to respond.

Out in the corridor, Jim Kirk waited at the lift. He turned at the sound of her footsteps and smiled. She smiled back, feeling slightly dazzled. True, the man was good-looking in a take-home-to-mother sort of way, but Ciana preferred more exotic types and had been exceptionally unimpressed by the holo in Kirk's file. Yet, in person he had a certain . . . magnetism, an appeal that had nothing whatsoever to do with his appearance and everything to do with the man himself. She averted her eyes, suddenly aware that she had been staring, and disgusted with herself for such unprofessional behavior. All right, so she was attracted to the man—but she refused to let it interfere with the job they both had to do.

She had not lied to Kirk when she had said she was using him. The truth was, she *needed* him to get that promotion, and the fact that she needed him—she, who had never needed anyone in her entire life—made her at once protective and jealous of him. Jealous, because she hated to be put in an inferior position to anyone. She had always been brighter, tougher, faster than any of her peers, and nothing had ever held her back from getting exactly what she wanted.

Until now. She could still see the image of Nogura's round, placid countenance, his dark eyes hooded and for once not quite meeting hers. Ciana had applied for the assignment as diplomatic liaison to the Federation, and it had not occurred to her for as much as an instant that she would not get it, just as she had so easily gotten every other promotion in her sterling career.

Why, Admiral?

She had gone to him at once. She dealt with every problem in her life the same way, by confronting it head-on. *Why did you refuse me this assignment? You knew how badly I wanted it.*

And Nogura had raised his face up from whatever he had been reading at his desk and said simply, *Lori. This was a diplomatic post. You lack the proper experience.*

Lack the experience! I've got ten years as top diplomatic adviser in the Fleet!

Nogura shook his head. *You know that's not the same as direct experience. Theory is one thing—telling diplomats what to do is one thing. Being a diplomat is another.*

She was not going to give up so easily. *Then what do I need, Admiral, to get the experience? What other position should I apply for? Just tell me and I'll—*

He waved his hand at her to silence her, and in a rare display of defensiveness said: *Enough, Ciana. I did not give you the assignment because you were not the most qualified applicant. It's that simple.*

She stopped, stunned. He had never cut her off like that before, never refused to give her his reasons. She drew in a breath, released it, and forced herself to speak more calmly. *Heihachiro, I have known you since I was a child. As a friend, I would appreciate some frankness here. Why didn't you give me the assignment?*

Nogura was quiet for a moment, and then he said: *Lori, you lack . . . subtlety. You come from a military family; I knew both your parents very well. They thought in black and white. You think in black and white. No shades of gray whatsoever . . . and diplomacy is all shades of gray. That, combined with your somewhat . . . tenuous control over your temper, makes you unfit to be a diplomat.*

She hadn't blushed since she was a girl, but standing in front of Nogura's desk, her face had grown suddenly warm. *Thank you, sir,* she told him. *I appreciate your honesty with me.* And she turned on her heel and left before Nogura had a chance to see her anger.

Now, looking at Jim Kirk, she felt a pang of envy. *Watch him,* Nogura had said. *Learn from him.*

The lift opened, and together they stepped inside.

"Reception east," Ciana said. The lift began moving horizontally.

"And I had thought this was going to be a good day," Kirk said somewhat wistfully. "I take it you overheard our conversation, Admiral." He was referring to Riley, of course.

"I heard." Her eyes were focused straight ahead, on the seam between the lift doors.

"I hope you were able to help him. Do you think he'll stay?"

"I think he'll stay."

Kirk sighed. "He obviously needed to talk to someone, but I was frankly too angry to be much help." From the edge of her vision she could see him watching her. "I'd like to thank you for being so understanding with him. It's kind of you to take such an interest in your personnel."

She gave a tight little smile and said nothing.

"Report, Lieutenant." Lieutenant Commander Ingrit Tomson looked out over the sea of screens that together gave a composite view of Starfleet Headquarters. It was the third time that hour she had asked for a report, but then, she had good reason: only her third day as chief of HQ Security, and already she faced a situation that would have made a veteran nervous. She was responsible for the safety of one hundred and twenty Council delegates, one of whom had already received an anonymous death threat. Tomson was experienced enough to know that it was probably a crank, but her instincts told her that it very often paid off to take cranks seriously.

"All stations reporting secure, sir." Lisa Nguyen glanced down at her console and touched a finger to her earpiece.

"What about sensors?"

"Sensors are in working order and also report secure, sir."

"Very good, Lieutenant." Tomson stepped up behind her new second-in-command. Seated at the console, Nguyen came only as high as Tomson's hip, so that Tomson had to bend down to rest a hand briefly on the young almond-skinned woman's shoulder. For the ultrareserved Tomson, the gesture was the equivalent of a bear hug. "Good to have you back after all this time."

Nguyen glanced up and behind her and smiled. "Thank you, sir. It's good to be working with you again." Although Nguyen had been working at HQ for almost two years now, she had only recently been transferred to HQ Security Central at the new security chief's request.

Both she and Tomson started slightly as Lisa's intercom buzzed. Ever since the news about the Galakhi delegate, everyone in Security was a little jumpy.

It was Zheng at Central Comm. "Local communication coming through for you, Lieutenant."

"Local?" Lisa sounded surprised. Behind her, Tomson frowned. With today's stepped-up security, the only calls expected were internal.

"From spacedock," Zheng answered. "A private comm."

"Put it through, Zheng," Tomson said over Nguyen's shoulder.

"On visual."

The head and shoulders of a black human male appeared on Nguyen's console screen. "Surprise." He grinned broadly, teeth flashing beneath a carefully groomed mustache.

"Stanger!" Nguyen cried, clearly delighted. "How are you?"

"Busy. I'm aboard the *Victorious* and we're getting ready to ship out. But before I left, I wanted to congratulate you first." He paused and looked at her with genuine fondness. "You look great."

"Thanks. I'm enjoying it here in Security."

"Not *that*. Lamia said you were pregnant."

Nguyen laughed, blushing a little. "I only found out myself a few weeks ago. Sometimes I forget—"

"You'll get used to it. I'll be sending along a little shower gift pretty soon. But if we get too far out, you might not get it till after the baby's grown. I heard it was a girl.''

"That's right," Nguyen said proudly. Tomson cleared her throat. "Uh, Stanger, we're on yellow alert right now, so I can't talk. But Lieutenant Commander Tomson is right here, if you'd like to talk to—"

"That sour old battleax?" Stanger's handsome features contorted. "Now, why would I want to talk to *her?"*

Nguyen looked as if she wanted to crawl under the console. Tomson let the corners of her thin mouth curve up the tiniest bit, then forced a frown and stepped forward so that Stanger could see her.

"All right, Stanger," she snapped, trying hard to sound honestly irritated. "Just what the hell are you doing annoying my people? Or don't they give the security chief anything to do on the *Victorious?"* Part of her was enjoying Nguyen's discomfort too much to let on, but at the sight of Stanger, it was all she could do to keep a straight face. Before the *Enterprise* crew disbanded, Stanger had served as Tomson's second-in-command after Nguyen had taken personal leave. Six months' leave had turned into a permanent assignment at Starfleet Headquarters when Nguyen decided to join a group marriage. Of course, in all the time Nguyen had known Tomson, she had never dared joke with the lieutenant commander. It was, Tomson decided, at least one good thing she had learned from Jonathon Stanger.

"Tomson! I should have known you'd be listening in. Are you being as hard on your new second-in-command as you were on me?"

Nguyen had finally worked up the nerve to glance back at Tomson's face, and was beginning to realize she was being put on.

"No need," Tomson said, deadpan. "Nguyen's already a good officer. She doesn't need any breaking-in. Unlike others . . ."

Stanger smiled and dropped the teasing tone. "I can believe that. Look, sir, I called to congratulate you on your recent promotion."

Tomson could no longer keep from grinning. Next to her, Nguyen relaxed and smiled too. "I appreciate it, Lieutenant. And congratulations on your position as security chief."

"Thanks," Stanger answered. "I just wanted to touch base

with everyone before we shipped out. We're probably going to be out—''

Tomson did not see Nguyen tense next to her, but she could feel it. She didn't even apologize to Stanger for the interruption. "What is it, Nguyen?''

"Sir . . . we just lost one of the B5 console screens.''

The Federation Council meeting was being held on level B5.

"Stanger, good luck.'' Tomson cut off the visual without giving him a chance to reply. "Malfunction?''

Nguyen's smile had vanished. She pressed a control on her panel. "Yes, sir. Computer verifies a simple malfunction.''

But there was a hesitancy in her voice that Tomson felt as well. There was nothing all that suspicious about a screen malfunction . . . except that it was occurring now, when all the delegates were arriving, on level B5. "Raise Zingje for me.''

Zingje's voice came over the intercom. "Lieutenant Zingje here.''

"We've just lost your screen, Lieutenant.'' Tomson leaned forward over the intercom on Nguyen's console. "All quiet down there?''

"All squared away, Lieutenant Commander. But we'll keep an eye open for any trouble.''

Tomson straightened, her pulse racing. The loss of just one screen was probably a coincidence, but not one she felt good about right now. "Contact Harker's party on level one and tell them to get down to B5.''

"Aye, sir.'' Nguyen was already entering Harker's code into her intercom panel when she stopped abruptly. Tomson saw and was just about to say something when she followed Nguyen's gaze.

The second screen for B5 went gray, and then the third, and the fourth.

"Raise Zingje!''

Nguyen entered Zingje's code with lightning speed. A deafening burst of static came over the intercom. Nguyen pulled out her earpiece and covered her ears. "The channel's being jammed!'' She was shouting, but Tomson could barely hear her over the screeching noise.

"Then raise *anyone*—'' Tomson began, but the effort to make herself heard was too great. She elbowed Nguyen aside and tried to contact another security patrol, any security patrol. She went through fourteen codes in a matter of seconds.

The static was on all channels.

She tried Central Comm. Static.

Tomson slammed a fist down on the console for one self-indulgent instant of frustration, then pushed herself away, toward the exit. "You have command!" she shouted over her shoulder at Nguyen.

"Sir, let me go—" Nguyen protested, but Tomson was already on her way down.

EIGHT

☆

Uhura walked into the wing of the building that housed Starfleet Command. She was ready for the crowds and the extra security checkpoints. Everyone in the Academy was well aware of the Federation Council's arrival; the Djanai/Inari dispute was debated in political-science classes, the conflict's origin was detailed in galactic-history classes. Tactics for protecting the delegates made exam material for security cadets. In her communications practicum, there'd been no real discussion of it, although Uhura had often arrived in the simulation room the past week to find the cadets involved in a lively argument on the subject.

Today she had a three-hour break between simulations, and it was too early on in the semester to have any real work to do. This was her chance to do two things she'd been putting off. Not fifteen minutes before, she had called Kirk's office to find the admiral (how hard it was to even think of him by that rank!) was out, but on HQ grounds. She'd been sorry to miss Kirk, but then, she'd been pleased and surprised to see Kevin Riley answer the signal, though the young lieutenant commander looked like he hadn't had any sleep since his promotion. Even though the admiral was tied up, Riley told her, there was a chance she could catch him on his way back to his office. He was greeting delegates. Give it half an hour.

She gave it fifteen minutes, and then left the Academy wing

to head for Command. In fact, she had come to HQ to do more than congratulate Kirk on his promotion. It had been more of an afterthought, actually. She looked down at the *kissar* cradled in one arm. If she was lucky, she'd be able to get it past the main checkpoint, and then she could look for the Vulcan delegation. Riley had verified that they'd already arrived. Uhura knew that she would be stopped, and her burden examined; and while she knew she could rely on her clearance to get her past any checkpoints, she was not so sure it would get the exotic-looking kissar past.

Her last day on the *Enterprise,* she hadn't been able to bring herself to say good-bye to anyone. She was stubbornly optimistic by nature, and found depressing situations a major annoyance. Besides, she was going to see most of these people again. Kirk had made it clear he would insist on another ship, and Uhura had already made up her mind that she would be on it. And when her shipmates became maudlin about the end of the five-year mission, Uhura reminded them that the next one was only a few months away.

She didn't pack up until the last minute, so that she would be very busy at the end, instead of moping around the ship like Leonard McCoy and a couple of others. When they were finally in spacedock and everyone was leaving and sniffling into handkerchiefs, Uhura was in her quarters madly stuffing suitcases. And when the door buzzer sounded, she expected to see Jim Kirk in the doorway, here to tell her the name of the new vessel they'd all get assigned to. She did not expect to see Mr. Spock.

He stood in the doorway, dressed in civilian clothing, one tidy carryall slung over his shoulder, while Uhura stood agape in the midst of four open suitcases and piles of unpacked things.

"Mr. Spock." She was too surprised to say anything but the obvious. "You're still here."

He nodded and glanced at the general chaos without saying anything.

"Well," Uhura said brightly, "I'm sure we'll see each other again very soon."

"In case we do not"—Spock held out something that had been tucked under one arm—"I would like to give you this."

She took it from him. It was a Vulcan harp, carved from *trihr* wood, a hard, almost-black wood that reminded Uhura of ebony. At first she mistook it for Spock's own harp, a family heirloom, and words of protest rose to her lips. After she held it and ran

her fingers over its polished surface, she realized he had had a
new one made for her.

"Mr. Spock. It's beautiful," she breathed. "I don't know
what to say."

"You are not supposed to say anything. You are supposed to
play it."

She laughed softly and ran her fingers over the strings.
Chords leapt into the air and lingered. "Thank you. I'll treasure
it. When I see you again, I'll play for you."

"I shall look forward to that," Spock answered. He began
to move away.

"Take care, Spock."

And he was gone.

When Kirk didn't get another ship, Uhura transferred to HQ.
It was a temporary career move, she promised herself. She knew
James Kirk. Admiral or not, he would eventually have command
of another ship. As for Spock, she expected him to do the logical
thing and accept the teaching position at the Academy. She kept
her word, of course; she took lessons from a tutor at Berkeley
and learned to play the harp. And she had a modern version of a
kissar, an African lyre, made for Spock, a gift to welcome him
when he arrived in San Francisco.

The ground level of Starfleet Command was a huge open
area, all glass walls and sweeping expanse of burgundy carpeting.
If you weren't careful, the glass could give you the optical illusion
that you were actually still outside in the gray drizzle, on the city
street with the other pedestrians. Today they seemed an exten-
sion of the crowd inside.

Uhura made it through the first checkpoint—the invisible
scanners that identified her to Security Central several levels
below and checked for hidden weapons. She wondered what the
scanners had made of the kissar. It was a handsome thing,
roughly the size of a classical guitar. The bowl was made the
traditional way, from a calabash gourd, the surface of which was
intricately etched. To Uhura, the lyre's most striking feature was
its neck, made from two ridged and twisting antelope horns. The
horns were not real—though, centuries ago, they would have
been authentic—but carved from wood; it was an omission Spock
would appreciate. Between the horns, eight strings hung suspended from a bridge of wood.

The kissar must have given the scanners pause. Still, no one stopped her until she arrived at an official checkpoint in front of the reserved lift that went to level B5, where all the delegates were headed. The area was cordoned off, forcing people to go in single file past the guards, who used hand-held scanners. It made sense, Uhura decided. If the central scanners were somehow sabotaged, the hand-held ones would remain unaffected. She stepped behind a Terran diplomat, and when it was her turn, smiled at the guards.

One of them, a Changed humanoid with black-velvet skin, stopped her before she could step onto the lift. "Ah, excuse me, Commander." He stepped forward with his scanner.

She turned slowly to look at him, and raised a brow so disdainful it would have made Spock proud.

"I'm sorry, sir, but are you essential personnel?"

She feigned cold irritation. "Don't I look it, Ensign?"

He was slightly flustered. "Sir, forgive me for asking, but only essential personnel are allowed—"

"Ensign," she said in a deadly authoritative tone, "I am to personally present a gift to Ambassador Sarek. Do you really want to risk his not getting it?"

"May I ask what this is, sir?"

"Why, a kissar," she stated, as if it were transparently obvious to anyone, and when he still looked confused, she added, "A musical instrument. Of course."

"Do a retinal scan," the ensign's companion suggested.

"Sir?" he asked by way of permission. She nodded, and he turned the scanner on her face and watched the readout. "Commander Uhura," he said respectfully, "if you'll swear you've been assigned to deliver this personally to the Vulcan ambassador, then we'll let you pass. But we have no record of this, sir."

"I've already said it once," she said huffily, hoping he wouldn't remember that that wasn't *exactly* what she'd said. "Of course, if *my* word isn't good enough, then you can verify it through Admiral Kirk's office—"

"Let her go," the other guard said.

"Sorry for the inconvenience, Commander." The ensign gestured Uhura on.

She haughtily stalked past them onto the lift. The doors closed over her, and she giggled. *Uhura, honey, you really should have been an actress.*

* * *

Did Ciana have any idea, Kirk wondered, *of the effect she had on others?* He was trying very hard not to become any more impressed with the vice admiral than he already was, but it was becoming all too easy to fall under her spell. The main level of HQ was crowded on the way to the first checkpoint, but Ciana never hesitated, never broke stride, just kept walking very quickly, as if there were no one in her way. Somehow, miraculously, the crowd always parted at the last minute to let her through. She exuded authority the way that Nogura did: naturally, without conceit, and without ever misusing it. She simply knew she had it, and others recognized it. Kirk found himself becoming envious, and wondered if, other than the occasional flare of temper, Lori Ciana possessed any flaws at all.

"I may as well start briefing you on our upcoming assignment now," Ciana said as the security guards waved them past the first checkpoint. She'd never even looked up, never slowed down. "We'll be going to Djana next week—that is, if the Federation Council votes to remove the peace-keeping force, as we expect. But first, I have something of a personal question for you."

She lowered her lids the smallest bit and glanced sideways at him—not at all coyly, but rather defensively, as if daring him to make something of it.

"Ask away, Admiral," he said lightly, though he was completely unable to guess what that question might be.

"Nogura seems to think you're hellacious diplomatic material. I know it must be true"—*was he imagining it, or was her tone slightly grudging?*—"since starship captains have to think diplomatically on their feet. So my question is: Just what is the big secret to diplomacy?"

The question startled him with its naiveté, so that he almost laughed; but one look at Ciana's serious countenance sobered him. He shrugged. "There's no big secret, Admiral."

She frowned at that, but remained determined to get some sort of answer from him. "Well . . . what advice would you give someone, then?"

"Just . . . listen to the other side, try to see their point of view—then ignore it and trust your instincts."

Still scowling, she stopped in mid-stride and blinked at him. "Trust your *instincts?* That's a pretty simple solution for solving complicated problems. And what do you do if your instincts don't conform with regulations?"

Jim finally had to smile. "Very simple, Admiral. In that case, you follow your instincts and break the rules."

"Just like that," she said scornfully.

"Just like that."

"Right-brained diplomacy." Clearly displeased with his response, she shook her head and started walking again; Jim followed, careful not to show his amusement at her reaction. "Just follow your instincts. I suppose this leaves out proper preparation, such as studying all the information available on a particular situation."

"Not at all," Jim countered. He'd heard of Ciana's reputation as a perfectionist and a stickler for detail; she probably didn't believe he could have made it through the stack of flimsies and still master the data well enough for her exacting standards. "In fact, I'm well-prepared on a number of different political situations. Go ahead—ask me questions about Djana. Test me."

A blond eyebrow quirked. "All right," she answered, "I will. What's the proper form of address you'd use with the Djanaan ambassador?"

It was a trick question, one he was ready for. "First off," Jim said, "it's Djanai, not Djanaan; a Djanai would find the Standard bastardization of the term offensive. Djana is the planet, Djanai the adjective and plural noun, meaning the inhabitants. The proper term of address is to use the vocative case, which is to put the word 'U' before the given name. Except that *this* particular ambassador prefers Terran tradition—so I would address him as 'Ambassador.'

"Then, of course, there's the political unrest between the two groups: the Djanai and the Inari. The Inari were those Djanai who left their native planet to settle the neighboring planet Inar, which, two hundred years ago, became uninhabitable—and so the Inara returned to Djana and, being more technologically advanced, took over the government." He glanced slyly at her. "Any other questions, Admiral?"

She sighed, beaten, and then not quite smiled at him. "Well, I *would* like to know whether you intend to refer to the ambassador from Djana as Djanai to his face."

"Only if I wanted to precipitate an interstellar incident." Kirk smiled. "He's the *Inari* ambassador; he represents the Inari population of Djana. Until recently the Djanai have appeared uninterested in politics."

Ciana finally smiled back, and slowed at the second checkpoint, because of the short line that had formed. At the sight of the vice admiral, however, both guards snapped to attention, then signaled for her and Kirk to come through before the others. Ciana stepped onto the lift and gave them a curt nod as the doors to the lift closed over her and Kirk.

The lift started to move down. "So you think we should take our advisers out," Ciana said, her tone now conversational rather than professorial, "and leave the Inari to the mercy of their own terrorists, not to mention the Orion pirates—"

He wasn't sure whether she was baiting him for the fun of it, testing him to see what he knew, or really arguing with him. He suspected, from the good-humored expression on her face as she looked straight ahead at the lift doors, that it was the first. "Our advisers don't keep the Orions away, Admiral. Our Border Patrol does."

"Some Council members would like that to stop too. After all, what does an association with Djana get us except a lot of very cheap alcohol?"

She gave him that funny sideways glance again, but she was smiling.

"Admiral," he said admonishingly, but returning the smile, "I think you know the answer to that."

"Really?" She looked back at the lift doors.

He sighed, a very small respectful sigh in consideration of the fact that she was a superior. "It's a Federation stronghold close to Romulan territory. Strategically speaking, it makes good sense to have them on *our* side."

"Quite frankly, Kirk, I suspect the Romulans already have their foot in the door. I wouldn't be surprised if they're encouraging the unrest. Call it . . . instinct."

The lift doors opened and they stepped forward into the reception area. Ciana ignored the guards that snapped to attention, and busied herself with peering into the crowd. There were already more than a hundred beings in the large chamber. Kirk had hosted diplomatic functions before on the *Enterprise,* but he had to admit that HQ put on a more impressive show. Long tables laden with food and drink and exotic flora from each of the delegate planets lined the walls, which were decorated with banners representing each planet. In the center of the chamber a fountain sent up a spray, brilliantly lit to reflect the United Federation of Planets' logo.

"There." Ciana gestured with her head and briefly rested a hand on Kirk's arm. "The Inari delegate. His name is Ewu."

Less than one and a half meters tall, Ewu gazed up earnestly at the Earth ambassador's face as the two conversed. The Inari was a stocky barrel-chested creature whose build, hidden by a long, simple robe, reminded Kirk of a Tellarite. The similarities stopped there, for by strictly human standards, the Inari's demeanor was warm and personable, and his features homely but vaguely endearing. His dark, whiteless eyes were situated above a long brown-skinned face that looked like a cross between a cow and a sheep with too-short muzzles. A race of intelligent ruminants, Ciana's report had said. Four stomachs and a need for constant grazing had produced a society dependent upon agriculture. Silage was big business on Djana, along with its by-product, alcohol, which the Inari and Djanai could not digest but were more than happy to export to those who could.

Kirk watched as Ewu cast an occasional wistful glance at a tray of fruit on a nearby table. Jim smiled inwardly, remembering the time his brother Sam had gotten the family milk cow, Raisin, rip-roaringly drunk on apples. Poor Raisin's digestive system had efficiently converted all the fruit sugar to alcohol.

"Come," Ciana said, drawing him by the arm. They made their way over to the Earth banner, where various dishes of Earth cuisine were displayed on the table beneath.

"Admiral Ciana. Good to see you again," the Earth ambassador said delightedly, and extended her hand. Dressed in a scarlet sari trimmed with gold, she was delicate and dark-haired. Next to Ciana, she seemed petite; next to Ewu, she became a giantess.

Ciana shook her hand. "Ambassador Bhutto." She turned, hands folded across her chest, and bowed in Ewu's direction. "Ambassador Ewu."

Ewu set his plate down on the edge of the nearby table and returned Ciana's gesture. The hands across his chest were four-fingered, with the two outer fingers ridged with what looked to Jim like vestigial hooves.

"Admiral Ciana." Ewu's voice was incredibly low and resonant, coming from deep within his broad chest.

Ciana gestured toward Kirk. "May I have the pleasure of presenting Admiral James Kirk to you both? Ambassador Indira Bhutto of Earth, Ambassador Ewu of Djana."

Kirk shook Bhutto's hand and bowed to Ewu. "I've been studying much about the concerns of your people, Ambassador Ewu."

"Ah," Ewu said. He seemed to be smiling, although Kirk

was not sure if it was his natural expression or if he had been practicing it for his visit to Earth. The Inari picked up his plate again with his hooved hand and, holding it close to his face, gracefully scooped up a piece of fermented silage with his long, flexible tongue. The humans, well-seasoned interstellar travelers, did not bat a lash at the action, although Kirk could feel Ciana's careful gaze on him. Ewu munched loudly and thoughtfully for a moment, then said in a kindly voice, "I'm interested in what Starfleet thinks about our situation. Are you in favor of maintaining a peace-keeping force on our planet, Admiral?"

Bhutto leaned forward, interested. Clearly she and Ewu had been involved in a friendly argument over just this question.

Kirk cleared his throat. "I'm not sure that the peace-keeping force has done you any good at all, Ambassador. But I do think you're entitled to some sort of Federation protection, if the majority of your citizens want it."

"Ah," Ewu repeated with a triumphant glance at Bhutto. "I agree with you there. After all, we are an important source of alcohol for the Federation. Even the Saurians cannot compete with us—"

"The alcohol is not the point, Ambassador. The Federation is morally bound to protect any planet whose citizens request it, regardless of whether there is any profit in it."

"I like this man," Ewu said enthusiastically to Bhutto and Ciana, and drew his lips back to reveal a hard, toothless upper ridge of gum. "Why don't you put him in charge so that my people don't have to live in fear of the rebels and the pirates?"

Bhutto smirked. "You didn't listen, Ewu. Admiral Kirk is siding with me. Sounds like he's against the peace-keeping force."

"I think," Kirk added, "the real question is whether the majority of Inari . . . and Djanai citizens *want* protection."

A smile played at Ciana's lips now.

Ewu's upper lip curled. "My understanding of your culture is that criminals lose their rights of citizenship. It is the same in mine. Last week the rebels destroyed two cargo ships filled with alcohol for export. Both crews were killed. Do you find that humorous, Indira?"

"Ewu, please, of course not." Bhutto's dark, beautiful face emanated compassion.

"I think that Admiral Kirk's question is whether the peace-keeping force has helped to stop the terrorist attacks," Ciana offered. "If it hasn't, then maybe it's time to try other methods."

Ewu was on the verge of a reply when the Inari aide appeared at his side. The aide, a much younger male with dark golden skin instead of brown, was visibly nervous. "Forgive the intrusion," he told the group, "but the Vulcan ambassador has requested a meeting with Ambassadors Bhutto and Ewu. He says it is urgent."

"When?" Ewu said, his eyes still on Kirk and Ciana.

"Now, Ambassador."

"Urgent?" Bhutto raised a dark brow. "That certainly doesn't sound like Sarek. If he says it's urgent, I suppose we'd better go." She set down her glass on a nearby buffet.

"Tell him I'll be there in just a minute, Umul." Ewu looked to have no intention of budging. "I want to ask the admirals some questions. Tell Sarek one minute."

"Ambassador," Umul began, with very undiplomatic exasperation, but a sharp glance from Ewu silenced him. "I shall return shortly," Umul amended.

Bhutto shook Kirk's hand, then Ciana's. "A pleasure meeting you, Admiral Kirk. Admiral Ciana." The sari whispered as she turned and followed the diminutive Umul.

The lift was programmed to go directly down to B5, so Uhura could not have stopped at another level if she'd wanted. The doors opened onto another checkpoint with two security guards, but apparently they had been warned of her arrival. They nodded and waved her on.

Beyond the checkpoint, the reception chamber assumed intimidating proportions. The Vulcan delegation, with characteristic punctuality, was already there; Uhura could see two Vulcan aides passing by the huge fountain in the center of the room. But where was Sarek? She had hoped to drop off Spock's gift first, before she spoke to the cap— (*No,* she corrected herself, *to the admiral. You don't know any captains anymore*) to the admiral. One, because it was awkward carrying this thing around, and two, because it would be even more awkward explaining to the . . . admiral whom the present was for. She had a feeling Kirk might not be in the mood to make light conversation about Spock these days. It had been a shock to all of them to learn he wouldn't be coming to San Francisco.

Uhura peered at the long rows of refreshments and the

people milling around. Perhaps if she used some logic . . . After all, Sarek would be in a logical place, wouldn't he? Whom would the Vulcan most be interested in talking to before the meeting? Either the Inari delegate, she decided, or no one. She spotted the Inari banner and wandered down to the table loaded with Inari delicacies. An aide gestured at what he obviously considered a sumptuous spread. Uhura smiled but shook her head. She could be a consummate diplomat when the situation called for it. In an emergency, she could even eat fermented dried hay and look like she enjoyed it—but this was not such an emergency. She would let the hay pass. Sarek was nowhere to be seen.

She headed for the Vulcan banner next. In front of the austerely set table, Sarek of Vulcan gave a curt nod to the Andorian delegate, who left looking disappointed at his inability to spark a debate.

"Ambassador?" she asked tentatively when she had ventured into Vulcan earshot. After her years on the *Enterprise,* Uhura was intimidated by virtually nothing anymore, but the sight of Sarek, hands clasped behind his back, face serene yet severe, was enough to make her hesitate . . . even if she did consider him an extremely handsome man.

He turned his head, and while his expression remained just as severe, his tone was welcoming, almost . . . friendly, as if many years of association with humans, including his wife, had finally had some effect. "Lieutenant Uhura." He paused. "Although I see you are Commander Uhura now. My congratulations on your promotion."

"Thank you, sir." Uhura straightened with dignity. She had met Sarek only once, very briefly, during a Council reception aboard the *Enterprise* years before. Even knowing of Vulcans' legendary memories, she had been unsure whether Sarek would remember her. That he did eased the last traces of awkwardness she felt. "I am deeply grateful for the opportunity to work with your son, and I would like very much to return a kindness he showed me." She held out the kissar. "I had meant to give this gift to him when he came to San Francisco. Would you see to it that he gets this?"

Sarek took the instrument from her and turned it in his hands with the reverent appreciation of a musician. "This is an extremely well-made instrument, Commander." He ran his fingers over it. "And quite delicate. I can see why you were reluctant to ship it."

Uhura beamed. It only made sense that Sarek was gifted musically, since he was the one who had taught Spock to play. "Yes."

"I will see to it that Spock gets this. I am sure he will appreciate such a fine gift."

"Thank you, Ambassador." Uhura bowed from the shoulders. For a Vulcan, Sarek had great finesse in dealing with humans. She could understand now why his government had pressured him to come out of retirement. She opened her mouth to say more, when an Inari aide appeared, tugging at the Vulcan's sleeve like a small child.

Sarek faced him gracefully, without so much as a hint that he considered the action inappropriate.

"Forgive the intrusion, Ambassador Sarek." The short, thick-bodied creature folded his arms over his chest and bowed low, apparently quite unaware of the discourtesy he had committed by touching a Vulcan. He seemed very young for his position, Uhura thought, and very nervous. "But it is quite urgent. Our ambassador has requested a meeting with you and the Earth ambassador. Please allow me to escort you there."

"Excuse me," Sarek told Uhura. He seemed completely unmoved by the Djanai's agitation. "I hope to return shortly."

"Of course," Uhura answered automatically. She did not have much more to say, but Sarek turned too quickly for her to take her leave. She watched the tiny aide lead the tall Vulcan toward the fountain, and heard Sarek say:

"There is nothing so urgent that it cannot be addressed inside the Council chamber, my friend."

Uhura followed, far enough away to be unseen, yet close enough to keep an eye on Sarek. It had occurred to her to try to find Kirk, but she did not want to be rude to Spock's father, and she knew from experience that these receptions did not last long, presumably to preclude the delegates from becoming argumentative before they were herded into the conference chamber for the vote. It would be easy enough to find the admiral after all the delegates were safely behind closed doors. Uhura sidled unobtrusively up to the Andorian table, next to the fountain, where Sarek stood with the lyre in one arm and waited for the Inari ambassador.

But the aide arrived with someone else Uhura recognized, Ambassador Bhutto of Earth, then left again, still looking frazzled. Uhura helped herself to a champagne flute of sparkling Thirellian water and watched the ambassadors from the corner of one eye.

Sarek greeted Bhutto in the Vulcan way, fingers of one hand spread to form a V. "Ambassador." Uhura concentrated so that she could just make out what he was saying over the noise of the crowd.

Bhutto returned the salute with admirable skill. "Ewu is coming, Ambassador. I'm afraid he's embroiled in a pre-conference debate with Admiral Kirk." She gestured in the direction the Inari was scurrying.

Uhura craned her neck. Admiral Kirk! Her gaze followed the back of the dark-robed little aide. Beyond him, under the Earth banner, James Kirk seemed to be enjoying a lively discussion with the Inari ambassador while Vice Admiral Ciana watched with a polite smile. Uhura was tempted to wave her hands and shout to get his attention, but for decorum's sake she contented herself with a private grin. At least she knew he was here, and she'd be able to see him after the delegates had cleared out.

"I am in no hurry," Sarek was saying. "But I was under the impression you and Ambassador Ewu were."

Bhutto's forehead creased. "Not at all. In fact, I wanted to ask you what was so urgent that it couldn't wait for the meeting."

"I was hoping you and Ewu would answer that question, Ambassador."

"Wait a minute." Bhutto's smile was slightly dazed. "I thought you were the one who called this meeting, Sarek."

Sarek shook his head. "Not I. There has been some misunderstanding. The Inari aide brought me here saying that you and Ewu were anxious to speak to me about something—"

Her pleasantly confused expression hardened to one of suspicion. She turned her head and watched the receding back of the Inari aide as he made his way back to Ewu.

"If you will excuse me, Sarek," she said in a tone that boded ill for the little aide, "I'm going to find out what's going on here." The hem of her sari danced as she strode off after the Inari. Sarek was alone.

Uhura saw her chance and took it. "Ambassador Sarek," she said as she approached him, "I forgot to ask if you would convey a message along with the kissar for me."

That was just before all hell broke loose.

* * *

"What you're suggesting," Ewu was saying with friendly vehemence, "is that we let the peace-keeping force go and hope that the attacks don't increase. Or am I misunderstanding you?"

Kirk shook his head, still smiling. In spite of Ewu's refusal to understand, there was something he liked about the hard-headed Inari. "No, I'm suggesting we remove the peace-keeping force *but* replace it with an alternative . . . such as a negotiated peace."

"Negotiated peace!" Ewu snorted, then broke off at the appearance of his breathless aide.

"Ambassador," Umul pleaded, tugging desperately at Ewu's sleeve. Kirk thought he saw anxious tears in the young Inari's eyes. "You must come. *Please*. The Vulcan is becoming impatient."

"Ambassador Sarek impatient?" Ciana sounded amused. *"That* would be a first."

"Ambassador Sarek," Kirk said aloud, then fell quiet. Of course Sarek would be here. Perhaps he should speak to him, give his regards to Spock . . .

"Oh, all *right*, Umul." Ewu brushed Umul's hands off his robe. "But you mustn't go around touching people's sleeves here. How could you forget your training so quickly?" He glanced up at Kirk and Ciana. "Please forgive his bad manners. This is his first Council meeting. I'm afraid he's overanxious." He gave Umul's shoulder a pat. "Calm down. The Vulcans won't eat you. They're vegetarians." To Kirk he said: "I would like to continue this discussion sometime, Kirk."

Kirk shot a glance at Ciana. "You'll get the chance," Ciana said. "If the peace-keeping force is withdrawn by Council vote, Admiral Kirk is the alternative. He'll be the Federation negotiator."

"Negotiator?" Ewu shook his head. "We don't need a negotiator. What we need is—"

"Ambassador!" Umul gave Ewu's arm a jerk. "There is no time—"

"I'm coming, I'm coming." Ewu crossed his arms over his chest and bowed to Ciana and Kirk. "Let us hope the peace-keeping force is not withdrawn, Admirals." He turned to follow his aide.

Kirk leaned over and whispered to Ciana, "So how did I do, Admiral?" She'd been watching him like a silent hawk all this time—to learn, Kirk wondered, or to judge?—and from her cryptic smile Kirk couldn't tell whether she approved of his remarks to the Inari.

"Not bad," she answered in a low voice so that only Kirk could hear. "Maybe now I'll let you have that cup of coffee you never finished."

He grinned, but it faded quickly when he saw the look on Bhutto's face as she marched toward them. She stopped Umul and his captive before they'd had the chance to advance more than three meters toward the fountain. "Ambassador," she said loudly, for Kirk and Ciana's benefit, "would you mind asking your aide what kind of trick he's playing on us?"

"Trick?" Ewu boomed. "Umul, what does she mean?"

"Trick?" Wide-eyed, Umul stared back at them. There was a disturbance some thirty meters behind them. Kirk looked and recognized Tomson, his former security chief aboard the *Enterprise*. She was as agitated as he'd ever seen her. She spoke to the four guards at the checkpoints in front of the conference chamber. Umul saw her too. The sight of Tomson made him panic; he grabbed Ewu's arm and began to drag him toward the fountain.

Ewu yelped and started swinging at the smaller Inari, but Umul was younger and more determined. They started moving closer to the fountain as Ewu began cursing earnestly in Inari.

Kirk and Ciana recovered from the initial surprise and rushed to Ewu's rescue, but Umul waved them back. "Get away! Get away, or I'll kill him!"

Both admirals hesitated.

"How?" Kirk demanded. He could see no weapon, and there was little chance of Umul throttling the ambassador to death before someone stopped him.

"With this." Umul held the gasping Ewu in a one-arm headlock, then fumbled with his free hand and pulled a tiny silver box from the pocket of Ewu's robe. He waved it menacingly at them.

"What is *that?*" Ciana sounded more indignant than worried. "And how the *hell* did he get that past our scanners?" But she ventured no closer.

The ruckus caught the attention of everyone in the room, including Tomson. She and her guards rushed over and took aim. Tomson knelt down on one knee barely a meter away from Umul and pointed her phaser at his head.

"Unhand him," Tomson said slowly and very calmly.

"You can't hurt me." Umul's normally bass voice had become tenor. "If you kill me, he dies too."

"I can stun you both," Tomson answered evenly. Her trigger finger twitched. Umul saw it and his eyes grew wilder.

"Just let me go," he pleaded, and jerked his head in the direction of the fountain, where Uhura, openmouthed with amazement, and Sarek stood watching. Kirk met her gaze and they stared at each other in mutual recognition, but neither dared smile.

And then something very strange happened. Uhura gasped; then she and Sarek began to shimmer . . .

. . . and then they disappeared.

Tomson grabbed her communicator with one hand, flipped it open, and shouted into the grid, "Nguyen! Trace that bea— *Dammit!*" She threw the useless communicator down in disgust, her weapon and her gaze still on Umul. "Zingje!"

A dark-skinned guard behind her snapped to attention. "Sir!"

"Get downstairs and see if Nguyen can get a trace on that transporter beam."

Umul watched the two disappear in the beam and emitted a low moan. He pressed something on the silver box, which began to hum.

"No!" Ewu bellowed, pulling himself free with a strength born of mortal terror.

"It's on overload!" Tomson yelled. "Get down!"

She had just enough time to say it before the room filled with a blinding flash.

NINE

☆

Barely an hour after the incident, Jim Kirk stood next to Ciana and watched as the chief of Security Central squirmed in the chair in front of Nogura's desk. The hot seat, Ciana had once referred to it jokingly, and Jim was beginning to understand why. Nogura's dark gaze was fixed intently on Tomson. There was nothing of the grandfather in him now; Nogura angry, Jim realized, was a terrifying sight. Not that he displayed his temper, but you could practically feel the black cloud emanating from him.

"Our signals were jammed from outside, sir," Tomson said huskily. Limp strands of yellow-white hair strayed from the normally tightly wound knot at the nape of her neck, and there was crusted blood on her forehead. She exuded a faint aroma of pineapple; when Umul's weapon overloaded, it had sent food and dishes flying onto those nearby. It had also killed the young Inari, and left Ewu, who had broken free at the last moment, with severe head wounds. His recovery was in doubt.

"Two minutes," Tomson continued mournfully. "That's all the time they needed to get the ambassadors to their prearranged coordinates." She hugged herself tightly, and Kirk saw that her ghostly pale hands trembled.

Next to him, Ciana tensed. Jim had wrenched his back pulling her down before the explosion, but she was uninjured. In fact, except for a few cuts and food stains on the back of her uniform, Ciana was entirely unshaken by the whole incident.

Except that she was a tightly wound coil of anger, and that anger at the moment was directed at Ingrit Tomson. Ciana clearly felt it unforgivable that anything should have been allowed to go wrong.

Nogura looked up at Ciana. "Go ahead." His deep voice was stern but level. The voice of God, Kirk thought. "You wanted to say something, Lori."

"I can understand how someone could jam our communications," Ciana said heatedly, "but no one has explained to me why they were able to get a transporter beam into the reception area. In the first place, how the hell did they know what level the conference was on, and second, how could they possibly get a beam past our shields?"

She and Jim were to the right and slightly behind the seated Tomson, but Tomson didn't turn her head to face Ciana. She focused her eyes glumly at a spot on Nogura's desk. "The shields weren't up yet, Admiral."

"Weren't up yet!" Ciana sounded disgusted.

"Some of the delegates hadn't arrived," Tomson explained dejectedly. "It made no sense to keep raising and lowering the shield every time someone else arrived. In five more minutes, the last of them would have been there."

"She's right," Kirk volunteered. "That would be standard procedure." He felt sorry for her; if anyone could be trusted with the safety of one hundred and twenty Council delegates, Tomson could. She had served under him for four years on the *Enterprise,* and Kirk's recommendation had gotten her this promotion. It wasn't her fault she was running up against some bad luck the first week on the job. And then he had a curious thought: *First, Riley wants to resign . . . then Tomson lets the Vulcan ambassador get taken hostage. Good Lord, if this keeps up, I'm going to stop giving out commendations.*

"Thank you, sir," Tomson said, grateful in the midst of her misery.

"That *still* doesn't explain why the kidnappers knew the coordinates." Ciana made a sweeping gesture with one hand, then let it drop and slap against her hip bone, punctuating her frustration. Unsettled, Jim looked at her. Vice Admiral Ciana was the closest thing to perfection he had ever met; he hadn't realized that she demanded it from others as well.

"There will be no displays of temper, Ciana." Nogura fastened his cold gaze on her. When Nogura started using last names, he was not happy. "I am just as upset about the situation as you are."

"Sorry, Admiral." Ciana folded her arms over her chest in unconscious imitation of Tomson and stared outside at the gray mist. Beads of moisture clung to the outer transparent wall.

Tomson closed her eyes, then opened them. For the first time since Kirk had known her, she seemed near tears. "It was an inside job, Admiral." She looked up at Nogura. "Umul could have gotten the coordinates after he arrived this morning, then contacted his people."

"Why wouldn't we have picked up an unauthorized communication?" Ciana said, less hostilely, casting a quick glance at Nogura.

"It could have been authorized, sir." Tomson twisted her long white neck and met Ciana's gaze with some of her old aggressiveness. "He could have used some sort of password or code that sounded like a normal conversation. We allow delegations to send messages as long as they use our closed channels."

Nogura nodded almost sympathetically. "I'm sure that's how it was done. We'll get Central Comm to go over today's records." He leaned forward and folded his hands on top of the desk so that they rested near the unidentifiable ceramic handiwork of his great-grandchildren. "But, Commander, if Admiral Ciana will permit me"—and here he shot her a meaningful look—"I have a question of my own. How did the Inari get that weapon inside the reception area?"

The flush started at Tomson's collar and worked its way up her cheeks. "That was entirely my fault, Admiral. It belonged to Ambassador Ewu. Prior to the reception, he came to me and asked if he could carry it on his person."

Nogura's thin white brows rushed together. "You let a delegate carry a *weapon* into a Council meeting? Commander, that is very irregular."

The color of her cheeks deepened. "I know that, sir. But the device in question was not actually a weapon. It was a personal shield, sir. Ewu was very concerned about his safety, and in spite of my attempts to reassure him, he insisted on carrying it. He was very persuasive, sir."

Kirk imagined that he was.

"But he misrepresented its capabilities to me. He assured me it could not be used as a weapon. I had no idea it could be put on overload. I took him at his word. I suppose I didn't want to offend him, sir." She bowed her head. "I made a serious mistake in judgment. I should have had our people look it over. I accept whatever disciplinary action you choose to take, Admiral."

Nogura stared at her for a full thirty seconds of awful silence. That, Kirk thought, was punishment enough for anyone. "For now," Nogura said finally, "I want you to return to duty and supervise the search for the hostages. But stop by sick bay first and get that cut cleaned up."

"Thank you, sir." Tomson stood, dwarfing them all. She nodded briefly in Kirk and Ciana's direction, but kept her eyes downcast. "Sirs." She left quickly.

Ciana's anger seemed to leave with her, but the vice admiral's expression was still troubled. "The Council has postponed the vote, sir."

"I'm not surprised." Nogura toyed with one of the desktop ceramics, finally looking as if circumstances had gotten the better of him. "After this, the outcome of the vote may very well change. The peace-keeping force might remain after all." He shook his head. "If Ewu dies . . ."

"If Ewu dies, the Djanai/Inari situation will get worse." Ciana stepped behind the hot seat and gripped the back of the chair with both hands, so tightly that her knuckles turned white. She leaned toward Nogura. "But things have already gotten out of hand if the native terrorists are attacking Inari cargo ships and the Inari ambassador—"

"There's got to be a damn good reason why, after a century of silence, the Djanai have started attacking," Jim said. From what he'd read, a group of dissident Djanai had migrated centuries earlier to the neighboring planet Inar. When Inar suffered a nuclear catastrophe that caused its axis to shift, the starving Inari came home and started developing Djana.

"Whatever the reason, they're desperate. And they've got the Vulcan ambassador and a member of Starfleet, Commander . . ." Nogura frowned. It was the first time Jim had ever seen him forget a name.

"Uhura," Jim said, feeling chilled at the sound of his own voice saying it.

"Commander Uhura," the older man repeated. "I'm sorry, Jim. I know she served under your command."

"Five years."

Nogura shook his head again. "Comm Central reports the

kidnappers have already made their terms known. They demand that the Inari be relocated.''

Ciana gasped. ''Off Djana?''

''Off Djana.'' Nogura sighed at the impossibility of it. The Inari ran the government, the industries, shipped the exports . . . Were it not for the Inari, the native Djanai would not belong to the Federation, nor would they need to. The Romulans and pirates would lose interest. ''That's why I'm going ahead and sending both of you to Djana without waiting to see the outcome of the Council vote. We've got to show the kidnappers that the Federation takes them seriously . . . if we're to save the hostages' lives.

''Your assignment is twofold: one, to negotiate for the re- lease of the hostages; and two, to bring about bona-fide negotia- tions between the Djanai and the Inari.'' Nogura paused. ''The situation there has steadily worsened over the last century, and the blame can be laid at our—Starfleet and the Federation's— door. Djana is a remote, unimportant planet with a small popula- tion, and therefore it's never had a full-time ambassador—only an 'ambassador-at-large' assigned to two other solar systems, one Miguel Andrews, who seems to have remained abysmally ignorant of the developing hostilities between the two groups. Andrews is in hiding to avoid being the target of another Djanai attack, so he will be of no use to you. However, we've got a terrorism specialist, Geoffrey Olmsted, who'll be linking up with you after you arrive on Djana. If an assault team becomes necessary, Geoff will coordinate it. He and his personnel are highly trained and first-rate. Geoff is gathering information on the Djanai terrorists and will be briefing you on them.

''But publicly, get the assistance of the Inari Council if you can, to help you get in touch with the kidnappers. The word is, their intelligence-gathering methods are on a par with ours, so use them if you can . . . though, up to now, the Council has refused to listen to the terrorists, or any of the less radical Djanai. According to Andrews, getting them to agree to listen to Djanai demands and negotiate in good faith is going to be tough, if not impossible. Andrews called the Council 'belligerent.' If they refuse to help you, if they refuse to sit down and listen to the Djanai—do what you have to. I'm giving you *carte blanche* on this one. Scare them, if you have to—because the situation is bad. Our intelligence reports that the Romulans are supplying the terrorists with weapons—and if we can't get the two groups to sit down and hammer out an agreement of some sort, we're going to lose the entire planet—the entire system—to the Empire.'' Nogura sighed again and ran a weary hand over his forehead. ''Solve *this* one, Lori, and I just might change that recommendation.''

Kirk felt a sudden burst of energy at the thought of a chance to leave his desk, to finally do what he wanted to do. He took a step forward. ''When do we leave, Admiral?''

''Tonight,'' Nogura said.

Spock was asleep when the comm signal sounded, in a deep, dreamless state but nonetheless with subconscious awareness that T'Sura was with him, even though at this moment she lay sleeping in her family home on the other side of the city. Perhaps awakened, now. *Parted from me, and never parted . . .*

There seemed to have been no time elapsed from the moment the signal woke him to the time he answered it. The sound, his coming to full consciousness, the motion of rising from bed, walking to the comm and snapping the viewscreen on, all seemed to be one fluid, instantaneous motion.

''Spock.''

Amanda was calling from Earth, where she was taking advantage of Sarek's Council meeting to visit relatives in Minnesota. But her face, her eyes, the tilt of her head, told Spock that something was terribly, urgently wrong, even if the fact she wakened him four hours before Vulcan's dawn did not. Amanda never miscalculated the time difference.

He knew immediately that something had happened to Sarek. Nothing else would bring Amanda to this degree of agitation. In the split second before she spoke again, Spock felt certain that his father had suffered another heart attack.

''There was trouble at the Council meeting. Your father has been kidnapped.'' She reached out and distractedly brushed back a gleaming silver lock from her forehead. Her long hair was down on her shoulders. On Vulcan, Spock had seen it down only when she brushed it out before bed.

''Was he harmed?''

''We don't think so.''

''Kidnapped by whom?'' The news was far too surprising for him to react emotionally.

''Starfleet thinks they're Djanai.'' She pressed her lips together tightly. It did not stop their trembling.

''I will come on the next shuttle.'' His teaching position was no concern, as it would not begin for another three weeks, but he was to take his leave of Sekar today. He would notify T'Sura and see if she was able to take care of his obligations to Sekar, to Llewellyn and McCoy.

Yet part of him knew that she, too, had been jolted from sleep. She sensed the danger to the family, even if she was unaware of the details. And somehow the knowledge brought Spock comfort.

"Why, Spock?" Amanda tried very hard to sound as if she were not on the verge of collapsing the moment the communication ended.

"I thought you might not want to be alone."

"I'm not alone. Doris is here with me. Starfleet has promised they'll tell us as soon as they know anything."

"Then I will come and offer Starfleet my assistance," he said, knowing what her response would be. Still, it would not stop him from doing it.

Her features hardened. "No. I won't have you involved with this too. At least I know you're safe where you are." Spock started to speak, but she continued. "They told me James Kirk is in charge of the rescue mission."

Spock blinked. It was the one thing she could have said that would reassure him.

"Please stay," Amanda said. "Stay on Vulcan and do whatever you were going to do. You must remember, you're a private citizen now. You would be in the way."

It did not have the comforting effect she intended it to have; nevertheless, Spock knew that it was true.

"You know what your father would say: *Kaiidth.*"

Spock nodded. What was, was. There was no point in agitating oneself over what one could not control. Based on that piece of ancient Vulcan wisdom, Sarek had hidden a serious heart condition from his wife for years, saying, when she scolded him for keeping it a secret, "There was nothing you could have done about it." And so there was very little Spock could do to expedite his father's rescue. The knowledge that Jim Kirk was involved would have to suffice. Nevertheless, he said, out of quite logical concern for the anxiety in his mother's eyes, "But I shall remain at home so that you can contact me should you need to."

"Do what you were going to do," Amanda repeated firmly. "I can find a way to get in touch with you."

Spock hesitated. "I was escorting a former shipmate of mine

to Gol . . . he indicated a desire for retreat. I had planned to spend a night there." Going to Gol meant cutting oneself off from all contact with the outside world. There were no comms, public or private, in the mountains.

"You must take him there, then. You can't refuse a guest."

She was correct according to the rules of Vulcan hospitality. However, under the circumstances, Spock felt the rules could be breached. "You would not be able to get in touch with me for two days, Mother."

"And how will that change things for Sarek?"

In the midst of his concern for his parents, it occurred to Spock that his mother had developed a talent for using logic to her advantage. He also realized that she was employing the human trait of asking a question to which she did not expect an answer. He sighed.

"Very well, then. I shall go to Gol."

Dream. Dense, warm fog. She was floating in and out of consciousness, sometimes in a white-gray place, vibrating, moving. Sometimes, nowhere, very, very dark.

Uhura stirred. It was hot and humid, and she felt sticky. The muscles in her neck and calves ached. She was half-lying someplace small and cramped, unable to stretch out her legs or rest her head. She tried to stretch, but her feet pressed against a wall. She opened her eyes and saw a gray metal bulkhead, sensed a slight hum. A ship.

She sat up, struck her head on the low ceiling, and rubbed it, cursing, as she looked around her. There was not much to see. She was in an enclosed bunk of some sort, and on her left was a hatch. She pressed what looked like the control panel. Nothing happened. The door did not open. And then she remembered the reception, and the Djanai aide, and the stunned surprise of feeling herself caught up in a transporter beam.

It made no sense at all.

"Hey!" She pounded on the hatch. "Hey! Someone let me out of here! There's been some sort of mistake!" The sudden movement left her breathless and a little dizzy. She put a hand to her temple. *Drugged. I've been drugged.*

A window appeared in the middle of the hatch, and a Djanai face stared back at her with huge whiteless eyes.

"There's been some sort of mistake," Uhura repeated. "If

you wanted a hostage, you've got the wrong one. I'm not with any delegation. I'm Starfleet. I'm not even a captain.''

The Djanai stared at her for so long she became annoyed.

"Don't you speak Standard?"

"You'll do," he said shortly, and the window disappeared.

TEN

☆

Midday was hot and intensely bright, but inside her cooler (not cool by Earth standards) dark cell, Keridwen put a hand-rolled cigarette in her mouth. Dressed in a knee-length white tunic, she sat cross-legged on the stone floor and bent forward, touching the end of the cigarette to an orange candle's flame. She puffed until the cigarette caught, then straightened. The first pull of smoke gave her a coughing fit; it always did. Unadulterated tobacco was expensive and scarce on Federation planets, and Keridwen found no glamour in smoking nicotineless cigars. She'd bartered for the hand-rolled pack on Arcturus, and smoked when the risk no longer mattered: on special occasions, or times when she was particularly upset.

This was not a special occasion.

She, Spock, and McCoy had arrived at Gol in the early morning, barely an hour after sunrise, before the desert had a chance to heat. Keridwen had insisted on taking them in the scout. It was small enough for intraplanet trips, and besides, the idea that she could leave again at any minute calmed her.

Keridwen inhaled again, and this time she did not cough. The acrid smoke stung her eyes and the back of her throat, but at the moment, the discomfort was oddly soothing.

She had lied to Spock about the card, of course. She'd known it meant Death the moment she saw it—and that it was somehow tied to the upside-down image of the Magician. It was a bloody strange knack she had, one that she had never been able to talk to anyone about. Not even the psychologists knew. When she was old enough to be told about her *psi,* she'd worried that she suffered from some type of madness.

It happened first with her grandparents, when she was twelve. She'd known three weeks before it happened, but at first she thought it was some kind of waking nightmare. She told no one; no one would have believed her, and afterward, when they really did die, what good would it have done to know? Hindsight, they would have said. Coincidence. We all experience a hundred premonitions a day, but most of them never come true. The one time one does, it's simply chance. . . . When she felt the same terror for her aunt, and then, years later, for her father, she kept it to herself. And each time, she would tell herself that she was wrong . . . until someone else died.

Sometimes she could sense good coming. Sometimes she told people, then. Most of the time, she didn't. Those she told always wanted to know more, always wanted to know the bad along with the good. After a while, she learned not to tell at all. Still, she wanted to understand what was happening to her. School gave some explanations, but no one could explain how an esper-blind person could be precognitive. Most of her professors did not believe precognitive people existed, and she did nothing to try to change their minds.

Michael had been the hardest. She'd had a crush on him less than a week when she felt compelled to read for him. It was at the very beginning, when the relationship could have gone the route of a giddy flirtation or turned into something more serious. Michael was not family, and because he was not family, the cards helped her. She did that sometimes when she could not sense alone. She laid the cards out for him—a parlor trick, she told him. He was very impressed at the accuracy with which she painted his past and present. She turned over the future, hoping to find herself there, and instead saw Death.

She told him the same thing she told Spock, and tried to believe it herself. But she hadn't just seen it. She'd *felt* it, the same cold heaviness, just as she had for her grandparents, for her aunt, for her father . . .

She had wanted very badly to take the coward's way out and tell Michael she didn't want to see him anymore. But some foolish part of herself had whispered that perhaps if she stayed with him, took care of him, watched over him, she could somehow avert the future she foresaw. . . .

And so, stupidly, she had let herself fall in love with him. And three weeks later, the cards proved right. And now, to feel the same ugly chill, to see Death grinning up at her from a stranger's cards . . .

It was all happening again, and here she was falling in love with Leonard McCoy.

Trends, her mind countered with the same explanation she'd given Spock. And it was true, according to all that she had studied about tarot and divination. *The cards reflect trends, which can be altered. Your actions can change this future.* But *which* actions? On impulse, she'd volunteered to go with them to Gol, suddenly afraid to leave them. Perhaps, on Gol, she could learn what to do to keep the cards from coming true. There was great wisdom here, and instinct told her that the solution lay with the Kolinahru.

The heavy stone door to her cell slid open a crack.

"Keridwen?"

"Damn," she whispered. She took the cigarette from her lips and clumsily knocked the ash into the candle. The flame jumped. She set the cigarette carefully on the floor, with the lit edge resting on the candleholder. "Come in, Leonard."

The door opened very slowly before McCoy stepped inside, gasping with the effort. "Those damn doors are gonna give me a hernia. Couldn't you hear me, Dwen? Skinned my knuckles knocking."

"No," Dwen answered curtly. She was not in the mood to talk to him.

"Well, if you would leave it cracked, I'd—"

"I wanted privacy."

He failed to get the point. He blinked at her. "Dwen, do you realize you're sitting in the middle of the floor staring at a candle? These navel-watchers must be getting to you." He paused and wrinkled his nose. "That candle smells awfully noxious."

Dwen sighed. She knew McCoy had come to Gol partly to get away from her. Obviously her solicitousness was beginning to grate on his nerves; he'd begun to suspect, quite correctly, that she was falling in love with him. She'd caught the expression of utter despair McCoy wore when she'd asked Spock if she could come with them to Gol. Only, things had changed now. She needed to be alone to think, and McCoy was an unwelcome distraction. She put the cigarette in her mouth and pushed herself to her feet.

"I thought *you* were the one who needed to get away," she said around the cigarette.

"Good God, what are you doing with that?"

"Smoking." She inhaled deeply and blew the smoke in his direction. She wanted to seem rude and insulting, so that he would leave in a huff, but it was very difficult not to smile warmly at him as he frantically fanned the smoke away. He was so very much fun to tease.

"Where'd you get that?" McCoy demanded. "That's *real* tobacco—with nicotine in it! Smells terrible."

"Arcturus. Wonderful, isn't it?"

"Keridwen, that's *bad* for you."

"Leonard, I smoke two or three of these a year. I doubt I'll die of lung cancer. Did you come here for a particular reason, or just to irritate me?"

"I was bored. It's too hot outside to walk, but if you go down to the base of the mountain, they've got hot springs. We can take the inside route down and then go for a swim. Besides"—he ran a hand over his perspiring forehead—"it's cooler down there."

She leaned down to flick ash into the candle. "Maybe later."

"I thought you were all excited about talking to these Kolinaroo guys. I expected to see you down there talking to them this morning."

"Kolinah*ru*, Leonard. The vowel sounds are clipped; think of Japanese."

"Kolinaroo," McCoy repeated, cheerfully mangling the pronunciation.

Dwen grimaced, but was too depressed to fight. "Whatever you call them, they're all meditating right now. I can't interview for the next hour or so."

"I see. Trying to get on their wavelength with the candle, eh? But you still wasted two whole hours this morning when you could have been talking to someone."

She was becoming honestly irritated now. She drew on the cigarette and blew smoke through her nostrils. It seemed to disconcert him a little. "You're very observant, Leonard. Now, why don't you leave me the hell alone?"

"Dwen." His face and voice became full of concern. "In all

the months I've known you, I've never seen you like this. Is it that you're really worried about something happening to Spock?"

"Spock's a stranger." She shrugged. "Why would I be concerned about him?" But inwardly she smiled. Leonard McCoy really was a very good man. She'd been concerned about his reaction to losing Natira. And once the tour ended, he seemed to be sliding down into depression again. But when he worried about someone other than himself, he was good as new. Only problem was, from the look in his eyes, the "someone other" was Keridwen herself. *This will never do. Three days ago I would have killed for him to look at me like that. To look at me at all. But now* . . .

McCoy refused to be put off by her remark. "You yourself said," he continued gently, "that anything in those cards could be changed. There's no reason for you to be upset."

"I'm not upset," she said coolly, but she didn't look at him.

"Dwen . . . Spock and I are very good friends. I don't believe in those infernal cards of yours, but the way you're acting is beginning to make me nervous."

"I'm sorry." She relented a bit. "I don't mean to scare you. What I told Spock was true: the cards merely indicate trends, and the Death card usually means loss, not literal death. If Spock doesn't want the future I read for him, all he has to do is act."

"And do what?" McCoy wanted to know.

"I don't know. Spock must figure that out for himself." She wandered toward the balcony and squinted out at the intense brightness. "Honestly, Leonard, if I knew the answer to your question, I'd tell him." She hugged herself tightly. "I'm sure Spock will be just fine. Besides, I thought you didn't believe in those 'damn silly cards.' " She glanced at him over her shoulder, then faced outside again.

"Well, if it's not Spock you're upset about, then what's bothering you? Ever since you read those cards, you've been as nervous as a chicken in a fox's den."

She kept her back to him. "It's personal. It's got nothing to do with Spock or the cards. I just want to be alone, that's all."

"If you're sure, Dwen." She could tell from his voice he was trying not to sound hurt.

"I'm sure," she lied. More than anything, she wanted to unburden herself to him, to have him reassure her that everything was all right. But it would be too cruel to him . . . and all his reassurances would be lies. Nothing was going to change what was going to happen. And still a part of her fought it, wanted to change it. This time she could not accept it. "Please. I'll see you downstairs later . . . maybe suppertime."

"All right," McCoy answered quietly. She didn't turn around to watch him go.

Dressed in the white robes of a student, Spock walked through the great stone archway into the desert outside. The community's garden sat at the mountain's base, where it could be irrigated by the underground springs and receive the morning sun and afternoon shade. The garden ran several meters long by several meters wide, and consisted of mounded rows of plants colored russet, scarlet, and white.

His return to Gol brought Spock a sense of familiarity and peace. He had made the correct decision here; he felt, for the first time in his life, a Vulcan among Vulcans. Even now, he sensed an awareness of T'Sura, a closeness, a sense of belonging, of family, that he had never experienced with T'Pring. Perhaps it was due to T'Sura's openness, or the fact that this was something T'Sura had wanted, but T'Pring had not.

There was even a measure of satisfaction now in participating in the time-honored custom of taking leave of a friend. Spock walked to the edge of the garden, where Sekar was on his knees harvesting vegetables for the evening meal. Around his waist he wore a cloth sack that hung in front like an apron. The sleeves of his robe were rolled above his elbows, and the muscles of his thick forearms rippled as he dropped the vegetables gently inside the sack. The scene was an ancient one: for fifty thousand seasons, postulants had harvested food in the same manner, in the same hostile stretch of sand.

"Sekar," Spock said.

Sekar stopped and peered up at Spock; his concentration on his task had been such that he had not noticed his visitor earlier. "Spock." He rose.

"I have come to take my leave."

It was the first step in the ritual. It obliged Sekar to give the traditional answer and step forward from the garden. The briefest surrender of mental shields, a simple mind-touch, a shared memory, and any mutual obligation the two ever had to each other would be fulfilled. The encounter would not take long. Spock had prepared himself carefully; Sekar's role, as postulant, was to have spent the last several weeks preparing for all those who would come this day to take their leave of him. Sekar stood for a moment of uncertainty in the garden. Spock waited.

Sekar did not move. "I am required to finish several tasks for the community today. I regret that I do not have the time to meet with you now. However, this evening I will take my leave of you."

Spock would not have been more shocked had Sekar laughed aloud at him or slapped his face. For Sekar to refuse to complete the ritual at the moment of asking was contrary to custom and the rules of courtesy. It ran counter to all Spock had been taught. For one fleeting second Spock asked himself if he had totally misinterpreted the relationship between himself and Sekar, or if he, Spock, had somehow overstepped his rights in asking Sekar's leave.

Spock decided that he had not. This left him with no possible explanation for Sekar's rudeness, except madness (which did not seem to fit the circumstances) or the chance that Sekar feared lowering his mental shields. The latter explanation seemed to him most likely, but even should Sekar crave privacy, it did not excuse him from taking leave of a friend.

"At what time this evening?" Spock asked him finally. There seemed no other logical reaction to Sekar's request for postponement.

"Two hours after sunset." Sekar's face was placid and composed, the face of a Kolinahru, as if he were totally unaware that he had just behaved in a most un-Vulcan and unseemly manner toward an old friend.

"Very well," Spock answered. Sekar went back to his gardening and did not look up again.

"Dammit!" McCoy sat tangled in a bedsheet and rubbed his right elbow, which had just made contact with the uncompromising stone floor. The narrow ledge that doubled as his table and bed was sheer torment. Besides being unpadded stone and dadblamed hard, it was too narrow for him to stretch out on comfortably. The Vulcans had provided him with a thin sheet—as a tongue-in-cheek joke, McCoy decided, and one in bad taste, at that. His upper-level room was warm during the day, but not unbearably so, and McCoy had assumed that since the desert cooled off at night, the room would too. That was before he learned just how efficient the black rock was at holding the heat. The cooler it got outside, the warmer it got in McCoy's room.

The dry heat evaporated his sweat but left him parched. He'd already drained the pitcher of warm, sulfurous water the Vulcans had left him and stripped down to his skivvies (he had nothing against sleeping in the nude, but he wasn't about to do it with the open-door policy they had around this place). He'd folded the sheet on the stone ledge in a pitiful attempt to cushion it. And then he'd noticed the light coming from the open balcony . . . straight into his eyes. He got up to close it and discovered two things: one, that there was no way to close the balcony off, and two, that on a clear desert night the starlight shone almost as brightly as a moon.

Grumbling, he had stalked back to bed, thrown himself down on it (much to his immediate regret), and tried like hell to fall asleep. He'd almost gotten there, too, when he'd forgotten where he was, rolled over just a little too fast, and . . .

Pain. He gingerly examined the offended elbow. It was going to be a very nasty bruise.

McCoy got up slowly and untangled himself from the sheet, then spread it out on the floor. The floor had to be at least as comfortable as that damnable ledge. Why hadn't he thought of this in the first place? He doubled the sheet over, then smoothed it out and lay down on it, trying to pretend the light didn't bother him. Some retreat *this* was turning out to be. If he could just make it through the night, he'd get Dwen to take him back in the morning. In the tourist quarter, you could at least get a glass of whiskey on nights when you couldn't sleep. Even a Glenfiddich would have tasted good now. Here, all you could get was vegetable stew made from something that looked like purple brussels sprouts and tasted worse. McCoy's stomach rumbled at the thought.

And it was too damn early to be trying to sleep. He was doing it out of sheer boredom. Yeah, he had wanted to get away, but he wanted to go someplace where he could *do* something. Take a walk, at least, and look at the pretty scenery. Play a round of golf—he *was* a doctor, after all. A golf course on the Sash-i-shar Desert, McCoy thought. The Hell Country Club, where golfers who lied about their golf scores go. The thought almost made him smile in the middle of his meanness.

He'd counted on Dwen to keep him company, at least, but she was wedged in her cell tighter than a terrified tortoise. He'd been so desperate for entertainment that he'd actually gone looking for Spock, but Spock was off somewhere being Vulcan.

Hadn't even thought to bring tapes with him . . . of course, they didn't have the wherewithal here for that. He should have brought a book with him, an old-fashioned paper book.

He rolled over onto his side and tucked his hands under his head, since he had no pillow. The ShanaiKahr Hilton it wasn't. It reminded him of the monastery back on Earth. He'd gone there on a retreat after his first wife, Jocelyn, had left him. Only *that* monastery had had real cots, with real pillows and real blankets, and the weather had been cold. He'd complained then, but it seemed luxurious now compared to this warm stone floor. It seemed to be generating more heat by the minute. McCoy groaned and rolled over, so the one side could cool off while the other heated.

Maybe the restlessness was a good sign. Maybe it meant he was over Natira. But no, he still felt a stab at the thought of her name. Still, he hadn't been that restless at the monastery. He'd still been so bitterly heartbroken over Jocelyn that boredom was out of the question. He sat in his cell all day until the monks came to remind him to eat. Such was not the case here (although remembering the purple brussels sprouts, he wished it had been).

He sighed. The source of his unrest was Dwen, of course. And this damn thing with Spock, although the business with the cards didn't seem to bother the Vulcan at all. He hadn't even mentioned it again. But ever since that night, something seemed to be eating at Dwen. She wasn't the same . . . and he realized with surprise that it wasn't really the fact that she seemed shaken up over Spock's tarot reading. McCoy devoutly refused to believe in any of that nonsense, and if Dwen wanted to be a sucker and frighten herself, that was her business. No, he refused to be afraid of Spock dying just on sheer principle. It was the fact that he really missed Dwen's company. It was one thing for him to be tired of having her around, and want to be alone . . . but it was quite another thing altogether for her not to be there when McCoy wanted her to be. He definitely did not care for the feeling.

Just the same way you treated Natira, you selfish bastard. Expected her to twiddle her thumbs while you were off doing what suited you. Well, you're not going to treat Keridwen that way. He sat up, surprised and disgusted with himself. *Good Lord, man, aren't you ever going to learn? Just getting over one woman, and here you are worrying about another.*

A bead of sweat trickled down his forehead, sidestepped a brow, and stung his eye. That did it. McCoy jumped up and put on his clothes: faded khaki pants and a blue flannel shirt. He'd gotten them to go camping on the Steinhatchee back when he and Jocelyn were first married. He wore them every chance he got, too, and they were nice and broken-in, the kind of clothes that brought a body comfort, like old friends. The flannel shirt would be just right for outside, since the desert was cooling off. Maybe he'd take a nice stroll out in the chilly air. He pulled on his boots and slipped through the doorway. He tiptoed down the hall, mindful of all the Vulcan ears behind the other half-open doors.

He paused at Keridwen's door, which was open just a crack. Inside, yellow-orange candlelight flickered. "Dwen?" he whispered. "You still awake?"

No response. With a grunt, McCoy pushed against the door's formidable stone mass until it stood half-ajar. "Dwen?"

She was sitting inside, just as he had found her earlier, staring into the flame of the now-melted-down candle. She seemed to be in a trance; her face was slack, aglow with orange light, her eyelids almost closed.

He spoke louder this time. "Dwen . . ."

She came to with a jerk; her lids opened as she put a hand to her heart. Her eyes seemed wild.

He hung back awkwardly, one hand still on the door. "Gee, I'm sorry if I startled you. I was just thinking about going to cool off in the scout, and wondered if you felt like joining me."

"No," she answered abruptly, staring at him with her hand still over her heart. In the dim wavering light, with that long, disheveled dark hair, she looked like an ancient Amerind shaman in the throes of a vision from the spirit world.

Feeling wistful, he said, "I really wish you would." When she said nothing, just sat looking at him with that oddly disturbing expression, McCoy added, "Well, if it's locked, I'll need the override combination. That is, if it's all right with you."

"It's all right. And it's unlocked. This is . . . this is V—" She faltered, and he realized that her eyes were filling up with tears. She was staring at him with a mixture of honest affection and sorrow.

Her expression touched and alarmed him deeply. "Dwen," he said softly, and moved toward her. He sat next to her on the warm stone floor and put a gentle hand on her shoulder, all without knowing he had done so. "Dwen, dear, are you really that upset about this thing with Spock?"

". . . V-Vulcan after all," she finished, then turned her face away from him, toward the darkness, and whispered harshly,

"Dammit. Dammit, Leonard, why couldn't you just leave me alone?"

"Be*cause.*" He took her by both arms and very gently turned her to face him again. "Because you've been a good friend to me, Keridwen, and you helped me through a very rough time. And I want to help you now, if I can."

Her voice was anguished. "There's nothing you or I can do, Leonard. There's nothing anyone can do."

"Nonsense," he countered firmly, still holding her arms. "You said so yourself, Dwen—the cards only show trends. The future can be changed."

She shook her head, her expression miserable. "It's more than just the cards, Leonard. The cards only reaffirmed what I felt. You see, I . . . I *know.* You'll think I'm crazy, but it's a weird talent I have. I just *know.*"

It was the way she said it—quietly, but with utter conviction—that made McCoy catch his breath and ask, "You know when people are going to die?"

She nodded and hung her head; the black hair hung forward, veiling her face. Staring down at the candle, she said, "It's happened to me before—dozens of times—and it's never been wrong. I don't know how to explain it; it's just a cold gray feeling that descends on me. It was there, at the ShanaiKahr Hotel, at the table . . ."

McCoy was scarcely able to believe what he was hearing; as stunned and disbelieving as he was, somehow he managed to say, "Even if it's all true, Keridwen . . . well, this sounds rather callous, but . . . you hardly know Spock. Even if you're worried about my reaction because he's my friend, it hardly explains the way you've been acting."

She emitted a long, shaky sigh and looked up at him. "This time, it was very strange. It seemed for a moment to hover over us all—even me—and then it moved around the table. It skipped over the fiancée, touched me, then settled over the two of you."

"The *two* of us?" McCoy stared at her, not sure he wanted to comprehend what she was saying. "You mean Spock and . . . *me?*"

"Yes," Dwen said softly, looking at him—or so it seemed to McCoy—as if he were already dead. "Spock. And you."

McCoy looked away, thunderstruck. For one brief instant he allowed himself to believe, and felt a thrill of honest fear. And then common sense kicked in. He rose angrily to his feet, disgusted that he had very nearly allowed himself to be frightened out of his wits by a lot of mumbo-jumbo. "Enough, Dwen. This is ridiculous!"

She was close to panic. "Please don't go out into the desert tonight, Leonard! Stay here, where it's safe. Gol is safe, I can feel it—"

"Listen to you, Dwen; you're babbling! For God's sake, I had no intention of going into the desert at night anyway . . . I'd have to be missing a lot more brain tissue to want to do that! I was just going to the scout; it isn't that far away."

She struggled to her feet; he reached down to help her up, and left his hands on her shoulders. "Dwen . . ." His tone became soothing. "How many times have you correctly predicted someone's death?"

"Six times that I know of," she said, becoming calmer at the fact that he wasn't leaving. "Though I've felt it for dozens of strangers—people just passing by—with no way of checking on what happened to them."

"Only six?"

"Yes, six. Isn't that enough? My grandparents, my mother and father, an aunt, and . . . a friend."

"And all of them died?"

"Yes. Three became ill; one committed suicide; two died in freak accidents."

McCoy shrugged. "But we all have premonitions, Dwen. Grandparents get old and sick, and we begin to see death coming for them . . . and each time we see a loved one off, we wonder if it's going to be for the last time. Everyone has thousands of premonitions—what if something goes wrong, what if the shuttle crashes?—but it's only the ones that come true that we remember."

She shook her head resolutely. "No. It's more than that. . . . It's impossible to explain. And there was no way anyone could have guessed about those six deaths."

"Dwen. I realize you're upset and worried about me, and . . . well, frankly, I'm flattered. But I'm not going to die anytime soon, and that's a promise. I refuse, in spite of any premonitions you or anyone else might have. And Spock . . . well, I've seen Spock in a lot of tight situations, and he's always been able to take care of himself."

Her face was taut with worry; in a gesture of concern that

touched McCoy, she reached a hand to his cheek. "Oh, gods, how I wish I could believe that."

"Believe it," McCoy said adamantly, and patted her hand. She smiled sadly and withdrew it. "After all, you said it was different this time—it's different because this time it isn't going to happen."

"But please, promise me you won't go out into the desert—"

"I'm *going* to the scout, and that's that." He felt a minor flare of irritation at the thought of returning to his hot, uncomfortable little cell . . . and Dwen's was no cooler. Perspiration was beading on his forehead; he wiped it away with the back of his hand. "I'm not going to stay in this infernal heat. Maybe what you foresaw was my being roasted to death on a bed of hot stones."

She didn't smile. "Then please, be very careful, Leonard."

"I always am," he said lightly, and touched her cheek.

Back outside in the corridor, McCoy forced himself to forget about Dwen's dire prediction. Death, indeed! The only dangers here at Gol were heat and boredom—though both, McCoy reflected with grim humor, were rapidly escalating to lethal levels. He had never been a superstitious man; in fact, he had always done his best to prove superstitions wrong, and now was no exception. Other than his real concern for Dwen, McCoy crept down the hallway with a light heart: relief from the heat was not far away.

The corridor ended with a flight of stairs. Running down the stairs got to him. He was eight flights up, and by the time he made it to the bottom floor, he was gasping.

It hadn't even been dark two hours; to McCoy it felt like eight-thirty in the evening. But the main hall, with its austere furniture designed to discourage idle sitting, was eerily deserted, lit only by an old-style Vulcan oil lamp. *Peace and quiet. You wanted it, now you've got it in spades.* McCoy's steps echoed in the silent gloom. There were three different passageways leading from the main chamber, but the doctor was hard-pressed to decide which one led to the outside. They could have at least put up an exit sign. Navigation was definitely not one of his talents; McCoy could get lost faster and more efficiently than anyone else he knew. Even though he had entered the retreat just this morning through one of these portals, tonight they all looked the same to him.

He chose the one to his right and started down it. Oddly, the corridor began to feel claustrophobic. There were no cell doors, and it became darker and narrower as McCoy progressed. Definitely the wrong way; he was about to turn back when he fancied he heard someone. Maybe that someone could tell him the way to the outside. He kept walking, the dark fading with each step, until the corridor dead-ended. McCoy found himself confronted by a white-robed Kolinahru standing before a door that stretched to the ceiling and was as wide as the two of them put end to end.

McCoy was startled. The Vulcan clearly was not.

"Guests are not permitted in this area." The Vulcan's tone was neutral, entirely without inflection. He gazed serenely at McCoy, and though he was unarmed, it was clear he guarded the doorway.

"Bluebeard's Castle," McCoy said under his breath; then, louder, in response to the guard's curious look: "Never mind, just talking to myself. Humans do that from time to time. I'd appreciate it if you could tell me how to get outside."

"The desert is perilous at night." The guard's hair was streaked with gray. Middle-aged, McCoy guessed, but his eyes seemed far more ancient.

"I know that. Just tell me how to get there. Theoretically."

"Go back down the corridor. When you arrive at the main hall, take the second passageway on your right."

"Thanks." McCoy started to turn away, but couldn't resist. "Say, what are y'all hiding in there? A few skeletons?"

The guard looked at him.

"Just kidding." McCoy gave him a little wave and walked very quickly back down the hall. Something about that guard and the room gave him the willies. Just what the hell would Vulcans be hiding in there, anyway?

He found the second passageway to the right, and in less than a minute he was standing outside, reveling in the chilly, though thin, air. It was refreshing, but he felt suddenly drained. He'd been taking tri-ox since coming to Vulcan, to compensate for the lower-oxygen atmosphere. It helped with the heavier gravity too, but the stairs must have done him in. He'd have to take some when he got back to the room . . . if he could ever bring himself to go back to the little cell with its hard stone floor.

Keridwen's scout was parked with the other visitors' vehicles less than a kilometer away, hidden behind a cleft of rock. The Kolinahru were very fussy about anyone marring their view, and so everyone had to trek through the desert on foot. McCoy rubbed his hands, thinking of how he would set the environment control to Earth normal conditions and sleep in perfect comfort.

Buoyed by the idea, McCoy started on his way. The rock formation was visible for miles, so there was no chance of getting lost. He could just make it out, thanks to the brilliant starlight.

The desert was beautiful and terrifying at night, and McCoy walked as fast as he could without gasping. He was mindful of Vulcan's nocturnal predators.

He made it to the scout without incident and stepped inside. The air inside was hot and stale, but he switched on the controls, and in no time the environment of the cabin reached temperate Earth normal conditions. McCoy felt lighter in the lessened gravity, and he filled his lungs with oxygen-rich air. Now all that remained was the matter of food and drink.

Keridwen had a small servitor, not much of a selection to speak of, but it was stocked, and McCoy chose a roast-beef sandwich and a gin and tonic, since it was the only liquor available on the program. Gin and tonic it was, then. The tumbler that appeared was ice-cold, sweating, and admirably tall. McCoy settled back into a thickly cushioned seat, sipped his drink, and gave a blissful sigh. He'd sleep here, then make his way back to the retreat while it was early. Tomorrow they'd leave, and every-thing would be much better.

In his enthusiasm, he drank up the gin and tonic a little too quickly, and finished off two more before he felt relaxed enough to crawl into the partitioned-off bunk in the back of the vessel and fall into a deep, contented sleep.

Sekar stood motionless in the dark passageway and was afraid. While he believed with his heart and mind that there was no shame in feeling so, only in acting so, his years of exposure to Vulcan training and philosophy made the acceptance of emotion difficult. Some time ago he had realized that he would never be free of the bonds of his heritage; even when he left Gol, the burden of nonemotion would go with him. Even if he succeeded in freeing others from Surak's influence, he himself would never be completely free. He had been too long among the Kolinahru, had absorbed too many of their precepts into his very bones. Now that the time for freedom had come, he had to search very deep within himself to find that other Sekar, Sekar the Free, Sekar the Declared.

He had been so long among them that he had come very close to forgetting his original purpose. Only the fear of facing the High Master herself tomorrow startled him from his complacency. Master T'Sai would touch his mind tomorrow, and she would not accept the margin of privacy that other mind-links allowed. There would be no hiding the true Sekar from her. He had no choice but to fulfill his mission tonight.

Even so, he had struggled with it, put it off. His treatment of Spock had been dangerously abnormal and served only to arouse suspicion and jeopardize his success. The fact that Spock was awaiting him at this moment forced him to act. In the garden he had wanted to tell Spock everything, had wanted his childhood friend to understand what he had to do. As a child, Sekar had learned to hate the rigorous Vulcan code of nonemotion, and as he grew older, he searched for a way to release his people from its cruelty. It did not take him long to find those who agreed, and who were willing to use him to that end. *For you, Spock, especially, I do this. How our people have made you suffer! How we have all suffered for the sake of one man's philosophy. . . .* But to speak would have endangered the very freedom Sekar sought.

He breathed deeply to calm himself, then continued his way down the passage until he stood before the entrance to the Hall of Ancient Thought and Storil, this night's Watcher. The office of Watcher dated from a less scrupulous era, when the katras of High Masters needed protection from those who craved power. A Watcher still guarded the entrance to the Hall at all times, though now the position was an honorary one.

"Live long and prosper, Brother Watcher." Sekar formed the Vulcan salute with his right hand.

Storil returned the gesture. "Live long and prosper, Sekar. What do you seek?"

"I wish to take my leave of you." It was an odd request, as Storil was not friend or family, and already a full-fledged adept, having passed through the rites of Kolinahr himself. Yet Sekar was within his rights; it indicated that he considered himself to have formed an emotional attachment to the older Vulcan, one that he wished to sever now. Sekar could probably mind-touch with only a small risk of being discovered, but, as with Spock, it was a risk he was unwilling to take.

If Sekar's request surprised the older Vulcan, Storil did not show it. He spread his hands in a gesture of invitation. "I am prepared, Sekar. Take your leave."

Storil stepped forward and, closing his eyes, placed his fingers on Sekar's temples. Sekar moved as if to reciprocate, but his left hand fastened quickly on the vulnerable spot between Storil's neck and shoulder. The older Vulcan dropped unconscious to the floor.

Sekar hesitated. It would facilitate his escape to kill Storil, or at least wound him severely enough to prevent his return to consciousness for the next several hours, before the next Watcher arrived to take his place. He could break the older man's neck quickly, painlessly . . .

But his training held him back. Sekar stepped over Storil's unconscious form and pushed with all his strength on the great stone door of the Hall. It slowly rumbled open. Only rarely was the Hall entered, by those who wished to save the wisdom of the dying or consult that of the dead. But Sekar was interested in helping the living. He went inside.

The vast dark chamber was softly lit, not by lamps, but by the luminous white glow surrounding the vrekatras, the shells that encased minds from a once-living host. Sekar trembled with awe. Before him on stands of black trihr wood shone hundreds of vrekatras, the wealth of Vulcan's knowledge, both secular and mystical. On each stand a name was carved in Vulcan script. The vrekatra Sekar sought was very old, having gathered dust some fifteen thousand seasons since it was brought to Gol by the retreat's founder, Sotek. A controversy had arisen among the Kolinahru even then: many protested the placement of this katra in the Hall of Ancient Thought; many felt this katra did not merit such an honor. But Sotek stood firm, and the deed was done. And over the centuries, no Kolinahr adept dared to disturb the contents of this particular vrekatra . . . until now.

In the darkest recess of the Hall, Sekar discovered the vrekatra half-hidden by shadows, a testament to the Kolinahru's eagerness to deny its existence. Beneath the shimmering orb, the legend read

He knelt before it and wondered if the great mind within were still intact after millennia of neglect. He had heard tales of katras that mysteriously perished inside their orbs, and he remembered his fear: How terrible, indeed, to come this far, risk this much, all for nothing!

Gently he approached the field in the traditional manner, using both hands to reach for the globe as he would for another's temples in the act of mind-meld. The field dimmed in response, permitting his fingers contact with the hard shell of the vrekatra.

"Master Zakal," he whispered. Joyfully, he sensed an intelligence stirring, as if awakening from a long slumber.

Master Zakal, I have come from the Declared. We ask your aid in the struggle against the followers of Surak. Will you freely consent to join us?

YES!

The force of Zakal's entry hurled Sekar backward onto the floor. Sekar felt in the midst of a great sandstorm that raged so mightily against him that he cried out in anguish. The power of Zakal's hatred overwhelmed him. He struggled to retain his own identity; Zakal devoured his mind, his body, and only his Kolinahr training kept Sekar from sheer oblivion.

Master, his mind screamed. The effort required to think that one word was enormous.

His struggle eased. Zakal was silent, listening.

I have a plan of escape. We shall go to the Declared. But you must let me up. I need control of my body. The Watcher will awake soon, and the others will discover us . . .

Sekar was lifted to his feet, as if by a great invisible hand.

Thank you, Master. He used the archaic expression that had died out shortly after Zakal's time. Tentatively he took a step and found that control had indeed been returned to him. But the crushing weight of Zakal's mind was still with him. Sekar ran lightly through the great Hall, past the open portal. He would have continued past the supine form of the Watcher, but Zakal jerked Sekar's body to a halt. Sekar understood instantly.

Master, no. It is not necessary—

IT IS NECESSARY.

Sekar balked. He watched as his own hands suddenly reached out toward Storil and rolled the unconscious Vulcan over, felt the audible *crunch* as the Watcher's neck snapped under the pressure Sekar's hands applied to it. Sekar's face twitched. His mind recoiled in shame from what had been done.

IT WAS NECESSARY, Zakal told him. DO YOU TRULY WISH TO
FREE VULCAN?

Sekar did not answer. *Let us go quickly, Master. I know of a
place in the desert where we can obtain a vehicle.*

GO.

Empowered by Zakal's will, Sekar felt as if he flew through
the desert. No time seemed to elapse between the time Sekar
knelt over Storil's dead body and the time he stood behind the
rock formation in the desert, trying to choose the best vehicle for
their escape.

THIS ONE. Zakal nudged him in the direction of the largest
craft. WE HAVE A LONG WAY TO GO.

Sekar entered the craft and found, to his delight, that it
possessed warp drive and a small transporter. He had not expected such good fortune; he had expected to have to change
vessels at least once. Oddly enough, the environmental controls
were on and set to Terran comfort levels. Sekar quickly lowered
the oxygen content of the air and warmed it, then began preparing
the craft for takeoff.

Inside his head, Zakal laughed.

Master?

YOUR NAME IS SEKAR.

?

AMAZING. AFTER ALL THIS TIME, THEY STILL HAVEN'T RUN
OUT OF NAMES.

ELEVEN

☆

In the gloomy low-ceilinged hallway just outside the Inari Council Chamber, Ciana spoke softly into Kirk's ear. "I guess this is my big chance to see the famed Kirk instinct in action."

She was half-smiling, but it was a brittle smile, and Kirk heard the slight edge of bitterness in her tone, though she clearly did her best to hide it. He knew that Lori was used to being the expert, the one who showed others how it was done; now she was having to sit back and learn from someone else—who, all the more annoyingly, happened to be a grade lower in rank. Not that she had protested in the least; the Djanai/Inari society was strictly patriarchal, and Ciana herself had the good sense to suggest that, since Kirk was the male, he would be better received and should therefore do most of the talking.

"Let's see how rusty it is after six months' leave," he said, for her sake trying not to appear overconfident. He drew in a deep breath. He wasn't nervous, but he felt excited, on edge, exhilarated . . . and despite her apparent cool poise, he knew that Ciana did too. Her eyes were a little brighter, a little wider than normal, her speech a little faster, more clipped. After all, this was her big chance too. What had Nogura said?

Solve this one, Ciana, and I just might change that recommendation.

Kirk squared his shoulders and shot Ciana a glance. "Well, wish me luck, sir."

"Break a leg, Jim," she said, and smiled in earnest; and then: "Watch your head!"

He ducked just in time to avoid hitting his head on the low archway, and recovered well enough so that no one noticed—he hoped.

Since arriving on Djana, Kirk had been impressed with the advanced native technology—and the total lack of interest in art and design. The Inari Council Chamber was reminiscent of every other example of Djanai architecture Kirk had seen: small, circular, dimly lit, with a claustrophobically low ceiling that came within inches of Kirk's head. There were no paintings, no colors anywhere save drab, dark earth tones. The furniture was nonexistent except for a low, crudely constructed table of dark wood that sat at the far end of the room. Its function, apparently, was to hold refreshments for the Council members.

The members themselves sat in a semicircle on the thickly padded floor, their orange-colored robes fanned out around them. Although no computer terminal was built into the room, each member carried with him what Kirk at first mistook for a notepad—but which no doubt accessed a central government computer.

As Kirk and Ciana entered, one of the Inari, his arms crossed over his chest, rose and bowed low. "Vice Admiral Ciana, Admiral Kirk. I am Ruwe, spokesman for the Council." He gestured to the open end of the circle. "Please, sit with us."

Kirk and Ciana returned the well-rehearsed gesture, then lowered themselves to the floor. Ruwe picked up a flask from the floor, and, holding it in both hands, proffered it to Ciana. "A gift to the representatives of the Federation."

"Thank you, U Ruwe." Ciana carefully used the honorific. "As the Federation's representatives, we are impressed by your graciousness." She held the flask so that Kirk could admire it; he smiled and nodded. Though he had spent the time on the shuttle reviewing Djanai/Inari custom and language, he was unable to read the hieroglyphs on the bottle; nevertheless, he had no doubt as to what the flask contained.

"Our finest grain alcohol," Ruwe remarked proudly.

"I would like to mention that our staff will very soon be transporting down a gift which we hope will please the Council," Ciana responded, and as a gratified reaction stirred through the room, Kirk smiled again. The Federation "gift" was a bushel of

Washington apples; a fair trade, considering what proof the bottle of alcohol probably was.

"We look forward to that," Ruwe said with evident relish. He returned to his place among the others, but remained standing. "The members of the Council: U Loru, U Wera"—he pointed to each one in turn—"U Mol, U Ona, U Kalon, U Erun." Ruwe took his seat as the others nodded politely at Ciana and Kirk. At Ruwe's gesture, Kirk and Ciana also sat on the floor, which was surprisingly comfortable.

"With the Council's permission," Kirk began, well aware that the six members of the Council were intently studying him, "we would like to proceed to the business at hand."

"By all means." Ruwe nodded. "We are interested in hearing your strategy for recovering the hostages. Since you brought no troops with you, we assume you will be taking advantage of the peace-keeping force."

And here we go, Kirk thought. He kept his eyes fastened on Ruwe, but on the periphery of his vision he could see Ciana give him a look; clearly she was having the same thought: the Council was not going to go out of its way to make things easy. Kirk shook his head. "No, the peace-keeping force will be unnecessary, U Ruwe. If military action is needed to rescue the hostages, we have a small group of our own trained personnel. But we're not here to fight with the Djanai—"

"We're Djanai, too," one Council member snapped, but Ruwe shot him a threatening look.

Kirk continued. "We're not here to fight with anyone. We're here to get our hostages back, and we want to use the safest methods to ensure their return."

"Which are?" Ruwe asked, not quite pleasantly.

"First, we need to talk to you—to get as much information as possible about the terrorists, about the entire situation, before attempting to contact the kidnappers—"

"*Con*tact them?" Ruwe tilted his head; he seemed to have trouble understanding.

"To negotiate."

The room became uncomfortably still. Kirk looked around at the shocked, disapproving faces of the Council members. He gave Ciana a glance that said, *I think that was the wrong thing to say.*

I know it was, Ciana's expression said.

"The Federation must *not* negotiate with them." Ruwe's

voice turned cold, and his heavy brow furrowed. "They are murderers and terrorists. If they learn you are willing to listen to their demands, it will only spur them to more violence."

A ripple of assent traveled through the group.

"U Ruwe," Kirk began, "we've heard only one side of this—"

"You have sympathy for kidnappers? For those who almost killed our ambassador?" His voice was strident.

"No." Kirk kept his tone calm. "But if we can do anything to keep anyone else from getting hurt, we will." He paused. "With all respect to the Council, there must be some reason the acts of violence have increased in recent years."

"I can tell you why. They—a handful of dissident natives— want us off-planet, Admiral. We constitute a third of the population, and are solely responsible for any civilization here, but they do not appreciate what we have done for the planet. And Djana belongs to us as much as it does to them. Our ancestors were born here. We call ourselves Inari, but we have as much right to the name Djanai. We have taken a planet that lay fallow and we have turned it into an agricultural paradise. Would the Federation rip us from our homeland and send us to some barren rock to silence a small group of protesters?"

Seeking encouragement, Kirk looked over at Ciana, but her expression was opaque. "No, U Ruwe. We would not agree to that. But refusing to acknowledge the kidnappers' demands will encourage violence. Talking to them doesn't mean we're going to give in to any of their demands."

Ruwe's broad shoulders rose in what Kirk took as a gesture of adamance. "If you do not agree to ship us off-planet, then the kidnappers will refuse to deal with you at all. You will quickly find yourselves at an impasse." Kirk tried to speak, but Ruwe's voice rose. "Just as we have, Admiral. Or did you think that we had not tried?"

Ciana suddenly broke her silence. "U Ruwe, we respect the fact that you have tried, but—"

Ruwe ranted on without giving her so much as a glance. Ciana's mouth stayed open for an instant, then thinned into a grim line as her left brow rose and stayed there.

"There is no dealing with them!" The Council head was on his feet now. "We have tried talking to them, but they are not interested in negotiating! The help we need is military, not diplomatic. We were quite clear in our request. Neither Starfleet nor the Federation has the right to dictate how we are to solve our internal problems. If Starfleet is unwilling to give us the type of help we asked for, then I am sorry, but you have come a very long way for nothing."

"The fact," Ciana told him coldly, "that a Federation diplomat and a Starfleet officer have been kidnapped makes it our business. This has escalated into much more than just a local problem." Her eyes were narrowed with anger; on a sudden hunch, Jim tried to catch her eye, and surreptitiously patted his midsection to mean *gut instinct*. If Ciana saw and understood, she didn't let on.

Kirk rose abruptly to his feet, an act which drew murmurs of surprise from the seated Council.

"U Ruwe," he said with perfect composure born of inspiration, "I'm sorry if there has been a misunderstanding. If the Council wishes, we will leave immediately." He turned to Ciana and gestured toward the door. *Trust me, Admiral.*

She stared hard at him for a second, then seemed to decide to play along. She rose and slowly started for the door. Kirk followed. Halfway out, he turned and addressed the silent Council over his shoulder.

"Of course," he said, "this means that we will notify all Federation vessels, including Starfleet and the Border Patrol, to avoid Inari space." *Carte blanche,* Nogura had said, and Jim hoped like hell he meant it, because this was an outright threat: *Refuse to cooperate, and we will leave your trading vessels open to attack.*

"You can't do that!" Ruwe boomed. Other Council members were struggling to their feet and voicing protest as well. "The Federation has guaranteed us protection! We have rights—"

Ciana turned and gave Ruwe a look that made him cringe. "By law, we cannot withdraw the peace-keeping force on your planet. But there is no Federation law that says Starfleet *must* protect your trading vessels—"

"Untrue!" Ruwe bleated, but his expression was sickly; Ciana had him dead to rights, and he obviously knew it.

"No. Such protection is a *courtesy,*" Ciana snapped. "And courtesy needs to extend both ways, doesn't it, U Ruwe?" She turned and walked toward the open archway without looking back to see if Kirk was following.

They were almost outside by the time Ruwe leapt forward and cried, "Wait! Let us discuss this further."

For the split second before they both turned to face the Council, Jim caught a glimpse of the fleeting grin on Lori Ciana's face, and knew it matched that on his own.

The Council, naturally, agreed to cooperate—or, at the very least, to provide them with background information on the suspected kidnappers, a secured suite from which to base their operations, and any technical help needed to free the hostages. Through the entire discussion with Ruwe and the Council, Ciana wore a scowl; the anger etched on her features was so convincing that even Jim began to think she was honestly furious with the Inari. For his part, Jim did his best to appear as irate as the vice admiral.

After they succeeded in getting the necessary reassurances from Ruwe, Kirk and Ciana took their leave of the Council with grim courtesy—Ciana all the while clutching the gift of liquor—after which they returned to the wing (now well-protected by every conceivable security device) where the Inari housed visiting dignitaries. They walked through the corridors in silence until Ciana stopped in front of their suite. After a retinal scan identified them as current occupants, the door slid open. Ciana motioned Kirk inside with a curt gesture.

He stepped inside. She followed, and as the door closed, she put up a hand before he could make a sound, and went back into her bedroom. When she came out, she said, "All right. Anything the Inari—or anyone else—try to pick up from this room will be so scrambled you could serve it with bacon and toast." And she sat down on the low settee in the middle of the room and began to giggle. Just a small chuckle at first, but as it grew in volume, it proved infectious. Jim welcomed the release of tension; he sank down on the awkwardly low settee (it was, after all, designed for shorter, stockier bodies) a platonic distance from the admiral and laughed.

Ciana ran her fingers like a comb through her thick silver-blond hair, pushing it back off her forehead, and after a time, managed to catch her breath. At the realization that she still clutched the bottle of Djanai liquor in one hand, she smiled and set it down on the low table next to the settee. "I'd better get rid of this before I'm tempted to drink some." She looked over at Kirk, her eyes bright. "For one dark moment there, I was afraid we were going to have a class-one interstellar fiasco on our hands."

He smiled back. "I wasn't."

One corner of her mouth quirked wryly. "The famous Kirk instinct, of course?"

"Of course."

"Well, I congratulate you on that instinct—and I, for one, must admit that in this case, our instincts were operating on the same wavelength. Did you see the look on Ruwe's face when you told him we'd leave his precious cargo ships to the mercy of the pirates? Did you hear the Council's great collective gasp?" She grinned at the thought.

He raised a brow as he turned toward her. "From your initial reaction, I thought you disapproved."

"Not disapproved—I was just surprised. I think I was being overcautious—afraid to speak up, because it was my temper talking, I suppose. But they deserved a good scare, the bastards. That business Ruwe said—about thinking we had come to give military instead of diplomatic aid—that was an outright lie. He knew damn well what we had come to do. Nogura showed me the entire transcript of their conversation. There's no doubt the esteemed Council was trying to confuse us."

"What would they gain by it?" Kirk asked.

She raised her shoulders and dropped them again. "I'm no psychic—but if I were Ruwe and wanted some military help tracking these people, maybe an argument like this would give me the upper hand, so that Starfleet would have to soothe the Council's injured feelings by giving a little military aid." She shook her head. "I don't mean to sound judgmental, but the more I learn about this culture, the more convinced I am that complete honesty is not necessarily considered a virtue here." She paused. "And speaking of instincts, Jim—I have a very uncomfortable hunch that we'd best not trust the Inari very far. They could turn on us." She stopped abruptly and said, "I'm sorry."

"For what?" Jim asked, though he knew the answer; she had called him by his first name, and he'd enjoyed it, and was already trying to decide whether to respond in kind or to ignore it.

"For calling you 'Jim' without asking first. I don't mean to sound condescending. It's Nogura's fault for using everyone's first name. I've gotten into the habit of thinking of you by that name."

"I like it," Jim said quite honestly. "If I happened to call you 'Lori,' would you find anything condescending about it?"

"That would be fine." The briefest dazzle of a smile lit up her face, and was gone; and in that short time, Jim came to know that the attraction he felt toward Lori Ciana was returned in full.

"Well," Lori said at last, "I suppose the Inari will be linking our system up with their terminals any second now. For now, we'd best get to work."

Far into Vulcan's night, Keridwen sat in front of the burning candle and drowsed in and out of a wakeful slumber. From time to time as she relaxed and drifted off, a cold panic clutched her and reminded her of Death in Spock's cards.

This time, she was roused to alertness by soft stirrings coming from the dark hallway outside . . . barely audible rustling, the scuffling of sandals against the stone floor. Keridwen blew out the candle and stood so that she could see through the crack in the doorway.

Outside, white-robed Kolinahru moved swiftly through the corridor and disappeared. On their way to some secret ritual, Dwen thought at first, but an urgency to their movements convinced her something had happened to disrupt the peacefulness of the mountain retreat. She watched for a moment as one, two, three . . . finally, a dozen or more passed by at irregular intervals, as if summoned from sleep to some emergency.

Odd. She would have liked to wander down to Leonard's room to see if he had a clue as to what was happening, but she remembered with a pang of guilt that he had gone out into the night desert to retreat to the comfort of the scout—and as there had been no reason to bring communicators from the ship with them (after all, there was no one left on the scout to communicate with), there was no way to get in touch with him at all, not even to see if he had made it aboard safely. She had been tempted to join him, to make sure he was all right, but fear had immobilized her. Fear that if she went with him, she might unwittingly make death come faster for him, or both of them. Fear that if she stayed on Gol, the same might happen. There was nothing she could do except trust her instinct that she should remain in her cell.

Gods, how she hoped that Leonard was right, that this was the first time she had been wrong, and that all her fears for their safety were ridiculous. But she'd spent hours in meditation trying to figure it all out, and was still no closer to dealing with the fact of Spock's cards. She half-smiled at the image of herself and McCoy enjoying a gin and tonic in the scout's cool cabin. At least a chat with him would have brought some relief from this damnably somber mood. . . .

Another flash of white as a Vulcan passed in front of her cell. But this was all too interesting to ignore . . . she felt the anthropologist in her claim ascendancy. If this *were* some sort of secret ritual—an ancient one, based in the old magic . . . She almost giggled nervously at a sudden compelling brainstorm. *This* was why she had felt she should remain in her room and not follow McCoy out into the desert. She had always felt that the answer was here, with the Kolinahru—and now it was time to follow her instincts and, quite literally, the white figures gliding quietly down the hall. Follow them, and find the answer. . . .

And it would all be very easy—the Vulcans supplied their guests with the same white hooded robe as the Kolinahru wore. She hadn't worn hers because it had been too warm. But now . . . now all she need do was pull the hood over her head, and she could be taken for one of them in the dimness; she had the right coloring for a Vulcan. And even in a group of them, her all-too-human thoughts could not be sensed by the strongest of telepaths—one side benefit of the accursed esper-blindness. They'd probably mistake her for an advanced adept with perfect mental shields.

This time she did laugh softly, and ran to the ledge where the white robe lay, carefully folded. She put it on and drew the hood as far forward as possible so that her face was hidden, then slipped out into the hall and did her best to imitate the urgent stride of the Kolinahr student in front of her.

They walked for what seemed like kilometers down dark halls and then down flight after flight of hand-hewn stairs. Keridwen was almost breathless by the time they reached the ground floor. Their contingent of about twenty students was met by other similar-size groups, and when they reached the central meeting room, Keridwen estimated their number had swelled to more than one hundred. They stood silently, expectantly, in the meeting room, and seemed to queue up for something; it took her a moment to notice that a panel in the wall had been pushed aside, and the Kolinahru were filing two-by-two into the gap.

Keridwen's heart pounded. A hidden meeting place. So this *was* a secret ritual, conducted in the dead of night to shield it from the curious eyes of visitors! She waited with the others, and when her turn came, walked side by side through the passageway with a male student. He did not look at her, but she pulled her hands up into the long bell sleeves to hide their trembling.

The room was actually a cavern—nature, not Vulcan hands had carved it from the rock aeons ago—lit only by oil lamps placed high on ledges to shed light on the mute assembly below. Keridwen was disappointed to see no religious artifacts or symbols, but there was a rise of flat stone in the cave's center: a stage, or perhaps an altar. She was among the last to enter, and only seconds after she found her place in the crowd, the stone door rumbled shut.

A slender figure made its way to the platform and stood above the assembly. T'Sai, Keridwen knew, even before she drew back the hood to reveal her white hair. Dwen had heard of the High Master but had never seen her. Yet the dignity with which T'Sai moved, her utter lack of urgency, and the respect with which the other Kolinahru regarded her convinced Keridwen that this was the revered High Master. Even in the cavern's gloom, T'Sai's placid face was incandescent, beatific. The face of a saint, Keridwen thought, and she would not have been surprised had a halo appeared behind the aged woman's head. If only she could have a private audience with T'Sai, she could tell the High Master about the shadow of Death that followed her everywhere, and T'Sai would be the only being in the universe who would understand, and know what could be done. The Vulcans themselves seemed mesmerized by the Master's presence; the crowd was so still that Keridwen could not hear even a breath.

"Kolinahru," T'Sai said at last, giving the R the guttural trill only Vulcans could. The Master spoke in even, melodic tones, and although Keridwen's Vulcan was rusty, she could understand enough of T'Sai's words to know that there was indeed some grave emergency. What that emergency was, Keridwen was not exactly sure: apparently someone named Sekar had—she must have gotten it wrong—stolen something that belonged to someone named Zakal (a visitor, more than likely; not a Vulcan name). Keridwen thought at first she must have gotten the object and subject reversed: it surely made more sense for a visitor to have taken something from one of the Kolinahru . . . but then, what did the Kolinahru have worth stealing? But from listening, it became clear that Sekar was in fact the subject, and had stolen Zakal's . . . Twice T'Sai used a word Keridwen did not know:

"katra." It seemed the Kolinahru were alarmed because Sekar might take Zakal's katra to the Romulans, and the outcome of that would be disaster.

The Romulans? Then "katra" must mean something danger-ous . . . a weapon, perhaps. And what were the Vulcans doing with a dangerous weapon? Keridwen took a step forward, listen-ing avidly. This was getting interesting!

Then T'Sai used another strange word: *ska-oot*. The word didn't sound Vulcan . . . probably borrowed from another lan-guage. Sekar had taken ska-oot too. And then T'Sai used a word Keridwen recognized with a start: her own name, Llewellyn. My gods, they had stolen her scout! She gasped and raised a hand to her mouth; the students on either side looked at her with mild surprise. A second realization hit much harder.

"I'm Llewellyn! Good gods, Leonard McCoy is on that vessel!" She blurted it out in Standard, and even when every eye in the place was focused on her, she was far too upset by the fact to worry about her discovery by the Kolinahru.

"Who is this?" T'Sai asked in Vulcan. She was entirely unruffled.

Keridwen lowered her hood, but before she could answer, another voice spoke. She recognized Spock, in front of her in the crowd. He was not Kolinahru, but apparently whatever summons had drawn them all here had drawn Spock as well.

"My guest, T'Sai," he said. "I did not know she had come. But I take full responsibility for the fact."

"You are sure of what you say—that the human McCoy is on your ship?" T'Sai asked her in Standard.

Keridwen nodded.

"You have heard things which no outworlder may hear," T'Sai intoned.

For one ridiculous instant Keridwen was afraid. *Relax. These are Kolinahru . . . what will they do to you?* But the fact that she was the only human among them, and in a secret place where no one would ever look, frightened her. After all, the Kolinahru would never want humans to know that they were capable of stealing, not to mention hijacking and kidnapping. In this place, in another time, such a discovery would no doubt have sealed her death.

"I beg forgiveness," she said weakly in Standard. There were no suitable words for such an apology; yet, how could the Kolinahru blame an outsider for answering the silent summons?

"I saw the others in the hall, and for some reason, I was strongly drawn to follow them here. Leonard McCoy is my friend, and perhaps I sensed danger to him . . ." Now was clearly not the time to mention any anthropological interest.

T'Sai's eyes were hooded, but her tone seemed to indicate acceptance of Keridwen's excuse. "Those who are drawn, are drawn. But you must pledge never to speak of such things."

"You have my word on it," Keridwen promised eagerly. "But what are we going to do about getting Leonard and the scout back?"

"I will see to it that your friend and your vessel are returned to you. Only be patient. There are far greater sorrows that must be averted first."

The Romulans getting their hand on this katra thing, of course.

"I ask permission to accompany you," Spock said to T'Sai. "Leonard McCoy is my guest here and my friend. I am bound to do what I can. And Sekar . . ." He paused. "Sekar was also once my friend."

"Agreed," T'Sai told him. "But thee may lose thy life . . . or worse."

Wondering uncomfortably what could be worse than losing one's life, Keridwen said, "I also ask permission to accompany you. It's my friend and my vessel we're after."

T'Sai's radiance seemed to dim at the thought. "There can be no outworlders involved."

"I'm a licensed pilot—" Keridwen began, but Spock interrupted her.

"High Master T'Sai, Dr. Llewellyn may be of some use to us."

There was the slightest rustle as the others turned to look at him.

T'Sai's expression had not changed from the moment she had stepped on the platform, and it did not change now. But she stared intently at Spock without speaking, as if shocked into silence.

"She is esper-blind," Spock continued. "Zakal could neither sense her presence nor influence her telepathically. I submit that having such a pilot would be a great advantage."

Confused, Keridwen glanced from T'Sai to Spock. But Zakal was just Sekar's innocent victim, wasn't he? Wasn't it Sekar they were pursuing? Just what the hell *was* this katra thing, anyway?

T'Sai was not pleased. "If Dr. Llewellyn is esper-blind, then how was she summoned by the mind-tree?"

"Dr. Llewellyn claims to be precognitive," Spock replied, "and I can attest to her total lack of esper-capacity."

"Fascinating," T'Sai breathed. "Dr. Llewellyn, if you will swear by whatever beliefs you have that you will never reveal anything that transpires in the course of this rescue, then we will permit you to accompany us."

Keridwen smiled ironically. For the first time, her psychic handicap had actually worked to her advantage . . . for whatever strange reason. She raised her arm, palm facing heaven. "By the goddesses and gods, I swear."

TWELVE

───────────── ☆ ─────────────

McCoy woke sweating, with a pounding headache over his left eye and some queasiness, the legacy of three double gin and tonics the night before. The air seemed thin and miserably hot, and for a moment the doctor imagined he was back in the grim stone cell on Gol . . . until he remembered he was on Dwen's scout. Either the environmental controls had failed or Dwen's brand of gin had some peculiarly nasty aftereffects. The doctor groaned, eyes still scrunched closed, and raised himself to a sitting position. All he had to do was make it to the servitor. Since it served double gin and tonics, it must also hold the cure for them.

He stretched cautiously and opened his eyes. He must have been asleep for hours . . . but a glance at his wrist chrono proved useless. He hadn't reset it since leaving Earth, and he could never remember the time differences. He pressed a toggle on the bulkhead next to his bunk. A viewscreen appeared, showing blackness littered with streaks of stars. McCoy blinked, but the sky remained out of focus. He snapped the screen off. So it was still night . . . and from the looks of it, too dark to be anywhere near dawn. He must have dozed off for a couple of hours at most. He lowered himself again with a pained sigh.

And realized the ship was *moving*.

He sat up so fast that the dizziness made him clutch his head. *For God's sake, take it easy. You overslept, that's all. You*

*overslept and Dwen and Spock found you and decided to head
back to the capital for whatever reason. . . .* Which suited McCoy
just fine. Couldn't have stood another minute in that hot, dull
place.

He used the bulkhead next to the bunk to brace himself, and
rose unsteadily to his feet. The servitor was just across from him.
Brilliant of them to design it that way. He stumbled over and
discovered, with deep and humble gratitude, the code for the
hangover medication. His throat was as parched as Vulcan's
damnable desert, but in his haste he swallowed the pills without
water and forced them down through sheer determination.

McCoy turned to look at the scout's helm. Spock was in the
pilot's chair, still dressed in one of the white Kolinahr robes, but
Keridwen was nowhere to be seen. McCoy frowned and stepped
back to peer up at the top bunk. Not there. Then where the hell
was she, outside on the hull?

Headache easing, he moved toward the front of the scout.
"Spock." It came out a croak. He cleared his throat and tried
again. A little better this time. "Spock, where's Dwen? And why
in blazes did you reset the environmental controls?"

The Vulcan in the pilot's chair swiveled to look at him.

"God Almighty." McCoy clutched at the back of a passenger's chair to keep from dropping to his knees. "You're not
Spock."

"Obviously," the Vulcan said, and turned back to stare at
the viewscreen.

"Who *are* you?"

"Unimportant." The Vulcan was thick-necked, burly
enough to be thoroughly intimidating, and perfectly composed in
the face of McCoy's dismay. *How,* the doctor wondered, *could I
ever have mistaken him for Spock?*

"Where are Dwen and Spock?" McCoy demanded.

"I know no Dwen. Spock is not here."

"And why the hell are *you?*"

"I had need of this spacecraft," the Vulcan answered matter-
of-factly. "I . . . borrowed it."

"*Stole* it, you mean." Shock and anger brought McCoy a
burst of energy. "This ship belongs to Keridwen Llewellyn, and
you just said you didn't know her. You couldn't have asked her
permission. Therefore, you stole it."

The Vulcan considered this calmly for a moment and then
said, "Very well. I stole it. But it was an emergency." He glanced

archly at McCoy. "And I regret that I did not realize until after takeoff that you were aboard. Your loud snoring alerted me to the fact."

"Snoring!" McCoy was ready to contest that, but it was an obvious attempt to get him off the track. He knew damn good and well he didn't snore—though Jocelyn had often accused him of it back when they were married. "Look, just what kind of emergency would require you to steal someone's ship?"

The Vulcan ignored him and looked back at the viewscreen.

"At least tell me where the hell we're going! What are you with, the Vulcan Secret Service or something?"

"Something." The Vulcan suddenly grimaced spasmodically, and an eerie light appeared in his eyes.

McCoy took a step backward. He had to force himself to ask: "Are you all right? I'm a doctor."

The Vulcan's expression smoothed and became placid again, but it seemed to McCoy that he nevertheless grinned ironically. "It is nothing you can help, Doctor." He turned his attention back to the scout's control panel.

Something damn strange about this Kolinaroo. Didn't even *act* like a Vulcan. With the feeling that things were going to get a whole lot worse than they seemed now, McCoy persisted. "I've got to get back to my friends, and *soon,* understand? I don't care *what* the Vulcan government needs this fool spacecraft for. Besides, my friends are going to come looking for me."

"Let them come," the Vulcan said in a way that made McCoy very uncomfortable. "I will release you at the first possible opportunity."

Release you . . . McCoy understood then that he was a prisoner.

The Vulcan turned his head and gazed into the doctor's eyes. Despite the heat, McCoy felt suddenly cold. "You're tired," the Vulcan said. "Go back to the bunk and sleep now."

McCoy went back without a word and lay down on the bunk. His head swam, but not from the gin and tonics. There was something seriously wrong with that Kolinaroo, something that made McCoy think he was . . . dangerous. A ridiculous notion to entertain about a Vulcan, but he couldn't shake it. If only he knew whether Keridwen kept a weapon hidden somewhere on board . . . but maybe a weapon wouldn't do him much good against this particular Vulcan. McCoy thought of his captor's powerful bulk and shuddered.

And I thought it was strange to be having a friendly talk with Spock and his fiancée. This *is Strange with a capital S.*

He was just beginning to wonder if Spock and Keridwen had noticed him missing yet when he fell hard into a deep, unnatural sleep. It was as if he had been drugged. He fought it, fought also to hold on to the eye-opening memory of his strange and desperate situation. From time to time he became fuzzily aware of the Vulcan speaking to someone else.

But there was no one else on the ship, was there?

At one point—perhaps minutes, perhaps hours later—McCoy managed to open his eyes and roll to the edge of the bunk. From where he lay he could just see the pilot's back as he spoke into the subspace radio. In Vulcan, McCoy thought at first, but somehow different from the language the doctor had been listening to the past few days. The stress seemed different, and so did some of the sounds. McCoy groaned aloud as the realization hit home.

Dear God, that wasn't Vulcan, it was *Romulan!* His kidnapper was a Romulan spy. He *knew* there was something weird about that guy. . . .

The pilot must have heard him. He finished his conversation, then walked back to where McCoy lay helpless, unable even to raise his head.

"You heard," his captor said. It was not a question.

"You're Romulan," McCoy slurred. Talking was next to impossible.

"No. Merely a sympathizer. But now we cannot release you as we had planned."

"We?" Suddenly his lips and tongue were loosened, and McCoy found he could sit up. "Are you royalty, or is there someone else on the ship I haven't met yet?"

The Vulcan didn't answer.

McCoy tried his best to look defiant, though he felt his insides turning to mush. "So what are you gonna do? Kill me?"

"Not yet," the spy answered, and McCoy's heart skipped a beat. "Your friend Spock is pursuing us. We have learned from Sekar that he could be very useful."

"Who's Sekar?"

The spy shrugged. "No one of importance."

"If you're not going to kill me yet, there are two things I'd like to know. One, who *are* you, and two, where the hell are we going?"

"We are going to ch'Rihan, in the Romulan Empire, to bring the Declared the Lost Powers." And the Vulcan/Romulan grinned, such a wide, hideous grin that the doctor recoiled involuntarily. "For I am Zakal, High Master of the mind-lords of Kolinahr, dead these past fifteen thousand seasons."

Rh'iov Rrhaen, commander in the Praetor's service, paced up and down the narrow stretch of floor that had served as his command base these past few weeks. There was just cause for his anxiety. Hours had passed since he last received word from the Djanai that their two prisoners were in tow and would soon be safely incarcerated in the underground base on Ulla, the smallest of Inar's moons. Secretly Rrhaen feared the Djanai would find some way to jeopardize his real purpose here—which had nothing whatsoever to do with the dispute between the Inari and the Djanai.

Rrhaen was a consummate diplomat—one reason he had received this particular assignment—but at present, he had every reason to doubt that his mission would succeed. Outwardly, he maintained a respectful attitude toward the Djanai, but privately he despised them. Rrhaen was a meticulous man, given to logic and detail, but the Djanai were a headstrong, superstitious lot who steadfastly refused to follow orders precisely (even though Rrhaen had always been careful to give the illusion that he was not giving orders, but help)—such as the idiot Umul, who'd managed to get himself killed. *And good riddance,* Rrhaen thought. The Djanai, with their big teeth and eyes and long, sloping profile, reminded him of a cross between a Romulan primate and a human. At times they seemed no more intelligent than either: they were slaves to their customs and religion. In Rrhaen's view, religion was a tool created by the state to control the simple-minded. Only fools believed in anything higher than themselves. Religion was to be tolerated, but never taken seriously. Yet Rrhaen was self-possessed enough never to reveal his scorn to the Djanai.

Still, as much as he hated playing diplomat to inferiors, he realized that this assignment was a delectably sweet one. His name would be recorded for future generations, both Romulan and Vulcan. Up to now, Rrhaen's military career had therefore been an unspectacular one, punctuated by several near-successes. But this would secure him a promotion, perhaps even a position on the Presidium. He owed the Djanai gratitude for being a patriarchy, one that the Empire decided would relate better to a male authority figure than a female one—a fact which enabled him to beat out several better-qualified female candidates for the job.

The door behind him rushed open. Rrhaen stopped his pacing and wheeled around.

What he saw brought both irritation and relief: Kel, the leader of the Djanai resistance (if anyone could be called leader, the way these creatures vacillated and called on their elders for advice), back in native dress again, bare-chested, his oiled hair free down his back.

"Kel. You're late. When you failed to contact me, I became concerned. Was the mission successful?" Despite his best efforts, a faint note of recrimination surfaced in Rrhaen's tone.

Kel's chin lifted in a gesture Rrhaen read as arrogant. The Djanai was slow to answer: Elements! How these creatures were slow, slow in breathing, eating, speaking, moving, living! "The mission went well, rh'iov Rrhaen. If I did not contact you, it is because I am unaccustomed to remembering such things."

Always "rh'iov Rrhaen," as if Kel did not realize that "rh'iov" was his title and not his name. Rrhaen compressed his lips and struggled hard not to vent too much of his frustration at once. Kel was late, but he was here, thank the Elements, and looking as if the mission had not been a particularly disastrous one. Let the Djanai show their stupid pride by ignoring Rrhaen's time constraints. In a matter of months, if Rrhaen were patient, perhaps Kel and the others would be calling him *Governor* rh'iov Rrhaen. Rrhaen forced a smile. "Of course not. It doesn't matter. I'm just nervous because you are late. And the prisoners—all went as planned?"

"Not exactly," Kel answered, and leisurely blinked his large black eyes. There was an agonizing pause before he continued. "The prisoners are incarcerated, but we stopped to—"

Consult the elders, Rrhaen's mind filled in, before Kel could even say it.

"—consult the elders. Ema had a vision of a large white bird over the moon Ulla. A bad omen. It would have been bad fortune for us to take them there, so we brought them here instead. That is what I came to tell you."

Rrhaen's brows rose in disbelief, then rushed together. "Here? Kel, there are no facilities for prisoners here! There's no brig. Where have you put them?"

As he awaited Kel's answer, Rrhaen's mind ticked through the possibilities. Other than this cramped office, Rrhaen had temporary sleeping quarters. Couldn't put them there—they might see something. And hopefully, the Djanai had enough sense not to put them in the transporter room, where most of the weapons were housed—

"In the conference room," Kel replied at last.

"But there are no force fields to hold them there!"

Kel tilted his great chin even higher and peered down his long expanse of face at Rrhaen. "My men are strong and capable of watching the prisoners, rh'iov Rrhaen. They will not escape. And facilities make no difference. This is the place where Djana wills them to be. No harm can come to us in this if we do as Djana wills."

"Kel, you may have just jeopardized this entire mission." Rrhaen staggered to the chair behind his desk and collapsed into it, covering his eyes with his hands. He could not explain to Kel what the Djanai had done wrong—that they had jeopardized Rrhaen's *true* purpose here, that of welcoming a certain Vulcan defector and escorting him and his most valuable prize into the waiting arms of the Presidium itself. There could be no chance of a Federation prisoner accidentally learning of this . . . and surviving to tell others. There was only one thing to be done. Rrhaen's mind worked to find some excuse, some lie to explain to Kel what he was about to ask the Djanai to do . . . and failed. When he spoke again, his tone was weary. "Kel . . . I must ask you to trust me—I cannot explain fully. You must kill your prisoners. They cannot know of the presence of a Romulan base here. If they live and are released, they will reveal our location— and that simply cannot be permitted. They must die. Do you understand?"

Kel thought about it. "No. I do not understand, rh'iov Rrhaen. Useless deaths bring Djana's wrath. And on a level you can understand, if we kill the prisoners, Starfleet will have no reason to bargain with us."

"Then simply lie to Starfleet as long as possible." His voice rose with frustration. "Tell them the prisoners are still alive. You would still be able to achieve your objectives."

"That would not be honorable," Kel said.

Rrhaen slammed both hands down on his desk and lunged to his feet. "Who *cares* if it's honorable? Elements, Kel, we cannot risk anyone from the Federation discovering what we are doing!

We can't afford to give them a single chance. Honor has nothing to do with it—'' He broke off, nearly weeping with the futility of communicating to the mind hidden behind Kel's great thick skull. There was no longer any point in continuing the ridiculous pretense that he was here out of the Praetor's kindness.

"Kel, you must kill the prisoners quickly—in a matter of hours. Or we will withdraw every weapon, every scrap of support, even destroy these bases we've built for you."

Kel appeared entirely unmoved. Elements, the man had fewer reactions than a mollusk! "I will have to—" Kel began.

"Consult the elders," Rrhaen finished with him. "I know, I know. But remember this—if the counsel of your precious elders includes anything other than executing the prisoners as ordered, the Empire will see to it that all of you are killed."

Which, Rrhaen silently assured himself as Kel left the room, *is precisely what I intend to do with the lot of you as soon as the prisoners are dispatched.*

Kel was a proud man, born of an independent people who had never acknowledged defeat. He stood now outside rh'iov Rrhaen's office contemplating what the commander had said. Kel did not like this one who called himself the Romulans' representative, had not liked him even before Rrhaen's ultimatum. Kel knew that the rh'iov secretly considered him a fool, but Kel was not angered by it; he knew that he was not a fool. Fools lose their tempers, just as Rrhaen had. The rh'iov was not so shrewd as Kel had thought—he had inadvertently revealed to Kel how he really viewed the Djanai: as simpletons, as slaves who trembled and followed orders when the master shouted.

No one ruled the true Djanai. Kel's people had long ago learned the foolishness of attempts to do so: how could one control another's heart? Even though Kel was responsible for guiding the Djanai resistance, and the others tended to defer to his judgment, he knew how absurd it was to think of himself in charge. He consulted, he did not order. It was the only way to win true cooperation. And when a consensus was reached, and the elders' opinions given special weight, the decision was made.

Clearly it was not so with the Romulans. Rrhaen was misguided enough to think himself in charge, and that by threats he could force Kel into doing what the rh'iov wanted . . . as if Kel were frightened of losing these accursed weapons, this accursed base, along with its accursed technology. *Take your base,* Kel had wanted to say, *and your weapons and your force fields and your invisible fast ships, and tell your people we have no more need of your help.*

But he had said nothing because the elders claimed there was justice in using technology to fight Inari technology: the two evils would cancel each other out, and Djana would become whole again. Kel could not argue with such wisdom, and the majority approved, so it was done . . . but in Kel's heart, he doubted. And each day he felt himself becoming less of a Djanai and more of an Inari, learning to operate Romulan and Inari ships and weapons, breathing in the stench of artificial things . . . forgetting what it felt like to till the land, to breathe sweet air and feel soft grass beneath his feet. The others did not speak of it, but he knew from their increasingly grim faces that they felt it too.

Kel understood now what Rrhaen and his people wanted with the Djanai. They were not offering help in return for open trade; no, they looked at Djana as something to dominate, to possess, as if a people and its planet could be owned. The Romulans were as bad as the Inari, as bad as the Federation, who kept the Inari here.

Kel did not relish killing, nor did he flinch when it became necessary. But he could not permit his hostages to be killed. If the Federation were wise, it would insist on proof its people were alive before bartering. To kill them now would be the worst sort of stupidity. He knew that Rrhaen was in charge of some vast secret project for the Romulans, and was desperate to see that it went smoothly—but that was Rrhaen's concern, and not Kel's. Kel would make sure that his prisoners stayed out of Rrhaen's way, but that was the extent of his obligation to the Romulans.

If Rrhaen insisted on the prisoners' deaths, then Rrhaen himself would have to die. Kel did not fear the vengeance of the rh'iov's superiors. When they discovered Rrhaen's death, Kel would claim he was killed by an escaping prisoner. And then, if necessary to appease them, Kel would agree to execute one— only one—of his hostages. The woman, he had already decided. She was clearly less important than the other, the Vulcan.

But first he went to seek the advice of the elders.

THIRTEEN

☆

Uhura squinted her eyes as the slight disoriented feeling of dematerialization came over her. Normally she felt nothing at all at being transported—she was a natural-born space traveler and she'd never experienced the dizziness others complained of while beaming. She'd never gotten spacesick in her whole life, not even after antigrav maneuvers, and took great pride in the fact. But after the unpleasant surprise of dematerializing in Starfleet's reception chamber, she found the process disconcerting. She even felt a little dizzy.

Stop it. You sound like Dr. McCoy.

If she was dizzy it was because of the sedative they'd used on her. It was finally beginning to wear off—apparently they wanted her to be able to stand on the transporter pad without help—but it had left her with a faintly queasy headache.

She opened her eyes again to a different transporter room, a larger one this time. Perhaps they were on a larger vessel now, or in some sort of military installation. The muscular Djanai next to her gripped her arm tightly and motioned her forward. She moved forward, encouraged somewhat by the presence of Sarek nearby, flanked by another, even burlier Djanai. The Vulcan seemed entirely unruffled by what had happened, and Uhura did her best to imitate his dignified air. But it was difficult to ignore the rapid beating of her heart. There was no telling where the Djanai were taking their prisoners; Uhura prayed only that it would not be worse than the tiny cubicle on the ship.

Think Vulcan. Logically, there's no reason for them to hurt you. Remember, they wouldn't have brought you this far if all they were going to do was kill you. And Starfleet will make sure nothing happens to you. Besides—and this thought comforted her more than anything—*you had the good luck to get kidnapped along with the Vulcan ambassador. God knows there must be a hundred people already working on this.*

And then she made herself think of something other than where she was going. Such as her students; what had they told them back at the Academy? Would they tell them the truth about what happened to her?

My God, would anyone at Starfleet think to tell the director so they'd know to find a substitute? Maybe the Djanai would let her call in to be sure the class was covered—*Better, that's better.* She smiled inwardly at the absurd notion and forced herself to relax a little, even though the Djanai had stopped in front of a door and gestured their two prisoners inside.

She flinched a little mentally as the doors opened, expecting to see a brig, or at the worst, an interrogator. But inside lay . . . a conference room?

Her guard gestured her to sit; at the other end of the table, Sarek's Djanai did the same. Uhura sank into the too-low but infinitely comfortable chair with disbelieving relief. Not bad. Not bad at all. She straightened, waiting for the guard to lean forward and apply restraints, whether a force field or the manual kind, but the Djanai walked back to the entrance and consulted his companion. He turned back and asked his prisoners a question.

"Are you hungry?"

Uhura's eyes widened a little, but she quickly regained control and glanced over at Sarek, who did not seem to think the question odd.

"Yes," the ambassador answered.

Uhura had been far too frightened to think about food, but it had been hours—perhaps even an entire day—since she'd last eaten. "Yes. Some food would be nice."

Her Djanai exited, leaving the other to guard them with an implacable expression.

Yes, Uhura told herself, *if you've got to be kidnapped, be sure to do it with an ambassador. At least they'll treat you right.* She folded her arms on the table and leaned forward. She was finally relaxed enough to remember Spock's kissar—Sarek had been carrying it when he was caught up in the beam. Panic seized her. *Ridiculous of you to be upset about it. Here you are, taken hostage by a gang of terrorists, and you're worrying about Spock's gift.*

Well, yes, dammit, she was. The lyre was custom-made, one of a kind. And if the Djanai had let anything happen to it, she'd . . . she'd . . .

She'd be very angry, that's what. But at the moment she was in no position to threaten.

"Excuse me," she said to the guard, who eyed her suspiciously. Really a very beautiful man, though not human-looking at all. His skin was deep red-brown, the color of cinnamon. He wore no shirt, and the muscles on his arms were so well-defined he looked to Uhura more like an idealized sculpture than a living, breathing being. She was getting used to the heavy jaw and the slope of the nose and forehead, and could recognize that his culture would consider him handsome. "But what happened to the musical instrument Ambassador Sarek was carrying when you . . . you ah, beamed us out of Starfleet Headquarters?"

The guard tilted his head back and studied her calmly for a moment before answering. "I know nothing about it."

Sarek spoke up. "After I was sedated, it was taken from me. I have not seen it again. Presumably it is in the care of our captors."

The guard glanced at them both. His manner was serenely distant, and Uhura could sense no hatred, no hostility, emanating from him. Yet at the same time, she saw that the Inari phaser in his hand was aimed at her, and she knew he would not hesitate to kill her if she gave him cause. "I have not seen it," he answered at last. "But perhaps I will ask those in charge—when my watch is finished."

"Thank you." Uhura managed to smile warmly at him. "It would mean a lot to me."

The guard's head turned as the door opened and his companion reappeared bearing a tray of food, which he set on the table between the two prisoners, then stepped back to watch as they ate. Uhura scanned it eagerly, realizing that she was in fact terribly hungry. There were two plates, heaped with fruit—some Terran and some Vulcan, in fact, to be sure the prisoners found something appealing to eat. Not the type of treatment she'd been anticipating at all. Uhura helped herself to a plate and a glass of

what turned out to be strongly medicinal-tasting green tea. There
were no utensils, but the pieces were easy enough to eat with the
fingers. Uhura picked up a slice of pineapple and bit into it. It
was tart and sweet and juicy. She discreetly wiped her chin on
the back of her hand.

She had almost cleared her plate when the door opened again
and a third Djanai stepped inside. His complexion was saffron-
colored, his long oiled hair several shades darker. Uhura decided
that the differences in skin pigment weren't racial, but an individual variation, like eye color. This Djanai seemed older than the
other two, and they greeted him with special respect. Like the
others, he wore simple loose breeches woven from rough fiber,
but his were elaborately adorned with beads and tiny feathers.
He stood sideways to the guards, careful not to block their view
of the prisoners, but the two younger Djanai listened intently,
their eyes focused on their leader, their phasers still aimed at
their prisoners. From the tone of the older one's voice, a problem
had arisen.

Uhura slowly lowered a half-eaten piece of melon back onto
her plate. If she moved quickly, while they were distracted—

"What you are thinking of is foolish," Sarek told her softly.
The Djanai, still engrossed in their conversation, did not seem to
notice. Apparently they did not realize that the Vulcan's hearing
was acute enough to hear them.

She glanced sharply at him. Had he read her thoughts? And
then she realized that her entire body was tensed, telegraphing
her intention. She sighed and relaxed. It would have been impossible anyway. She would never have made it to the door. "I just
wish I knew what they were talking about," she whispered.

"I understand enough Djanai to explain the gist of it. The
one is consulting our guards for an opinion concerning a course
of action." Sarek paused, listening. "Fascinating."

"What is it?" Uhura picked up her piece of melon and took
another bite.

The cinnamon-colored guard was speaking impassionedly
now, and the other was bobbing his head in agreement. Sarek
leaned closer and lowered his voice so that she had to strain to
hear. "They referred to someone called rh'iov."

Uhura stopped chewing and stared at him. She did not speak
Romulan, but she knew a few words. "Rh'iov" was one of them.

Sarek continued, his words barely audible. "I cannot understand all they are saying." He paused. "But I believe this rh'iov has ordered our execution."

She swallowed hard. The melon slid down the wrong way, triggering a coughing fit, and the Djanai stopped speaking to stare at her. "Are you all right?" the saffron-colored one asked.

She nodded, gasping, tears in her eyes. Sarek watched her quietly, but said no more. Saffron went back to speaking, the two guards' heads huddled close to hear him. She coughed a few more times and swallowed some of the green tea. It helped.

What else are they saying? she wanted to ask Sarek, but she wasn't sure she had the courage to hear the details of her own end. The Djanai conference seemed to be winding up, but if Sarek had caught any more information, he wasn't volunteering to share it.

So she was going to die. She should feel frightened, and, true, part of her mind was frozen with mortal terror . . . but mostly she felt an odd sense of unreality and indignation. These calm, silent men had no right to take her life, or the ambassador's. Silly, insignificant things came to mind. She had classes to teach . . . and then there was Spock's kissar. Such a beautiful, elegant thing; Siobhan had taken three months to carve it. Knowing how much skill and love went into its production, Uhura couldn't bear to think of Spock never seeing it, never knowing of its creation; of strangers ignorantly mishandling it, tossing it aside like a piece of garbage. The thought brought tears to her eyes. Silly of her. Here she was, facing death, and the one thing that made her want to weep was the loss of a musical instrument. Certainly there were worse things to cry about.

But she couldn't think of one. She had always enjoyed life, and there had definitely been times when she faced worse ends than this one. Except that she had always escaped.

The door opened again, but it was not the saffron Djanai leaving. She looked up at the figure of the Romulan rh'iov Sarek had mentioned. He was an older man with streaks of iron gray in his hair, and the bitterness in his face and demeanor was reflected in his voice. At the sight of him, Uhura knew that Sarek had been correct; the Romulans would never let the hostages know of their involvement here and then permit them to live.

"Kel," he snapped at the saffron one. Calmly, deliberately, Kel turned away from his men to peer at the rh'iov. It was quite clear that the Romulan considered himself in charge here, and just as clear that the Djanai did not.

The Djanai answered in Standard. The part of her that was not horrified beyond belief found the situation perversely funny. The only way the rh'iov could communicate with the Djanai was in Standard, the language of the Federation. "Yes, rh'iov Rrhaen?"

"I've come to make sure you carry out my order."

Kel gave his men a look that said: *His order. This poor benighted soul thinks we're going to carry out* his *order. I suppose we should humor him.* To the cinnamon guard, Kel said, "Take the food away, Ela."

Ela tilted his head in acknowledgment and moved to the table. He stacked the plates onto the tray.

"Stay, Ela," the rh'iov said. The implicit threat in his tone would have frozen most in their tracks, but Ela kept moving as if he hadn't heard. The Romulan dropped a hand toward the phaser on his belt.

Kel's phaser was already in his hand. "He must clear the plates, rh'iov Rrhaen. It is our custom. We have shown our guests hospitality, but if we are to kill them, we must remove all signs of graciousness."

Rrhaen stared reluctantly as the door closed over the departing Ela. "Very well." With his phaser, he gestured Kel and the remaining guard away from the door, toward the seated prisoners. "But on my authority as rh'iov of the Romulan Empire, I must insist that you now execute the prisoners as ordered."

I'm not afraid, Uhura thought crazily, but the hair on the back of her neck rose. There was no more time now: she had to take action or die. Kel and the guard faced their hostages and raised their phasers. The Romulan took his place behind them.

She could rush them, she supposed. Wouldn't make much difference, except that she would die a little faster and call it suicide. And it wouldn't buy Sarek enough time to do him any good.

"Would you please stand?" Kel asked politely.

Uhura jumped to her feet. "Please . . . I beg of you, don't kill the ambassador. I'm military personnel—I'm expendable. But if you kill the ambassador, you'll have all of the Federation—and Vulcan—against you."

"She is quite correct," Sarek affirmed amiably as he rose from his chair.

She couldn't help but shoot him a dirty look for that.

"The Federation is already against us," Kel said. "And

Vulcans do not believe in revenge." He glanced sideways at his fellow Djanai. "On my order," he said loudly, taking aim again.

If she were going to die, she at least had to die for a good cause. She threw herself, arms spread to make a wider target, in front of Sarek.

Behind the Djanai, she saw the Romulan raise his own phaser and take aim at Kel. *Behind you,* she almost screamed, knowing full well that Kel would interpret it as a pitiful attempt to distract him and would ignore it.

"*Now,*" Kel shouted.

She scrunched her eyes shut and prepared for the blast.

Instead, the hiss of the door made her open them again. Ela had returned. He stood in the doorway, phaser held high. His reactions were much faster than those of the rh'iov. He fired before the Romulan took aim. For one millisecond the rh'iov's form radiated such intense brilliance that Uhura averted her eyes. When she looked back, Rrhaen was gone.

There was a moment of terrible uncertainty before the other two Djanai lowered their weapons.

"Forgive us," Kel said. "We did not mean to frighten you, but the deception was necessary. Please sit. If you like, Ela will bring back the food."

Uhura shivered, unable to do anything more than gape at them. She felt no relief; that they had so coolly dispatched the Romulan proved that the moment she was no longer needed, she would be just as callously killed. She stumbled toward her chair, but before she made it, her legs went weak under her. She sank to her knees.

Sarek lifted her firmly by the arms and deposited her in her chair. "The food will not be necessary," he told Kel. "But you could bring some hot tea."

She felt suddenly, horribly cold, and only dimly aware of the fact that Sarek was standing over her, and her teeth were chattering. At some point, a cup of very hot green tea appeared in front of her. She sipped a little, and when she could speak again, said, "Tell me, Ambassador, that you didn't know that was going to happen." She glared up into his serious face. "Or I will kill you myself."

He blinked. "Djanai is an illogical language, full of metaphors I do not understand. I did not know that was going to happen. However, in the future it would be best for your safety if you could refrain from heroics.''

''You've got a deal.'' She deflated with a great sigh and laid her head wearily on the table.

FOURTEEN

---- ☆ ----

The drugged feeling had worn off altogether, and McCoy decided it hadn't been a delayed reaction to the gin. No, that Vulcan had hypnotized him, confirming his worst suspicions about the lot of them. Now the doctor sat propped up in the bunk, alternating between helpless panic and boredom. He had no desire to go sit in the passenger chair behind Zakal; it was bad enough back here, occasionally peering out at the Vulcan's broad, powerful back. There was no point in even considering escape . . . since the Vulcan probably wouldn't sleep. And there weren't any weapons McCoy could see, not even anything heavy with which to hit Zakal over the head.

The doctor craned his neck to glance again at his captor, and sighed. Not that he could inflict any damage to that huge skull anyway. It would probably take an antimatter reaction just to knock the Vulcan unconscious. Even if McCoy did manage to catch him off guard and knock him out, there was the delicate matter of navigating the ship. McCoy couldn't pilot himself out of a wet paper bag; hell, he probably couldn't copilot with Keridwen standing over his shoulder.

The last thought brought a wave of self-pity. He missed Dwen . . . and others. If only Jim or Spock were here. Now, *they'd* be able to figure a way out of this mess. Think. What would Jim do in this situation? But McCoy drew a blank. *Aw, the hell with it. I'm a lover, not a fighter—*

Correction. You're not much of a lover these days either.

The doctor gave up on the notion of escape and went back to trying to figure out just what was wrong with the Vulcan. Zakal, he'd said his name was, but that sure didn't sound like any Vulcan name McCoy had ever heard. Then there were the facial grimaces, the erratic behavior, that gruesome smile. Maybe Zakal had been lying when he claimed not to be Romulan. Of course, the man was acting weird even for a Romulan spy. Could be a medical reason: a brain tumor, say, triggering a psychosis. That sounded a bit more plausible than the explanation he'd given that he was some sort of dead Vulcan ruler. McCoy would have given his eyeteeth for a mediscanner—but his was back in a tiny stone cell somewhere in the Vulcan desert.

What other organic causes for psychosis? A hormonal imbalance, say . . . McCoy suddenly groaned aloud. No, not again. He'd already put up with *one* Vulcan undergoing pon farr, and that was enough, thank you. But this guy was certainly acting irrationally enough . . . and it would account for a lot of his behavior. Still, if it were a case of pon farr, then why would Zakal be hell-bent for the Neutral Zone—unless his bride was meeting him on the other side?

McCoy had a quick flash of memory. Wait a minute— Keridwen had a first-aid kit somewhere in the scout. He remembered her saying she'd learned to read a mediscanner. Now, if he could just figure out where she kept it . . .

His gaze fastened on the storage compartment across from the bunk. It was the only logical place for it. The doctor slowly swung his legs around and lowered his feet to the floor.

Zakal did not seem to notice, or if he did, did not care. The Vulcan had been quietly transfixed by the control panels the last few hours, without twitching, grimacing, or muttering under his breath. Now was the time for McCoy to make his move.

He rose quietly and tiptoed over to the compartment. With painstakingly slow movements he raised the lid. The fates were with him: inside, stuffed under some bundled clothes, was the first-aid kit. McCoy opened it and found the small mediscanner. He closed his fingers around the bit of square synthetic metal and gingerly withdrew his arm from the compartment.

The scanner was half the size of McCoy's hand. It was no more than a cheap over-the-counter model meant to be used in household emergencies. It couldn't do a detailed hemoanalysis, and it probably couldn't tell the difference between a Romulan and a Vulcan. But it could tell you if your kid's leg was fractured or if you had a brain tumor. And it just might be able to tell if the Vulcan's blood chemistry was as wildly out of kilter as Spock's had been.

McCoy hid it in his palm, folded his hands behind his back, and strolled nonchalantly up behind the seated Zakal. The doctor leaned over the Vulcan's shoulder, feigning an avid interest in the control panel. He waved the scanner once, quickly, over the Vulcan. It bleeped softly before McCoy could palm it and hide it behind his back again.

Zakal glanced at it and raised a brow; McCoy held his breath. But the Vulcan simply turned back to his controls, apparently unimpressed by what the doctor had done. Perhaps he felt that it made no difference.

McCoy felt encouraged. His captor was behaving like a normal Vulcan again; perhaps the derangement had been only a temporary one. Now might be the time for questions. The doctor cleared his throat and asked in a friendly, conversational tone, "How much longer before we get to where we're going?"

To his surprise, the Vulcan answered. "Approximately three-point-four-seven hours." His tone was completely rational.

McCoy was confused. Had he slept longer than he'd thought? "You mean we're already in the Neutral Zone?"

"By no means." Zakal didn't seem to mind explaining; in fact, he did so as calmly and with as much emotional detachment as Spock himself. "We are stopping well before that—at Arcturus, to be precise, since this vessel is not equipped with a cloaking device. It will be necessary to obtain one before entering the Neutral Zone." He glanced sideways at McCoy. "As you probably have surmised."

"Um," McCoy said. If Zakal were feeling this logical today, maybe he'd listen to the voice of reason. McCoy directed his warmest smile at him. "About this Neutral Zone thing—you know, the Romulans aren't going to take too kindly to my being there. If you'd just let me off on Arcturus, I'd have a whole lot better chance—"

"—of informing the authorities before I have a chance to escape to the Neutral Zone," the Vulcan finished calmly. "I cannot risk that, Dr. McCoy."

When did I tell him my name? McCoy puzzled; since it was going so well, he kept trying. "Look, Zakal, you could just leave me someplace . . . deserted. Someplace where it would take me a while to get to the authorities. That way, you'd have time to get away. And even if I *did* manage to get to the authorities, I swear I wouldn't do anything to try to stop you—"

The Vulcan turned his head sharply and stared at the doctor with narrowed eyes. "My name is Sekar. Who told you about Zakal? Has he spoken to you?"

"Uh, er, no," McCoy stammered pleasantly, and took a big step backward. *Bet you aren't really High Master of the whatcha-macallit of the Kolinaroo, either.* "No, not at all, I just must have gotten confused on the name. Your name's Sekar. Yep. Sure. Exactly what I meant to say in the first place. Well, I'd certainly appreciate it if you'd consider what I just said, Sekar." *If you can.* McCoy scurried quickly to the safety of the bunk and peeked at the scanner readout.

Nothing. McCoy sighed and dropped the scanner on the bunk. Not a reading beyond the norm. The Vulcan was perfectly healthy.

Except that he was certifiably insane. Lost his shields. Taken a spacewalk in the asteroid belt without his helmet. Beamed down one too many times.

And there wasn't a damn thing McCoy could do about it, except sit on his bunk and pray they made it to Arcturus in one piece, then pray for a chance to escape . . . and hope like hell that Spock wasn't far behind.

And, of course, consider the possibility that Dwen's premonition had been right, after all.

Spock returned alone to ShanaiKahr in a borrowed vessel; within two hours he returned with a sleek Vulcan shuttle equipped with warp drive and transporter. By then dawn was already breaking, and McCoy and his kidnapper had been gone for hours. It was too late, Keridwen knew, ever to see McCoy (or the scout, as if that mattered) again. She had not misread the cards, had not misunderstood her premonition; it had foretold McCoy's death all along, followed by a second: Spock's. And what was to keep her and T'Sai from following?

The Vulcans failed to share her despair; they busied them-selves with preparing the craft for takeoff. Keridwen sat in the pilot's seat and grunted as Spock called out the systems check-off; all the while, she fought a growing sense of futility that threatened to spill over into tears. Dammit, she loved McCoy— at the very least, as a dear friend, and that only because she hadn't had the opportunity for anything more. She interrupted Spock's calm voice in the middle of check-off.

"But how will we *find* them?" It was almost an angry sob. "Has anyone picked them up on sensors? Has Vulcan Space Central put a bulletin out on the ship?"

Spock stared over at her in mild surprise. "No. A bulletin would be against our best interests."

She stared at him, convinced he had taken leave of his senses. "Then how can we possibly find them? They could have gone in any direction. Tracing a small craft like that will be impossible!"

Spock studied her for a moment, then returned his attention to his control panel. "All systems functional," he said. "Ready for takeoff."

"And which bloody heading?" she cried, frustrated at his refusal to answer.

A voice behind them intoned, "Mark four-one-four."

Startled, Keridwen turned her head. Behind her in one of the passengers' seats, T'Sai sat, eyes closed, hands steepled in an attitude of prayer. Keridwen had thought the older woman was meditating, and wondered why the High Master needed to accompany them at all. Even if T'Sai felt responsible, she could only get in the way: after all, what help could the frail, elderly woman possibly be? Keridwen had several times been on the verge of saying so to Spock, but held back for fear of seeming rude.

"Heading mark four-one-four," Spock repeated, entering it into the navigational computer. He glanced over at Keridwen, and though his face did not show it, she fancied she detected faint amusement in his eyes. "High Master T'Sai will be directing us."

"I see," she said dubiously, though she didn't see at all, and turned back to her own control panel. "Mark four-one-four, then." Her anger began to dissipate. While she might not know where Leonard was, the Vulcans seemed to. Their calmness brought a strange comfort, though at the same time she felt trapped, unable to elude the feeling that her presence aboard the craft was preordained. She could watch the unusual turn of events, but was powerless to do anything but sit and let things happen around her. Now that the wheel of fortune was in motion, there was nothing she or anyone else could do to slow its inexorable turn.

But when it stopped, would Spock and Leonard McCoy still be alive? Or was she merely helping to hasten their deaths?

She busied herself with the thousand small details that demanded attention during takeoff; she waited until the small craft sailed beyond Vulcan's stratosphere, out of planetary orbit, then the EriB system, and safely reached warp drive before she turned in her seat to look at T'Sai. The Master was still in a trance. She was concentrating, Keridwen knew, on the Vulcan inside the scout. Incredible, to know that a mind could reach out that far, and for a moment she was jealous, but it faded quickly. *T'Sai may have the world's highest psi rating, my dear, but there is one skull she'll never be able to penetrate: yours. And that's why you've been allowed to come.*

In a way, she was sorry T'Sai was in an unreachable state. There were some questions she wanted to ask the High Master—professional curiosity, she told herself—but she wanted the answers just as much for Keridwen herself as for Dr. Llewellyn, the anthropologist. Dwen swiveled in her chair to glance over at Spock. He no longer wore the white robe, as T'Sai did; he was dressed in a Vulcan civilian's dark gray pants and tunic.

"Spock," she said, since there was nothing more for either of them to do but stare at the stars on the overhead viewscreen, "I swore I would never reveal anything I learned on this . . . rescue attempt, and my word is as good as any Vulcan's. I don't see how I can help you without knowing what it is we're up against. And I'll probably figure all this out anyway, before it's all over. So just what is this 'katra' that Sekar stole? Is it a weapon, something secret the Vulcan government has been working on?"

He was silent at first; and when he answered, his gaze was still on the viewscreen. "Nothing like that. Although I suppose you could call it a weapon, since it is being used as such." He hesitated. "It is a . . . spirit. That is the closest translation for it in Standard."

Her jaw dropped. "Spirit?" It was so far removed from any answer she had expected that she was temporarily rendered speechless.

Eyes still averted, Spock shifted in his chair. "The spirit of a Vulcan, Zakal. He died some two thousand years ago, at the very beginning of the Reformation."

"Ye gods," Keridwen breathed softly. The anthropologist in her half-smiled in wonder. "But how . . . ?"

"His spirit—" Spock began, but broke off. "The word does not translate well into Standard. 'Spirit' is not quite the right term. Katra includes one's mind as well . . . all the knowledge accumulated in a lifetime."

A Vulcan lifetime of two and a half centuries. A great deal of knowledge indeed.

"His katra was preserved," Spock continued, "as are all those of the Kolinahr High Masters. Unfortunately, his knowledge of mental powers was great, while his scruples as to their use were . . . nonexistent. He was a great enemy of Surak's. His own students turned against him, however, in favor of the new pacifism, and imprisoned him. Had that not happened, Surak would undoubtedly have had much more difficulty in gaining philosophical control over the masses. There are those who say that the Reformation would have failed utterly."

She frowned, puzzled, still not understanding why the Vulcans felt such urgency over this stolen katra. "I can see how a High Master could exert a great deal of influence over his students, and even public opinion—but why fear Zakal's knowledge being taken to the Romulans? Surely they have their own methods for mental control. Why, even we humans—"

Spock interrupted with an intensity she had never seen in him. "Humans today cannot conceive of the type of power wielded by the ancient High Masters. As I mentioned to you once before, in ShanaiKahr, these were the mind-lords—from your anthropological perspective, the most powerful of all magicians. They controlled the populace utterly, through terror. It is recorded"—and here Spock paused, and his expression became oddly detached—"it has been recorded that Zakal of ShanaiKahr killed his enemies simply by willing it. The methods he chose were particularly gruesome; one was to cause the temperature of the victim's skin to rise, so that it spontaneously ignited and burned."

Horrified, Keridwen raised a hand to her lips and tried to imagine it. "Incredibly destructive mental powers . . . and the Romulans—"

"When the Romulans separated from the Vulcans," Spock continued, "none of the old High Masters went with them. Those on Vulcan, after Zakal's death, chose to align themselves with Surak. The discipline underwent a radical change in philosophy. The path of Kolinahr still harnesses great mental powers—but, for the sake of peace, applies them inward, to the control of one's mind and emotions, rather than using them to control individuals and the outer environment.'' Spock's expression darkened. ''For the Romulans to gain control of these powers—for *any* war-loving race to gain control of them—'' He suddenly shook his head. ''I can discuss this no more, and would prefer to refrain from speaking of him as much as possible. T'Sai is attempting to guard us and the ship from Zakal's telepathic powers. I can do what I can to shield my own thoughts, but it greatly increases our chances of being detected.''

''All right, then, we won't speak of him.'' Keridwen experienced something new: a real sense of the power of esper-blindness, and for the first time in her life, she was honestly glad to be so. ''To make things easier, then, let's change the subject.'' She was glad to do so—the very thought of Zakal's powers, harnessed for evil, was giving her gooseflesh. ''Since I came to Gol to learn more of the religion, and the High Master is currently indisposed, would you be willing to answer a few of my questions—just to pass the time?''

''It is more a philosophy than a religion,'' Spock answered, ''but I will answer your questions, if I am able.''

''Good. Now, this katra business—is everyone's katra preserved?''

''Not everyone's. Normally just the High Master's, or those possessing special knowledge, and then only when the death is foreseen and the preservation can be arranged. It is not always possible.''

''And what happens to those katras that cannot be preserved?''

''They are 'set upon the winds'—which means that they are lost.''

''Then the spirit is destroyed?''

Spock shook his head. ''No. The spirit can never be destroyed, but all the knowledge, everything that makes up a specific personality, is lost forever.''

''So the ability to keep this knowledge gives you the right to trap a spirit for eternity.'' She said it without thinking, and winced when it came out sounding judgmental. But she let the remark stand. She could see that the phrasing disconcerted him a little.

''It is considered an honor,'' he replied with the faintest hint of defensiveness. ''The katra is then able to help the living.''

"And if the katra is not tr . . . excuse me, not preserved, where does it go?"

"It disappears."

"Lost forever?"

He shrugged. "There is some disagreement even among the Kolinahru masters on that point. Some say it is lost forever; some say it is born into a new body, to learn new lessons, to acquire new knowledge."

"Interesting." She rested an elbow on the console's ledge and leaned toward him. "Reincarnation. So many different cultures share that belief, it's considered something of a religious universal. Which do you believe?"

"I have no evidence to lead me to choose one conclusively over the other. But I tend to agree with the former, that it is lost forever. I have no memory of previous lives."

"But of course you wouldn't, according to the argument," she said, trying to sound neutral, "since memory would probably not be retained in such an instance."

He gave her a curious glance. "And which explanation would *you* choose, Dr. Llewellyn?"

The question flustered her a little. "I . . . I'm not sure anymore. I used to believe that we're born again."

He raised a brow. "I must admit I have never understood the aversion so many species seem to have toward death. My opinion is that the theory of reincarnation was created in response to it. But is being alive such an advantage? Is not one life sufficiently full of obstacles to discourage anyone from attempting another?"

That made her smile. "I think that's the whole point, Mr. Spock—to learn from the obstacles. Different lives, different obstacles, different lessons. Frankly, it doesn't do anything to allay *my* fear of death. In fact, just think of all the different times you'd have to go through the experience of death." The smile faded; she shuddered. "Hundreds, perhaps thousands of times; each time, the experience just as frightening, just as unknown as the first time because you'd have no memory of it." She paused and forced her tone to become lighter. "Sorry. I didn't mean to sound so morbid."

He'd been regarding her intently; now he turned back to stare at the viewscreen as he spoke, and Dwen thought, *Whatever he's about to say, he's reluctant to speak about it.* "Dr. Llewellyn," he began somberly, "you have been most preoccupied since reading the tarot cards for me. I surmise that you believe the Death card that appeared in fact heralds my own death. While I do not believe as you do, I would like to point out that even if I knew my death to be approaching, I would not consider it alarming. I do not fear it, as I said before. All must die . . . and even if the cards were correct, it makes no difference to me, or in how I would live my life. Certainly it is nothing you should feel concern—or guilt—over."

She looked away. "It isn't guilt that I feel, Mr. Spock . . . and it wasn't only your death I foresaw."

He turned his head sharply to frown at her. "Do you think the cards may have been referring to Dr. McCoy?" His reaction was quick, but controlled, Vulcan. Yet though he tried to keep his tone disinterested, Dwen heard the concern in it, and was touched. *He cares for Leonard too, in his own way.* She tried to look unwaveringly at him as she answered, and found she could not.

"I believe so," she said, and then, more desperately, "Dear gods, I pray not."

And with fear she recalled the card that touched Death:

The Magician, ill-dignified. . . .

FIFTEEN

☆

The ship was no longer moving.

McCoy woke to that realization and pushed himself to a sitting position on the small bunk. *The gin and tonics,* he told himself at first, and tried to shake off the lingering effects of another odd trance-sleep, blinking until his blurry vision cleared . . . until, with an unpleasant jolt, he recalled that he was the captive of a madman.

"We've stopped," he said aloud thickly, half to himself, half to his captor, in the hopes that Sekar/Zakal (or whatever name he went by at the moment) would respond with the location. Were they on Arcturus already? If so, those were the shortest three hours McCoy had ever spent—in fact, he could remember nothing that had happened after he'd asked Sekar where they were headed.

McCoy struggled to the edge of the bunk and craned his neck to peer at the pilot's chair.

It was empty.

He felt a surge of relief mixed with exultation, but warned himself: *Calm. Calm. Be calm. It's too good to be true. He's probably just in the head or something—*

"Sekar?" he called as he rose unsteadily to his feet. "Zakal?"

No reply. Struggling against hope, McCoy walked to the

back of the ship and knocked hesitantly on the door of the head, then pushed the control.

The door slid open. The head was empty.

"Well, hallelujah!" McCoy crowed with as much energy as he could muster. "I've been abandoned!" His steps were lighter, faster as he moved again to the front of the ship and settled into the padded pilot's chair. He would hook up with the nearest Federation vessel—and in his self-indulgent imagination, he pictured himself saying to Dwen: "About that little premonition of yours, Dwen—well, it was dead wrong!"

The thought made him smile. It took him a minute or two to figure out the subspace radio controls and get the transmitter working. "This is a class-one distress call," he began, but a shrill burst of static made him grimace and cover his offended ears with his hands. It continued agonizingly until McCoy managed to switch it off.

After a pause, he tried again. Same thing.

But McCoy's spirits were not easily daunted; he rose and headed for the hatch. Even if this was Arcturus, there had to be a public comm station nearby. Eagerly, confidently, McCoy strode facefirst into the closed door of the hatch.

It was a painful, undignified experience that left him sprawled on his backside, rubbing his nose. "Dammit," McCoy swore, and pushed himself to his feet again. This time when he approached the hatch, he did so gingerly, with his right hand stretched out. When his fingers touched the seam in the door, it did not open.

He was still a prisoner.

All hope forsaken, the doctor took two and a half steps backward and sagged into the soft, contoured embrace of the copilot's chair. The Vulcan had locked him in the ship—and trying to coax the computer into opening the door, McCoy knew, would be a pointless exercise in frustration. Sekar/Zakal had probably programmed it to respond to his voiceprint or retinal scan—in which case the computer would ignore all others—and gone out in search of a cloaking device. Arcturus, all right—but McCoy had no way of knowing for sure.

And there was no chance of escape. McCoy slumped in the chair, leaning forward until his forehead rested against the padded control panel.

Maybe, the thought began in his head; McCoy immediately tried to quash it, but it resurfaced again: *Maybe this is exactly what Dwen foresaw. Me, cut down in the prime of life by a crazed Vulcan.*

Spock, of course, would have deemed it poetic justice.

The thought made McCoy smile grimly; he thought of Spock and Dwen, and tried to guess what the two of them were doing now. . . . And he honestly, sincerely hoped that, even if Dwen *were* right about his, McCoy's, dying, that she had been wrong about Spock's.

He lay with his head resting against the scout's control panel for what seemed like a very long time . . . and fell asleep.

McCoy woke to find himself still leaning against the control panel, his head resting on his folded arms. What wakened him this time was a sound at the hatch—a strange, sharp hum followed by a loud *bleep,* and then silence.

He perceived all this in less than two seconds, and raised his head—stiffly, because his neck and shoulders ached from maintaining the awkward position—to peer in the direction of the hatch. Just as he did, it opened.

He fully expected to see Zakal (or his alter ego, Sekar) returning with the cloaking device—and therefore, he saw nothing.

Nothing, that is, until he adjusted his vision *downward,* to where the stocky, diminutive figure of the Tellarite stood.

To McCoy's eyes, accustomed as they were to Terran standards of beauty, the Tellarite's short, stubby body and porcine facial features were repugnant, though his thick fur (which covered most of him) was a striking autumnal shade of burnished copper. McCoy stood up, his mouth agape, entirely unable to make any sense out of what he saw.

You're not Zakal, he almost began—but it was a stupid, obvious thing to say, and the years he'd spent around Spock had taught him to avoid saying stupid, obvious things. For a second he and the intruder stared at each other in awed silence.

And then the Tellarite aimed a weapon at him—a type of phaser McCoy had never seen before, four times the size of a standard Fleet-issue phaser and about one-third the size of the Tellarite. The intruder growled in a language the doctor recognized as being *not* Standard. Clearly he meant for McCoy to move away from the control panel.

Under normal conditions, the sight would have inspired real

terror in McCoy; now he grinned hugely at his attacker, scarcely able to believe this turn of good luck.

"You want to steal the scout, don't you?" McCoy asked, his voice rising giddily.

The Tellarite emitted a nasty snarl in response and gestured with the oversize phaser; cheerfully the doctor raised his hands in the universal signal of surrender and moved away from the copilot's chair.

McCoy beamed, a veritable fount of goodwill. "You're more than welcome to it, friend." He took a cautious step backward, toward the hatch. The thief crossed over to the pilot's seat, keeping the phaser trained on McCoy the entire time.

"Believe me," the doctor continued, "you can take it—no shooting necessary. Please, *please,* take it and enjoy it. My pleasure." McCoy bobbed his head and held his hands out in what he hoped was a gesture of generosity as he inched his way toward the exit. He heard a *swoosh* as the hatch opened behind him.

"Thank you," he said, still grinning, to the thief. "Thank you, and bless you."

The Tellarite cocked his head, his squinting deep-set eyes narrowed with suspicion and puzzlement.

McCoy took a final step backward and sank onto damp, marshy ground as the scout's outer hatch closed over him. He half-expected to find himself in Sekar/Zakal's grasp, but he was alone—alone and free in the Arcturan night.

The doctor turned and ran before his accidental benefactor had a chance to change his mind. Fortunately, he could see where he was going, even though it was night: the sky was cloudless and full of moons—three large ones, and all of them full. Which was an altogether good thing, as the ground was thick, slippery mud that came ankle-deep and was littered with garbage. The Vulcan had landed the scout in what appeared to be a huge flat garbage dump/swamp/occasional landing strip. A half-dozen other vehicles dotted the expanse—but the field was otherwise deserted. Several times McCoy encountered refuse—bits of what looked like ship wreckage, and other things too abominable to guess at—all of which he definitely would have tripped over had he not seen it first. At one point he *did* fall—over what seemed to be a human skull.

Arcturus was definitely an interesting place.

McCoy broke into an uncomfortable, sticky sweat—not from

fear, but because the atmosphere was hot and heavy, and so humid that a fine mist hung in the air; around McCoy's head was a loud whine—mosquitoes, no doubt. The doctor had spent his boyhood in Georgia, and was well-acquainted with swamps and the accompanying wildlife. But this marsh was especially noxious, exuding the cloying, dank aroma of swamp mixed with decay and sewage; McCoy realized, with a grimace of disgust, that the field was probably used as a latrine by those who landed in the strip and who, returning intoxicated from the bars, could not trouble themselves to make it back to their ships.

He slowed just enough to shoot a quick glance behind him; oddly enough, Dwen's scout was still there. He'd figured that the little Tellarite would have taken off and been in warp drive by now—but this was no time to get curious. With a flash of guilt, he hoped like hell that Dwen had good insurance.

In front of him, at least a good half-kilometer away, shone the bright glow of a city. Arcturus or not, a public comm station couldn't be far away. He'd get himself to a pub comm, flag down the nearest Federation vessel, and see Dwen and Spock again.

McCoy's giddiness at his newfound freedom was tempered by a growing sense of apprehension as he approached the city. Like most of his shipmates, he'd never visited Arcturus; like most of his shipmates, he'd heard enough hair-curling tales about the place to know its dangers. For, as the time-worn saying goes, Arcturus is the place where everyone goes to make deals. There is good reason for this. Nestled cozily in the center of a major pirate corridor, Arcturus had stubbornly resisted all overtures from the Romulans, the Klingons, and even (a halfhearted one) the Federation. In the known galaxy, the planet was infamous for being a rarity, an anomaly: a bona fide anarchy.

There was no Arcturan government; therefore, there was no bureaucracy, and no red tape. There were no laws, and certainly no such thing as extradition of escaped criminals, which made Arcturus a very popular place with the unjustly and justly accused . . . and bounty hunters. If any part of the planet could have been said to be ruled to any degree, by anyone, it was a fleeting phenomenon related to who had the deadliest weapon at any given moment. The most apt credos for the planet were: *Every [your species here] for him/her/itself* and *[Your species here] eat [your/their species here]*. Or so McCoy had heard.

Technically within the bounds of Federation territory, Arcturus was usually given wide berth by both Starfleet proper and the Border Patrol; and the planet was close enough to the fringes of both Romulan and Klingon space to allow for free exchange among the three great empires. While it could honestly be said that Arcturus was the one place in the galaxy where Klingon, Romulan, and human were free to meet and ignore the hostilities between the governments (not to mention enjoying the more lucrative aspects of illegal trade between their empires), and the natives all spoke your language (despite the total lack of public education, every Arcturan was nevertheless versed in several languages—although they insisted on overlaying their own grammar on whatever language they happened to be speaking), the reality was hardly a utopian dream. The doctor had heard much of the swift and bloody fights that erupted in the bars, and knew the natives were unprejudiced as to the outcome: they regarded their human, Klingon, and Romulan visitors with equal contempt.

It was into this unhealthy milieu that McCoy stumbled. After some time, he made his way through the treacherous mud, steering clear of one obviously intoxicated group of Klingons who staggered three abreast and paused occasionally to throw back their heads and roar at the moons.

At last the doctor's feet made contact with something firmer: the rough, uneven surface of an unpaved pedestrian road. McCoy lifted his boots out of the mire—it let go with a loud slurping sound—and onto the street; the ankles of his pants were wet and heavy with the evil-smelling sludge.

In front of him stood the city, a collection of sleek and shining edifices that contrasted shockingly with the squalor outside. Indeed, the dirt street in which McCoy stood was littered with refuse and debris—some of it heaped high in fly-covered piles. As he neared the city, the smell began to change from that of sewage and swamp to rotting garbage mixed with something unnatural and offensive that the doctor did not recognize: industrial pollution. He paused for a second to take in the spectacle: the city actually glowed—not from streetlamps (there weren't any), but from the fact that each building was veiled by its own force field. As McCoy drew even closer, he saw that in front of the nearest glowing building stood two armed and surly guards—one human, dark-skinned, and grizzled, his face shining with sweat, the other possibly Arcturan, his translucent chalk-white skin covering his formidable bulk. Both were dressed in vests and breeches made of tanned animal hide.

McCoy approached them with what he hoped was an ingra-
tiating smile. "Excuse me, sirs . . ." He'd never been on Arcturus
before, but he'd heard that all the natives spoke Standard. He
addressed himself to the human. "My name is Dr. Leonard
McCoy, and I desperately need—"

The human stared at him with opaque black eyes; if he
understood, he gave no sign. The hulking Arcturan curled his
pale upper lip, revealing toothless black gums, and snarled at
McCoy with all the conviction of a trained guard Doberman.

Disconcerted, McCoy backed off, but kept trying. "—to get
to a public comm. I was kidnapped, you see, and I—"

As he spoke, the human raised his phaser and casually
picked out a spot in the middle of McCoy's forehead.

The doctor gulped audibly, raised his hands, and backed
away as fast as he could without startling anyone. The guard
lowered the phaser and cackled derisively as McCoy darted back
into the dark street.

Frustrated, the doctor stood for a moment contemplating his
alternatives; there seemed to be none, since every building he
could see before him was secured by a force field and two guards
out front. Maybe, McCoy told himself, Standard was simply the
wrong language to use here. He found himself remembering the
old cliché about Arcturans: they speak a lot of languages, but the
only one they really understand is money. Of course, offering a
bribe was going to be a trick, because he didn't have his ID on
him, and it was going to be tough if not impossible to promise
someone credits without it.

With little real hope of success, the doctor prepared to
approach the same two guards, when he heard the sound of
feminine laughter several meters to his left. He turned toward it
and caught a whiff of something reminiscent of patchouli—only
stronger, and more offensive—and saw, draped in shadow, three
tall figures. One of them stepped closer, into the city's glow.

She was, at least to McCoy's best guess, female, though she
stood a millimeter or two taller than he, and she was broad of
shoulder, hip, and face. Like all Arcturans (that is, all the *holos*
of Arcturans McCoy had ever seen—this was his first encounter
with a live one), she was humanoid, and the ghost-pale skin of
her forehead was heavily creased with folds of excess skin,
reminding McCoy of a certain Asian breed of dog. Her earlobes
were pendulous, full of more holes than a sieve, and heavily laden
with dozens of earrings and sparkling beads. She was quite bald

save for the crown of her head, on which sat a shock of platinum
hair and an exotic ornament made of iridescent peacock feathers,
and she was provocatively clad in a low-cut garment—too short
to be honestly termed a dress, too long to be called a vest—of
patchwork fur and bright metallic spangles. On her feet were
shin-high matching boots, the high heels of which were sharp and
pointed enough to be dangerous.

At the sight of McCoy, her thick lips stretched in a smile (or
grimace, depending on one's cultural point of view).

"You here are new?" she purred in pidgin Standard. Her
voice was low and pleasing, despite her garish appearance. Mc-
Coy did his best not to react to the fact that her two front teeth
were missing. Behind her, her companions giggled and made
inviting noises.

"Yes, yes," McCoy answered eagerly, though he recognized
the question as a variation on a very ancient pickup line. He
almost, in his desperation, asked her how to contact the *local*
authorities, until he remembered where he believed himself to
be. "Is this Arcturus?"

"This is." She turned back to smile at her tittering companions, as if to say, *Can you believe this one's stupidity?*

"I need very badly to get to a public comm station. I've got
to get in touch with Federation authorities—"

The Arcturan threw back her head and laughed; the earrings
clinked, the feather sprays fluttered languidly in the humid
breeze. Her friends, their faces still hidden by darkness, echoed
her laughter. "Public comm!" sneered one; "Federation authorities!" howled the other.

The Arcturan stopped laughing and grinned at him. "On
Arcturus, you will find pub comms not. *Private* comms, yes.
Money much more."

McCoy glanced out of the corner of his eye at the two males
guarding the building; this female was definitely his best bet.
"The money doesn't matter. If you can just get me to a comm,
any comm, as long as it works, I'll pay you—anything you want.
Name your price."

She lowered her eyelids and studied him coyly; the furrows
in her brow deepened. "Money you have *now?*"

"No," he admitted, disheartened at the thought that his ID
was at the moment very far away, baking in an empty cell in the
Vulcan desert, "but if I can just get to a comm, I could get some
for you. See, I can call my bank and they can verify my voice-

prints—and retinal scan, if the comm has one—and I could get right into my account—"

"Interested *not* I," she sniffed, and began to turn away.

"Honestly, I'll pay you a hundred credits—"

She and her friends were heading back for the shadows.

"*Two* hundred," McCoy begged, following.

She stopped with her back to him. "Three hundred and fifty."

"Three *hundred* and—" McCoy began, outraged, but desperation quickly brought him to his senses. He stopped his tirade before it began and sighed. "All right—I promise, I'll get you three hundred and fifty credits out of my account."

She turned and twined her thick muscular arm around his. The pseudo-patchouli smell became nauseating. "Done. Three-fifty." She gave him another gap-toothed grin, apparently meant to be inviting, but it failed to have the intended effect on McCoy. He responded with a sickly little smile.

She gestured skyward with her white chin, up at the moons racing through the mist. "Night of three moons full. Every six years, one time only. Three full mean very strange, very wonderful things tonight." And she looked meaningfully at him.

"I can hardly wait," McCoy said.

She took him back to the entrance of the first building, where the human and Arcturan guards stood. She was clearly known to them: the Arcturan nodded at her, then glowered distrustfully at McCoy; the human winked and leered familiarly at her. He, too, was missing a front tooth; McCoy began to wonder if it was more a matter of fashion than a result of the violent local life-style.

"Picked up another stray, have you, Ziza?" the human asked good-naturedly. So, he understood Standard perfectly after all. "That one's too small. I'd throw him back if I were you." He and his partner stepped aside to let her and the doctor by.

"He's rich enough," Ziza retorted airily, her earrings and the spangles in her vest jingling as she swept past them. McCoy repressed a shudder at the sudden calculating light in the guards' eyes as they registered this new information.

The building's entrance was now visible, though still barred by the force field; in front of it stood a detached retinal-scanner unit. *Then why the guards?* McCoy wondered, but scarcely had he finished the thought before he recognized its stupidity. If the Tellarite had so easily broken the lock on Dwen's shuttle (and

Lord, she was going to kill him and make her own prophecy come true when she found out McCoy had so happily abandoned it to the Tellarite's care), then how much more easily might someone break into a building—or, at the very least, jam the sensitive scanner?

Ziza leaned over the scanner; for a few milliseconds her pale face was lit up by the scanner's glow. Seconds after that, the green glow around the entrance dissolved. Ziza grasped McCoy's upper arm with a strength that was painful, and propelled him toward the entrance.

The massive door—adorned with ornate and vaguely lewd bacchanalian scenes that looked like something carved by a drunken Hieronymus Bosch—rumbled and parted. McCoy and Ziza stepped inside; or rather, Ziza stepped inside, and gave McCoy a firm push.

McCoy caught his breath, stunned by the smells, the sights, the sounds. The room was dark, darker than it had been outside, and at first he thought the building was on fire; the air was thick with smoke that stung his eyes. Added to Ziza's overwhelming perfume and the none-too-sweet aroma drifting up from his ankles was the smell of something burning, and for some odd reason, familiar. . . .

Tobacco cigarettes, just like the one Dwen had been smoking (how long ago? days?) in her cell, though there were some exotic undertones to the odor, making McCoy think there were probably other illegal substances contributing to it.

He coughed, on the verge of gagging at the interplay of smells. Next to him, Ziza giggled, spangles tinkling in concert with her laughter.

"You soon will use to it," she said, and pointed with a long silver nail at something directly ahead. "There. The bar."

McCoy squinted. Through the haze and the darkness he could see that the room was crowded with more species of beings than a Federation Council meeting. There were humans, Tellarites, Cygnusians, a Klingon, and a Horta getting chummy with a group of Andorians . . . even a stray pair of Romulans, neither of whom, fortunately, bore any resemblance to the demented Zakal. Most were in tight clutches, seated at tables, heads (or what passed for them) together, talking earnestly.

The noise, like the smells, was similarly overwhelming—it was a veritable Tower of Babel, through which was pumped slick,

incongruously sanitized Muzak, slightly too loud, so that everyone had to shout to be heard.

"What? Where?" McCoy asked, unable to tell what Ziza
was trying to indicate in the moving sea of sentient creatures.

"Bar."

McCoy blinked and wiped tears from the corners of his
burning eyes. So there was—a long, old-fashioned wood bar
hidden for the most part by the large number of warm- and cold-
blooded bodies propped against it. Behind it, pouring from an
unlabeled bottle into the Tom Collins glass gripped in his clawed,
stub-fingered hand, was a seven-foot-tall Gorn, his bright green
scales flashing iridescent mauve each time he moved. His thick,
powerful physique was partially covered by a leather-and-fur
tunic that McCoy had decided was the native Arcturan costume.

"Bartender," Ziza told him, and gave his backside an encouraging little pat. "Ask him."

The doctor stared for a moment at the huge reptile's slow,
lumbering movements, at the sharp claws and teeth as potentially
deadly as a phaser, and meditated on the animosity between his
own species and the Gorn's . . . and the fact that he was not yet
completely out from under the shadow of Keridwen's prediction.

"Go." Ziza nudged him.

McCoy swallowed and gathered his determination. He had
to get to a pub comm; after all, the longer he stayed on Arcturus,
the greater the chance of running into Zakal—who by now had
probably discovered the theft of the scout, and would not be in a
particularly gracious mood. The doctor took a step forward into
the crowd, murmuring his apologies.

There was a sudden commotion at the table where the
Klingon and the Horta were sitting with the Andorians. The
Klingon, who previously had seemed intoxicated by the idea of
interstellar friendship, not to mention his drug of choice, rose
abruptly, overturning his chair. The room quieted—save, of
course, for the obscenely cheerful Muzak—as he drew out a
phaser and pointed it at one of the giggling Andorians.

Just as swiftly, the amorphous Horta (whom the Klingon had
mistakenly trusted) produced a phaser from deep within himself,
and by rather clumsily manipulating it with the edge of his stony
bulk, produced a blinding burst of red light.

The Klingon's midsection erupted in a blaze; he looked down
in great surprise and annoyance to view his own demise as
tongues of flame ate their way from the center out, leaving in

their wake a hole through which McCoy could see the other side of the room. The flames raced to the outer edges of the Klingon's form, leaving nothing but his head; as they danced up his neck, he opened his mouth and, more from anger than pain or fear, let loose a bloodcurdling roar that reverberated long after he was gone.

All this took approximately one second; afterward, the Andorians and some of the humans in the crowd applauded. Conversation resumed, and the incident was forgotten by the time an Arcturan child dashed out with a hand-held vacuum to sweep up the dulling embers—the last remnants of the Klingon's temporal existence—from the floor, then disappeared again.

His fears thus reinforced, McCoy continued toward his goal. He struggled through the cluster of tables pushed together with no allowance for passage, then took on the challenge of elbowing his way to the bar proper—no small feat, since the way was packed at least four deep. The doctor soon learned that the Standard phrase "excuse me" had no meaning whatsoever on Arcturus. At least, not to the Tellarite standing at the outermost fringes of the bar. After shouting the phrase until he was hoarse (which didn't take long in the smoke and the stale, unfiltered air), McCoy gave up, ducked his head, and dug in with both elbows.

It took some time before he saw light and finally leaned against the wood bar—which was filthy and slightly sticky to the touch—next to a tall, gawky Aurelian, his delicate wings folded tightly against his back and shoulders so as to avoid accidentally hitting someone on either side of him, and thus instigating an incident similar to the one with the Klingon. The wings were huge, featherless, covered with a membrane so delicate that a network of fine green veins could be seen beneath. The Aurelian glanced at McCoy with casual irritation, then took a long drag off the cigarette held to his beak by thin, long fingers—and blew a thick cloud of smoke in McCoy's face.

The doctor choked on it, but otherwise ignored it; he had seen the belt slung low on the Aurelian's bony hips and decorated with no fewer than three phasers and a monstrous Klingon dagger. McCoy craned his neck to look for the bartender, who was holding out his claw for payment from an unseen patron at the far end of the bar. McCoy raised an arm. "Bartender—"

The sound was swallowed up in the noise. McCoy tried waving, but if the reptilian noticed out of the corner of his huge protruding eyes, he gave no sign. After collecting from the customer (and the tip must have been small or nonexistent, for the Gorn emitted a threatening hiss after counting the paper and solids in his hand), the bartender plodded his way back over to McCoy, put his gigantic hands on the bar's filmy surface, and leaned forward. He stood so close that the doctor could feel and hear his hot, rattling breath, and stared expectantly at McCoy with round amber eyes—*bug eyes,* McCoy would have called them if he'd been feeling particularly suicidal—that had vertical black slits for pupils, like a cat. The Gorn made no attempt at speech—McCoy decided he was incapable of it—but his posture was quite communicative.

What'll it be?

"I don't want a drink," McCoy half-shouted over the din. "I'm looking for a pub . . . er, a comm station. I understand you know where one is."

The Gorn drew back his head and hissed, spraying McCoy with warm viscous spittle that had a foul, slightly fermented smell to it. The doctor's instinct was to recoil, but he forced himself to hold still and appear unimpressed. "I'll pay you well," McCoy said.

The Gorn drew a little closer—interested, McCoy decided, though he could no more read the creature's expression than he could a gila monster's—and held out his hand to reveal a thickly padded soft white palm.

McCoy felt a twinge of digestive discomfort. "I don't actually *have* the credits on me. I, uh, need to access my account from the comm—"

The Gorn roared and reached out with a clawed hand; the doctor turned and was seriously contemplating flight, except that something soft and pale and furry barred his way.

Ziza smiled. "Rrk," she said sweetly to the furious bartender. At least, that's what it sounded like to McCoy: like someone trying to trill a French R and choking on it, or a cat coughing up a furball. "It's okay, Rrk. This one is with I. He not pay, then I pay." And she fluttered her curled white lashes at the Gorn.

Rrk growled softly, as if reluctant to give this puny outworlder any help—but then he went to a small nearby opening in the bar, squeezed his bulk through, and motioned for McCoy and Ziza to follow. As slow-moving as Rrk was, it was almost impossible for McCoy to keep up with him; for though the crowd parted immediately to let the ominous-looking Gorn through, it closed just as quickly behind him, so that Ziza and McCoy had to fight their way through.

Rrk headed away from the bar and the crowd, toward a deserted alcove. Against one wall, glowing pale green under the protection of its own mini-force-field, was an interstellar comm station. Whoever owned the force-field concession on Arcturus, McCoy reflected, was a very wealthy individual.

Rrk produced a small black damping device hidden within the leather-and-fur vest and aimed it at the comm station. The field disappeared with a barely audible high-pitched pop. The Gorn turned to Ziza and said in a voice that was something between a hiss and a growl: "Three minutes, five hundred credits."

"Five *hundred*—" McCoy began, wondering whether his bank account would survive his little visit to Arcturus, but the Gorn silenced him with a look.

"If you fail to pay me or you damage the equipment," Rrk rumbled, "I'll take it out of both your hides. Understood?"

"Understood," Ziza said gravely. McCoy nodded with enthusiasm.

Rrk grunted and lumbered off.

"Why do I get the feeling," McCoy muttered, studying the Gorn's thick black claws that tapered to lethally sharp points, "that he was *not* speaking figuratively?"

"He wasn't." Ziza, amused by it all, reached out to give the doctor a push in the direction of the comm. "Call."

McCoy went over to the wall and leaned over the retinal scanner. Upon sensing a customer, the scanner came on and silently drew a white beam of light over McCoy's right eye. After a pause of several seconds, which seemed like forever to McCoy—though he realized they were very far from home—the terminal screen lit up with the words:

McCoy, Leonard E., M.D.
Identity verified
Credit access available
Please enter your secret code number

"Macoy," Ziza cooed behind him. "Handsome name for handsome man."

McCoy repressed a shudder and, keeping his eyes on the screen, punched in his personal calling code. Lord, he wasn't looking forward to *this* month's bill. It took him a full minute of waiting to get the interstellar operator on audio—during which time he panicked and swore, while Ziza stroked his arm and assured him that such delay was normal—who seemed to find it hysterically funny that someone on Arcturus would want to try to flag down a Federation vessel.

"Contact with Federation vessel impossible," the operator giggled in his nasal, high-pitched voice. "You here are new, yes?"

"I here am new," McCoy snapped, "and I've just about had it with this barbaric, backwater inefficiency! I've already wasted over a minute of valuable time. What in God's name do I have to do to get in touch with Starfleet or the Federation?"

"Earth you could call," the operator suggested.

Over the hysterical laughter that followed, McCoy shouted, "Fine, dammit! Then get me Earth. Get me . . . get me Starfleet Headquarters in San Francisco. Admiral James T. Kirk."

There was a pause, and then the operator spoke, his tone serious but sly. "How much?"

"What do you mean, how much?" McCoy said. "This is a *comm* station—you're an operator. This is being billed to my personal account."

"Connection with Earth *very* difficult. Using regular equipment, probably impossible. Special effort necessary."

McCoy lost his temper. "Special effort my—"

The channel crackled and seemed on the verge of closing.

The doctor recalled his desperate situation. "Wait a minute—"

"I listening."

"All right, you've got me over a barrel. How much do you want?"

"Earth very far. Two hundred credits."

"One hundred."

The signal began breaking up again.

"All right, damn you, two hundred credits." McCoy rubbed his forehead at the onset of a headache caused by the very idea. "You've got my account number."

"Visual signal without delay, fifty credits extra."

"Fine, fine—what's fifty extra credits between friends? Make it two hundred fifty, then. But I don't have any more time to bicker, all right? I've got to get through to Earth right away."

"Thirty seconds," the Arcturan said, "especially for visual." And then there was nothing but static.

"If it takes another thirty seconds, I don't want it," McCoy said to the quivering gray nothingness that illuminated the terminal screen; but there was nothing he could do now but hold his breath and worry about how much of his three-minute time limit had elapsed. Let's see: there was a minute waiting for the operator, then the past forty-five or so seconds that they argued, and then, if a no-delay visual took another thirty seconds, all he had left for trying to get hold of Jim and explaining his situation, not to mention arranging the rescue, was a mere forty-five seconds. Would it be enough?

Ziza laid a warm, beefy hand on McCoy's shoulder and stroked the length of his arm, all the way to his wrist. "Relax, Macoy. I like you. Maybe money no problem."

But the simper on her face and the manner in which she touched him made McCoy even more nervous. Glancing quickly at her, then back at the comm screen, he asked tersely, "Where are we, Ziza?"

Clinking earrings, laughter. "I said already. Arcturus, silly."

"No, I mean the name of this city."

"Arcturus again."

"Do you mean to say that everywhere on this planet is called Arcturus, or do you mean that just this particular city—"

An image—blurred and choppy—coalesced on the screen in front of him, a sight so beautiful, bringing such relief, that tears formed in McCoy's burning eyes. It was the image of a very young Vulcan female from the shoulders up. She wore a red Starfleet uniform and balanced a subspace earpiece in her delicately pointed left ear. She touched her fingers to it briefly.

"Starfleet Headquarters."

Salvation. Civilization. Yet at the same time, McCoy was irritated. Here he was paying two hundred and fifty credits to talk to Jim directly, but the Arcturan hadn't bothered to link him up with the admiral's office. McCoy wasted no time.

"This is an emergency. I need to get in touch with Admiral James T. Kirk *immediately*—"

In spite of the Arcturan operator's promise, there was still a slight delay on the channel; for a few seconds the Vulcan's image froze on the screen, and McCoy began to repeat his request before he realized what was happening. As he spoke, she interrupted with, "One moment, please."

It actually took far less than one moment. The screen flashed and went gray again as Kirk's office was signaled. McCoy noticed that his hands hurt; he looked down and saw he was gripping the edges of the comm panel tightly. The seconds were ticking away. By the time he got Jim, he'd have fewer than—

A new image came on the screen—and with deep regret, McCoy noted it was not Jim Kirk's, but that of a younger, bearded man.

"Admiral Kirk's office. Commander Kevin Riley here."

Though agitated, McCoy smiled in recognition. "Riley! Riley, this is Dr. Leonard McCoy. I'm in some pretty serious trouble and I desperately need to get in touch with Jim."

Another delay, and then the young man's face relaxed in a wide grin. "Dr. McCoy! It's been a long time. How are you?"

"There's no time for that, Riley. Listen, I need to talk to Jim *right away*. Every second counts. Is he there?"

Riley's image froze on the screen as another maddening pause made McCoy want to scream. And then Riley came to life again. "No, I'm terribly sorry, Doctor. The admiral's off-planet on a mission, and it would take some time to get in touch with him. Is there anything I can do to help?"

McCoy's throat constricted at the news that Jim was gone, but he calmed himself and said, "Yes. Riley, this is going to sound crazy, but . . . I've been kidnapped by a Vulcan. He's certifiable. And he's been in touch with the Romulans—I think he's trying to smuggle them some sort of secret 'power,' some sort of weapon, maybe. I just managed to escape and I'm calling from Arcturus, from the city I think they call Arcturus too. Anyway, I wanted to be hooked up with a Federation vessel, but they won't do it for me—"

As he spoke, Ziza started stroking his arm affectionately again, and whispered something in his ear McCoy didn't register, then giggled loudly. McCoy tried to push her away; it wasn't helping his story sound any saner.

"A *Vulcan?*" Riley interrupted, his expression one of disbelief. He'd evidently said it right after McCoy had said he'd been kidnapped by one, but because of the time delay, McCoy didn't hear the interruption until just now.

"You heard right," the doctor said. "A Vulcan, but he's space-happy. Look, Riley, I'm *not* drunk and I'm not having a psychotic interlude. I need your help before this Vulcan finds me. Could you try to get someone to route a ship this way?''

Riley's face had frozen into an expression of skepticism, as if he suspected the doctor of a practical joke. But he said finally, ''I'll see what I can do, Doctor.''

''Look, Riley, I'm not kidding. This Vulcan is dangerous. I honestly think he might hurt some—''

Ziza grabbed his wrist painfully hard. He turned on her, furious. ''Dammit, can't you see I'm—''

But the words to complete whatever he was going to say flew out of McCoy's head forever. For it was not Ziza who gripped him tightly; the doctor turned and found himself staring into the dark, slightly insane eyes of the grinning Vulcan Zakal.

SIXTEEN

———————— ☆ ————————

"Help, Riley!" McCoy yelped as Zakal pulled him away from the screen, nearly dislocating the doctor's arm from its socket.

Ziza reached out to block Zakal with pale, thick arms. "Leave he alone! He belongs to I!" She drew a knife with a long, evil-looking blade from a sheath hidden in her vest and threatened the Vulcan with it.

Zakal turned to frown at her with mild irritation, as one might regard a pesky insect. A look, nothing more.

Ziza dropped the knife, fell to her knees, and screamed.

"Doctor? Are you all right?" Riley asked behind them, on the comm screen.

Ziza rolled on the floor in agony, clutching her midsection.

"Stop hurting her!" McCoy cried, though he could not understand exactly *how* the Vulcan was doing so. "It's me you want! Let her go!"

A thunderous roar reverberated at the entrance to the dark alcove; McCoy looked over Zakal's shoulder and, with a mixture of awe and an emotion very much approaching relief, saw the Gorn.

Rrk's amber eyes caught the dim light and seemed to glow with fury; in a flash of insight, McCoy understood that the Gorn had feelings for Ziza, which explained the ease with which she talked him into letting the doctor use the comm. Rrk emitted a low, dangerous rumble and headed with surprising speed directly toward Zakal . . . and McCoy.

"Wait a minute!" The doctor raised his hands in a gesture of innocence. "I didn't hurt her! *He* did it!"

Ziza was still writhing on the floor; she looked up at the three of them and moaned.

The Gorn was not particularly interested in assignation of blame. McCoy cringed and covered his head as Rrk wielded his long, deadly claws and leapt at the human and the Vulcan.

Fearlessly Zakal fixed his eyes on Rrk and took a step toward him.

The Gorn froze in mid-leap. The sound of his high-pitched squeal raised gooseflesh on McCoy's arms.

"Dr. McCoy!" Riley shouted behind them, and then the three minutes were up and the channel went dead. An operator with a Terran accent came on audio. "Thank you for using TSSR. Your account has been charged two thousand, eight hundred and forty-three credits. If you wish to make another call, please reenter your code."

An impossible thing began to happen as Rrk and the Vulcan stared at each other, transfixed: the Gorn began to melt.

It was as if his skin became liquid; it sloughed off him in languorous waves, leaving behind reddish-brown muscle and bone, and collected on the floor around his feet in brilliant green puddles flecked with mauve. The slick and glistening internal organs in his abdominal cavity were exposed; some still pulsed and quivered. Rrk emitted a horrified, horrifying death wail and sagged into a great heap.

McCoy was too sickened, too stunned to think, to move, almost even to breathe. He couldn't look at the poor Gorn for more than a split second, but Zakal he stared at for a long, long time. The Vulcan was smiling with childlike enjoyment. Nearby, on the floor, Ziza seemed to recover and began to weep softly.

There were only two possible explanations, McCoy told himself as he allowed Zakal to lead him through the suddenly hushed bar. The first was that he, McCoy, had gone certifiably insane . . .

. . . and the other—that he had not—was far too horrible to contemplate.

Geoffrey Olmsted, Federation specialist in xenoterrorism and leader of the most feared assault team in the galaxy, looked to be anything but. He was middle-aged, small, soft, and pear-shaped, with a slight waddle to his walk. Minutes after arriving in Ciana's well-protected quarters at the Inari Council building, Olmsted complained of feeling chilled and drew out an old-fashioned beige cardigan sweater from the black satchel he carried with him (and which, Kirk had assumed, was stuffed full of secret documents and weapons). Give the man a pipe, and he would fit the stereotype of college professor beautifully—although in the course of the briefing, it became clear that Olmsted's political views were nowhere near as liberal as a professor's. Obviously brilliant, he was nevertheless a right-wing extremist who saw anti-Federationists and Romulans hiding behind every bush and tree. At first Kirk, who prided himself on his moderate views, was annoyed; but then he came to see that Olmsted's beliefs were a practical necessity for someone in his field, born of many kill-or-be-killed situations.

Still, it was hard to look at this plump, balding little man with the benevolent round face and believe that he was a highly efficient killer who trained others to be the same.

"My contacts have set up a face-to-face between your group and a Djanai representative. Their leader, in fact—name of Kel," Olmsted said. He was sitting on the too-low settee next to Ciana and across from Kirk, tapping the end of a stylus against the writing tablet in his lap and somehow managing to look quite comfortable in the undersize Inari furniture.

"Why a face-to-face?" Ciana asked, and leaned forward, hands resting just above her knees. "Isn't that unnecessarily risky—for both groups?"

Olmsted tapped his stylus and sighed, not with irritation at the naiveté of Ciana's question, but at the absurdity of the situation. "In a different place and time, I'd say yes. But the Inari talent for technology is unsurpassed—and they have a protective force field which absolutely cannot be damped. You'll be perfectly safe. I assume that's why the Djanai asked for this meeting—because they're using the same protection. But to answer your first question: the Djanai *asked* for a face-to-face—and to refuse would be very bad form, especially since we don't anticipate any tricks. You see, the Djanai are extremely religious—which makes them very difficult to deal with—and apparently they believe the only way they can bargain is in person. Their religion scorns technology; like our Amish, they believe their god wants them to keep it simple. One of the reasons we're in this mess is that, a century ago, in its haste to help out the Inari, the Federation ignored the less technologically advanced group, the Djanai. Since the Djanai were none too communicative, and refused to talk to our field ethnographers, we know very little about them. They mistrusted us because of our technology—same reason they refuse to mix with the Inari. They feel that the Federation was the source of the problem.''

"Who's their god?'' Jim asked, shifting in his chair, which was so low he couldn't even cross his legs.

Olmsted's small eyes brightened. "It's rather interesting: Djana, the spirit of the planet itself. These people are farmers, so the land and certain animals are sacred. You can imagine how they felt about the Inari coming in and taking over the land.''

"But the Inari didn't just take over the land,'' Ciana objected. "When the Federation relocated them on Djana, it resettled them in uninhabited areas.''

"What it *perceived* to be uninhabited,'' Olmsted corrected her, folding his short arms and resting them on a soft shelf of cashmere-covered stomach. "The Djanai are used to living on large expanses of land—and setting aside sacred places used exclusively for worship. Unfortunately, the Inari settled on some of the sacred lands. Their version of the same religion had changed radically in the centuries spent on Inar; they perceived the Djanai use of the land as near-criminal waste, and promptly began developing it.

"As a result, the Djanai now feel hemmed in as, over the years, the Inari have encroached on the sacred lands. The fact that the Djanai have resorted to the use of technology and are communicating with the Federation directly indicates that they've been pushed to final extremes. So''—he unfolded his arms just enough to point the stylus at Kirk—"that's what you have to bear in mind when you talk to them. They're liable to be very rigid in their demands, which boil down to: Get the Inari *out,* or else.''

"I think the important thing is to try to win their trust at this first meeting,'' Kirk said.

"Absolutely.'' Ciana nodded; consciously or unconsciously, she was mimicking Olmsted's posture—arms folded at midsection, though she lacked the padding on which to rest them. "That's our objective—to simply convey to them that we feel we've made a mistake, we're willing to correct it, and we ask them to consider sitting down with our people and the Inari to work out an amicable solution. All provided, of course, that they promise to arrange the safe return of our hostages.''

Olmsted's blue eyes narrowed in disapproval. ''As far as the consideration of negotiation goes, I'd play up the notion of consensus, if I were you. Ask them to go back to their people and get a consensus on sitting down to negotiate. Remember, their leaders don't quite have the power ours do. It's a different setup. Kel is more of a spokesman, but it would be wise to bear in mind that he's going to have to get a consensus on every single issue before he can agree or disagree with you. Pretty much the same thing is done in the Inari Council—though the delegates wield somewhat more power.

''And a second thing: I'd avoid mentioning the Inari at all in that first meeting, because the Djanai won't react at all nicely to the thought of sitting down with them. In fact, they're likely to cut off all communications with you at the mere mention—''

He broke off as the comm terminal signaled. Ciana rose gracefully, without using her hands to push herself up out of the low divan, and stepped across the room to stoop in front of the terminal. It was a closed channel, which meant either HQ or the Inari Council was trying to get in touch with them.

''Ciana here,'' she said, and then frowned, puzzled. Jim couldn't see the screen, but he could hear the voice—a very familiar one. ''Hold on a second,'' Ciana responded, and turned her head to give Jim a curious glance. ''Your chief of staff wants to talk to you.''

Jim stood up. ''Excuse me,'' he said to Olmsted, who nodded pleasantly. He walked over to the terminal, set at Inari eye level, so that he had to scrunch his neck down to see the screen.

As Ciana passed by him, she muttered almost inaudibly, ''This had better be good.'' She was referring to the fact that this particular channel was reserved for Nogura and the Council, and anyone else who happened to use it had better have a damn good reason.

Riley's anxious face peered out from the screen at Kirk.

''What is it, Riley? Crisis at the office?''

He'd said it half-jokingly, but Riley did not smile. ''Not exactly, sir. But I have some rather upsetting news that I thought you would want to know about.''

Someone's died, Jim thought, looking at the bewilderment

on Riley's face; and in that split second, he had time to hope desperately that it was not his mother, Winona.

"It's about Dr. McCoy."

A strange numbness descended on Jim. *My God, Bones is dead.* "What's happened?"

"He's been kidnapped," Riley said, and the answer was so contrary to what Jim expected that he could not make sense of it. "He escaped for a little while on Arcturus—"

"Arc*tu*rus!"

"—and called here looking for help. I called Nogura right away, Admiral, since Dr. McCoy's a civilian now, and it would take Nogura's approval to send a Federation vessel there to rescue him—but I'm afraid that as I was talking to the doctor, his kidnapper found him—"

"Who the hell would want to kidnap McCoy?"

"A Vulcan, sir."

Kirk's eyebrows shot up. "Riley, if this is your idea of a bad joke, it's coming at the *wrong* time. This is a closed channel—"

"Honestly, sir, that was my reaction too—at first, I thought Dr. McCoy was drunk or something, but then I saw the Vulcan come up behind him, and then he hurt the woman. Or at least I'm pretty sure he did, because I heard screaming and—"

Kirk put his hands up. "Riley. Riley, slow down, this isn't making any sense."

Riley took a deep breath. "I'm sorry, Admiral. But I'm afraid that no matter how many times I repeat it, it's *still* not going to make any sense."

"Let's start from the beginning, shall we?"

"All right. I was fielding your calls this morning—the new yeoman won't start till next week—and Dr. McCoy called looking for you. It was a very bad signal, and the HQ operator confirmed that it was coming from Arcturus. Anyway, McCoy seemed very upset—like I said, at first I thought it was some sort of joke, but as McCoy was talking to me and asking for help, the Vulcan—"

"The one he says kidnapped him?" Kirk interrupted.

"Yes, sir, that one. The Vulcan . . . Sir, I'm not sure how to explain, but he looked . . . berserk. Dangerous. And he was violent. Dr. McCoy was with a woman—"

Kirk immediately thought of Keridwen Llewellyn.

"—and the Vulcan starting hurting her. I couldn't see how, but it was quite evident that he did. She fell down and started screaming, and Dr. McCoy started yelling at the Vulcan to stop, that he would go with him, just leave the woman alone. And then the channel was closed.''

Kirk stared for a moment at Riley, studying the young commander's expression. Riley clearly was dead earnest . . . and, hopefully, had too much sense to interrupt Kirk and Ciana during a critical mission with a feeble attempt at a practical joke. Yet it all sounded far too absurd for Kirk's mind to accept the idea. It took him a full minute to come up with a rational response.

"So what happened with McCoy? Is Nogura going to help him?"

"Ah . . . no, sir. Nogura contacted the Vulcans. They actually know about it. They verified McCoy's story, but said they would take care of it. They have a rescue mission under way, led by Mr. Spock.''

"Spock," Kirk repeated weakly. He'd been standing over the terminal, hunched over, hands resting on the desk; now he sank into the child-size chair. "Leading a rescue mission. But he's a civilian now. Riley . . . are you *sure* this isn't some sort of joke?''

"Positive, sir. Nogura said that, judging from the Vulcans' reaction, this was a pretty serious matter. McCoy's apparently in a lot of danger.''

"I see." Kirk thought for a moment. "Commander, could you transfer me to Nogura?''

"Yes, sir, right away.''

"Wait a minute, Riley—''

Riley paused and looked at Kirk expectantly. "Yes, Admiral?''

"You did right to call me.''

Riley smiled faintly, though he still wore a trace of that haunted look he'd worn when he tried to resign. "Thank you, Admiral.''

His image faded to dark; it was another thirty seconds before Nogura's appeared on the screen.

"Yes, Jim, what is it?" The head of Starfleet's expression was as implacable as ever, but there were dark smudges under his eyes.

"I just heard from Riley about McCoy. Was he serious?''

"I'm afraid so, Jim." Nogura gazed soberly at him for a beat, then said, "According to McCoy, the Vulcan—or Romulan spy, most likely—had some sort of secret weapon he was taking to the Romulans. It could be nothing—just a Vulcan with a brain tumor spouting a lot of nonsense—but it's got my attention. You see, the attack on Starfleet Headquarters was not an isolated event. Several terrorist attacks occurred simultaneously, at various trouble spots in Federation space. The guiding force behind them all, according to our intelligence, is the Romulans."

"Are you saying that this affair is a smokescreen to hide Romulan activity?"

"In the case of Djana, the unrest is real enough and must be dealt with . . . let's just say the Romulans nurtured it and appear to have timed the event for their convenience."

"If McCoy's life is in danger," Jim said, and then stopped. For the first time since he'd thought Riley was calling to tell him someone had died, the somber reality of it struck him. He reworded his request so that it would better appeal to Nogura. "If all this *is* just a smokescreen, Admiral, then doesn't it make sense to go after McCoy and his kidnapper ourselves? Deal with the source? God knows, we've gone out of our way to steal weapons from the Romulans—it's certainly to our interest to stop them from getting their hands on another."

Nogura shook his head. "What you neglect to mention, Jim, is that we have no way of knowing for sure that McCoy's kidnapper is anything but a crackpot. It's all conjecture. And besides, the Vulcans are taking care of this; I'm sure they'll deal with it very efficiently. Did Riley mention to you that Mr. Spock is heading up the rescue?"

"Yes."

"Then you can rest assured that your friend McCoy will come out of this without a scratch." Nogura paused; a glint of humor flashed in his tired eyes. "In spite of any confrontations we may have had, I honestly like the doctor. Speaks his mind and doesn't give a hoot what anyone thinks. Very refreshing. Only, don't tell him I said that. I'm confident he'll be all right, with Spock in charge."

"Still, sir, don't you think—"

"Jim, your mission is to remain on Djana and see to it that negotiations begin."

"And I have no intention of abandoning that mission, Admiral. But once we fulfill our mission"—he was careful not to say "I" and "my," as Ciana and Olmsted were listening—"once we get the Inari and Djanai to sit down together, I request permission to see if I can assist Mr. Spock."

"Jim, if you two manage to get those groups talking, I wouldn't care if you both took a week off to go bar-hopping on Arcturus."

"Thank you, Admiral. Kirk out."

Nogura's image faded; Kirk rose with difficulty out of the low chair and turned to see Lori and Olmsted watching him.

"I'm sorry, Jim," Lori said as he retook his seat across from her. "I know that you and Dr. McCoy were close."

You were *close*. Her use of the past tense threw him; she was speaking as if McCoy were dead. But that couldn't be what she intended. No, she had said it because his and McCoy's friendship belonged in the past, back with his memories of the *Enterprise* . . . and the realization was not a pleasant one. Jim shrugged. "You heard Nogura. It's being taken care of." He smiled politely at the rumpled Geoffrey Olmsted. "Now, where were you?"

Olmsted perked up visibly. "I was just saying that when you first meet with the Djanai, you shouldn't mention the Inari, or they're liable to walk out on you. Leave that for later."

"Noted and filed," Jim said. He was focusing hard on what Olmsted was saying, trying to force his mind off the subject of Leonard McCoy. "I'll say nothing to them the first time around." Ciana nodded in agreement.

"Good." Olmsted beamed, revealing deep dimples on either cheek. "Then I'll explain the setup for tomorrow morning's meeting." He struggled to sit forward, and arranged the writing tablet on his lap at an angle so that both Kirk and Ciana could see. "You'll be meeting the Djanai on their own sacred ground."

Ciana took a breath and was about to interrupt; Olmsted raised a plump, uncallused hand. "It was the only way they would agree to a meeting. A prearranged location, perfectly safe. The Djanai will be here . . ." He marked an X on the tablet. "And you'll be here." He made another X a short distance away, then circled them both. *Scientific proof,* Kirk almost quipped, but he held his tongue and managed to repress a smile.

"You'll be enclosed in your own force field, Admiral Kirk, courtesy of the Inari Council, and it is absolutely impenetrable. I'd stake my own life on it. The location's been examined and will be so again before we beam you down. You'll of course be monitored at all times, and we'll beam you up at the first sign of trouble. The degree of risk will be infinitesimal."

But Ciana was frowning suspiciously. "Who'll be operating the force field and transporter?" At Olmsted's look, she said, "I don't want any foul-ups—such as finding out at the last minute we've got a Djanai sympathizer in the ranks. That's what caused this whole mess to begin with.''

"No chance of that.'' Olmsted met her scrutiny with an openness that was impressive. "My people are very thorough—since, most times, their lives depend on it. There will be no Djanai sympathizers slipping through the cracks. And most of the equipment will be operated by my own people.''

Ciana made a small noise of approval, but her expression remained troubled.

"Well.'' Olmsted picked up the satchel near his feet and slipped the writing tablet and stylus into it. "Any other questions?''

"You haven't located their headquarters yet, have you?'' Lori asked.

"No,'' Olmsted answered confidently, "but my people are scanning for them. No matter how well they've hidden themselves, we'll find them. We've got the latest equipment, the best people. It's only a matter of time.''

"Let's hope so,'' Ciana said. She rose, causing Jim and Olmsted to follow suit. "If I think of anything before tomorrow morning,'' Lori said, shaking Olmsted's hand, "I'll buzz you.''

"And remember, if negotiations fall through, my rescue team is standing by.'' Olmsted reached across to give Jim's hand a single firm shake. "Nice meeting you, Admiral.''

"Same here,'' Jim said; he and Lori watched Olmsted go.

The second the door closed over the rotund little man, Lori turned toward Jim. Her arms were folded, and she ran her hands slowly over her upper arms, as if she were chilled; there was apprehension in her eyes. "What you said about trusting one's instincts . . .'' she began.

"What?'' Jim blinked at her. His mind had been racing back and forth between tomorrow's meeting with the Djanai and the plight of Leonard McCoy.

"Trusting one's instincts,'' she repeated, looking at him with concern. "I've got a bad feeling about tomorrow's meeting, very bad''—she pointed at a spot just below her solar plexus—"right here. Jim, I don't think you should go alone.''

He finally registered what she was saying and smiled, a small ironic smile. "I thought we'd reasoned that one out, Lori. I'm more expendable, more experienced in the field. And it simply doesn't make sense to risk us both. Nogura would never be able to replace you.''

Without false modesty, she replied, "I understand that. Normally, I'd follow logic—but this is the great instinct experiment, remember? And this particular gut feeling is very strong.'' She patted the spot.

"That's fear, Admiral," he said, his smile softening. It occurred to him that she was standing very close. "That's one instinct you have to learn to ignore.''

"No matter how strong?"

"No matter how strong.''

"There's something else. Maybe instinct, maybe not; stronger than the fear.'' She was looking at him intently; for an instant so fleeting it might have been his imagination, she seemed very vulnerable. "I've been debating for some time whether to mention it to you.''

"Fire away. I'll give you an honest reaction.''

"*Will* you?" she murmured, and in the split second before she spoke, Jim knew exactly what she was going to say. "I'm very attracted to you, Admiral Kirk." She smiled. "There. I've said it.''

As promised, he gave her that honest reaction.

He took her into his arms and kissed her.

SEVENTEEN

☆

It was quiet aboard the Vulcan spacecraft; the only sound other than the low hum of the engines was the slow, steady drone of T'Sai's breathing. The cabin lights were dimmed to conserve power, giving the impression of night.

Keridwen was staring glassy-eyed at the lights on her control panel when she had the brief sensation of a warm, almost feverish hand resting on her left shoulder. She looked over, her reaction dulled by fatigue, at Spock sitting in the pilot's chair across from her. He was studying her face with concern; yet, at this distance, it was impossible for him to have touched her.

"You need rest, Dr. Llewellyn," he said gravely. "Perhaps you should lie down for a while." He was quite right; it had been hours since they had left Vulcan, and a full day since Keridwen had gotten any sleep. She smiled at his concern and his oddly endearing formality; she liked Leonard's Vulcan friend, in spite of her efforts to remain detached.

"Perhaps I will take a break." Dwen got up and stretched, yawning as she glanced over her shoulder at T'Sai. The High Master, her stern ancient visage as cold and composed as a death mask, was still in deep trance; she had uttered no further commands for the past few hours. Dwen turned back to Spock and said conversationally, "If we continue on this heading, we'll be at Arcturus soon."

"Yes." Spock glanced at his control panel. "I anticipate

another seventeen-point-four minutes to landing." He entered a code into his control panel; the vessel began to slow for approach.

"Unfortunately, being human, I can't get much of a nap in," she said regretfully, and peered up at the overhead viewscreen as the Arcturan system came into view. The natives of said system could hardly be termed linguistically creative; they had endowed their sun, their planet, and their single sprawling metropolis with a single name, which Standard, with its imperial tendency to ignore native terms if they were difficult to pronounce and to substitute its own ancient names for the stars, translated as Arcturus.

And poor Leonard, if he was still alive, was down there somewhere in that sordid mess, in the clutches of an evil mind-lord. Dwen drew in a sudden breath. What if Leonard were being tortured?

Dear gods, I can barely stand the thought of his dying . . . please, not that. She squeezed her eyes shut at the mental vision of Leonard McCoy screaming, writhing in agony amid flames . . .

She blotted out the thought. Aloud, she said ruefully, "I've been to Arcturus once . . . and had hoped never to have to come here again. The place lacks charm."

Spock busied himself with his controls and did not answer.

"One question," she said, walking over to stand behind Spock's right elbow. "When we do find this Zakal—what will we do with him? I mean, if he's so terrifically dangerous . . ."

Spock's expression was impenetrable. "T'Sai and I will deal with that."

"Will you find a way to—what did you call it?—set his katra upon the winds?"

To her utter surprise, Spock, keeping his face toward the screen, said: "No."

She was aghast. "But someone like that—who has killed so many of your people, who is capable of such incredible violence . . . whose aim is to destroy your civilization—you would try to keep him alive?"

Spock finally turned to face her; there was something ancient and disturbing in his dark eyes. "Your culture has a rather trite way of putting it: Two wrongs do not make a right. Moreover, a promise was made by a student to preserve Zakal's katra. I'm sure you're familiar with the Vulcan belief that a promise must be kept at all costs."

"Loyalty has its limits, Mr. Spock. But what will you do with his katra—if you manage to recapture it?"

His eyes flickered in response to the implicit in her question: *if you survive to recapture it.* "It would be returned to . . . a place of safekeeping," he said.

She shook her head in disapproval. "One can be too merciful, Mr. Spock."

"Surak would disagree."

"I'm sure he would. He succeeded because he lived in such violent times; it was necessary to go to the peaceful extreme to get the pendulum swinging back toward the middle. Since you've mentioned one old Terran saying, I'll mention another: Unrestrained mercy leads to weakness and allows evil to flourish. Zakal is already dead—what's the harm in allowing his spirit to join his body?"

Spock was frowning; she could see that he was considering her words, but she also knew they would do little to change his mind. "Your concepts are most interesting," he said, "but Zakal was defeated once already by those who followed Surak's methods. It therefore follows—"

He stopped in mid-sentence as a low moan came from T'Sai. Both Spock and Keridwen turned their heads sharply to regard her; but the older Vulcan's expression was unchanged.

"Zakal," Spock said abruptly. His tone chilled Keridwen to the core. "We must speak no further of him."

"I'm sorry," Dwen apologized, stricken as she realized the danger her words had caused. "It's my f—"

"You are esper-blind," Spock answered quickly. "He cannot sense you. The fault is my own. Let us talk no more of it."

Keridwen nodded and walked back to her own station; concentration on the landing seemed the best way to master her fear. Behind her, the High Master groaned again, this time forcefully, and shuddered in her chair.

Amazingly, Spock ignored her; he was staring down at a flashing red light on his control panel, a faint crease between his brows. "Dr. Llewellyn, the outer hull is beginning to superheat . . ."

"What?" Keridwen slid back into her seat and checked her own monitor. The temperature of the outer hull registered near one thousand degrees Celsius. "That's im*pos*sible—" She knew it was a stupid thing to say the instant she said it; it was quite

clear what—or rather, *who*—was responsible. *It's all my fault. If I hadn't started talking to Spock, this wouldn't be happening.*

T'Sai moaned and rocked in her chair; like Spock, Dwen forced herself not to look at the High Master; instead, she kept her focus on her control panel, watching helplessly as the temperature of the hull climbed over fourteen hundred degrees.

"Auxiliary coolant system activated," Spock said calmly; nevertheless, the temperature inside the cabin was rising; Dwen felt perspiration creeping out onto her forehead and back.

The collision alarm sounded. Dwen jerked slightly at the noise. The automatic airlock had just sealed off damage to the outer hull. The computer interpreted the hole as being caused by a chunk of ice from a passing asteroid, but the scanners picked up nothing—no asteroids, no debris, not so much as a pebble, certainly nothing that could have caused such a gaping hole.

The metal had simply overheated, and then crumpled on its own.

Impossible.

"We need to land before there is further damage." Spock raised his head from his monitor and looked steadily over at Dwen. Arcturus the planet was now visible on the overhead screen.

Dwen nodded, stunned but able to focus, and consulted the navigational computer. "Preparing to enter orbit around Arcturus; descent spiral plotted and locked in." She was about to reach for the subspace radio controls until it occurred to her: this was, after all, Arcturus. There would be no space traffic controller, no one to talk them down. Like everyone else, they would simply have to trust their scanners to warn them of nearby vessels—and pray there was no malfunction.

The vessel went smoothly into orbit, and began its descent without incident . . . but then Dwen sensed, even before the controls told her, that something was wrong. Their velocity, instead of decreasing as it should, began to *increase.*

Zakal, she thought instantly, and then, again: *Impossible.* But the limits of the possible she had known all her life no longer seemed to have any meaning.

Damn you, Zakal. Briefly her fear gave way to a powerful surge of hatred for their Vulcan tormentor. Aloud, she told Spock, "Decrease speed."

He touched his controls and looked over at her. "The controls are not responding, Dr. Llewellyn. I shall attempt manual override . . ." He did so as he spoke, then looked up to face her again, his expression unreadable. "It seems I am unable to access manual override."

"Gods and goddesses," Keridwen said blankly, not really aware she was speaking aloud. "At this speed, we'll burn up."

"Correct," Spock answered matter-of-factly. "However, I have a suggestion: would you attempt to access manual override yourself? And I shall assist T'Sai." Without waiting for her answer, he settled back in his chair and closed his eyes.

Keridwen stared at him for an instant, then came to herself and began to punch the code for manual override into her control panel. Nothing happened.

The ship was spiraling downward, faster and faster; Arcturus loomed ever closer on the overhead. Dwen was perspiring heavily—a glance at the screen revealed a hull temperature of twenty-six hundred degrees. She drew a hand across her slick forehead; a drop of sweat stung her eye.

So that's it, then. It's Spock and I who're going to die, after all. And it seemed monstrously unfair that an event so momentous as her own death should happen so swiftly, so matter-of-factly, with so little fanfare. *At least,* she told herself fatalistically, *this means Leonard should be all right.* She closed her eyes and, without hope, tried one last time to access the override.

It worked. She felt the ship slowing and opened her eyes. The temperature of the hull was now two thousand degrees and dropping.

"We're all right," she breathed, and turned her head to look over at the Vulcan beside her. Spock's expression was composed, peaceful in the face of death. He opened his eyes slowly, and for a moment they seemed vacant, as if he had not yet extricated himself from a dream . . . and then they cleared and became cognizant again. "Spock," Dwen repeated, louder this time, "the controls are on manual. We're going to be all right."

Spock grunted and glanced down at his panel. "The controls do seem to be on manual, but we are far from all right, Doctor."

She came to the same conclusion the instant before he said it; the craft was indeed decelerating, but was only seconds away from Arcturus's atmosphere. Spock gave Dwen's thoughts voice. "At our current rate of descent, incineration is unlikely; however, impact is likely to be a pro—"

"Prepare for crash landing," she interrupted. There was no more time to be afraid, to think—only to react. Her fingers danced swiftly over the controls, cutting entry velocity to the minimum as the craft hurtled through the uppermost layer of Arcturus's atmosphere. "Get restraints on T'Sai, if you can, then take care of yourself. This is not going to be one of my smoother landings."

As if cued by the mention of her name, T'Sai stirred. "Landing coordinates: 437 by 562.1." She spoke in a voice that was strong and clear, and then fell silent again.

Dwen repeated them to herself silently and entered them into the navigational computer while Spock rose from his chair to attend to T'Sai. Dwen activated her own cushioning field; impulsively she reached her hands beyond its pale golden glow for the control panel . . . and withdrew them again. There was nothing more she could do except watch . . . and wait for the impact. Darkness flew by on the overhead, darkness and occasional pearl-gray swirls of clouds; they were coming down on the planet's night side.

Leonard is down there somewhere.

She repeated it silently, like a mantra; somehow, the thought held back the fear.

Even though she had braced herself, when impact came, it was far stronger than she had anticipated. It slammed her against the controls, despite her restraints. Her head snapped forward, causing her dark hair to swing forward and a shock to run down her neck, into her back. She was vaguely aware of Spock and T'Sai nearby, being buffeted in their seats.

When it was over, she straightened and rubbed the back of her neck gingerly, and was pleased to find herself uninjured. Spock recovered first. Keridwen, still a heap on the floor by the panel, gave him a dazed smile as he helped her to her feet. She glanced back at the passenger's chair; miraculously, T'Sai was sitting in it, looking only minorly disheveled.

Dwen caught her breath and said to Spock, "That wasn't quite so bad as I expected. Where exactly are we?"

He moved to the overhead, took a look at it, and then leaned down to study his scanner. "We seem to be in a low wetland of some sort . . . very nearly a marsh."

Keridwen took a step toward him—her legs felt shaky and undependable—and looked herself. "Soft ground, eh? Must have helped to reduce the impact."

"Undoubtedly." Spock straightened and headed for the hatch.

"Where are you going?" She was a little embarrassed at the note of alarm in her voice; but the way her knees were knocking, she doubted her legs would let her get very far, and she felt a real pang of fear at the thought of being left alone (or with T'Sai, which was essentially the same thing) on the ship.

"Outside, to survey the damage." Spock exited through the hatch without further comment.

"Why not just use our scanners?" she protested, but he was already gone. She glanced uncertainly at T'Sai, who sat, her dignified face in repose, eyes closed once again. Dwen sighed, and followed Spock.

She paused a moment in the open hatch to gaze out at the night sky, which to her Terran eyes seemed abnormally, gloriously bright, ashine with the light of three round lemony-white moons. The air outside smelled of sewage, and was warm and heavy with moisture; beads of water hung suspended, creating a fine mist. It was rather like stepping into a steambath. Dwen took a tentative step out into the night—and sank shin-deep into evil-smelling mire. She raised one foot: the soft desert boot came up out of the muck with a loud sucking noise.

"Ugh!" Dwen exclaimed, crinkling her nose. The mud had gotten inside her boots and was squishing between her toes. "What did the High Master do, give us the coordinates for a public latrine?"

Spock did not respond; he did not seem to have heard the question at all. He was staring, arms folded, at the fore hull of the ship as it gleamed silver in the moonlight.

And then she saw it: a hole, almost a meter wide and over twice as long. The metal surrounding it was scorched.

"Dr. Llewellyn," Spock said gravely, keeping his eyes focused on the damage, "it would be best in the future to avoid . . . such conversations as we had. The fault is entirely mine; and here are the results."

He stared at the hull a bit longer, then went back inside the craft and left Keridwen to gape at its scarred, blackened surface.

"Why are you keeping me alive?" McCoy asked. He was sitting in the passenger seat behind the Vulcan, who was at the scout's controls; as the doctor spoke, he pressed the control that dissipated his cushioning shield. His captor had brought him back to Keridwen's ship and installed a cloaking device with a speed

that Spock would have envied, then taken off. Barely a minute
ago, the scout had pulled free of Arcturus's orbit.

After witnessing what Zakal had done to the Gorn bartender,
McCoy dared not ask about the puddle a half-meter to the left of
the pilot: it was a scorched, unidentifiable mass that could have
been garbage—except that it was dotted with tufts of brilliant
copper fur. The doctor feared for his life as never before . . . save
for those moments when he seriously questioned his own sanity.
What he had seen done to poor Rrk was clearly impossible. . . .

And yet, over there on the floor was more tangible evidence
McCoy could not ignore. Supposing—just supposing—that Zakal
had used a "secret weapon" of some sort. An invisible mind-
weapon . . . and the doctor could testify as to its incredible
power.

Then God help us all, McCoy thought grimly, *if he manages
to get it to the Romulans.* If there was just some way to stop
him—maybe now, while he was distracted with the controls. . . .

Zakal—or was it Sekar now?—shifted his focus from his
monitor to McCoy.

"I would advise against trying," the Vulcan—Sekar this
time, for his expression was one of formal reserve—said calmly,
glancing at McCoy over his shoulder. The answer, rational though
it was, made the hair on McCoy's forearms and the back of his
neck lift. *Then it's true . . . he can read my mind.*

But maybe not—maybe it was just a clever guess, or maybe
the doctor's expression had given him away. As an experiment,
he addressed a thought to Sekar. *You know everything I think,
don't you?*

"I do," Sekar answered aloud, causing McCoy to draw back
against the padded chair. "There is no longer any advantage to
be gained by attempting to hide the truth from you. You already
know of Zakal's presence, and have seen what he is capable of;
it is through him that we sense your thoughts."

McCoy swallowed air; his mouth had become drier than the
Sash-i-shar Desert at midday. "You haven't answered my question," he persisted with a boldness he did not feel. "Why are you
keeping me alive?" A tiny part of his brain kept telling him to
shut up; if he kept asking, Sekar/Zakal might just decide there
weren't any good reasons for letting him live, after all. Still, he
had to know . . . and he encouraged himself with the thought that
if Zakal had wanted to kill him, he would have done so long ago.

It was still Sekar, serenely Vulcan, who answered. "We do

not kill you, Dr. McCoy, because it would serve no purpose"—
here the corner of the Vulcan's upper lip twitched slightly—"and
because you may prove useful to us."

"Useful?" McCoy said, but he did his utmost to sound
unsurprised—no point in convincing Sekar otherwise. "How?"

"You know much of Starfleet, something the Declared"
(McCoy had caught on to the fact that the Declared meant the
Romulans) "will appreciate . . . and what you do not know, your
friend who follows knows. He will be greatly appreciated as
well."

Spock. So, Sekar—or Zakal—could sense even a Vulcan's
thoughts . . . at a very great distance. McCoy's fear deepened.

Sekar's face shifted subtly; an odd light shone in his eyes,
and he grinned evilly at McCoy. "He follows with T'Sai, High
Master of the Kolinahru. I shall enjoy my revenge on that daugh-
ter of Khoteth. Perhaps you will even live to see it." And,
apparently pleased by McCoy's terrified expression, Zakal threw
back his head and laughed.

"I will tell you the real reason I have not killed you, Dr.
Leonard McCoy, regardless of what that fool Sekar thinks. It is
because you are harmless and you amuse me. And when you
cease to amuse me, you will die."

The revelation brought McCoy little comfort.

Jim Kirk materialized in the open field and marveled at the
beauty surrounding him. In the far distance aubergine mountains
lifted snow-covered peaks into a deep Terran-blue sky. The plain
where Kirk waited alone was carpeted with pale gold stalks of
wild grain, with the exception of the clearing in which he now
stood.

The view was only slightly obscured by the shimmering
white Inari force field that surrounded him. Geoffrey Olmsted
had beamed him from the transporter in Ciana's secured quarters; at this instant, Lori and Olmsted were monitoring Jim's
every move. Yet even with the knowledge that the Djanai Kel
would be appearing any second, Kirk had to work to keep his
entire mind focused on the present moment—and not on Leonard
McCoy or Lori Ciana.

"Admiral? Do you read us okay?" Lori's voice asked him.
It was her formal tone, used for Olmsted's sake. Kirk instinc-
tively raised a finger to the tiny receiver in his ear.

"Loud and clear."

"Reception on this end is good." She paused, and said, more warmly, "Break a leg, Jim." He imagined he heard her smile.

"Thanks, Admiral." He grinned faintly. After what had occurred yesterday between him and Lori, he could no longer deny how he felt about her . . . yet at the same time he was concerned as to how this new relationship would affect their mission. Lori was handling herself professionally so far: although last night she had repeatedly expressed her premonition of danger about the meeting with Kel, this morning she was strictly business. It was the mission and nothing else, and she was all confidence—if she still felt any misgivings about sending Jim alone, she did not show it. And for that, he admired her even more.

Kirk forced his mind back to his present situation as he heard the hum of a transporter beam. A burst of light appeared a meter directly in front of him, and Kel gradually materialized into view.

The speaker for the Djanai had the same height and build as a Tellarite—short, stocky, and muscular. His skin and waist-length hair were brilliant yellowish-orange, and he was shirtless, wearing only crudely made trousers decorated with shells, bits of polished wood, and bird feathers. Kel's eyes, huge and black without a trace of white in them, regarded Kirk with exceptional serenity. Like Kirk, he stood shrouded in an Inari force field.

Kel did not speak, but waited patiently for Kirk to speak first.

"Kel," Kirk said by way of greeting. Olmsted had advised him to skip titles—they meant nothing to the Djanai—and to avoid the Inari custom of bowing with arms crossed over the chest. "My name is Kirk. I speak for the United Federation of Planets and the organization called Starfleet."

Kel digested this without the slightest movement. And then he responded, "I speak for Djana and her children. Djana has instructed us to take hostages, and thus make our wishes known to the Federation." He spoke extremely slowly, but Kirk knew better than to mistake his slowness for a lack of intelligence. Jim sensed great shrewdness behind those implacable black eyes.

Kirk tried to slow his rate of speech to match Kel's. "And those wishes are?" He knew the answer Kel would give this particular question—and had prepared a reply.

"Djana and her children desire the removal of the Inari. They have desecrated the land, and stolen it from her, so that her children live there no more; and they have killed her sacred bird, the *lewa,* which is seen no more in these fields.''

"We wish to talk to the Djanai about how to accomplish this. What specifically have the Inari done to your people that made you take Federation hostages? They took your land?''

"As I said—not our land, but Djana's. It is not ours to give— but it is not the Inari's to take. The number of our people increases, and we are crowded because there is always less land. The Inari build their distilleries on it. They took the land we live on and the land we worship on—sacred land, but the Inari have no regard for it. They tear up the land and destroy the nests of our sacred bird. We can permit this no longer. Djana has instructed us to act.''

"Then let us agree, for the sake of both our peoples,'' Kirk said, "to sit down together and make a plan, so that the lewa is no longer slaughtered, and your people are no longer crowded.''

Kel paused to consider this.

"Way to go,'' Ciana said into his ear.

Thanks, Kirk told her silently, but he was careful not to smile, not to let his expression shift the slightest bit. He waited while Kel studied the distant mountains.

"Perhaps,'' Kel replied at last in his deep, resonant voice, "but first, the Federation must promise—''

Kirk stopped listening; with utter disbelief, he watched his own force field fade, then disappear with a resounding *pop.* Kel stopped speaking and stared at him with apparent surprise.

"What the *hell* is happening?'' Ciana shouted angrily into the receiver. Jim knew the question was not for him, but for Geoffrey Olmsted. "Hold on, Jim, we're beaming you up right away—''

He and Kel stood motionless and looked at each other for what seemed like a full minute. Jim could hear Ciana and Olmsted swearing in the background, something about a malfunction.

"Where's that transporter?'' Jim demanded aloud—a split second before he felt himself caught up in the transporter beam. He relaxed in relief; so the technically inept Djanai had found a way around the ''impervious'' Inari force field after all . . . and he could just imagine the hell Olmsted was catching from Ciana at that very moment.

As he materialized on the platform, he opened his mouth to say to Lori, *Damn good instincts there, Admiral.*

And closed it again without saying a word, for Ciana and Olmsted weren't there.

Instead, Jim found himself in an unfamiliar transporter room, face-to-face with two strange Djanai. One of them stepped forward and raised a Romulan phaser at him.

"Your communicator, please." He gestured with the phaser at Kirk's left ear.

Reluctantly Kirk removed the tiny device and handed it to him.

"Thank you," the Djanai said. He dropped the receiver onto the floor and crushed it to powder under his boot, then looked back up at Kirk. "Please remain on the transporter pad."

And before Kirk could protest, he was caught up in the beam again.

EIGHTEEN

––––––––––––––––––– ☆ –––––––––––––––––––

In Ciana's secured quarters, Geoff Olmsted eased up on the transporter control. Ciana stood next to him, watching anxiously, shifting her weight from foot to foot. The space above the transporter pad where Kirk had stood only moments before glimmered faintly, then faded to nothingness.

The expression on Olmsted's chubby face was grim. "He's not there, Admiral. They beat us to the punch."

"Then trace him—"

"Too late." Olmsted shook his head. "We've lost contact. They must have destroyed the transmitter."

"Dammit!" Ciana exploded, and brought her fist down on the console so hard that Olmsted flinched and her hand hurt, but she was too furious to acknowledge it. "How the *hell* could this happen, Geoffrey?"

"I don't know," Olmsted admitted, but his tone was decidedly unapologetic.

"I thought you said the Inari field was impenetrable." She was bitterly angry with herself: she had *known* all along that something like this would happen; why the hell hadn't she just pulled rank on Jim and gone herself? *So much for listening to my instincts. Jim was wrong—it wasn't fear at all. I should have insisted on negotiations via pub comm . . . anything but this.*

She stopped herself right there. Guilt was a waste of time, and right now there was no time to waste.

"The Inari field *is* impenetrable," Olmsted was saying. "Believe me, if anyone—Romulans included—came up with a damper for this field, I'd be the first one to know about it. And that, my dear Admiral, you can bet your life on."

Like Kirk bet his, she almost snapped, but an idea, half-formed, began to come to her. "Malfunction, then?"

Olmsted shook his head. "No way. Checked it out myself this morning. Admiral, this wasn't a screwup; this was deliberate."

"But if the Djanai didn't damp that field, then who—?"

"What makes you think the Djanai had anything to do with it?" He shook his head and folded his arms tightly across his chest. "No, this was sabotage. The field was programmed to fail at that specific time.

"Dammit, I *told* you about screening out Djanai sympath—" she began. And stopped, as in a flash she understood exactly what had happened. She and Olmsted gazed knowingly at each other. He was right; he had committed no mistakes, had allowed not a single Djanai sympathizer near any of the equipment.

Without another word, Ciana walked across the suite to the comm terminal. She took a deep breath and composed herself before bending down to punch in Ruwe's private code.

He answered immediately, as she expected.

"Admiral Ciana. Did your meeting with the Djanai go well?"

"No, U Ruwe."

Ruwe's enormous dark eyes widened. "Oh, no! What has happened?"

His reaction struck her as comically dramatic. "Admiral Kirk has been kidnapped by the Djanai." Her tone was as disinterested as that of a newsreader's.

"How terrible! How awful!" Ruwe raised his four-fingered hands in a gesture of dismay and helplessness. "But not so unexpected. At the risk of seeming impolite, Admiral, I must say that I warned you about dealing with them. Killing is all that they understand, and they won't stop until they've captured you too." He drew closer to the screen, his voice full of sympathy and concern. "I suppose you'll be sending in Mr. Olmsted's assault team, then—"

"No," Ciana said.

Ruwe shrank away. *"No?* Well, then, will you be using the peace-keeping force?"

"No." She waited a beat before continuing. "U Ruwe . . ." she began.

Ruwe, you little cow (it was the most bigoted, demeaning term she could think of to call him, and it felt good), *I can see right through your act . . . and before this is over, I swear I'll tack your lovely hide on my office wall as a decoration.*

"U Ruwe," she said aloud, her face an impassive mask, "we're aware that *you* sabotaged that force field. The Djanai had nothing to do with it—they simply reacted faster than we did."

"Untrue," Ruwe bleated, but she saw the fear on his long brown face.

"You're a bad liar, Ruwe," she told him, purposely avoiding the polite use of the vocative. It was an insult, to be sure, but right now Ruwe needed insulting. "We have proof. Very damning evidence, in fact." A lie not quite as big as Ruwe's—but then, Ciana was more skilled at deceit. "The Federation isn't going to take kindly to this at all. In fact, I'm personally seeing to it that you and your Council are hauled up before the Federation on charges of sabotage. Of course, this means you'll lose Starfleet protection for your trading vessels."

Ruwe stared at her with large moist eyes; his chest was heaving. He said nothing.

As much as Ciana wanted to do or say anything to hurt the Inari for what he had done to Jim, she managed to control herself. This moment presented an opportunity that was too good to waste.

She swallowed and imagined she felt some of the anger—and the fear she felt for Jim—drain from her body. If she wanted to get him back safely, she couldn't risk giving in to either. *All right, Jim, I won't act out of fear . . . but let's hope like hell my instinct's still in good working order.*

"However, U Ruwe," she said in a quiet, even voice, "I will consider not informing my superiors immediately—or bringing charges—provided you swear that you and the Inari Council will assist us in every way possible in recovering Admiral Kirk . . . and that you and your people will sit down and honestly try to settle your differences with the Djanai."

Ruwe moved as if to speak, but she cut him off. *"Before* you make that promise, bear in mind that I have already dispatched a sealed report to my superiors, to be opened in the event I am captured, injured, or killed. It informs them of your treachery . . . and they will no doubt follow my recommendation that the

peace-keeping forces and all other Federation protection be withdrawn from Inari space." She finished and gazed steadily at him.

Ruwe did not meet her eyes. Several seconds passed before
he said weakly, "I will inform the Council of what you have said,
Admiral Ciana."

Not a confession, but it would do for now. She closed the
channel without further comment.

*You do just that, little cow, while I contact Nogura to tell
him that I have failed . . . and lost Jim.*

Ciana leaned heavily against the terminal and covered her
face; her fine hair brushed against the backs of her hands. She
did not know if Olmsted watched, and she did not care.

Kirk took care to memorize the way back to the transporter
room as a third Djanai guard led him through a maze of narrow
corridors. To Jim's eyes, the location looked suspiciously like the
interior of a Romulan vessel. They were either on a ship, starship-
class because he could sense no movement—possible, but unlikely that it was anywhere in Inari space if the hostages were
held here; the energy cost of maintaining a cloaked vessel for
such a long time was enormous—or in some sort of permanent
underground facility. Any minute, Kirk expected to be face-to-
face with one of the Praetor's loyal soldiers.

He imagined Lori was giving Olmsted all kinds of hell right
now. She was probably frantic with worry (though he already
knew her well enough to know she'd never show it), and for that
he was sorry.

Not that he was worried himself in the slightest; his mind
was too preoccupied with studying his surroundings and considering methods of escape. At the moment, escape seemed unlikely
if not impossible. The Djanai, though shorter, was sturdier, and
held a phaser against the small of Kirk's back. Besides, Jim told
himself, he wanted to find out where they were headed first; he
hoped it would be to the other hostages.

He got his wish. The Djanai nudged him toward a door and
motioned him inside. Kirk expected to see a brig with holding
cells; instead, what he saw was a room filled with pirated standard
Fleet-issue furniture: an oval conference table and several chairs.
Perfect, he thought ironically, for negotiations.

At one end of the table, Uhura sprang from her chair,
grinning hugely. "Capt . . . Admiral Kirk!" Her smile faded
somewhat as she saw the phaser-toting Djanai behind him.

At the other end, Sarek, still dressed in his somber charcoal tunic with the bright ambassadorial medallion, displayed no surprise. He nodded sedately at Kirk as the guard greeted a second armed Djanai who stood watch over the prisoners. The two guards motioned for Kirk to sit midway between Sarek and Uhura. The first guard left after a few words of explanation to his fellow, who seemed as surprised to see Kirk as Uhura had been.

"Sir . . ." Uhura lowered her voice to something less than a whisper. "So they captured you too? Are they still taking hostages from Starfleet Headquarters?"

"Actually," Kirk answered with a sheepish expression, "the idea was to rescue you. Our plan seems to have backfired."

"In that case," Sarek said dryly, "you will forgive me if I do not say that I am glad to see you."

"The feeling is mutual, Ambassador. Though I'm glad to see you're unharmed."

Sarek gave a nod. "Has the Council voted on the issue of Djana's peace-keeping force?"

"No, they've postponed the vote." Kirk studied the Vulcan and Uhura; not only were they unharmed, they were unrestrained, and apparently well-fed; large platters of half-eaten fruit and untouched green silage sat at either end of the table. "You two seem to be doing all right for yourselves."

Uhura cast a quick glance at their captor, who was watching with disinterest that verged on boredom; Kirk assumed he didn't understand a word of Standard. "They're involved with the Romulans, Admiral . . ." She lowered her voice even further. "In fact, one seemed to be in charge here. They just had a disagreement of some sort with him and killed him."

"I see." Kirk looked over at the sienna-skinned guard, who gazed placidly back at him. "Excuse me, sir—do you speak Standard?"

"He does," Uhura volunteered.

Kirk addressed the Djanai again. "I'm James Kirk. Do you have a name?"

The Djanai did not have a chance to respond before Uhura said, "Ela. His name is Ela."

Kirk shot her a "Do-you-mind?" look; she shrugged apologetically. "Ela," Kirk told him, "I came to Djana because I wanted to help your people live in peace. I don't want to die before that happens."

Ela stared at him with the same disinterested, benign expression. Kirk swallowed his frustration at the lack of response and continued.

"Ela, before I was captured, I was talking with your"—he almost said the word "leader," but caught himself in time— "your speaker, Kel. I asked him a question, but I never heard his reply. I would like to know his answer now. May I speak with him?"

Ela remained maddeningly silent, but his hand dropped to his belt—a modern equipment belt that contrasted sharply with the handmade fabric of his trousers—and pressed a control on his communicator. Kirk waited patiently until, after several minutes, the Djanai who had escorted Kirk from the transporter appeared. Ela spoke into the Djanai's ear; the Djanai thought for a moment, then left the room again without speaking.

Moments later, Kel appeared.

"James Kirk." His voice came from deep within his powerful chest. "You wish to hear my answer to your proposal. It is this: the Federation brought the Inari to Djana, and now the Federation must take them away. When that happens, then Djana's children will hear what the Federation has to say."

"Kel, you said that your people want your sacred lands back . . . that you want an end to the overcrowding, and the killing of the lewa. If the Federation can see that these things are done, would you be willing to talk to the Inari?"

"I would prefer Djana to take my life," Kel answered calmly, "than to speak with the Inari."

And he turned and left.

At T'Sai's bidding, Spock went alone into the city to procure a cloaking device, leaving Keridwen and the High Master on the craft. Dwen had argued in favor of her accompanying Spock. If both of them went in search of the cloaking device, chances were better that at least one of them would make it back. But Spock clung stubbornly to logic. Arcturus held many dangers; if Dr. Llewellyn went with him, and both of them were killed, T'Sai could not pilot the ship, and all would be lost.

Fine, Keridwen had said. *I'll go alone, then.*

Spock shook his head. If she went alone and were harmed, then Spock and T'Sai's chances of being detected increased dangerously. Perhaps Dr. Llewellyn did not realize that having an esper-blind pilot prevented the ship from being led off-course, even destroyed. No, Keridwen must remain on the ship.

And so she did. The entire time, T'Sai stayed in her trance, never moved, never stirred, while Dwen paced the ship and worried. She had suspected, of course, that since Sekar wished to take Zakal's katra to the Romulans, it would be necessary to cross over into the Neutral Zone . . . yet the dangerous reality of it had not fully registered in her consciousness before now.

Within an hour, Spock returned with what appeared to be a fully functional cloaking device. He appeared slightly disheveled, but volunteered no information as to how he accomplished his mission, and Dwen did not ask.

They immediately went aft and set to work installing it.

Crouching next to Spock in the engine compartment (it was too small to honestly be called an engine *room*), Keridwen reached a hand out to steady the device while Spock connected it to the power source.

The result of that touch was remarkable.

It was Death itself: cold, dark, impassive. Spock's face and voice faded until Dwen could see and hear nothing; she gasped, and found no air, only blackness. She was drowning in the void of space.

She drew her hand away as if she had touched fire. The vision faded. Even so, for a moment she could not catch her breath. As her vision cleared, she saw that the cloaking device had tilted alarmingly on its side and that Spock was staring at her with concern. He waited until she recovered somewhat, then asked:

"Dr. Llewellyn . . . are you all right?"

She nodded. When she was able to speak, she said, "Yes. I'm all right." And to prove it, she lifted the cold metal device and held it upright for him. Spock frowned at her, but continued his task without further questions, as if he understood what had happened and knew there was nothing to be gained by discussing it. Dwen managed to hold on to the device until Spock finished his work.

Amazingly, her hands trembled only a little.

The intensity of the experience had faded somewhat the second time she touched the cold metal surface, but it was still like brushing up against Death.

Or, more accurately, as if Death had presented itself to her, and was awaiting her reply.

It did not take them very long to install the device and for

Dwen to check Spock's work and pronounce it good. Afterward they laid in a course for the Neutral Zone.

"Nogura here." The head of Starfleet's image appeared on the terminal screen and peered expectantly at Ciana.

"The Djanai have Jim," she said abruptly. She'd already decided there was no gentle way to break the news, and she had steeled herself for Nogura's reaction. Even so, the look of shock and disappointment on his face made her wince inwardly, though her outward appearance was one of calm control.

"How could this happen?" Nogura asked heavily. Lori's mental filter adjusted the question so that she heard: *How could you allow this to happen?*

She worked hard to keep the guilt from showing on her face. "The Inari double-crossed us, Admiral. They didn't want us to negotiate with the Djanai, so they rigged the equipment to fail right when Jim was meeting with the speaker, Kel. I'm ashamed to say that the Djanai reacted faster than we did, sir. Maybe the Inari tipped them off somehow. All blame for the incident rests squarely on my shoulders."

He listened without comment, and did not contradict her last statement, a fact she found surprisingly painful. For a moment, neither spoke. And then Nogura asked, "Have Olmsted's people located where the hostages are being held yet?"

She shook her head. "Not yet, sir. I'll contact you when they do."

Nogura's expression was colder, more reproachful than Lori had ever seen it. *If he had any confidence in my diplomatic ability before, he's lost it all now.* "All right, then," the old man said, and his voice was flint-hard to show he would tolerate no argument on this point. "The second they locate the hostages, send Olmsted's people in. I won't risk losing Jim too."

"Sir, the Djanai didn't do anything but take advantage of the situation. They may still be willing to negotiate. I see no reason to jeopardize the success of the entire miss—"

"It's a little late to still be worrying about the success of your mission, Ciana!" he thundered, no longer trying to conceal his anger. "You could at least concern yourself with the fate of the hostages instead of your career."

Her jaw dropped; blood rushed to her face and neck. When she could speak, she said in a voice that quivered, "Dammit, Admiral, I *am* thinking about the hostages—more than you know.

I'm also thinking about the entire population of a planet. If we send in the assault team now, we're doing exactly what the Inari wanted us to do. I don't care to let them pull the strings.''

"I don't intend to let them do that. But I'm going to get the hostages out first, then deal with the diplomatic problems,'' Nogura said. She tried to speak again, but he waved her silent. "I've already given you an order, Admiral: as soon as Olmsted's people locate the hostages, they're to rescue them—at any cost. That's all I have to say. Nogura out.''

The screen went gray. Ciana stared at it, heaving with anger. *Nogura, you old fool, can't you see this is killing me? Don't you know I'm dying to do something, anything, to bring Jim back safe?* But she was right not to send Olmsted's people in immediately, and she knew it. Furthermore, she was convinced Jim would do the same thing if their positions were reversed. If she could just be patient enough, the Djanai would contact them again . . . but to take swift revenge against them would only make them more mistrustful of the Federation.

"I'll tell my people, then,'' Olmsted said quietly behind her. He had been listening.

"No,'' she said. She turned to face him.

He crooked a brow at her. "But Fleet Admiral Nogura just said—''

"I don't give a damn what Fleet Admiral Nogura just said. You're directly answerable to me, and I say: go ahead and put your team on alert. But when you locate the Djanai hideaway, you don't strike. You come to me first, and I'll tell you if and when to go in.''

Olmsted considered this and asked, "Why, Admiral?''

"Instinct,'' she said.

Sitting at the conference table with Sarek and Uhura, Kirk had a pretty good idea of the reaction Lori and Nogura would have to his capture: to send in Olmsted's assault team as soon as the hostages' location was pinpointed. Which meant that there was very little time for him to salvage the mission and gain the Djanai's trust—and that, given Kel's response to Kirk's offer, meant that it was time to take desperate action.

Jim cast a nonchalant glance at the bored but wary Ela, who stood watch by the door, keeping his large Romulan phaser aimed in his prisoners' general direction. What Jim needed was a distraction that seemed innocent enough so that Ela did not signal the others for help—and that yet provided an opportunity to separate the guard from his phaser.

Jim gazed with feigned casualness at Uhura on his right, then Sarek on his left. Their guard did not seem to mind if the hostages conversed . . . but Jim's problem was how to convey what he was plotting to the others without awakening Ela's suspicions. He'd simply have to risk a distraction—and hope like hell the others caught on soon enough.

Jim let out a loud groan and clutched at his chest as he pitched forward against the hard surface of the table.

Uhura reacted before any of them. "Captain! Admiral!" She scrambled to his side and bent down to peer at him with concern. Still moaning, Jim kept his head on the table and, with his face toward her and away from Ela, winked.

Blessedly, she caught on at once. "It's his heart!" she cried with convincing dismay, and gestured for Ela to have a look. The Djanai, his expression only mildly curious, moved behind the table, past the seated ambassador, to the center, where Jim sat writhing in imaginary anguish, Uhura still next to him. Ela kept his phaser chest-high, and kept it trained on Jim's head as he cautiously investigated.

Jim waited for an opportunity. If the guard came close enough, or lowered the phaser for just an instant . . . Jim raised his head from the table and reared back in his chair, as if in redoubled agony. But Ela was unwilling to take any chances. He wisely remained out of Kirk's reach, and with his free hand reached for the communicator on his belt. Jim prepared to lunge—probably a bad idea, but the best one he could come up with at the moment.

And then, with his peripheral vision, he saw a dark form towering behind Ela. The Djanai emitted a short, surprisingly high-pitched bleat, then sank to the floor. Kirk looked up to see Sarek gazing impassively down at the guard's still form.

"Thank you, Ambassador," he said, rising. "You read my mind."

Sarek handed him Ela's phaser. "Not so surprising," the Vulcan said dryly, "when you realize how many years I have lived with a human."

Jim took the phaser. There were at least two more Djanai on the base—another guard and Kel, and possibly a Romulan. Before they risked stepping out into the corridor, it only made sense to improve the odds. "Ambassador, if you'd be so kind as to repeat your performance . . ." Kirk gestured at the door.

Before he finished saying it, Sarek went over and flattened himself against the wall near the entrance. Jim knelt down next to the unconscious Ela and rolled his body to one side, to find the communicator fastened to his belt. Jim removed the communicator; he and Uhura dragged Ela's limp body under the table. The effort made them grunt; the Djanai, though short, was stocky and surprisingly heavy.

Once Ela was safely hidden, Kirk pressed the signal button on the communicator. He and Uhura scrambled to resume their places at the table and affected expressions of innocent boredom. Jim kept the phaser in one hand, but kept it concealed under the table.

The second guard took little time to respond. Within seconds the door slid open; the Djanai paused in the entranceway and frowned at two prisoners where there should have been three. He did not see the Vulcan beside him.

"Surprise," Jim said, and raised Ela's phaser. The guard raised his own weapon to fire, but by then it was too late. Sarek reached down, found the vulnerable spot at the junction of neck and shoulder, and applied pressure. The guard's all-black eyes widened in surprise, then rolled up in his head to reveal yellowish whites as Sarek eased him to the ground.

"We are most fortunate," Sarek said, rising. "I am not all that familiar with Djanai morphology, and was uncertain as to the precise location of the nerve—"

"We appreciate the guess." Kirk got up and stripped the communicator and phaser from the guard's belt and handed both to Uhura. Ela's communicator he kept for himself. He flipped the grid open and adjusted the frequency until he found the channel he was looking for. "Kirk to Ciana—"

"Jim! Where the hell are you calling from?"

The relief in Lori's voice was so great that he smiled. "The Djanai base, I would assume."

"Repeat, Jim. You're breaking up some."

He repeated it.

"Okay, Olmsted says he's got your location pinpointed. You're underground on one of Inar's moons. Are Sarek and Uhura with you?"

"Yes, and in good shape."

"Great. We'll have you locked into the transporter in just a sec—"

"No. I want you to lock onto Sarek and Uhura—but I've got sor..e business to finish down here first."

"For God's sake, Jim—"

"Without their hostages, I've got a hunch the Djanai might be willing to listen to what I have to say. Remember that little chat we had about instincts, Lori?"

"Damn your hide, Jim Kirk, if you get yourself killed—" But her tone was one of resignation.

Jim smiled. "Admiral, please, there are Vulcans present." He paused, then said very seriously, "It's our best shot, Lori, to try to pull this thing out. Let me try."

"Why not?" she said bitterly. "Nogura's ready to drum me out of the Service as things stand now. Besides, I get the feeling you're going to do what you please anyway." She sighed. "The old man's been breathing down my neck to send in Olmsted's team. I'm disobeying a direct order, letting you do this."

"Then I promise not to mess up."

She did not sound amused. "I give you twenty minutes, Jim—and if I don't hear from you by then, we're beaming you up. Is that understood?"

"Understood. And thanks. Uhura has a communicator, and Sarek's standing next to her."

There was a pause. "Got them," Olmsted's voice said faintly in the background, and then Lori said, "Yes, we've got a fix on them. And, Jim—"

"Yes, Admiral?"

"Take care of yourself."

"I always do. Kirk out." He closed the communicator and put it on his belt.

"Good luck to you, Admiral," Uhura said. She and Sarek began to shimmer; their forms became unearthly bright, then winked out of view.

Jim headed back out into the corridor. The base appeared to be very small. The narrow corridor from the transporter room led directly back to the conference room where Sarek and Uhura had been imprisoned; at that point the hall forked in two directions. Jim chose to go left.

That corridor ended in a doorway. He clutched the phaser tightly and moved toward the door. It opened; Jim pulled back, then ducked low and to the side, aiming the phaser with both hands at the room's center.

It appeared to be an office with a desk and terminal, and a small cot in one darkened corner. Kel lay on the cot. At the sight of Kirk, he jumped to his feet and reached for the weapons belt on the desk.

But Kirk was faster; he took a step forward and pointed the phaser at Kel's head before the Djanai could put a hand on the belt. Kel froze and stared uncertainly at his former prisoner.

"How many of you on the base?" Kirk demanded.

Kel's attitude was cooperative. "Ela and Mul. And myself. There are no others."

"The design of this base is Romulan." Kirk brought the phaser threateningly close to Kel's head. "That means that there is a Romulan in charge here. Take me to the Romulan."

Kel did not budge. "There is no Romulan in charge here. There *was* rh'iov Rrhaen, who thought he was in charge. We killed him."

Kirk debated silently for a moment, then said, "I wish to speak to the Djanai people, Kel. I want to discuss an idea that might help them, and let them come to a consensus. How can I do this?"

"First, you must talk to the Circle of Elders. They will tell the people; they will take the consensus, and tell me the results . . . and I will tell you."

Kirk gestured with the phaser at the comm terminal. "Contact them."

Kel balked. "It is too dangerous. To communicate with them would reveal our location."

Kirk showed him the communicator on his belt. "We already know the location, Kel—we're on one of Inar's moons—and your Federation hostages have escaped. Go ahead—look for them. You won't find them here." When Kel did not react, Jim continued. "The Federation doesn't want to harm your people, Kel . . . even though you have threatened harm to ours. It's time for you to listen to what we can offer you."

"But this is not the way it is done," Kel protested mildly.

Kirk considered the dangers of beaming down to Djana himself and meeting the elders in person . . . and shook his head. "It's time to break with tradition, Kel. This will have to do for now. Get them."

Kel sighed and spoke Djanai into the terminal; the screen brightened.

"No tricks this time," Jim said. "Like I said, my people know where I am."

Kel gave him a curious look. "There were never any tricks, James Kirk."

It took several minutes for the Circle of Elders to gather. Seven of the ancient Djanai assembled, dressed in the same type of hand-decorated breeches Kel wore; their oiled hair, streaked with white, fell almost to their ankles. They sat in a semicircle on the floor in a manner that reminded Kirk of the Inari Council.

"Wemu is the speaker," Kel said, then added as an afterthought: "They have come at great personal danger to themselves. Only the Inari have such communications equipment on Djana."

On the terminal screen, Wemu rose from his place in the center of the half-circle, and regarded Kirk with regal poise. The speaker's skin was ebony; his hair was a startling silver-white.

"I respect them for taking the risk," Kirk said, setting the phaser down on the desk between himself and the comm screen. "But I came to Djana with a message, and I will not leave until I am satisfied that Djana's children have heard it." He paused as a ripple of approval moved along the circle of Djanai. "I promise that I will not lie to you. And so, I must tell you that the Federation cannot promise to remove the Inari completely from your planet." This caused sounds of disapproval. "The Romulans have provided you with weapons, even this base," said Kirk, "but do they offer to remove the Inari for you?"

"No," Wemu said. "We hear what you say: Kel has explained to us that rh'iov Rrhaen's people were using us as a means of attacking the Federation. We will not be used as pawns in someone else's war."

"I'm glad to hear that, Wemu. So let me explain why it is so difficult to remove the Inari. First, there are no habitable planets nearby; the cost to move every Inari to a suitable one would be enormous, more than the Federation itself—or the Romulan Empire—could afford. Second, the Inari refuse to leave; they point out that they were also once Djana's children, and have an ancient claim to the land. But I have a suggestion that I would like the Djanai to consider, and to reach a consensus on."

"If you will not remove the Inari—" Kel began next to him.

On the screen, Wemu held up a hand for silence. "Let us hear first what the Federation has to offer, Kel."

Kel became silent.

"As I said to your speaker," Kirk continued, "maybe the Federation can return much of your sacred land to you. I'm going to propose to my people, and to yours, and to the Inari, that much of the Inari industry can be moved to Inar."

"But that planet can no longer sustain life—" Wemu began.

"No. And to make the entire planet habitable again would be far too expensive. However, certain areas could be enclosed and made habitable—and those areas could be used to contain the Inari factories and distilleries, instead of building them on your sacred land." Kirk paused, seeking their reaction, but the elders' expressions were unreadable. If he lost them now . . . "All I ask from you now, Wemu, is that you and the Circle of Elders sit down with the Federation to discuss this. Nothing would be done, of course, until both you and your people agree."

He picked up the phaser in front of him and, in full view of the Circle, handed it to a surprised Kel.

"Thank you for hearing me out," Jim said. "I've completed my mission here, and now I am happy to become your prisoner once again."

Kel and Wemu hesitated for what seemed like a very long time. And then Wemu said, "You have acted honorably. Put down the phaser, Kel."

With measured, deliberate movement, Kel set the phaser on the desk, not quite midway between himself and Kirk. "You are free to return to your people," Kel told him.

Kirk grinned.

On the screen, Wemu said, "I shall tell my people what you have said, and have their consensus. Kel will tell you how to contact us again."

He said more, but his words were drowned out by the whine of a transporter beam. Both Kel and Kirk reached for the phaser; Kel, closer, got to it first.

Kirk stood up. His first thought was that the twenty minutes had passed (it hadn't) and that Olmsted's team was beaming in to rescue him . . . in which case, he was ready to lunge in front of Kel to protect him.

His second thought was that the Romulans had discovered the murder of one of their own, in which case he was prepared to duck under the table and let Kel handle the situation with the phaser.

But it was neither. Two humanoid figures coalesced out of light—one that Jim at first mistook for a Romulan . . .

. . . and the other was Dr. Leonard McCoy.

NINETEEN

───────── ☆ ─────────

At the sight of McCoy, Kirk smiled and took a step forward. *Bones . . .* he started to say.

But he kept silent. The doctor's eyes were full first of recognition, then terror, then a warning—as if he were afraid to acknowledge his friendship with Jim.

The Vulcan—Jim decided that he was Vulcan, first because Riley had mentioned McCoy's "berserk" Vulcan captor, and second because he wore the white robes of a Kolinahr postulant—seemed perfectly composed, and not at all insane.

"My name is Sekar. Rh'iov Rrhaen has not responded to my signals. I sense that he is not here," he said politely, unfazed by the weapon Kel shoved in his face. "Could you stand aside so that I may consult his computer?"

"Rh'iov Rrhaen is dead," Kel said, "as you soon shall be." The Djanai's thick stub of a finger tightened on the firing control; Jim saw that the phaser was set on kill. *He's not a Romulan, Kel,* he almost cried out.

The words died in his throat. And in that split second before Kel fired, Jim saw the others' reactions.

McCoy paled and squeezed his eyes shut. The Vulcan, astoundingly, smiled.

And Kel . . . Kel threw back his head and shrieked as the phaser became molten metal in his hand.

The Vulcan continued smiling, and watched patiently as his

would-be attacker sank onto his haunches behind the desk, grabbing the wrist of his offended hand. The phaser oozed slowly onto the floor in a thick, molasseslike puddle; steam rose from it with a faint hiss.

"Now," Sekar said cheerfully over Kel's agonized moans, "if you will kindly move away from the terminal, please."

Jim helped the injured Djanai to his feet and led him back to the cot. The formerly yellow-orange flesh of Kel's palm was angry red and blistering in spots, the vestigial hooves on either side of his hands charred grayish black. Kel lay down with the wounded extremity resting on his chest. Jim looked up at the Vulcan's broad back as Sekar bent over the terminal. What looked like a star map of the Neutral Zone, labeled in Romulan script, flashed on the screen.

What the Vulcan had done to Kel with a glance was beyond all understanding, all belief, and explained the haunted look in McCoy's eyes. Even so, Kirk forgot his fear as he examined Kel's burns.

"He needs help," Jim said angrily to the Vulcan's back. "These are second- and third-degree burns."

"Jim . . . please be quiet," McCoy begged softly. Kirk shot him a look of disgust, on the verge of saying, *And here you are, a doctor . . .*

Until he saw, *really* saw, the expression on McCoy's white, drawn face, and understood. The doctor wasn't terrified for himself, but for Jim and Kel—terrified that Jim would draw the Vulcan's attention and get himself and the Djanai killed for his efforts.

Kirk looked down at Kel in grim silence. The speaker's wounds were excruciating—but probably not fatal. Once the Vulcan was gone, he would get Kel to a medic.

If the Vulcan let them live.

Apparently satisfied with what he had seen on the terminal screen, Sekar rose. "Come, Doctor. The transporter room would be that way." He pointed in the direction of the corridor.

And then Kirk's communicator whistled. Jim sat stiffly still and ignored it; after seeing what the Vulcan was capable of, he didn't want to bring Lori into this, not even at an apparently safe distance.

Yet he knew that if he didn't answer, Ciana had sworn to send in the rescue team . . . and he seriously doubted they were a match for this Vulcan who called himself Sekar. If he just ignored the signal long enough for Sekar to leave the room . . .

He let the communicator continue to whistle, and prayed like hell Ciana could read his mind.

Fortunately, Sekar seemed undisturbed by the signal. He stepped up to the door, which opened, and gestured the doctor through. Still ashen-faced, McCoy gave Kirk and the Djanai one last concerned glance and headed meekly into the corridor. Sekar followed.

"Bones," Jim whispered as the door closed over them; but for Kel and McCoy's sakes, he did nothing. And then the doctor and Sekar were gone.

In Ciana's secured quarters on Djana, Olmsted checked the chrono on his wrist. "Excuse me a moment," he said politely to Commander Uhura and Ambassador Sarek, both of whom he had been debriefing. The former hostages appeared to be in perfect health, but Ciana had already sent for a Fleet medic, just to be sure.

Olmsted struggled up out of the low chair and walked over to the other side of the large suite, where Ciana waited anxiously by the terminal. She'd sat on the edge of the low sofa the entire time, ready to jump at the slightest sound from the comm.

"Your twenty minutes are up," Olmsted said, and scanned the admiral's face for a reaction.

"What makes you think they're *my* twenty minutes?" she snapped. Olmsted didn't have an answer for that.

"Sorry," she said, running a careless hand through her short hair. Olmsted, she decided, in spite of the fact she sometimes jumped down his throat, wasn't a bad sort at all. She'd worried he would override her order and go straight to Nogura for authorization to send in his team. But he'd done nothing of the sort—had only sat and calmly debriefed Sarek and Uhura while they waited to hear back from Jim.

Now she could tell from the deep creases settling between his brows that his supply of patience was nearing exhaustion. His people were mobilized and ready on a cloaked fighter orbiting Inar's second moon as they awaited Olmsted's order to strike.

"Not yet," Ciana told him. "Jim may have just forgotten. Let me contact him."

She leaned forward to touch the terminal controls, and sent out a signal on the reserved channel.

Please, Jim, answer. For God's sake, be all right and answer.

No reply. She scanned quickly for a malfunction—there was none. The communicator was functioning; it was signaling at the other end. . . .

No one was there to answer. Yet Ciana couldn't believe that Jim would forget—or, for that matter, be stupid enough to let himself get captured again. In the short time she had worked with him, she had come to know him *very* well . . . because he was cut from the same cloth as she. No, something else was happening, something that none of them had foreseen.

"Do they still have Admiral Kirk?" Commander Uhura's soft, elegant voice asked behind her.

Ciana did not turn, did not answer.

"Sorry, Admiral," Olmsted said, and from his tone it was clear he meant it. He reached a plump, dimpled hand past her, toward the terminal controls. "I'm going to send my people in there."

She leaned to one side and blocked him. "No. One more time. I'm going to try again—"

"Admiral," Olmsted repeated firmly.

She repunched the code as he spoke. There was an agonizing pause as Jim's communicator was signaled at the other end.

And was unanswered.

Dammit, Kirk, I can't lose you again.

"Kirk here."

The relief was so intense she nearly sagged onto the controls, but caught herself and straightened at once. "Jim! What's going on?"

From his voice, she knew immediately that something bad had happened. "I'm with Kel," he said shortly. "Beam us both up, and have a medic standing by."

Kirk beamed into Ciana's quarters with one arm assisting Kel; as soon as he helped the Djanai off the platform, Kel, though clearly in great pain, waved Jim away with his good hand. "It is not fatal," he said.

But he grudgingly submitted to the ministrations of an Inari medic who awaited him.

Lori Ciana was waiting too; as she caught Jim's gaze, the smile started in her eyes and slowly moved down her face.

"Admiral," she said softly. And though she behaved with

the perfect decorum befitting her rank, she somehow made it clear to Jim that were it not for the presence of Kel and the medic and Olmsted, she would have thrown herself into his arms. As it was, he grasped her hand and gave it a brief strong squeeze; both dropped their hands as Olmsted walked around from the small transporter console.

"Glad to see you again, Kirk," Olmsted told him jovially, and gave him a friendly swat on the back. "For a minute there, I was sure I'd have to send my people in after you, but the vice admiral here wouldn't let me."

"That's because she has good instincts," Kirk said; Olmsted frowned curiously and was on the verge of saying something when Lori interrupted.

"What happened down there, Jim?"

"I escaped—obviously—and got Kel to let me speak with the Djanai Circle of Elders. They're going to talk to us, Lori. They're willing to sit down with representatives of the Federation."

She closed her eyes and let out a sigh of weary relief.

"Good job," Olmsted said, giving him another thump on the shoulder.

Lori opened her eyes. *"Damn* good job." But she eyed his face with concern; she had noticed that he hadn't yet smiled. "There's more, though, Jim, isn't there? Something's wrong. What?"

"It's McCoy," he said heavily. "Riley was right—McCoy's been kidnapped, and by someone extremely dangerous."

"I thought he said the doctor was kidnapped by a Vulcan."

Kirk nodded. "A Vulcan, by all appearances . . . but he did *that* to Kel's hand." He inclined his head in the direction of the Djanai and the medic. Kel had collapsed on a sofa, his good arm thrown up over his face, while the Inari ran a subsonic stimulator over the burned tissue of Kel's palm.

Puzzled, Lori squinted over at the Djanai, then back at Kirk, and frowned. "How did he do it? Burning phaser?"

Kirk shook his head. "He had no weapons on him that I could see, Admiral. He just . . . made it happen. He came and got information from the Romulan computers—a location, I think. And then he left, and took Bones with him."

"Is McCoy all right?"

"He seemed to be. But the question is, for how long? The Vulcan—if he *is* a Vulcan—is *not* sane."

Ciana was silent as she gazed at Kel and the medic; and then she seemed to reach a decision. "Jim, you know that I overheard your conversation with Nogura—the one about McCoy. The doctor's your friend . . . and your mission here is complete. As your superior officer, I hereby give you a new assignment—to assist the Vulcans in their rescue operations."

He gave her a look that was pure gratitude, but said: "Lori, I'd go on a second's notice—but I can't. We both know that. Our mission here is far from over . . . and besides, even if I took you up on the offer, the flak you'd catch from Nogura—"

"I don't give a damn about Nogura. He's mad at me already. And what you don't know, Jim, is that our Inari 'friends' "—she lowered her voice and glanced back at the medic—"have very good reason to cooperate with us now. In fact, I'm sure they'll be more than willing to listen to whatever proposals we come up with." She almost smiled. "Our friend Ruwe had your shield rigged to fail—"

"What?" Kirk was astounded.

She nodded, continuing. "So we would get upset with the Djanai, listen to the Inari stories about how impossible they were to deal with, and send in Olmsted's team. I think the idea was to so disillusion us that we would deal only with the Inari, and refuse to hear what the Djanai were saying." She finally did smile, showing the briefest flash of dimple. "You know, it's amazing how far a little blackmail goes. If I keep Ruwe's little secret—don't tell Nogura and don't remove Federation protection for their trading vessels—the Inari Council is willing to negotiate with us on a settlement."

Kirk's own smile was grim. "Congratulations, Admiral. Frankly, I'm beginning to think you don't need me after all."

"Oh, I need you, all right, Kirk. You took care of the Djanai, I took care of the Inari. I'd say it was a pretty effective partnership."

Kirk's grin faded; his tone became serious. "Of course, Nogura said I could help McCoy only if both sides were talking. They're not quite at that stage, Admiral—"

"Both groups are willing to talk to us. So we play intermediary. What's the difference?"

Jim thought about it, and remembered the look of stark fear in McCoy's eyes. "Lori . . . if I go, I want you to know that I'll consider this the favor you said you owed me. And I mean that."

He was referring to the time she had offered, in a year or two, to recommend him for command of the *Enterprise*.

McCoy's friendship was worth more, after all, than command, worth more than any lifeless collection of metal and bolts.

Still, part of him was hoping she would say, *I still owe you that recommendation, Jim; of course, this doesn't count as your favor.*

But she didn't. She said, "Fair enough. Just promise me one thing—"

He looked questioningly at her.

"Come back," she said.

McCoy decided that they had passed into the Neutral Zone. He had no real way of knowing, of course, and Sekar—it was always Sekar, the rational Vulcan, who piloted the scout—volunteered no information, and the doctor, afraid of rousing Zakal, did not ask. But McCoy had seen the star map labeled in Romulan on the terminal screen, and he knew that Arcturus wasn't all that far from the buffer of dead space separating Federation territory from the Praetor's Empire.

When he and the Vulcan had beamed down to meet Sekar's Romulan contact, McCoy had been astonished and glad and horrified all at once to see Jim again. Astonished, because even though the doctor had contacted Riley for help, Jim was supposed to be away on a mission. He was even more astonished when he realized Jim wasn't there because he was trying to rescue him, McCoy . . . the look on Jim's face had been one of sheer shock.

McCoy had been glad, for one lovely but fleeting instant, just to see Jim once more, because he had convinced himself that Keridwen's prediction was going to come true. After all, Zakal was a lunatic, a murderer, and McCoy had resigned himself to hopelessness, to wait for that awful moment when he failed to "amuse" the Vulcan sufficiently.

And he was horrified that Jim should get caught up in this mess. He prayed that Kirk would not be so foolish as to attempt a rescue (a pointless prayer, McCoy suspected, knowing Jim). Bad enough that Spock was following. Dwen had predicted *two* deaths . . . if Jim had been there, at the tarot reading, would she have predicted a third?

There was yet another reason that the doctor suspected Dwen's scout had made it to the Romulan side of the Zone. In the last hour, Sekar had fussed endlessly over the cloaking device, then become increasingly anxious, at times even pacing, and at other times uttering terse messages (apparently unanswered) into the subspace transmitter.

McCoy decided it behooved him to stay well out of Sekar's—and Zakal's—way, so he propped himself up into a sitting position on the bunk and stayed there. From time to time he drowsed, struggling vainly against the strange, unpleasant twilight state that was something less than sleep.

The shrill signal of the subspace radio woke him. Sekar began to chatter excitedly into the transmitter, in a language not quite Vulcan.

Romulan, of course. A Romulan vessel must have finally responded to Sekar's signal. McCoy sat forward, suddenly alert.

Sekar engaged the autopilot, rose, and headed back toward the bunk where McCoy watched.

"Dr. McCoy," he said, standing over him. It was definitely the Sekar personality, that of the ultrareserved, logical Vulcan, so that McCoy was not particularly frightened. But beneath that reserve was a mounting excitement even Sekar could not entirely conceal. "Would you mind stepping onto the transporter platform with me?"

McCoy was mightily tempted to point out the illogic of phrasing that particular command as a question, but held his tongue. He rose and took the four steps necessary to make it over to the claustrophobic transporter chamber—two pads scarcely large enough for an adult human and a small console mounted on the bulkhead.

Sekar spoke a few more words of Romulan into the transmitter grid on the console. The Vulcan waited for a reply—one remarkably free of static, indicating that they were very close to those responding—and then stepped onto the pad next to the doctor.

McCoy felt the gentle nausea of dematerialization and closed his eyes. He had no idea where he and Sekar would reappear; he would not have been surprised to find himself in front of the Presidium.

As it was, when he dared open his eyes again, he saw what appeared to be the transporter room of a Romulan Bird of Prey—a place he had been a very few times in his life, but those few were sufficient to etch themselves indelibly on his memory.

At the sight of Sekar, four Romulan centurions came toward the platform. Sekar—or Zakal, McCoy wasn't quite sure anymore

which—stepped forward with palms open in a display of friendship, and uttered a greeting. One of the centurions, obviously the
leader, replied politely and to the Vulcan's apparent satisfaction.
Two of them escorted Sekar in a fashion similar to that of a
Federation honor guard, and two of them drew phasers and
motioned at McCoy in a way that made it clear he was now their
prisoner.

The doctor experienced an odd sense of relief; at last he was
freed from Zakal's clutches, even if it only meant that he would
spend an unspecified amount of time contemplating the interior
of a Romulan brig. But at least now he had the hope that he
would be processed and released . . . after all, he had committed
no crime against the Romulans, had been forced to enter their
danged Neutral Zone against his will.

McCoy and his centurions followed a short distance behind
Sekar and his honor guard; at any moment McCoy expected to
be led in a different direction, toward his cell. Sekar would no
doubt be escorted and warmly introduced to the commander of
this particular vessel.

Yet when the centurions led Sekar down a long stretch of
corridor and through a narrow entranceway, McCoy's guards
followed. Perhaps, McCoy thought, he was being led along with
Sekar to see the commander, to be displayed as a sort of trophy,
after which the brig would certainly follow.

But as soon as McCoy stepped inside, he realized a trick had
been played on the unsuspecting Sekar. The centurions had led
them both to the brig . . . and Sekar now stood at the entrance to
the holding cell, his head turned to one side to stare over his
shoulder at his deceitful captors. McCoy, sandwiched front and
back between two centurions, caught sight of the Vulcan's face
and recoiled until his right shoulder blade made firm contact with
the phaser held by the Romulan behind him.

Sekar's expression was one of pure fury.

TWENTY

─────────────── ☆ ───────────────

In Ciana's quarters, Kirk waited impatiently for notification that the Inari vessel was available.

"You might find this interesting, Admiral," Olmsted said. "I've been scanning the area around the Djanai base, looking for any activity, and I've just picked up a vessel—Vulcan registry, from the looks of her." He peered up at Kirk. "I figured that if the Vulcans were on Dr. McCoy's trail, they might wind up in this area. Think it could be your friend?"

"Spock." Kirk grinned. "I wouldn't be surprised. Can you open a hailing frequency?"

"I think we can manage that," Olmsted said easily. He punched a few controls on the console, then stepped aside and motioned for Kirk to speak into the transmitter grid. "She's all yours."

"Thanks." Pulse quickening, Kirk leaned over the console. Maybe he wouldn't have to wait for that Inari ship, after all. "Admiral Kirk to Vulcan vessel. Come in, please."

No reply. He gave them fifteen seconds before trying again.

"Kirk to Vulcan vessel. Please identify yourselves."

Another five seconds passed, and then:

"This is Spock." The tone was terse, cool, without a hint of recognition.

Yet Kirk could not help smiling at the sound of the Vulcan's voice. "Spock!"

270

"Where are you signaling from, Admiral?"

"It's not important. Listen, I have good news. Your father has been released unharmed."

There was a pause, and then Spock replied, in the same strangely aloof tone, "I see. This is indeed good news. Has my mother been informed?"

"My guess is Starfleet has taken care of that by now." Kirk hesitated. "Spock . . ." His manner became gravely serious. "I know about McCoy. He tried to contact me at HQ—and I want to help. Nogura has given me authorization. Need a copilot?"

But the Vulcan's response was guarded. "I see you have inferred our situation, Admiral. However, I already have a capable copilot. And I'm afraid the craft is too small to permit another passenger."

Kirk would have felt no different had Spock slapped him in the face—but the situation was far too critical to waste even a second registering hurt feelings. "Spock, the Vulcan—or whatever he was—was just in this area. I saw him. And I know he's got McCoy with him. Whatever kind of weapon he's got, the Romulans have gone to an awful lot of trouble to get it. I'm coming along."

"I emphatically request that you do not, Admiral." Spock's voice was suddenly, surprisingly, full of passion. "The mission contains dangers you cannot fathom."

"I've dealt with the Romulans on their own turf before. And if it's that dangerous, then how can I let you go without my help?"

"I have . . . special assistance," Spock countered, "the nature of which I am not at leave to discuss. Admiral—" He broke off abruptly, as if unwilling to continue the thought; finally he said: "Admiral, if you insist on following, there is nothing we can do to protect you. I can only warn that the danger is great."

Kirk no longer attempted to hide his anger and frustration. "I'm not asking for your protection. Dammit, Spock, I'm asking to *help*—"

"Forgive me," Spock interrupted in the same odd tone. "Admiral, I can no longer continue this conversation."

"Spock—"

But he had already closed the channel.

Disbelieving, Kirk stared at the grid. He raised a fist, intending to slam it down on the console . . . and let it drop limply against the toggle that cut off transmission.

It was the same frosty reception it had been when the Vulcan called to say good-bye—as if Spock wanted nothing more to do with him, as if the Vulcan were suddenly ashamed of his human friends.

No, that can't be right—after all, he's risking his neck to save McCoy's, isn't he?

But then what could account for Spock's distant attitude?

Kirk turned away from the console. Whatever the cause, it didn't matter; he was going to follow the Vulcan ship anyway.

Since the first moment he had allowed Zakal into his consciousness, Sekar had struggled to maintain control of his body—indeed, most times the Master granted him full control, especially when Sekar's knowledge and expertise were necessary . . . though Zakal's outbursts, when he seized Sekar's body without warning, were most unsettling. Yet, from sharing Zakal's consciousness, Sekar learned that even the Master grew tired and required rest; apparently the constant monitoring and discouragement of their pursuers fatigued him.

And so Sekar generally maintained control. Sekar piloted the vessel, Sekar made the decisions affecting their journey's course. It was he who chose to beam down to Rrhaen's base even though contact with the rh'iov had been lost, he who accessed the star maps on the Romulan computer, he who decided the best alternate course of action was to flag down the nearest Romulan vessel and request transport to the Praetor himself.

Yet there were times when Zakal took unannounced, total control. It shocked Sekar that the High Master would do such a thing without asking permission; it was a contingency for which he had not prepared. He was even less prepared for Zakal's cruelty. True, Sekar disagreed with the Surakians and felt there were times when killing was necessary, even beneficial, to society. And he had told himself he was ready if, during his mission, killing became unavoidable. He also knew of Zakal's history; he knew the Master, in his time, had brought about the deaths of many.

He simply was not prepared to know that Zakal *enjoyed* it.

The incidents with the Tellarite thief and the Gorn in the bar were painful memories for Sekar. Zakal had overpowered him, pushed him aside as if he were an insensate object, a thing of no consequence rather than a living, rational being. And then the

High Master had killed without need, without compunction . . . worst of all, with utter delight. Sekar felt deep shame.

But now his anger overshadowed any sense of guilt. The Declared, the very ones he sought most to help, were those who betrayed him now . . . who promised to present him to the rh'iov of the vessel, and instead led him to a criminal's cell.

And in that instant of overwhelming anger, Sekar relinquished all control, and gladly, to Master Zakal.

Zakal watched quietly as the one centurion put McCoy into a holding cell and activated the force field . . . and then turned to point a weapon at him. Clearly the empty cell next to the weakling human was intended for Sekar.

Zakal smiled with pleasure at what was to come, yet his satisfaction was tainted with disappointment. These who called themselves the Declared were indeed of Vulcan ancestry, and Zakal sensed from the two specimens before him that they were passionate warriors who would not shrink from the battle to regain their home planet—for that, he was glad. But over the great span of time, their minds had weakened. They had lost the mental disciplines, and in these four, at least, there was not talent, not even the vaguest predisposition for sorcery.

If they are all like this, what chance have we of defeating the children of Surak?

The guard behind him—a slow-witted imbecile named Vrael, whose interest lay in the physical and whose mind was as easily read as an unrolled scroll—thrust his weapon hard into Sekar's back, in the tender region of the liver. Zakal registered the body's discomfort and Sekar's personal frustration at such mistreatment—and decided it was time to act.

He took control of the body and turned it to stare directly into his prodder's vacant eyes. "Do you know who I am?" Zakal asked politely, in perfect parody of Sekar's Surakian manners.

Vrael hesitated, uncertain whether it would be good form to answer a prisoner's question.

But the Master already knew his thoughts. "I am Zakal," he said in the colloquial dialect provided him by Sekar's mind. "High Master of the Kolinahru." He spoke quickly, before the other guards had an opportunity to interrupt, and in case Vrael did not recognize the name, Zakal communicated directly to Vrael's mind exactly who and what he was.

Vrael dropped his phaser and put his hands to his head. The

nearest guard retrieved it, and shouted at his fellow, a request to know what was happening.

But it was too late for Vrael to answer.

"Your brains are on fire," Zakal said.

Vrael screamed and reared back in agony, palms pressed hard against his temples . . . and then collapsed on the floor.

His companion, young and inexperienced, dropped to his knees to examine Vrael. The other centurions knew enough to keep their phasers trained on Zakal. Zakal could have easily overtaken all three of them at that point, but he knew it was unnecessary . . . and besides, he was so looking forward to their reactions.

An unholy mixture of blood and brains oozed from Vrael's ears and nose.

The young Romulan saw and fainted dead away. The other two stared, sickened and disbelieving, at Zakal.

"Please," the Master invited them. "Use your weapons."

Their hands trembled so that taking aim was impossible. One of them dropped his phaser.

Zakal laughed as he willed them all dead, then went to find the bridge.

Rh'iov Alrrae swiveled one hundred and eighty degrees in her command chair to frown at her communications officer. "*What* did you say?"

Rie's black hair was streaked with silver; she was old for her rank, too old to be assigned to a communications board, and clearly resented it. When she answered Alrrae, there was a trace of hostility in her tone. She turned to calmly repeat her entire sentence, word for word, to her commander; Rie was stupid, and a literalist. "The transporter room verifies that the prisoners are on board, Rh'iov; but I have just lost contact with Vrael."

Alrrae was on her feet now. She knew that Rie despised her, and she did not care. She would not have cared had she known her entire crew hated her and wished her ill. There was no silver in her hair; she was young, one of the youngest commanders in the Praetor's service, and one of the most ambitious. The Elements seemed to back her meteoric rise to power, and she fully intended to be a member of the Praetor's Inner Council before she reached middle age.

Now here was another sweet tidbit, another unasked-for gift to launch her to even greater heights: two Federation prisoners, one a Vulcan with a bizarre story, and she would not let them go so easily. "If Vrael does not respond, what of Ren?"

"Not responding, Rh'iov," Rie said sulkily, narrowing her eyes to show that she was quite aware the question insulted her intelligence. The main viewscreen showed the tiny scout, held in place by the Bird of Prey's tractor beam. Alrrae stared at it without seeing it.

"Notify the crew: first-degree alert. Inform them of two escaped prisoners, one Vulcan, one human. Send available centurions to the transporter room and the brig, then seal off Level Six."

"Yes, Rh'iov," Rie answered in the same defensive tone, and turned back to her station.

"Science Officer Trel." Alrrae stepped down from the command platform. "Adjust our scanners for a human, and scan all levels beginning with the sixth. Tell me as soon as you have him."

"Yes, Rh'iov." Trel, pale and slender, bent over his viewer. Its greenish-yellow glow bathed his expressionless face briefly; then he straightened. "Rh'iov," he said without emotion. At times, Alrrae was convinced Trel had been snatched as a babe from a Vulcan cradle. "The human is located on Level Six, as he should be. The force shield on his cell is operating correctly."

"Elements!" Alrrae swore. She was impatient by nature, because (or so she told herself) she was so much more intelligent than those around her, and their slow, stupid ways vexed her. "If the prisoners are in the brig, Trel, then why do Vrael and Ren not respond?"

Trel stared back down at his viewer and raised his fair golden brows in surprise. "Rh'iov, the Vulcan is not on the sixth level, but I have located four of our own . . . all dead. Apparently—"

He broke off, distracted by the sound of the bridge doors opening.

Alrrae pushed herself up out of her seat and turned to regard the intruder. It was, as her instincts had warned her, the Vulcan; he wore a long white robe of a vaguely archaic-looking style Alrrae did not recognize. He was of formidable size and heavily muscled, but Alrrae was unafraid. She and every one of her bridge crew carried phasers on their weapons belt; the Vulcan clearly carried no weapon at all.

Alrrae drew her phaser and moved forward until she was not quite arm's length from the Vulcan. She did not expect him to attack, but it paid to be cautious until she knew for certain with whom she was dealing.

"You are the rh'iov," the Vulcan said, undaunted by the phaser she pointed at the center of his chest. It was not a question; he seemed to be quite certain of her rank. "Greetings. I spoke with you earlier, on the scout."

"Yes," she replied carefully, although she wondered how he had recognized her; the communication had not been visual. She remembered the Vulcan's story, all right; a fantastic claim, that of a madman (or a Federation trickster); she was tempted to blow the little ship out of the Neutral Zone on the spot. Nevertheless, she did the smart thing—Alrrae *always* did the smart thing—and informed her High Command of the situation. Now she awaited their instructions.

"You claim your name is Sekar," she told the Vulcan. "You say you work for our Empire and that you have completed a mission for the Praetor—that you have brought us a prize. But I know nothing of your mission, Sekar; therefore, I am obligated to treat you as an agent of the Federation until I receive verification of your story from my superiors. Surely you can understand my position. Your vessel is, after all, of Federation registry—"

His face twisted angrily at that. *Oho,* Alrrae thought, *what kind of Vulcan is this?*

"Rh'iov Alrrae," he thundered, and her heart missed a beat because she had not told him her name. "I have waited ten thousand seasons to offer my help to your race."

"Help?" Alrrae let irony creep into her voice, an attempt to hide her unsettledness. No matter; he must have obtained her name from one of the centurions. "What sort of help do you propose to offer us?"

"The power to reclaim your birthright—the planet Vulcan." He paused dramatically, then said, "I am Zakal, High Master of the Kolinahru, mind-lord of ShanaiKahr. And I have come to bring the lost knowledge of the mind-rules to the children of the Declared."

I see, Alrrae came close to saying dryly, *and I am President of the Federation Council.* But instinct held her back. These were the words of a madman, all right, and yet . . . the Vulcan spoke with an authority that was persuasive.

And he *had* known her name. Alrrae's mind raced through the possibilities. Suppose, just suppose that the Vulcan were telling the truth. As a child, she had heard whispered stories of the ancient mind-lords' powers, of their undying souls hidden in secret caverns, deep beneath Vulcan's surface . . . and she had half-believed.

Now it occurred to her that some of the old legends might be true.

When the Vulcan had first contacted her vessel, Alrrae had forwarded his message to the High Command, requesting guidance and verification. And she would wait to hear back from them before taking any foolish leaps of faith.

"If you are who you claim," Alrrae said coolly, "give us proof." She folded her arms. "Surely you would not deny us that much; and if you are who you say, then I shall welcome you gladly."

"Proof," the Vulcan repeated. His lips twisted bitterly. "Very well, proof you shall have." He closed his eyes briefly, then opened them again.

"Rh'iov." Her helmsman, Ryllin, looked up panicked from his console. "The ship's self-destruct sequence has been initiated."

"Very good," Alrrae said softly, never moving her gaze from the Vulcan's face. "Ryllin, abort the sequence."

The sound of Ryllin's hands manipulating controls, and then his anguished voice: "Rh'iov, controls do not respond."

So . . . the legends were true, and the Elements had seen fit to grace her with a visit from a Vulcan mind-lord. "Lord Zakal," Alrrae said in the humblest tone she could affect—but before she could finish with *would you kindly return control to the helm, please,* Zakal spoke.

"Control is returned." And he smiled, but the expression made Alrrae's blood run cold.

Yet, if she could recruit him to her cause, if she could convince him to teach her his mental wizardry first, and no one else . . .

"And then you would kill me," Zakal said; Alrrae shuddered to hear her thoughts spoken aloud. "And use your powers to gain control of the Empire. I am afraid, my dear Rh'iov, that I cannot permit that. You are a dangerous woman, and besides, I need an example for the others."

In one horrifying flash he allowed her to see her own death approach. She faced it bravely, as a warrior ought, and did not scream; she could not have if she had wanted, for her throat had filled with blood.

Before the blood vessels in her eyes burst, the last thing she saw was the Vulcan, smiling.

Elements take you, old man. . . .

"And now," Zakal said cheerfully as he stood over Alrrae's blood-mottled corpse, "I wish to be taken directly to your Presidium, please."

For a moment, none of the stricken crew stirred.

"Then I presume," he continued, "that you all wish to die bravely, as your rh'iov did."

Another pause. And then, very slowly, Ryllin began to lay in a course.

TWENTY-ONE

☆

"It is time," T'Sai said.

Spock and Keridwen swiveled round in their chairs at the same time to see the High Master with her eyes open, regarding them serenely. Unlike Dr. Llewellyn, Spock was unsurprised; he had expected this. They had passed into the Neutral Zone some time ago, and now, cloaked and shielded, they had located Zakal and the ship aboard which Leonard McCoy, if he still lived, was a prisoner.

If in fact Zakal had permitted the doctor to live thus far, then even Spock would experience a faint wave of the emotion of surprise. Logically, it made no sense for Zakal to keep his human captive alive; though logic clearly did not govern Zakal's actions.

Dr. Llewellyn rose from her station and followed T'Sai aft to the transporter platform. Shortly after entering Romulan space, Spock had communicated to her that her assistance would be required in terms of the transporters; admittedly, while he could concentrate on shielding his thoughts from Zakal, his own control was imperfect, while Dwen's was infallible. Thus, even though she was human, she was the safer choice as transporter operator; Zakal would be all the more unlikely to sense T'Sai's impending arrival and try to prevent it.

Spock did his best not to find the fact somewhat galling. He busied himself with the scanners. He had chosen a research vessel for this particular mission precisely because its scanners

279

were sophisticated and extremely sensitive. It would be useful to know who else—if anyone—still lived aboard the ship that carried Zakal. Spock adjusted the scanners to differentiate between three distinct life forms: Romulan, human . . . and Vulcan.

No more than three seconds elapsed before the results showed on the monitor screen. Five life forms sensed: one Vulcan, three Romulans . . . and one human.

McCoy was still alive. Spock kept firm control of himself, harshly repressing the sensation of gratitude that tried to well up within him. In the past, Vulcans had been stronger empaths than telepaths; Zakal would be able to sense emotions faster and with greater ease than thoughts. Control was of paramount importance.

Spock distracted himself with the sensors, programming them to sweep a large area of neighboring space, to reassure himself that no other Romulan vessels lurked nearby—for the shields would have to be lowered when T'Sai was beamed over to the Bird of Prey. He was only peripherally aware that T'Sai had already stepped onto the platform and given the still-amazed Dr. Llewellyn the proper coordinates without consulting the ship's instruments. Spock ignored all this as best he could, to prevent Zakal from anticipating the High Master's imminent arrival.

Spock focused his attention on the scanner readout. It showed a tiny distorted section of space quite close to the cloaked research vessel. Spock's first thought was that it could be another Romulan vessel, forewarned of Zakal's intrusion—but the area of distortion was far too small to be a Bird of Prey; and if a Romulan ship were going to deal with Zakal, a more likely scenario would be that the Romulans would behave in a more direct fashion—by appearing, shields up against attack, and demanding an explanation.

No, it was most probably a Federation vessel.

"Kirk," Spock said aloud, and felt an honest surge of anger toward his former captain. Kirk had ignored his, Spock's, warning; the admiral, with his usual disdain for the unknown, had followed regardless, assuming that no matter what the danger, he was more than a match for it. His appearance now would only serve to jeopardize the mission—

A loud crackling sound behind him silenced the thought . . . and then the ship began to vibrate, as if the outer hull were being shaken by a giant invisible hand. Spock turned in time to see

T'Sai collapse on the platform. The transporter chamber rained red-orange sparks; there was the acrid smell of smoke.

"I don't understand," Keridwen cried as she struggled to lift the injured High Master and help her from the platform. She led T'Sai over to a nearby bunk. "The transporter seemed to be working perfectly. There's still no indication of a malfunction . . ."

But Spock understood all too well. In three long strides he made it to the bunk where T'Sai lay, and knelt down to examine her. She was semiconscious, not fatally wounded; but there were dark, ugly burns on her hands, face, and neck.

The whole ship was vibrating now, trying to shake itself apart.

"T'Sai," Spock half-shouted, loudly enough to be heard over the ship's groaning.

Her eyelids fluttered, then opened, and she gazed lucidly at him. The vibrations eased.

At the moment, Spock could not permit himself the luxury of guilt at what he had just caused. Zakal would sense that too, and destroy them all. It was clear that T'Sai was injured too severely to stand, much less walk; beaming her over to confront Zakal was now unthinkable.

"I will go," Spock said quietly, realizing as he spoke that he was no match for Zakal's talents, and that all was lost.

"No," T'Sai answered in a voice suddenly strong and not entirely her own. "Thee have not the power or the training, Spock . . ." And she looked up at Dr. Llewellyn.

Keridwen's eyes filled with a curious brightness. "Of course," she said huskily. "It only makes sense."

T'Sai gazed at her intently. "If you are willing . . . the advantage to us would be great. But the danger to you is greater."

Dr. Llewellyn appeared confused. "I don't understand."

T'Sai reached out and pressed warm, unsteady fingers against Dwen's forehead. It was not the politely shallow mind-brush Spock had attempted so long ago in the bar. T'Sai reached deep, and touched the inner core of Dwen's mind.

The effect on Dwen was one of euphoria . . . and astonishment at the revelation that she and T'Sai were not alone.

Throughout the journey, the High Master had been the silent, secret receptacle for the katra of another—a mind far more powerful, far more ancient than T'Sai's own.

We offer you the gift of magic, the great ancient mind said. *And yet, Dr. Llewellyn, the magic you offer us now is perhaps far greater than our own.*

The inner voice changed, became T'Sai's. *Be aware, Dr. Llewellyn, that what we offer is fraught with danger. For once your mind is joined to that of the Ancient One, the Other, the possibility exists that you will never be able to separate from each other . . . and your minds will be locked together so long as your body lives. Mind-meld has never been attempted with one who is esper-blind, because of the danger involved. I cannot be sure of the outcome.*

"I'm willing to risk it," Dwen said, "if the Other is too."

T'Sai's eyes closed. *He is willing to risk all, including the second death. Are thee?*

The question caused a sword-sharp image to flash in Dwen's mind. It was Death again . . . and this time, it was not the gray heaviness she had seen hovering over Spock and McCoy. It was detailed and concrete. This time she saw it clearly, and this time she was not afraid.

The Ancient One saw the image too, and did not shrink from it. It was a simple choice between Death and Life. They could choose to remain on the ship, and be safe . . .

And Spock and Leonard McCoy would die, and the evil would live.

. . . or there was another path . . .

Dwen and the Ancient One made their decision. "Yes," she said aloud. "Oh, yes."

And smiled.

After the meld was complete, Spock lowered the shields for the few seconds necessary to beam Dwen over to the Romulan vessel. T'Sai lay on the bunk, refusing to heal her wounds so that she might concentrate on protecting the ship. Both the High Master and Spock were uncertain whether their combined powers would be enough to protect the small craft; but Dwen had seen the future, and knew they would be safe.

The union with the Ancient One's mind was sheer bliss; all the knowledge, all the experience of a life span twice that of a human's, was as available to Dwen as if she had lived it herself. Each gained and lost something in the exchange—the Ancient One lost the ability to sense Zakal's thoughts—yet gained the freedom to move about the ship without Zakal's detection. Dwen gained the Ancient One's wisdom and power (*magic*, he had called it at first, though now Dwen saw it was not magic at all, merely the elegant, creative application of science) . . .

And the loss would be her own life.

She materialized on the engineering deck. It was the largest room on the ship, thus reducing her chance of materializing inside a bulkhead. It was also safer than beaming directly in front of Zakal—and beaming directly into the Bird of Prey's transporter, Spock had pointed out, would alert what remained of the bridge crew to her arrival. This way, Dwen could walk undetected on the ship . . . sabotage the phasers undetected, and perform the one task that would guarantee her mission's success—the one task she and the Ancient One had kept secret from both T'Sai and Spock.

Dwen moved stealthily through the vast engineering deck. At its far opposite end, in a partitioned area, a Romulan engineer sat with his back to her. Zakal had permitted this one to live, no doubt because he was necessary to the ship's function. But the Romulan sat half-slumped at his station, as if he were drugged, oblivious to his surroundings.

Dwen approached silently from behind. Following the Ancient One's instructions, she laid a cool hand against the warm flesh of the Romulan's left temple; with her right hand, Dwen found the vulnerable spot on the engineer's right shoulder and pressed. "Sleep," she whispered into his ear.

It worked. The Romulan slumped forward, unconscious, and in the millisecond between the time her left and right hands touched him, the Ancient One gathered the necessary knowledge. If Zakal had sensed anything, he might think that his prisoner had gone to sleep.

The engineer's knowledge was put to good use. Dwen bent over his slumbering form to reach the console. . . .

The ship's computer responded immediately to her touch. It was odd to hear and see the Romulan language and understand it . . . it was odder still to program in what she knew would be the manner of her own death.

When Dwen and the Ancient One finished their work, she straightened. It was time to find Zakal. Spock, familiar with the interior of a Bird of Prey, had given directions: the Vulcan life form was two levels up, on the bridge.

The human part of her was thinking of Leonard McCoy, in a cell somewhere nearby; yet the older, wiser mind in her knew that Zakal must be dealt with first. Far worse for him to go free than for Leonard McCoy to die.

And the human part of her had glimpsed the future. If she went directly to the bridge now, Leonard would be all right.

Dwen went straight to the lift, up to the first level, then made her way down the long corridor to the bridge.

The doors opened before her without hesitation. Even without the capacity to sense Zakal's thoughts, both she and the Ancient One knew instantly where he was.

The doors closed behind her as she stepped onto the bridge, her gaze fixed on the back of the dead commander's chair.

At the sound of the doors snapping shut, Zakal whirled the chair around and gaped at her, his expression one of utter astonishment.

Dwen's lips moved, but it was Sotek who spoke.

"Master? I have come."

TWENTY-TWO

───────── ☆ ─────────

Once in the Neutral Zone, Spock's scout-class research vessel
engaged its cloaking device, and Kirk, who had already raised
the Inari vessel's cloak, found it a challenge to follow. Scanning
an entire quadrant of space for an infinitesimal patch of distortion
that moved at warp speed, and then trying to keep up with it, was
clearly impossible. Jim adjusted the sensors on the two-person
vessel to cover a broader range, then asked the computer to
project the research ship's current course.

Less than half a parsec distant on this particular heading
sailed a lone Bird of Prey . . . which just happened to hold a small
Federation scout in its tractor beam. This was no doubt the vessel
Spock pursued.

Jim increased speed to maximum and laid in a course that
would keep him parallel to the Romulan vessel—and the tiny fast-
moving area of distorted space.

When at last he was within transporter range of either vessel,
Jim checked his scanners. The Bird of Prey was uncloaked,
unshielded, apparently unaware or unafraid of its pursuers. Curiously, the life-form readings indicated only three Romulans
aboard instead of the normal complement of twelve; either the
crew had deserted ship . . .

Or, more likely, been killed. There was also McCoy's mysterious Vulcan . . . and two humans.

That last bit of data threw him; Jim blinked and squinted at the readout again. No mistake. There were definitely two humans on board, one on the lowest level of the ship—in an area Jim knew from personal experience was most likely the brig—and one on the uppermost level, the bridge.

There were no other life forms near the brig; but the human on the bridge was surrounded by the Vulcan and two Romulans. The question was, which one was McCoy? The scanners on the Inari vessel were good, but they weren't *that* good.

Instinct told him McCoy was a prisoner in the brig—which meant he would be shielded from transporter beams, to prevent escape. Jim would have to beam over to release him, then transport the two of them back to the Inari vessel.

Except that he couldn't help wondering who the other human was.

And it made sense to stop the Vulcan before he reached his destination and turned over the weapon—whatever it was—to the Romulan government.

Logically, Jim began to reason with himself . . . and the phrase made him pause to smile before he continued with the thought. He let it continue in his former first officer's voice. *Logically, Captain, one should beam down to the brig first. Dr. McCoy could then be released and transported back before you proceeded to the more dangerous area of the bridge. However, if you beam directly to the bridge . . .*

Kirk stopped the thought there. The consideration of what might happen painted a vivid image.

He set the ship on autopilot and hoped like hell the Romulans didn't suddenly decide to make a drastic alteration in their course heading . . . and then he went over to the one-pad transporter and locked in the coordinates for the Bird of Prey's brig.

Zakal's face contorted with rage as he recognized his former student and foe. He leapt to his feet. "Khoteth!"

The sight of the Vulcan's anger was enough to make the two Romulans—the communications officer and the helmsman—cringe at their stations, but the weakling human female merely smiled at him.

It was Khoteth, all right—of that, Zakal was sure. But the circumstances were far different from the circumstances of that night fifteen thousand seasons before. For now, Khoteth's mind was closed, impenetrable. Impossibly, this woman had managed to bring Khoteth onto the ship without Zakal's knowledge—and that realization made Zakal *afraid*.

SEKAR, Zakal commanded, rousing the younger Vulcan's mind from its twilight state. Although Sekar was not yet a full-fledged initiate, his mental energy might prove to be of some use, after all. SEKAR, YOU MUST HELP ME NOW.

But he sensed Sekar's disillusionment. Ultimately, the young Vulcan proved himself to be a Surakian coward.

No, Master, Sekar answered. The response felt infinitely weary and detached. *I have seen your true essence . . . and I will no longer help you kill. You do not truly wish to help the Declared; you wish only to use them to defeat the children of Surak. Once you are done with them, you will terrorize them as well.*

Zakal roared silently, and ejected the ragged fragments of Sekar's katra from his body.

All this occurred in less than an instant . . . and then the woman's form began to glow, a soft blue, tinged with gold. She took a step toward him, and spoke aloud in a voice Zakal knew was Khoteth's own:

"And now, Master, your time has come again."

The two powerful enemies confronted each other again, this time for the final battle.

Rie had sat on the bridge at the communications console ever since the Vulcan intruder killed the rh'iov. She had been permitted to drag the commander's stiffening corpse out of the way, and prop it, half-sitting, against a nearby bulkhead. Alrrae's blood-filled eyes and mouth remained wide open; Rie thought her expression was one of rebuke, as if she were on the verge of saying, *Well? Why don't you or Ryllin do something? Why do you just sit there at your posts like cowards?*

Rie was not sure *why* she sat at her post; she only knew she could do nothing more. It was as if the Vulcan held her mesmerized; she dwelled in a waking nightmare where she was powerless to move, even to scream.

Yet, when the human stepped onto the bridge, everything changed. As Zakal rose from his chair, Rie felt the heaviness lift. She turned her head cautiously to peer over at Ryllin, who still sat at the helm. He caught her glance and gave a slow, almost imperceptible nod. He felt it too.

The bridge brightened as the human began to glow with a

strange blue light. A struggle was coming, Rie guessed, one that it was best not to become involved in. She shielded her eyes with cupped hands and peered again at Ryllin. He was taking full advantage of Zakal's distraction; his hands were a swift-moving blur above his console controls. Rie was a trained Romulan soldier; she did not have to ask what he was doing.

In the midst of his task, he paused to scowl curiously at his screen.

Don't stop! Rie wanted to shout at him. *The Vulcan must be stopped before he reaches the Presidium—*

But something was wrong; Ryllin simply continued to stare at his terminal. As discreetly as possible, Rie punched in her secret identification code. Perhaps the helm was malfunctioning; she could program the computer auto-destruct from her own station, if necessary.

What she saw on her monitor made her blink.

The auto-destruct sequence had already been initiated; she and Ryllin had not known, as the particular sequence was designed to deal with hostile intruders, so there was no countdown. Destruction would take place in a matter of minutes.

Rie tried to ignore what was happening around her. There was one last task to perform, a task she wanted to give her full attention.

She programmed the computer to send out a distress signal on a frequency monitored by all Romulan vessels. It warned of the ship's imminent destruction, and instructed all vessels to stay clear. The effects of the explosion would be felt over an area of roughly one square parsec.

Rie finished what she had to do. Then she waited.

McCoy lay curled up like a shrimp on the cold hard floor of the brig and waited for death.

His mood swung wildly from optimism to total despair. At times, he almost succeeded in convincing himself that Zakal had forgotten him, and that when they got to wherever they were going, he would be interrogated at length, and then sent home— wherever that was. At one time, *home* meant Earth, and then the *Enterprise;* what it meant these days, McCoy could no longer say.

At other times—like now—McCoy expected to die. He tried to approach the concept philosophically, the way Spock might— and failed. So he just lay there, helpless under the weight of a

cold gray panic. After all, he had witnessed the fate of his jailers
. . . and when no one came to replace them, he could pretty much
guess what had happened to the rest of the crew.

But there was one thing to be thankful for: McCoy no longer
experienced the semiconscious state the Vulcan had induced in
him earlier. It was as if Zakal had forgotten him, or decided he
wasn't worth worrying about. McCoy took the thought to its
logical conclusion. If Zakal arrived on ch'Rihan as he had promised, would anyone think to look in the brig in all the attendant
excitement? In his mind's eye, McCoy saw a little skeleton lying
curled on its side behind the brig's force field. . . .

The thought was almost funny, in a grim sort of way.
Starving to death in a brig would probably be a better end than
those he'd seen Zakal dish out.

McCoy reached the point in the cycle where he was just
beginning to think he'd be all right, when he saw a shimmer of
light on the other side of the force field.

It began to take humanoid shape. Someone was transporting
to a coordinate just outside the doctor's cell.

McCoy pushed himself to a sitting position and watched. He
half-expected Spock, but well before the materialization process
was complete, he recognized Jim Kirk. His first reaction was
gratitude; his second, fear. He did not want any of his friends to
get even remotely involved in this situation. Zakal seemed to
know all, sense all, and it was only a matter of time before he
registered Jim's presence.

McCoy got to his feet just as Kirk pressed the control that
dissipated the force field. They met in the doorway and grasped
each other's arms.

"Jim!" the doctor exclaimed with a mixture of gratitude and
regret. "Jim, I'm sure glad to see you, but I'm damn sorry to get
you mixed up in this. We've got to get out of here right away, or
he'll stop us—he knows everything that happens, Jim. He can
read people's minds . . ." He was vaguely aware that he sounded
incoherent.

"Take it easy, Bones." Kirk smiled and drew him out into
the corridor. "If you're talking about your Vulcan, he must not
be able to read *everyone's* mind; he certainly didn't know enough
to stop me from coming." Jim's voice was so full of confidence
that McCoy felt a smattering of hope. Jim hadn't sounded this
good since . . . well, since well before he gave up command of
the *Enterprise*. "Look, Doctor, I have to know—my ship's scan-

ners showed another human on board. Who is it? Is it the woman you were traveling with?''

"You mean Dwen?" McCoy asked feebly, horrified at the thought. "I have no idea, Jim . . . I guess she could have followed—after all, it was her ship that was stolen. . . ." *Not to mention a very close friend.* "Good Lord, I hope it isn't." He looked around the brig, at the dark, empty holding cells. "Then where is she? I mean, where did the sensors say the human was?"

"The bridge," Kirk answered shortly. "Along with the Vulcan and two Romulans."

"Dear God." McCoy swayed and groped blindly for the nearest support. Jim grasped his arm firmly and steadied him. "Jim . . . you're not thinking of going up there, are you? That's insane. Why don't we beam back to wherever you came from and then just transport the human off the bridge?"

Kirk's lips thinned. "Because I'm alone, Doctor, and we have to use the Romulans' transporters to get back. The minute we do, whoever's on the bridge is going to know about it, and raise their shields . . . and we'll never be able to get that person off the bridge." He paused. "You stay here, Bones. If I don't make it back in two minutes, activate the transporter. I've locked in the coordinates—"

"And then you're just going up there by yourself?" McCoy shook his head. "You can't do it, Jim. If you think you can merely walk in there and stun him with that phaser, you're wrong. He'll kill you before you know what's hit you. You don't stand a chance—this guy can *think* people dead. You've seen what he's capable of, Jim, and he's pure *evil.*"

Kirk looked at him steadily. There was no recrimination in Jim's gaze, but he said: "You're suggesting we simply get the hell out of here—without even checking to see who it is . . . leave a person who might be your friend up there with him . . . and let him take that kind of power to the Romulans."

"Yes," McCoy said uncertainly. "No. I mean . . ." He put his face in his hands and rubbed it as if to wipe away the confusion. "Hell, I don't know what I mean. If it's Dwen, God knows, I can't leave her there. And even if it's not—if it's some other innocent victim . . ." He sighed. There was no escaping death; he might as well embrace it. Running away only seemed to prolong the wait for the inevitable.

"All right," he said heavily. "I can't let you go up there

alone. Lead the way to the bridge, dammit. Just don't entertain
any hopes about leaving.''

But Kirk was already halfway down the corridor.

Sotek raised the shield around Dwen's body and waited for
the contest to begin. It was not long in coming; yet in the midst
of it all, Dwen felt a deep sense of peace that verged on euphoria.
The events of her life had all led to this moment, and were not
random, but braided together with meaning. And what she had
regarded as her greatest flaw had become her greatest talent.

In spite of his efforts, Zakal could not penetrate Sotek's
shield . . . and even if he did, he would never be able to penetrate
Dwen's mind, never be able to threaten the core of what she was.

Sotek wasted none of their energy on attack; he erected the
protective field, then waited for Zakal to exhaust himself.

Zakal likewise erected a protective shield, this one scarlet
tinged with gold—and began to wage war. With a swift motion of
his arms he gathered up his energy and hurled it at Dwen. Her
blue shield was engulfed by an orange-red wall of flame, the heat
of which was so great that the Romulan female sitting at a nearby
station was incinerated. Her hair and uniform blazed brightly for
a few seconds, then dulled to cinders as she slumped forward
over her console. Sotek and Dwen could not spare the energy to
grieve for her.

The fire wall stopped at the edge of the blue aura, where it
broke into small tongues of flame which swirled along the shield's
edges before fading away.

Zakal paused expectantly for Sotek's response. None came,
and the fact seemed to infuriate him even more.

It is Zakal's greatest flaw, Sotek communicated to Dwen.
*He cannot control his emotions—anger least of all. It is that
which will destroy him. He will attack blindly now, until he is
spent.*

There was an ominous rushing sound on the bridge as the air
grew hot and began to stir. Fine grains of red sand leapt into
existence and trembled, suspended on the wind—then hurtled
forward.

The wind increased, yowling, until the surviving Romulan
clung desperately to the helm, his uniform tunic rippling against
the skin of his back.

Zakal, Sotek said silently. It was their foe's name . . . yet somehow Dwen understood that Sotek meant the word in its ancient sense.

The Fury; the Desert Storm.

I have taken leave of my senses, McCoy told himself silently as he crouched behind Kirk, who was preparing to burst onto the bridge, phaser at the ready. *I have seen what this Vulcan is capable of—so what the hell am I doing here?*

He knew the answer, of course. He was there because he cared about Dwen and couldn't stand the thought that she might be in there with that madman . . . and he couldn't let Jim go onto the bridge and die alone, either.

With an awful thrill, McCoy remembered Spock's tarot reading, and the one card Dwen had been unable to explain. It was the card next to Death: the Magician, wrong-side-up.

The fear was strong and sickening. It left him weak, scarcely able to move. McCoy knew beyond any shadow of a doubt that if he followed Jim Kirk onto that bridge, he would die.

Even so, he couldn't let Jim meet his death alone . . . and he had to be sure that the human on the bridge was not Dwen.

In front of him, Jim tensed; McCoy prepared himself for what came next.

Kirk crouched low and propelled himself forward, through the double doors. McCoy followed at what he hoped was a safe distance.

The bridge was a swirling red hell.

Jim and McCoy were caught up in a hot wind so powerful that McCoy could not keep his footing, but dropped to his hands and knees. The wind lashed against him, stinging his cheeks and hands, cutting his bare skin. It took him some time to realize that the red swirls and the pain were caused by tiny grains of red sand of the type found on the Vulcan desert.

There was a sandstorm on the bridge.

The wind and sand blinded them. McCoy shielded his streaming eyes as best he could; next to him, Jim was also on his knees, still struggling to raise the phaser.

Something heavy bumped against McCoy. He cried out, startled, but the noise was swallowed up by the wind. McCoy looked down and saw the body of a Romulan female, covered with dark green buboes—subcutaneous hemorrhages. He reached out to find a pulse . . .

The skin of her neck crackled like paper beneath his finger-

tips. The dry heat and sand had leached every bit of moisture
from her body. McCoy drew away in disgust and tried once again
to look up, into the wind.

On the other side of the narrow bridge stood Zakal, en-
sconced in a protective sphere of fiendish red. The look on his
face was the one he had worn when the Romulan guards had tried
to put him in the brig. Amazingly, Zakal seemed unaware of the
intruders; his attention was focused on the patch of blue a few
meters in front of him.

Dwen. Amazed and horrified, McCoy drew in his breath . . .
and choked on the hot gritty sand.

As awesome and terrifying as Zakal appeared, Dwen seemed
every bit his match. Some miracle had transformed her from a
mere human to a magician as powerful as the Vulcan. Within the
shimmering blue field that protected her, Dwen's face was strong
and serene and content; she showed no signs of fear or weakness.

Yet McCoy was afraid for her sake. "Dwen!" he shouted, so
loud that his voice broke, barely loud enough to be heard over
the windstorm.

Behind the blue aura of safety, Dwen turned her head to
look at him. At first sight, she seemed so honestly glad that she
smiled . . . and then her expression of joy turned to one of fear.

The wind slackened as Zakal gathered up a ball of flaming
energy and launched it in the direction of McCoy and Kirk.

In that instant McCoy saw Death coming at him in the form
of a fireball. He had time to feel sorry he'd dragged Jim into this,
and to think the single thought:

Save yourself, Dwen.

He felt the heat of the approaching blast singe his lashes and
brows, and closed his eyes.

"No," Dwen said.

It was the moment of choice. Sotek had made his long ago:
he would gladly embrace annihilation to stop Zakal, but it was
Keridwen's body, and Keridwen who had to make the final
decision.

Even though she had seen the future, she knew it hinged on
choices, to the very end. At any point, she and Leonard could
exercise their wills and change the outcome.

Leonard could have taken the coward's way out, and not
come to the bridge. But he had come, and was willing to risk

death to save her. And now she had a choice: save herself and Sotek, or let McCoy and Kirk die.

Dwen made her decision.

Before the fireball could touch McCoy or Kirk, they were both suddenly enveloped in a soft blue glow. The wind and sand could not reach inside it; the flames hit the shield and dissipated.

The effect was, of course, exactly the one Zakal hoped for; the extra expenditure of energy caused Dwen's own shield to weaken. Zakal wasted no time in taking advantage. He launched another bolt of heat energy at Dwen. The shield dimmed; the impact knocked her to the ground. She tried to stand up, and found she could not.

"*Go,*" she said to the two humans. She had made her choice; now she could only hope that Leonard made the right one too. But he and Admiral Kirk lingered. "Protecting you drains me," Dwen said. "He knows that. Go—so I can hold him here. Otherwise, we are all dead."

The second bolt scorched her, leaving her body mortally wounded. Because of Sotek's strength, she was able not to cry out.

McCoy threw himself against the edge of the protective field; he shouted at Zakal with a voice that was full of anguish. "Leave her alone, you bastard! Leave her alone! If you want to make someone suffer, take me!" Tears streamed down his face, even though his eyes were sheltered from the wind and sand. The admiral grabbed his arm and tried to pull him back, but Leonard angrily shrugged him off.

"*Go!*" Dwen shrieked, but the doctor would not hear. For one bitter moment she tasted despair; McCoy and his friend would die with her and the others in the explosion that was coming . . . and her death would lose its meaning. Dwen began to weep, and even Sotek's wisdom could not comfort her.

And then McCoy's and Kirk's bodies began to shimmer and blink.

TWENTY-THREE

───────── ☆ ─────────

On the research vessel, Spock had picked up the Bird of Prey's auto-destruct warning.

Though T'Sai had told him nothing of Sotek, Spock had surmised what was happening when the High Master transferred Sotek's katra to Keridwen Llewellyn. Spock realized that the small Vulcan ship would be safe so long as Sotek engaged Zakal's full concentration; even so, T'Sai, though wounded, continued to shield the vessel from possible attack.

And Spock did his best to keep his emotions under control. His outburst upon detecting Kirk's vessel had enabled Zakal to injure T'Sai . . . and his imperfect knowledge of the mind-rules required them now to leave the fate of all Vulcan in the hands of a human.

But it had been Spock's understanding that Dr. Llewellyn and Sotek intended to return from their mission. Once he decoded the Bird of Prey's warning, he swiveled in his chair to look at T'Sai where she lay on the bunk.

"The Romulan vessel has just issued an auto-destruct warning," Spock said. He kept his tone as flat and unemotional as possible, but made it clear that he found this turn of events disturbing and wished for direction from T'Sai.

Her reaction was not one he had hoped for; she did not stir, but said: "All is as it must be. Dr. Llewellyn knew of the consequences. It was her choice, and Sotek's."

Spock turned back to his station. So, it was as he had suspected: together, Keridwen and Sotek could not overpower Zakal—yet they were a match for him, and Keridwen's esperblindness had permitted them to sabotage the ship without Zakal's knowledge. Inwardly he felt deep guilt and shame. T'Sai had just told him, in essence, that Keridwen had intentionally sacrificed herself. To attempt to rescue her now would be suicide: if he beamed her over from the Romulan ship, Zakal would sense it and destroy them all while Keridwen's molecules were in transit. . . .

And the secret knowledge would fall into the hands of the Romulan Empire.

"There are only two-point-four minutes left before the Bird of Prey destructs," Spock said evenly, without turning around. "I do not understand, T'Sai. If you were aware of the danger, why did you not warn me? We must leave the area soon to avoid being destroyed ourselves."

Yet the thought of leaving Dr. Llewellyn distressed him more than he wished to admit to himself. If there were only some way to save her . . .

"I shared Keridwen Llewellyn's mind," T'Sai replied. Her voice sounded weak and infinitely tired. "She knew what is, and what will be. I did not speak of it earlier because the time was not right."

Spock said no more. Instead, he indulged himself in one last scan of the Romulan vessel . . . and was surprised at the data on his screen. There were now three humans aboard, where earlier there had been only two.

Jim Kirk had beamed over to the Bird of Prey.

Spock's first thought was to warn the admiral—but using subspace communications was risky. If any of the Romulans—or Zakal—intercepted the message . . .

Spock almost considered beaming over himself. If he could beam down to the brig and free Dr. McCoy . . .

He checked the scanners. No life forms registered on the third level, with the exception of a Romulan in Engineering. The brig was empty. . . .

And the three humans and one Vulcan were all on Level One, bridge level.

This, Spock realized, would seriously jeopardize Dr. Llewellyn's plan. If McCoy and Kirk had followed their emotions

instead of logic, as Spock knew they had, and rushed up to the
bridge thinking to save Keridwen . . .

They would wind up killing her . . . and themselves.

Spock studied the sensor readout intently. There had been
only one human on the bridge until very recently . . . and that
human had, like the Vulcan nearby, emitted unusually high
energy readings. This, Spock decided, was Dr. Llewellyn.

The other two humans were therefore Dr. McCoy and Kirk.
And as Spock watched, something quite extraordinary happened.
The sensors began to detect an energy emission surrounding the
two.

Keridwen, trying to protect them. Perhaps Spock was already too late.

He went over to the transporter console.

"Dwen!" McCoy cried as he stood next to Jim on the
transporter pad of the research vessel and looked around him.
"Where's Dwen? You've got to beam her up right away!"

Spock could not bring himself to answer. The thought that
he had indirectly caused Dr. Llewellyn's death and was now
powerless to help her filled him with a strange bitterness that
negated any joy he might have felt upon seeing his friends. He
turned away from them and went back to the helm. There was
less than two minutes before the Bird of Prey self-destructed;
that left Spock with less than a minute to pilot the ship out of
danger.

"Spock!" McCoy demanded, his voice quivering with anger.
"Don't you hear me? Dwen's over there, and Zakal's killing her!
You've got to do something *now!*"

Spock brought the ship around one hundred and eighty
degrees; he plotted the most direct course out of the Neutral
Zone, and fed it into the computer.

"Spock . . ." Kirk was saying. Both he and McCoy had
stepped down from the transporter platform and followed Spock
to the pilot's console. "Spock, the woman's down there. Why
won't you answer us?"

McCoy reached a hand out and roughly grabbed Spock's
shoulder. "For God's sake, Spock, *can't you hear me?*"

The Vulcan turned and gave McCoy a look that made him let
go immediately. "I hear you, Doctor," Spock said. "I hear."

He turned back to the controls.

*   *   *

As Leonard and Admiral Kirk vanished from the storm, Keridwen's sorrow turned to joy . . . and the blue glow around her brightened against the swirling red dust.

She knew she was wounded, yet she and Sotek were so focused on their task that neither of them knew the nature or extent of her injuries, nor felt the pain. Only one thing mattered now to Keridwen: that she hold on, that she live long enough to distract Zakal while Spock and the others made their escape.

Sotek understood, but his satisfaction did not hinge on the fate of the few, as did Dwen's; he was concerned with the many, the followers of Surak . . . though for Keridwen's sake, he was pleased that the humans made their escape.

The Fury still raged, but Zakal was clearly exhausting himself. He threw no more heat bolts, and seemed to be biding his time until Dwen was too weak to maintain the shield.

Less than a minute before the explosion, according to Sotek's internal clock. Less than a minute, and their purpose would be fulfilled.

But Keridwen's body was in shock. Her consciousness fluttered alarmingly; Sotek tried to help her hold on . . . but the blue aura weakened. Zakal took advantage, and raised the wind.

Hold on, holdonholdon . . .

She did not know if the thought were her own or Sotek's, or if the sudden dimness on the bridge were caused by her failing eyesight.

Less than thirty seconds

But she was glad, very glad. All the pain that came before with Michael, with her parents, with her grandparents . . . all that suffering was not wasted; it had happened for a reason.

Only one regret, now: that she could not explain all this to Leonard and Spock. She wanted them to know that she was *happy* in this . . . but they would have to deal with what happened in their own ways. She could only hope that the paths they chose from this point led to good.

Twenty seconds

The storm eased. Zakal was laughing at her, at Sotek. He could see that she was dying. "How fortunate, Khoteth," he sneered, "that *I* never made a promise to save *you* from the second death."

Dwen let Sotek speak. "And how fortunate, Master," he gasped through Dwen's lips, "that my promise to you in that regard has been fulfilled. I have saved you once . . . I shall not do so twice.''

Ten seconds

Zakal's eyes widened as he contemplated the meaning of Sotek's words. He was on the verge of saying something when Keridwen interrupted.

"Taste *my* magic, old man . . .''

The bridge dissolved into white brilliance.

On the overhead screen, the Bird of Prey was receding . . . and the sight made McCoy half-crazed. Keridwen was there, with that madman, and Spock was acting as if nothing were wrong.

The Vulcan ship had just gone into warp drive, and was speeding away from the Romulan vessel. Both McCoy and Jim were trying to reach out for the controls, but Spock blocked them from the console. An ugly situation, but McCoy was desperate enough for violence. Out of the corner of his eye he saw Jim reach for the phaser on his belt; he silently cheered him on.

That's it, Jim! Stun the sonuvabitch and turn this ship around . . .

"*Stop,*" someone said. A female voice, weak with age, yet conveying such authority that McCoy and Kirk stopped immediately and looked for the voice's owner.

It was a white-haired Vulcan female; for some reason, she looked familiar to McCoy. She had been lying on the bunk, but had propped herself up in response to the argument. She wore the plain white robes of a Kolinahru, and McCoy noticed that she had untreated second-degree burns on her forehead and cheek.

"Spock is doing what he must," she said firmly. "Do not interrupt him. Keridwen Llewellyn also knows what she is doing. She volunteered to sacrifice herself.''

"But we can *save* her!" McCoy cried. "If we just beam her over here—''

"It is too late," the woman said. "Had Spock beamed her aboard with you, all of us—including Dr. Llewellyn—would now be dead. She hoped her death would win you your lives. If you turn the ship back now, you will make that impossible.''

"Why?" Kirk demanded angrily; if he were impressed by the elderly Vulcan's demeanor, he did not show it. "Just why is it that she must die? How will beaming her over kill us all?''

"There are some things," the woman replied, "which I am

not at liberty to explain." And she lowered herself back onto the bunk.

"*No*," McCoy said. His mind refused to accept what the Kolinahru was saying. Desperately he turned back to Spock. "Spock . . . we can't just let Dwen die!"

Spock's expression was slack, dazed as he sat in the pilot's chair and stared up at the overhead screen. "It is already too late, Doctor." His voice was faint, almost a whisper. "The Bird of Prey has commenced its auto-destruct sequence. If we return now, we will most certainly be destroyed."

McCoy followed the Vulcan's gaze to the viewscreen and staggered backward as he registered the content of Spock's words. He was only dimly aware that Jim caught him and lowered him into a passenger's chair. "This can't be," the doctor whispered. "It can't—it wasn't supposed to happen this way at all."

On the overhead, the Bird of Prey exploded into a dazzling burst of white light. Spock and Jim looked away. McCoy watched and let himself be blinded.

"No," he said. Grief crushed him. His chest heaved against its weight; his eyes burned with tears. "No," he repeated dully. Jim laid a hand on his shoulder. McCoy's mind noted the gesture, but was too stunned to comprehend its significance. "No, it should have been me. Not her, not Dwen. It should have been me."

The temporary blindness cleared. On the screen, the brightness had faded, leaving in its wake clouds of red dust, a small and angry nebula.

"It should have been me," the doctor said again, and as he looked away from the viewscreen, his gaze met Spock's.

The Vulcan's eyes were haunted.

It should have been me. . . .

In that moment, McCoy understood he spoke for both of them.

EPILOGUE

☆

"I must break the link," Spock said. "I wish to become a postulant in Kolinahr." He stood outside, in the merciless afternoon sunlight of T'Sura's garden.

"I know," T'Sura said. She finished tucking a seedling into the ground, then rose and wiped red sand onto the seams of her pants. Even over the great physical distance, the bond had held. She had known all that happened to Spock—not the details of the actual events, but she sensed his distress, his grief, his shame. She had known of this decision before Spock became consciously aware of it himself.

And she was not surprised. It was the pattern of her life: intimacy, followed by loss. Perhaps from the beginning, she had expected this new sorrow.

And she sensed Spock's resolve. This could not be averted; were she to plead, to bargain, it would be more difficult for both of them.

"Then let us dissolve the link." T'Sura reached a hand toward Spock's forehead; he reciprocated. Each one's fingers touched the other's skin at the same instant, and for a moment T'Sura shared the full clarity of what had happened: Spock's emotion that had caused T'Sai's injury . . . his inability to make reparation because of his lack of mental training . . . the realization that his own emotional outburst, combined with the unthinking emotional reaction of his friends, had cost Keridwen Llewellyn her life . . .

And the personal agony Spock endured as he watched helplessly while Keridwen was killed . . .

It was an experience T'Sura understood well. Yet she pulled away from him slowly . . . and he from her. They receded from each other level by level, until at last both drew their hands away.

The bond was severed. For a moment they stood staring at each other, strangers. And then Spock said something truly extraordinary.

"I am sorry."

He turned and walked out of the garden, back into the house. T'Sura knew that she would not see him again. She also knew that from time to time he would sense her presence, and she his. But such lingering effects would soon fade.

And T'Sura would be alone again.

SAN FRANCISCO, 9:00 A.M.

"Good morning, Admiral. And welcome back." Riley directed a smile at Kirk, who sat at his desk terminal and frowned at the plethora of bureaucratic communiqués that had accumulated during his absence. Instead of looking tired after his visit to Djana, as Riley expected, the Admiral seemed invigorated, even a bit younger than he had been his first day at HQ.

A subtle change had come over Riley as well. When Anab had left him, he'd thought he would die . . . but in that period of time since she shipped out, he had not. The work had kept him sane . . . and the memory of what Ciana had said shamed him into working harder still. And the pain lessened.

There was nothing he could do to protect Anab out there in the far reaches of space; there was no way to ensure she would come back to him. He could not control that. But he could control what became of the person she had left. In his more objective moments, Riley saw that Anab had tried to do what was best for him: forced him not to cling so desperately to security, forced him to decide what *he* really wanted.

He wanted to work for Jim Kirk. He wanted to earn the trust the admiral had already vested in him. He enjoyed the assignment . . . and though the specter of Lana Shemry—and Riley's guilt at being a survivor—would always be with him, the next time Anab called she would speak with a different Riley.

At the sight of his chief of staff, Kirk's frown changed to a tentative grin. "Riley. Still with us, I see."

The two weeks Kirk had given him to make a decision were not up. The admiral's remark was a test, Riley knew, to see where he stood.

"Yes, sir. I'm glad you mentioned it." Riley walked up to Kirk's desk and stood before the admiral with awkward formality, hands clasped behind his back. "About my . . . resignation . . ."

"Yes?" All traces of Kirk's good humor fled. His expression as he looked up at Riley was apprehensive.

"I'm sorry that I ever brought it up, Admiral. At the time, I was undergoing problems of a . . . very personal nature. The problem has since been resolved. Sort of." Riley hesitated. "Anyway, if you still want to have me, Admiral—I enjoy working for you. I want to do the best job possible. I want to make you glad you chose me."

As he spoke, the tension in Kirk's face eased. When Riley was finished, the admiral said faintly, "I think I already am. You're going to do just fine, Riley."

"Thank you, sir," Riley answered, greatly relieved at Kirk's response. He was going to say more when he heard the sound of the outer-office doors opening.

Vice Admiral Ciana came in through the outer office. Like Kirk, she appeared cheerful, energetic, not at all drained by the stressful events on Djana. She held a cup of steaming coffee in her left hand.

" 'Morning, Riley. 'Morning, Jim." She stepped up next to Riley and scrutinized him while taking a cautious sip of the coffee. "How's it going, Chief of Staff?"

"Fine, sir. Just fine," Riley said with genuine warmth. Like Anab, the vice admiral had hurt him in order to help him. As unpleasant as the memory of the encounter with Ciana was, Riley was grateful for it. He turned his head and addressed Kirk. "Admiral, I'll be back in a few minutes to go over the staff selections with you. I think you'll be pleased with the people we have."

"I'm sure I will," Kirk said.

Riley blushed faintly; he hadn't meant it to sound as if he were patting himself on the back. He'd been honestly thrilled by the highly qualified applicants who were available. "If you'll excuse me, sirs . . . ." He went back into the outer office.

Ciana took another sip of coffee, then said: "So, what's with him? Think he'll stay?"

"He'll stay." Jim leaned forward and stared at her in frank appreciation, relieved that he no longer had to hide his feelings from her. The brief voyage with Spock and McCoy—they had taken Kirk as far as Djana, then continued on to Vulcan—had been a bitter one. McCoy had been mute with grief, Spock stone-faced and distant. Jim felt that the bonds between the three were dissolving; they were moving apart, each to his own separate destiny.

His heart went out to McCoy. Spock's coldness he found hurtful, but he did his best not to dwell on it. Maybe it was better this way; maybe the Vulcan was trying to make things easier for all of them. After all, Jim's future was no longer entwined with Spock's, but lay elsewhere . . .

With Lori Ciana. Or so Jim hoped. And he had promised himself that once the permanent negotiating team took over on Djana and he and Lori returned to San Francisco, he would know whether Lori had reached the same conclusion.

"Riley will stay," Jim repeated. "What did you say to him that day, Lori? It had quite an effect."

Lori half-sat on the edge of his desk, her expression suddenly impish. "I used an old and venerable psychological technique. I threatened to strangle him if he quit. Works like a charm every time." She smiled into her cup.

Kirk grinned. "I thought you'd bewitched him—just as you have a certain admiral."

She set the cup down and reached out to touch his cheek. "The spell works both ways, Jim."

He put a hand on hers. "There's something I want to talk to you about, Lori." As he said it, the intercom whistled. "Perfect timing." He grimaced ruefully and pressed the toggle. "Yes?"

Riley's voice filtered through the grid. "You wanted to know when Nogura got in, Admiral. He's in his office, and anxious to see you both."

"Thanks," Jim answered unenthusiastically. He snapped the intercom off and looked sheepishly up at Lori, who sat watching with a bemused little smile.

"To be continued." Jim got up, came around the desk, and offered her his arm.

"To be continued," she replied, still smiling. Together they walked arm-in-arm to Nogura's office.

MIDMORNING, SHANAIKAHR PLAZA HOTEL

McCoy sat alone at a booth for four and stared across the bar at the empty table where Dwen had read Spock's cards. The room was bright with harsh sunshine that poured in through the windows and made it uncomfortably hot, despite the climate control set at Terran comfort levels. McCoy noticed the heat, but did not care. He was alone in the bar except for the surly Tellarite waiter and a red-nosed Earther who was already drunk at eleven o'clock in the morning, Vulcan Central Time.

McCoy himself was sipping room-temperature Thirellian mineral water. At first he'd ordered a Glenfiddich. When it arrived, he found he couldn't drink it.

Dwen was right—he'd been drinking far too much lately. A bad habit of his, trying to blot out unpleasant memories. And right now, the strangest thing had happened; right now, McCoy didn't want to forget. He wanted to remember Dwen, wanted to try to sort out what had happened.

He was still stunned with grief at her death, but was at the point now where he could function in spite of it. Impossible to believe that she was dead. Harder still to believe how she had died . . . and that her prophecy had been fulfilled, and she had substituted herself and Zakal for Spock and McCoy.

It should have been me. . . .

But it hadn't been. And if Dwen's prediction had been true, McCoy decided, then he had damn well better make every remaining second of his life count . . . because the thought of Keridwen dying in vain was too horrible to bear.

The very least he could do was stay sober and try to figure things out. Certainly there was something worthwhile he could do that didn't involve Starfleet. There was all that Fabrini medical knowledge. Maybe he could do some practical research with it—find a few more cures, maybe take the medical innovations to some less-advanced planets, where such new knowledge would normally be long in coming. Maybe save a few lives that would otherwise not be saved.

McCoy was lost in thought, trying to figure out the fastest way to get through all the red tape such a project would entail, when he became aware of someone standing beside him. The waiter, McCoy assumed, and said: "Nothing else, thanks."

"Dr. McCoy," Spock said.

McCoy glanced up, startled. The Vulcan looked drawn and severe in a cape and trousers of black; if McCoy hadn't known Vulcan customs better, he might have thought Spock was in mourning.

He had not seen Spock since their arrival back on Vulcan; in fact, they had not spoken a word to each other during the long journey back. Spock, McCoy knew, was enduring his own private hell, just as McCoy endured his.

"Spock," he said softly, and gestured at the seat across from his. "I didn't expect to see you again. Sit down."

Spock sat stiffly; his spine did not touch the back of the cushioned bench. "This will be our last meeting. I have come to take my leave of you."

McCoy did not understand right away. "I admit, it'll be a while before our paths cross again, but that doesn't mean—"

"I shall soon become a postulant in Kolinahr, Doctor. I shall not see you, nor any of my friends or family, again."

At first McCoy was too shocked to reply. And then he said the next thing that popped into his head. "But, Spock, what about your fiancée?"

"We have severed the relationship." Spock's tone seemed wooden, rehearsed.

"I'm sorry," McCoy said honestly. "I'm truly very sorry."

"I know," Spock said. The cold control wavered for an instant as he looked away, but it was there again by the time his gaze once again met McCoy's.

The doctor was too weary, too drained by grief over Dwen to react emotionally to the thought of never seeing the Vulcan again. A part of him simply could not believe; a part of him felt that whenever he needed help, Spock would somehow be there. He looked at Spock with a mixture of fondness and mild melancholy. "You know, Spock, I can't say I blame you. In fact, maybe those Kolinahr folks have the right idea. Maybe we'd all be better off without emotions."

Spock watched McCoy guardedly for a moment, then said, "And you, Doctor . . . what plans do you have?"

"Me?" McCoy tilted back his head and finished off the Thirellian water, then set the glass down. "I dunno. Maybe I'll follow your lead, Spock—maybe hide out in the wilderness for a while." He paused to lower his voice. "Look, I know I lost my head on the ship and said some cruel things . . ."

"You needn't apologize, Doctor."

"I just wanted you to know I'm sorry." And before the Vulcan had a chance to reply, McCoy blurted, "Spock . . . do you think it was true? Did Dwen really foresee our deaths?"

There was the faintest trace of bitterness in Spock's tone. "It scarcely matters. Whether she truly foresaw our deaths or not, the outcome is still the same: she sacrificed herself to win our lives."

McCoy contemplated this silently.

And then Spock rose, and parted the fingers of his right hand in the Vulcan gesture of salutation. "We shall not see each other again, Leonard McCoy. Live long and prosper."

McCoy stood, surprised by the sudden tightness of his throat. "Good-bye, Spock. Take care."

He watched as the Vulcan, a stark and lonely figure in black, walked out of the empty bar. And somehow, his heart refused to accept that this time was the last.